The Place I Call Home

Hartley Blaze

Yellow Rose Books
by Regal Crest

ISBN 978-1-61929-450-9

First Printing 2020

9 8 7 6 5 4 3 2 1

Original cover design by AcornGraphics

Published by:

Regal Crest Enterprises

Find us on the World Wide Web at
http://www.regalcrest.biz

Published in the United States of America

Acknowledgments

With thanks to those at Regal Crest Enterprises who have given me a shot at being published. Special thanks to Cathy for patiently answering all my questions and Micheala for helping me edit this novel into the best shape possible.

Dedication

To Mum. Wish you were here to see this.

Chapter One

I'M COMING HOME.

Caitlyn Swailes put down the letter and let out a tremulous breath. Five years. It's been five years and now she's finally coming home.

Home was Carshalton, a town in the London Borough of Sutton, in South London, with a historic village centre. It consisted of a number of neighbourhoods, the main focal point being the visually scenic and picturesque village.

Eyes on the letter, unable to look away in case it disappeared into thin air, she lifted a trembling hand from the table-top to brush back her fringe, blonde hair swiftly falling back to where it had been. *Jesus, I don't believe it!*

Baby blue eyes slowly drifted over to the kitchen doorway as her mother appeared. "Why didn't you tell me?"

Tricia Swailes blinked at her daughter as the question slowly registered. "This is the first time I've seen you since the letter arrived, honey."

"There is a little invention called a phone, Mum. You could have easily given me a phone call." Her gaze dropped back to the letter, fingertips delicately tracing the flowing script of familiar writing. "Has she written to you often?"

"Uh-huh," Tricia nodded. "Every couple of weeks a letter or postcard arrives, letting us know she's all right, where she is, and all that. A parcel arrives on birthdays and at Christmas." She sat down opposite her slouched daughter, watching her closely, trying to read what Caitlyn was feeling. "Darcy didn't write to you?"

Caitlyn snorted. "Nothing. Not even a damn postcard."

"Maybe she wasn't sure where to send one." The suggestion sounded lame even to her own ears.

"She could have sent it here, Mum. She must know you would have passed it on." She rubbed her forehead in frustration and again pushed away her fringe. She hated all the conflicting emotions bubbling within her, too many to deal with, all because of a letter she had longed for and dreaded. "I'm sorry, Mum. I shouldn't snap at you. It's Darcy I'm annoyed with."

"It's fine, honey. I understand." Reaching out to pat Caitlyn's hand affectionately, the petite woman stood and moved to switch on the kettle. "Would you like a cup of tea?"

"No," Caitlyn sighed, sitting back in her seat. "I'm...I'm going to go upstairs and tidy up a bit."

"Darcy's not arriving tonight, honey," the older woman chuckled. She dropped a teabag into a mug.

"I know. It just...it gives me something to do."

"All right then. I'll finish cleaning down here, then I'll make us some lunch. I'll give you a shout when it's ready."

Getting to her feet, Caitlyn walked over to her mother and kissed her cheek.

"What was that for?" Tricia asked in amusement.

"To remind you that I love you, despite my little outbursts."

She left the kitchen and made her way through the family home. Her childhood home held many memories, many good and many bad also. This was the home she ran to when life didn't make sense, the home she returned to when she had good news or bad to share, the home the whole family visited for a Swailes family get-together.

It was also the home Darcy Kenton came to. This house was as much her home as it was Caitlyn's.

Upstairs, Caitlyn walked into what had once been her eldest brother Jeremy's bedroom, memories filtering into her head as she looked around. Most of his stuff was long gone, replaced by Darcy's simple possessions.

Caitlyn found the room already neat and tidy, everything in its proper place, the carpet hoovered, surfaces dusted, the faint scent of lemon wood polish lingering in the air. She chuckled softly at her mother's antics.

Leaving the bedroom, she headed for her own. At one time pink, the room had been painted lilac as soon as she had hit thirteen and declared she needed a change. She took a seat on the edge of the bed, sighing as a swell of confusion, anger, and fear threatened to burst free. Why now? Why after so long without a single trip back would Darcy decide to come home?

Unable to answer the question herself, she turned her attention back to her bedroom, gaze taking in trophies and trinkets, posters and books, until her eyes settled on a neat line of photo albums standing proudly on her bookcase.

With time to kill until lunch, she stood and retrieved one of the albums. She got herself comfortable on the bed, opened the book, and was instantly taken back to her childhood.

The first page made her lips curl into a wistful smile as she laid eyes on baby pictures of herself and Darcy. She had known

Darcy her whole life, friends before they could even walk. "Six weeks old," read the caption under a photograph of the pair side by side in separate bouncers, their faces lit up in delight as they stared at the camera. "Happy birthday, Caitlyn," read another, the photo showing the pair with cake-smeared faces.

Caitlyn smiled and laughed lightly as she turned the pages, fond memories coming back to her as she went through the years. The girls grew from babies to toddlers, to five, six, seven-year-olds. She paused when she came across the photo of them in the back garden, Darcy's arm around her shoulders, her own arms around Darcy's waist.

They had been seven years old and it was the height of summer, they were dressed in shorts and T-shirts. "Best of friends," was the caption. Her insides twisted as she traced the plastic-protected photo with a fingertip, brushing over Darcy's bruised face. That was the summer she was old enough to realise just how different their lives were.

It was August 1999.

"Mum!" Caitlyn yelled out, racing down the stairs. "I'm going to knock for Darcy."

"Okay, honey," Tricia called back. "Hey!"

Caitlyn looked back as she reached the front door, seeing her mother standing in the kitchen doorway.

"Don't go far. Back garden, or..."

"The front. I know, Mum."

Tricia smiled. "How about we go to the park later?"

Blue eyes lit up with delight. "Can Darcy come too?"

"Of course, honey. You two rarely leave each other's side. In fact, I'm beginning to worry you might end up getting stuck together!" She pulled a face, making her daughter laugh and roll her eyes.

Leaving the house, Caitlyn trotted down the crazy paving path, hearing the usual sounds of summer in the neighbourhood. Children were laughing and squealing while they played, dogs were barking as they raced back and forth. "In the Summertime" was blaring out of stereos from houses and cars passing by, and the delightful smell of sizzling barbecues filled the air.

She loved summer. Freedom from school, her best friend's company, swimming, ice cream, and she was allowed to stay up an extra hour at night. In her opinion, summer was almost as good as Christmas.

Knocking on her friend's paint-chipped front door, Caitlyn

bounced from foot to foot as she waited for someone to answer, eager to get on with the day. She frowned when she got no response. Darcy was usually quick to answer the door. She liked to be outside more than Caitlyn did. She knocked again, a little louder, a little harder. She knew someone was home because she could hear the stereo on inside.

Yvonne Kenton swung open the door and squinted at the sudden bright light that greeted her.

"Hi, Mrs. Kenton," Caitlyn greeted cheerfully, despite the uninviting scowl on the older woman's face.

"What do you want?"

"Can Darcy come out and play?"

"She's not allowed out." She started to close the door.

"How come?"

The tall brunette sighed in annoyance. "Because I say so. Now go away."

The door slammed shut, making the small girl jump back. Her excitement from moments before gone, Caitlyn walked away from the house, unable to understand why Darcy wasn't allowed out. Maybe she had been bad. She frowned. That didn't add up because Darcy was never bad. Darcy was quiet and shy, always polite, and quick to offer help if needed.

Caitlyn headed along the side of her house to the back garden. The previous summer, she and Darcy had painted the Wendy House Caitlyn's father had built, a little place big enough for the two of them, a place where her older brothers weren't allowed to venture. The pair often camped out at night in it, curling up in sleeping bags next to each other and not falling asleep until the early hours as they talked, told stories, and dared each other to go outside and wander around in the dark.

Sitting in the little house, Caitlyn looked out one of the windows and across to Darcy's home. What had Darcy done to make Yvonne angry? How long would she not be allowed out for?

A gentle tap on the wooden door was followed by, "Honey?" from her own mother.

Standing, she moved to open the door for Tricia. "Hi, Mum."

Seeing something had upset her daughter, Tricia smiled lovingly as she held out a glass of orange juice. "I saw you come back alone. Is Darcy out?"

"No. She's not allowed out today." Blue eyes filled with tears as she remembered how mean Yvonne had been to her.

"Oh, I see." Tricia glanced over at her neighbour's house. "We'll still go to the park, okay? Let me finish cleaning up the house, then I'll pack us a picnic and we'll go."

"Okay."

Tricia pulled her daughter into her arms. "Don't be upset, sweetheart. I'm sure Darcy will be back out playing soon."

Left alone again, Caitlyn set her drink down on the plastic table and sighed as she looked around the Wendy House. She had been so happy and looking forward to the day ahead, but all that had changed now that Darcy wasn't allowed out. She wondered again what her friend could have possibly done.

Wanting to do something, she grabbed a brush and started sweeping the floor. Once she had finished that, she moved on to wiping down the cupboards her dad had put in and the table and chairs. Finished with her cleaning, she took out a packet of biscuits she and Darcy had bought with their pocket money and sat back down with a deep sigh.

A hesitant knock on the closed door drew her attention, her eyes lighting up when Darcy opened the door and poked her head in. "Darcy!"

"Hi, Caitlyn." Darcy walked in and closed the door behind her, before sitting opposite her friend.

Caitlyn's delighted smile slipped when her gaze fell on the bruise beneath Darcy's left eye. "I...I knocked for you, Darcy. Your mum said you weren't allowed out."

"It's okay now. She's um...she's taking a nap. So, I came out."

Caitlyn fiddled with her drink, tracing swirls against the chilled glass. "What happened to your eye?"

"I knocked it." Reaching out for a biscuit, Darcy avoided Caitlyn's gaze.

"How?"

"I don't know. I don't remember."

Caitlyn frowned, watching her friend closely, not believing her. "You don't remember?"

"Nope."

"Does it hurt?"

At this question, Darcy hesitated. "Not really."

"Didn't it hurt when you knocked it?" Caitlyn asked, determined to find out what had happened. She watched her friend shrug in response. "When my knee hit the table leg it really hurt," she stated, waiting for some sort of response. Sitting back in her seat, she decided to change the subject, seeing how Darcy was so reluctant to talk. "Do you want to play? My mummy's taking us to the park after she's done the cleaning, if you're allowed."

"Maybe."

"Caitlyn, are you ready to go to the park?" Tricia called out from the back door.

The little blonde jumped up from her seat, ready to rush off. She paused at the door when Darcy didn't move. "Are you coming, Darcy?" She reached out for her friend's hand.

"I better leave my mum a note." Darcy sighed as she got to her feet, a frown creasing her brow, dark green eyes filled with sadness.

Caitlyn smiled a beautiful smile as she pulled Darcy to her. "Let's get my mum to write it." She tugged Darcy out of the Wendy House and headed toward Tricia. "Mummy, look! Darcy's here!" she called out in delight, smiling broadly.

Tricia smiled, that dimming a little before brightening again as the girls approached. "Hello, Darcy. How are you today?"

"I'm fine, thank you, Mrs. S. How are you?"

"I am very well, thank you. Have you been in the wars, Darcy?" she pointed at the girl's face.

"I knocked it."

"Mum, can Darcy come to the park with us?" Caitlyn asked hopefully.

"If it's all right with Yvonne," Tricia replied. "You'll have to ask if you're allowed, Darcy."

"She's sleeping, Mrs. S. I...I don't want to wake her up." The girl dejectedly kicked at the neatly cut lawn with the toe of her trainer.

"I see. Well, how about if we wait until she wakes up? Then we can ask her if it's all right," Tricia suggested. "We don't want her to worry, do we?" She smiled as both girls shook their heads. "Right then, you girls get on with playing and I'll do some gardening. Then later, we'll go to the park and have a late lunch." She clapped her hands to shoo them away. "Go on now, unless you want to help me dig up weeds."

Giggling, the two girls ran off, heading back to the Wendy House, their sanctuary.

God, I miss you, Darcy, Caitlyn thought, tracing the photo with a fingertip, a sad smile on her lips.

"Caitlyn?"

Hearing her mother calling, she set aside the photo album and stepped out of her bedroom. "Yes, Mum?"

"Lunch is ready if you're interested."

Making her way downstairs and through to the kitchen, the

paediatric nurse smiled as she walked in, the familiar aroma of warm bread fresh out of the oven permeating the air. "You know, you could have told me you had already been up there cleaning."

"Where's the fun in that?" Tricia laughed. As her daughter sat down, she set a glass of milk and a neatly cut cheese and tomato sandwich in front of her.

"You do realise I'm not eight anymore, don't you?" she teased, eyeing the four little squares.

"Yes, love. But you and I both know you've never grown out of the habit of cutting your sandwiches into squares," Tricia smiled, brushing a hand through her daughter's golden locks.

"It makes them more manageable," she muttered defensively, feeling the heat of a blush on her cheeks.

Laughing, Tricia walked over to the counter to retrieve her own lunch. Taking a seat, she watched her youngest child pick up one of the squares. "What brought you over today?" she asked, once Caitlyn had taken a bite and couldn't possibly get up and leave.

Blue eyes rolled at her mother's tactics. Walked right into that hadn't she! Caitlyn finished chewing and reached out for her milk. "Can't a girl come over and visit her mother?"

"You're always welcome, honey. You know that."

"It's my day off and I had nothing else to do," Caitlyn tried, watching her mother's face to see if she believed that.

"You usually come around when things are bothering you at home or work." Seeing her stubborn daughter wasn't ready to talk, she changed the subject. She knew the news of Darcy's return home was bothering Caitlyn, along with whatever had made her come home in the first place. "You found something upstairs to keep you busy. I haven't heard a peep from you since you disappeared up there."

"I got looking through one of my old photo albums. Something smells delicious, are you baking?"

"Cookies. Luke's bringing Olivia over for dinner tonight. I'm not sure if Natalie will come along. I think they're having some trouble."

"I'm not surprised. He was never that serious about her when they started dating."

"I think it's safe to assume they wouldn't still be together if little Olivia hadn't come along."

"It's good that he's trying for her sake, though." Caitlyn picked up another square. "So, catch me up on everyone, Mum. How are Brian and Isabella?" She bit into the soft bread, glad the limelight had shifted from her.

"Brian's busy with work. You know how he is, determined to get promoted, as always. And Isabella..." Tricia smiled. "Izzy is preparing for their third little bundle of joy."

"Wow! Brian is a busy boy, isn't he? How far along is she?"

"Just over three months. She should be having an early summer baby, which is nice because at least she won't be in the last stages of pregnancy if we get any nice weather this year."

Caitlyn laughed and nodded in agreement. "And how's Jeremy? Still stressing over the restaurant?"

"Jeremy and Stacey are thinking of taking a trip to Disneyland."

Baby blues widened. "The one in Florida?"

"No, the one in Paris." Tricia laughed. "Can you imagine them getting their brood calmed down enough for a long plane trip to Florida?"

Caitlyn laughed and shook her head. "No, that's why I asked."

They finished their lunch, managing to catch up on everyone and everything, except what was going on in Caitlyn's life. The matriarch of the family wondered why her daughter was so reluctant to talk. She watched Caitlyn stand up and walk to the sink to dispose of her plate and empty glass, watched as she stood staring out the window at the back garden.

"You know, I can't believe my old Wendy House is still standing," Caitlyn chuckled. "Darcy and I were forever playing in there when we were little and climbing up onto the roof to star gaze or to just be high up. Now my nieces love it as if it were their own and still it stands strong."

Pleased Caitlyn was at least talking about something, Tricia smiled affectionately. "Your dad made it to last, honey. It has served this family well."

"I seem to remember you didn't think it would stand for a week!" Caitlyn teased.

"Yes, well, do you remember the incident with the spice rack?" Tricia laughed. "Are you looking forward to Darcy coming home?" she asked, knowing now where Caitlyn's thoughts were. "You seemed a little...upset earlier."

Sighing, the nurse turned and leaned back against the counter, knowing her mother wasn't going to drop it. "I guess...I am looking forward to her coming home. After so long away, it's about bloody time she came back!" She folded her arms across her chest, ignoring the pang of hurt that blazed through her. "I was upset," she admitted quietly. She met her mother's patient blue-grey eyes. "I'm supposed to be her best friend and she didn't think to once get in touch with me to at least let me know she was okay."

Tricia wasn't sure what to say. She knew something had happened between her daughter and Darcy to cause a rift, a big rift, but neither girl had ever confessed anything to her, so she wasn't entirely sure what had gone on. She reached out to rub her daughter's arm affectionately. "You know Darcy, honey. Stubborn. Always was, always will be."

Snorting, Caitlyn nodded, knowing the truth to that statement.

"Will you be staying for dinner tonight?"

"Yeah. If that's okay?"

Nodding, Tricia moved to hug her daughter. "Sweetheart, this is your home. You are always welcome."

"Thanks, Mum." Moving away from the counter, Caitlyn walked back to the table. "Is everyone coming over when Darcy comes home?"

"Yes. I thought Darcy would love a good old Swailes get-together."

"Darcy hates crowds of people, you bully," Caitlyn laughed.

"We're family, it doesn't count."

Blue eyes again drifted to the garden, memories stuck on her childhood. "I think I'll go and clean up the Wendy House," she said suddenly, a thoughtful look on her face. "Unless you've already beaten me to that as well?"

"No. It's on my list of things to do, but you go ahead, sweetheart." Her head tilted to the right as she regarded Caitlyn. "Honey..."

"Mm?"

"I understand you don't want to talk about whatever it is that's bothering you, but you're okay, right? You're not...sick or anything?"

"I'm fine, Mum. You know me, I'll talk when I'm ready." Caitlyn smiled as she walked over to her mother, hugging her tightly and kissing her cheek.

"All right. I'll be here to listen when you are ready."

"I know." Crouching in front of the cupboard where all the cleaning products were kept, Caitlyn sorted through them, finding what she needed for the intensive cleaning job she planned to do. Dropping the numerous bottles into the old bucket, dented by her brother Luke drunkenly treading on it years before, she added a few old rags and dusters.

"Put your coat on. It's colder than it looks out there," Tricia cautioned.

Wrapped up in her winter coat and beanie hat, Caitlyn took her bounty outside, before returning to the house for some warm soapy water. Then she got down to her task.

It was a nice afternoon, cold yet the sky was as blue as her eyes. She decided to start with the outside of the Wendy House, scrubbing clean the white walls and window frames. On her own, her thoughts drifted once again back to her childhood and her best friend.

"Let's play mummies and daddies," Caitlyn suggested. Taking Darcy's hand, she tugged her toward the Wendy House.

"Why?"

"Because I want to." She led the taller girl inside, squinting as her eyes adjusted to the dimmer light. "I'll be the mummy and you can be the daddy." Letting go of Darcy's hand, she put her hands on her hips as her gaze roamed around the small space. "I have to tidy up this mess!" she declared.

"Where?" Darcy looked around in confusion.

"And you have to go to work." Caitlyn scowled at her.

"Work?" Darcy asked, shooting her friend a baffled look. "What do I do?"

"I don't know, you decide. But it has to be a good job, so you make lots of money. Then you can buy me nice things." Seeing Darcy frowning, lips parting ready with a protest, Caitlyn turned pleading eyes on her best friend. "Please play, Darcy. We can pretend the Wendy House is our home and later I'll ask my mum if we can sleep out tonight, then you won't have to go home." She smiled. "You can stay with me."

Looking thoughtful, Darcy slowly nodded, a small smile curling her lips. "Okay." She walked over to the door. "I'm going to work now. Bye."

"Wait!"

Darcy turned back. "What?"

"You have to kiss me goodbye," Caitlyn explained, like it was the most obvious thing in the world.

"Why?"

"Because that's what my daddy does when he goes out in the morning."

Huffing in annoyance, Darcy plodded back over to Caitlyn and kissed her cheek, before turning to leave again.

"What's your job?" Caitlyn called out as her friend reached the door and pushed it open.

"I'm a pilot," Darcy grinned. "I'm gonna fly to the moon."

"You can't. If you go to the moon, you'll never be home with me."

"Yeah, but least the house would stay clean and you wouldn't have to cook for me."

It made sense. "Okay, fine. See you later." Once the door closed, Caitlyn picked up her brush and dustpan and began sweeping the floor again, singing softly to herself. Remembering her mother opened the windows and doors to let fresh air in the house, she did the same. Standing at the window, she frowned out at Darcy, who was sitting on the grass staring up at the sky. "What are you doing?"

"Planning my trip."

"Oh." Returning her attention to the Wendy House, she put away the dustpan and brush, then stood and nodded to herself for a job well done. Finished with cleaning, she decided to go and get her sleeping bag so she could set it up.

Picking up her empty glass from earlier, she stepped outside and frowned in confusion when she didn't spot Darcy anywhere. "Darcy?"

"Yeah?"

Spinning around, she looked up to see her best friend hanging upside down from a tree branch. "What...what are you doing?"

"Training."

"Training?"

"I saw a show about space travel once. They went upside down, so I thought I should practice."

"Oh. Okay."

"Where are you going?"

"To get the sleeping bags and ask if you can stay tonight."

"Want me to come?"

"You're at work, silly." She waved. "See you later." She walked away, glancing back at Darcy every other step to make sure her friend hadn't fallen out of the tree. Stepping through the double doors and into the kitchen, she looked up at her mother, who was standing at the sink. "Mum, can Darcy stay tonight?"

"If it's all right with Yvonne and Colin. We'll ask later, okay?" Taking the glass Caitlyn held out, Tricia put it in the sink for washing.

"Okay."

"Honey, what is Darcy doing?" Tricia asked, looking out the window at the upside-down girl.

"She's training."

"Training for what?"

"To fly to the moon. She says they go upside down, so she's practising." She headed for the doorway while her mother laughed. "I'm going to get my sleeping bag, just in case Darcy can stay."

"Okay, honey."

Racing upstairs to her bedroom to retrieve her sleeping bag and the spare one Darcy used when she stayed over, Caitlyn threw them down the stairs then followed, picking them up at the bottom and making her way back outside. She found Darcy walking funny across the lawn and frowned as she stopped to observe. "What are you doing now?"

Looking up, Darcy scowled. "You know, you can't keep disturbing me at work like this."

Caitlyn blinked in surprise. "Sorry."

"It's okay, if we're married and all," Darcy grinned. "I'm practising my walk for when I get to the moon."

"Oh. Anyway, you should come home soon. My mum said she's bringing out lunch for us."

"Okay." Turning around, Darcy plodded back in the opposite direction, stopping when she reached the Wendy House. She smiled over at Caitlyn. "I'm home."

"Darcy!" Yvonne Kenton shouted from her back door, making both girls jump. "What the hell do you think you're doing? I told you no going out." She stormed over to the fence that separated her garden from the Swailes'. "I am going to smack you so hard! What did I tell you? You never listen!" She glared over the fence at her frozen daughter. "What are you doing just standing there? Get back over here right now!"

"Hello, Yvonne," Tricia called out as she appeared at her own back door. "Everything all right?" She made her way over to the fence.

Distracted from yelling at her daughter momentarily, Yvonne looked in Tricia's direction. "Oh, hello, Tricia. I was just telling Darcy to come back home."

"She's okay here if you want a break. In all honesty, she keeps Caitlyn out from under my feet."

"I don't want her intruding. I did tell her to stay in the house." The inebriated woman ran her fingers through tangled brunette locks.

"You know how kids are at this age, they do as they please most of the time. At least my lot do!"

"I don't know how you cope with four," Yvonne muttered, eyes darting over to Darcy. "If you don't mind? Only for a couple of hours?"

Tricia smiled. "How about the whole night? Caitlyn asked me if Darcy could stay over. It would give you and Colin some peace and quiet for the evening."

"That does sound nice." As she smiled, Yvonne transformed into a completely different woman. "All right. If you're sure?"

Tricia waved a hand nonchalantly. "No problem at all. In fact, I was going to take them to the park in a little while, if that's okay with you?"

"Yeah, yeah, no problem." She had lost interest in the conversation, her eyes drooping as she glanced Darcy's way. "You behave for Tricia, you hear me?"

Darcy nodded, dark green eyes wide with fright. "Yes, Mummy. Th—thank you for letting me stay over." While her mother said goodbye to Tricia and weaved her way back into her house, Darcy slipped inside the Wendy House.

Yvonne Kenton, a she-devil in disguise, Caitlyn thought, looking at the old Kenton house. Why she took her bad moods out on Darcy, Caitlyn never understood.

"Are you all right, honey?"

Startled to hear her mother's voice, Caitlyn turned in Tricia's direction and offered a small smile. "Fine, Mum. I was just remembering Yvonne."

"Oh." Tricia shook her head. "I brought you out a coffee. How goes it with the cleaning?"

"I've finished the outside, maybe I'll let you do the inside. I don't think I fancy the knee and back ache I'm bound to get from crouching down in there." Dropping the cloth, Caitlyn wrapped her hands around the hot mug her mother handed her.

"What and I do!" Tricia exclaimed in mock outrage.

Caitlyn laughed. "You're my mum, it's your job." She sipped at the coffee and smacked her lips in appreciation. "Mm, good. Thank you."

"You're welcome. You know, I was thinking. Perhaps we should have a family get-together this Sunday. Have everyone over for a good old Sunday roast, catch up with each other and relax."

"Aren't you doing that when Darcy returns?"

"No. I thought of inviting everyone over for her homecoming meal. Aunts, uncles, cousins, Grandma and Grandad, they all love her as much as we do."

"Yes, they all accepted her right off, didn't they?" Caitlyn smiled at a memory from the past and nodded in agreement.

"They did," Tricia smiled. "What do you think about a Sunday get-together?"

"Sounds good, Mum. You know I love your cooking. So do my brothers."

"And what about Ian? Will he be able to make it?"

"Sure," she sighed quietly. "He loves coming over. Though God knows why, none of you are nice to him."

"Oh, honey, that's not true."

Caitlyn gave her mother a look of disappointment. "He tries. He tries so hard with all of you and you give him funny looks and laugh at him behind his back."

"We do not," Tricia replied in a higher pitch than usual.

Recognising a lie when she heard it, Caitlyn sighed and looked away, knowing nothing she said would change their minds. "I better get on. Otherwise I will change my mind and you'll have to do it after all."

"Do you want me to take that mug from you?"

"No, I'll put it on the little table, if it's still in there." Opening the door, Caitlyn peered inside, her nose wrinkling at the smell of stale air that greeted her.

"I keep meaning to replace it," Tricia admitted. "It's seen better days. Shout if you need anything. Or if you get stuck."

"So you can come running out with a camera! I think I'll pass." She smiled as she watched her mum walking away, her cheerful laughter drifting back to her. Turning her attention back to the job at hand, Caitlyn crawled inside the Wendy House. "This seemed a hell of a lot bigger when I was a girl!" She grimaced, putting her mug down on the table.

Shuffling over to the cupboards, she peeked inside and smiled when she found a packet of biscuits and a bag of marshmallows, her nieces doing what she and Darcy had done when they were young. She sighed wistfully as her thoughts again turned to Darcy and their childhood.

"Look, Darcy!" Caitlyn exclaimed excitedly, pointing up at one of a few clouds in the moonlit sky. "It's a puppy!"

"Where? I don't see a puppy. I see a...marshmallow man." Darcy frowned up at the cloud formation.

"It is not! It's a puppy. Look." She shifted closer to her friend, their bodies touching all down one side, their heads close together. "Follow my finger," she instructed. "There's the floppy ear, and a little bit over to the left is his eye, then down to his nose."

"If you say so, Caitlyn," Darcy laughed. "I see a marshmallow man. Look at his bulging belly, and those blobs out there are his big arms." She turned her head to glance at her friend and grinned when baby blue eyes turned her way. Looking back up at the sky, Darcy pointed. "Look at that one! That's a crocodile!"

"No, it's not," Caitlyn argued. "It's...."

"God damn it, Yvonne!" Colin Kenton yelled at his wife. "I work my arse off all day, and this is what I have to come home to!"

"Maybe we should go inside," Darcy suggested softly.

"Oh, you say you're working!" Yvonne slurred back. "For all I know you're fucking the dumb blonde you have working for you!"

"Oh, for God's sake! This again, Yvonne? Why is it I'm always the one cheating? We both know what type of woman you are. Out late, disappearing for days on end only to suddenly turn up again like nothing's different! Hell, I'm not totally convinced Darcy's even mine! She looks nothing like me!"

The sound of breaking glass echoed over to the two little girls lying on the grass. Caitlyn took Darcy's hand and squeezed. "Let's go inside the Wendy House," she whispered, afraid and knowing her friend was too.

Not saying anything, Darcy rolled over and started crawling toward the little house. Seeing Darcy had tears in her eyes, Caitlyn felt bad for her best friend and settled next to her on the sleeping bag, an arm wrapping around Darcy's waist.

"Do they argue a lot?" she asked close to Darcy's ear.

"They didn't used to," Darcy mumbled. "But now...my mum has a lot of drinks and gets mean." She swallowed hard. "She goes out and sometimes she...she doesn't come back for a while."

"Like the time you told me she went on holiday, but you didn't know where?"

Darcy nodded.

Her gaze settled on the dark smudge beneath Darcy's eye. "Darcy..." she trailed off, not sure she wanted to know if Yvonne had been the one to do it. "You can always come over to my house if they start shouting, even if it's nighttime."

"I can't knock on your door at night, it's too late. Your

mummy and daddy would send me home again. Or take me back and then I'd be in big trouble."

"You don't have to knock on the door." Caitlyn sat up excitedly, her idea making sense to her. "I'll leave my bedroom window open for you, then you can climb in. Remember? Last summer, Jeremy dared you to climb up the fence on the wall all the way up to the top and you did."

Nodding, Darcy smiled at the memory. "He said I couldn't do it, so I did."

"It reaches my bedroom window, Darcy. I'll leave my window open and you can come stay with me."

"Thanks, Caitlyn. You're my best friend." Sitting up, Darcy hugged her smaller friend.

"You're my best friend too, Darcy. My bestest friend. For ever and ever."

The two girls settled down as the late hour and active day finally caught up with them. Holding hands, they drifted to sleep.

Finding herself staring out the small window at the Kenton's house, Caitlyn shook her head in despair. "Poor Darcy." What would have happened if she hadn't had them next door? She shivered in horror. It wasn't worth thinking about. Glancing around the now cleaned and polished house, she smiled. "Not bad, even if I do say so myself."

Getting herself out of the Wendy House, she stood up and groaned as her body popped and protested when she straightened herself and stretched. She wondered if Darcy ever thought about her childhood. Or did she block it all out?

Stepping back inside the main house, she found the kitchen empty. Hearing little feet pounding along the hallway, she smiled as she realised her brother had arrived with his daughter. Caitlyn smiled brightly as a little strawberry-blonde charged into the kitchen sporting a beaming smile. "There's my favourite little princess!" she greeted.

"Aunty Caylin!"

Caitlyn picked up her niece and spun her around, making her squeal in delight, before she took a seat at the table, Olivia settled on her lap. "You've gotten bigger since I last saw you. What have you been doing? Anything fun?"

"Playin'."

Caitlyn laughed and looked up at the handsome man who appeared in the doorway. "Hey, Luke."

"Caitlyn!" the light blonde-haired man greeted in surprise.

"Rare to find you here. Everything all right?"

"Fine. Dropped in to visit with mum on my day off."

He nodded, knowing there was more to it than his baby sister wanting to see their mother.

"Leave those alone!" Tricia scolded her son as he reached out to snatch a cookie off the cooling tray. "I've only just taken them out of the oven."

Pouting, he walked over to the table and took a seat opposite Caitlyn and his daughter.

"Do you two want a cup of tea?" Tricia asked.

"Yes please, Mum. It's turned really chilly in the last hour," Caitlyn replied.

"Thanks, Mum," Luke added with a nod. He returned his attention to his sister, curious as to why she was really there, but knowing she wouldn't talk if he pressed. He tried a different topic. "Did you hear Isabella's expecting again?"

"Mum told me earlier." She smiled. "Did she tell you Darcy's coming home?"

Taken by surprise, the carpenter looked over his shoulder to his mother. "Darcy's coming back. When?"

Pouring the boiling water into three mugs, Tricia smiled. "Sometime next week."

"She wouldn't give you a specific day. Or a time?" His dimples popped as he grinned.

"You know she hates a fuss," Tricia laughed.

"And you would cause a fuss!" he chuckled.

"Hold on a minute," Caitlyn broke in, voice full of suspicion. "Why aren't you surprised mum got a letter from Darcy in the first place?"

A guilty look appeared on his face. "I uh...I knew Darce had been writing home."

"Did she write to you?" Caitlyn growled, a perfectly sculpted eyebrow lifted in question.

"No, she sent the odd postcard now and then and a present for Olivia near Chri—"

"She knows about Olivia?" Caitlyn interrupted, growing angrier by the minute.

Luke slowly nodded, his Adam's apple bobbing nervously. "Um, yeah," he squeaked out.

"But how? She had left by the time you and Natalie got together."

Luke looked over to Tricia for help, only to find his mother with her back to him, sensibly keeping out of it. "I bumped into her one afternoon. I was over in France soon after Natalie found out she was pregnant. I was sitting outside a café and she sat down opposite me, grinning goofily. A coincidence. She told me she was passing through and soon to be moving on."

"*Was* in France. Where is she now then?"

"Germany?" Luke questioned in Tricia's direction.

"Portugal," Tricia informed them. "She's been all over Europe, moving on when she grew restless or bored. I'll have to show you the postcards and trinkets she sent."

"Why didn't you show me before? Why is it only now I'm finding out she kept in touch?"

"It wasn't a secret, love. And I never hid them from you. Postcards were stuck on the fridge and a couple of the trinkets are in the living room in plain sight."

"Can we play, Aunty Caylin?" Olivia asked, growing bored of the conversation going on around her.

"Of course we can, pudding." Caitlyn smiled down at the four-year-old. Her emotions were once again all over the place and a distraction was just what she needed. "What would you like to do, play inside or outside?"

"Can we play in the outside house?"

"Course we can." She set the little girl on her own feet and got up herself. "We'll be outside if you need us." Her tone indicated how unhappy she was. "No gossiping about me, Luke. I swear, you're worse than an old woman sometimes!"

Luke watched as his daughter led his sister outside and across the lawn toward the back of the property where the Wendy House stood. "Is everything all right with her?"

"She hasn't said anything. I tried asking, but she had just found out Darcy was coming home and didn't take that news very well."

"Do you think she had another argument with Ian?"

"It wouldn't surprise me."

Sapphire eyes settled on his mother, a deep frown creasing his brow. "Do you think something happened between Darcy and Caitlyn?" he asked, having his own suspicions. "Before Darce left, they were barely talking to each other. And over the years, she hasn't been back home once. Something must have happened, right?"

Tricia sighed deeply, her gaze drifting outside to her daughter and granddaughter. "I know she hurt Darcy many times. I can only assume Darcy had enough and left to start anew."

"She's coming home now, though," he pointed out. Picking

up his mug, his attention shifted back outside. "Do you think they will finally get their act together?"

"We can live in hope, son."

"Perhaps they need a helpful nudge." He grinned at his mother. "Are you planning a family dinner?"

"Something like that. But no interfering, Luke. Your sister's with Ian and Darcy..." she frowned. "We don't know about Darcy."

"But..."

"If things are meant to be, it will work itself out in the end."

"And if it doesn't?"

Tricia sighed and shook her head. "Whatever will be, will be."

STANDING AT HER bedroom window with her arms wrapped around herself, Caitlyn stared out at the silent street below. It was late, or early, depending on how you looked at things. All the houses sat in darkness, most people asleep. Her fiancé, Ian Moran, was one of those lucky people. He was snoring away happily.

She couldn't sleep. Her mind kept playing over the letter, which had swiftly turned her perfectly ordered life upside down. When she had woken up that morning, the last thing she had expected to discover was that her lifelong best friend was return-ing home after years away. Finding out, she hadn't expected the swarm of feelings and emotions that left her a mess for the rest of the day.

Returning home to the two-bedroom house she shared with Ian, she hadn't told him Darcy was coming home. Instead, while they sat in front of the television, the couple talked of work, of upcoming plans with friends, of other daily life worries.

Now, as she stared out at the swaying trees, she wondered why she hadn't mentioned Darcy's homecoming. It wasn't as if she hadn't had the opportunity. She was supposed to love him, was engaged to be married to him, and yet she hadn't thought to tell him the most epic thing that had happened in her day.

She supposed it was because her reason for not marrying him sooner had always been that Darcy was absent and she didn't want to get married without her best friend there to be her maid of honour.

It was safe to assume Ian would think that now Darcy was returning, he and Caitlyn could finally think about getting mar-

ried. She was certain he would eagerly bring up the subject of
them setting an actual date for their wedding.

She frowned. Why was Darcy coming home now? Was she all
right? Why hadn't she written in all the years she'd been away?
Would everything be different now? After all, it had been five
years!

Ian reached out for Caitlyn as he rolled over. Only finding
cold sheets, he groggily opened his eyes and instantly came wide-
awake as he spotted someone standing by the window. "Hey," he
called out softly, realising who it was. He wiped at his eyes as he
tried to focus. "Honey, what are you doing?"

Lost in her head and the numerous questions she had, Caitlyn blinked over at Ian, surprised to see him sitting up in bed. He
sat staring back and she realised he'd said something. "I'm fine,
Ian. Go back to sleep."

"That isn't what I asked, but good to know." He pushed back
the covers and climbed out of bed. "I asked what you were
doing," he told her, shivering when the cold hit him. "Jesus, Caitlyn, it's freezing!" He picked up their duvet and walked over to
her, wrapping the warm covers around them both. "You look like
you're a million miles away."

"Couldn't sleep."

"It's late, sweetheart, and we both have work in the morning." He led them back to the bed. "Try counting sheep."

Settled back into bed, it wasn't long before Ian was once
again snoring while Caitlyn lay on her back staring up at the ceiling, still unable to sleep. She glanced at him. Did she really want
to marry him? She pondered. Surely if she loved him, truly loved
him, she would have married him regardless of Darcy's absence?

Chapter Two

DARCY KENTON STOOD outside on the balcony of her rented home in Portugal, looking down on the people going about their business. She liked people watching, easily picking out the tourists from the locals. It was a game that didn't require much thought on her part. As far as she was concerned, she had done enough thinking for one day, her rambling thoughts giving her nothing but a headache.

A warm arm curled around her waist, soft lips pressing against her neck.

"What are you thinking about, sweetheart?"

"Nothing at all. I was just people watching." Smiling, Darcy pulled Lauren Cansdell around her body until the redhead was standing in front of her, her girlfriend's back against her chest. Wrapping her arms around Lauren's slim waist, she rested her chin on a bare shoulder.

"How many tourists did you spot today?"

"Eight so far." She kissed her girlfriend's neck. "You look beautiful, baby. This dress really suits you."

"This old thing?" Lauren replied in her best southern drawl. "Why, thank you, Miss Kenton." She smiled as she earned herself another kiss. Seeing the amusement dim in Darcy's eyes, she knew that whatever was bothering Darcy had just returned to the forefront of her thoughts. She didn't ask. If Darcy wanted to talk, she would.

Darcy sighed heavily as her inner peace was once again disrupted by her rambling thoughts. "Do you think I'm doing the right thing, Lauren?"

"Do you?" the redhead retorted. "Honey, it was your decision to leave and your decision not to go back for the past five years, and I completely understand the reasoning behind your choices, but..." She sighed, wanting to tread carefully. "They are your family." She stroked the hands resting on her stomach. "Maybe it's time, babe. You can't stay away forever."

"I love you," Darcy murmured, lips curled up into an adoring smile. "You're always my voice of reason."

Lauren shivered at the sensation of soft, warm lips tracing the back of her neck. It was a particularly sensitive spot for her, and Darcy knew it. "Darcy," she groaned, her head tipping forward at the touch of a hot tongue. "Honey, as much as I would like to pursue this, I have to go to the market if you want to eat today." She turned in her taller partner's arms and smiled. "Maybe later?" she suggested huskily. Kissing Darcy's chin, she moved away, not waiting for an answer she was sure she already knew.

"Do you want some company, babe?" Dark green eyes watched Lauren collect her handbag and purse.

Lauren glanced over her shoulder in surprise and slowly smiled lovingly. "No, sweetheart. I know how much you hate shopping and crowds. But thank you for offering, it's very sweet of you." With a wiggle of her fingers, she was out the door.

Once the front door closed, Darcy turned back to face the view, gaze dropping to the street below, waiting for Lauren to appear. She grinned when her girlfriend stepped out of their building and waved when Lauren looked up at her and blew a kiss.

God, she is beautiful. Darcy watched the graceful redhead walk away until she lost her in the heavy crowd. Turning her attention to other sights, Darcy sighed deeply. She wondered, not for the first time and certainly not for the last, if she was doing the right thing. Maybe it would be best to stay away and leave it all in the past. She trailed her fingertips over the rough iron fence guarding the balcony, the radiant sun warming her but doing nothing to dispel her melancholy. But that was just it, wasn't it? She didn't want it to be the past. Caitlyn had always been a part of her life, and the Swailes family was her family.

Green eyes popped open, the little girl holding her breath while she tried to figure out what had woken her from a peaceful slumber. It was May 2002 and at ten years old, Darcy was a little older and a lot wiser. Then she heard it. Angry voices. Downstairs in the living room and getting louder and louder and drifting up to her bedroom.

As something shattered downstairs, Darcy sat bolt upright in her little single bed and swallowed down her fear. It was one of those nights. Again. Knowing it would only get worse, she knew what she had to do. Pushing back her covers, she climbed out of bed to recover her beaten up pair of Nikes she refused to part with.

Quietly, she made her way over to her window, jumping in fright when something else was smashed downstairs. Not hesitating, she opened the window and carefully climbed down the nearby drainpipe, making her way across the front garden and over the small brick wall to the house next door.

It was dark out, the only light coming from the streetlamps, and quiet, no one around at this late hour. Glancing back to her house to make sure she hadn't been spotted leaving, she waited a heartbeat, then another, before finally exhaling in relief when neither of her parents appeared at the door. Carefully placing her hands and feet, she climbed the lattice, which was nailed to the front of the Swailes' house, up to a window she knew would be open.

Climbing through the window, she saw a small figure sit up in bed. "Sorry, Caitlyn. I didn't mean to wake you," she whispered, kicking off her trainers.

"It's okay, Darcy." Caitlyn held up her covers so her friend could slip in beside her. "They fighting again?" She wrapped her arm around her friend as Darcy settled next to her.

Now that she was in the safety of her friend's house, the comfort of Caitlyn's arm around her, Darcy felt her throat tighten and tears flood into her eyes, threatening to spill, as she thought of the anger and venom she had overheard. "Yeah."

"You're here now, no one can hurt you. I won't let them." Caitlyn gave Darcy a tight squeeze.

Darcy let out a trembling breath. "Caitlyn, why do my parents fight all the time?" Her voice was small and tinged with hurt.

"I don't know."

"Your mum and dad don't fight. They ask you how your day was when you get home from school, you eat dinner together and talk, and your dad takes you places and plays ball with you and your brothers." She sighed sadly. "They were fighting about my mum going out again and coming back drunk," she confessed in a whisper.

"Oh."

"I don't know why she does it. Why does she go out and drink when she knows it upsets my dad? Why does she disappear for days and days, then come back like nothing happened? Why does she start shouting at him and...and at me?"

"I don't know, Darce," Caitlyn whispered. "But she shouldn't yell, not at you anyway. You're quiet and good."

Darcy sniffled, her emotions starting to get the better of her. "I heard my dad say he's going to leave," she admitted tearfully. "I thought maybe...maybe I could go with him and start again somewhere else, just me and him, but..." she trailed off as a tear leaked free from the corner of her eye and slowly rolled down to the pillow her head was on.

The dark bedroom remained silent and still when Darcy paused, Caitlyn waiting to hear something she probably didn't want to. "But what, Darcy? Are you going to leave?"

Darcy shook her head, squeezing her eyes shut at the ache in her chest, remembering the argument she had heard loud and clear. "Why don't they love me, Caitlyn?"

"They do love you, Darcy. They're your parents." Caitlyn sat up in bed and looked down at her friend. "I love you, Darcy. You're my best friend. Forever."

To the ten-year-old, it was enough for her. Smiling, Darcy waited for Caitlyn to lie back down then snuggled close, everything right in her world for the time being.

A fond smile curled Darcy's lips. How could she not love Caitlyn? She had made her feel loved, made her think her life was worthwhile, that she was special. Despite what was going on at home.

Darcy turned and walked inside the apartment, pausing long enough for her eyes to adjust to the dimmer light indoors. Despite being the end of November, the weather was pleasantly warm, and she headed into the kitchen to get herself an ice-cold beer. She wasn't really a drinker, not after what her mother had put her through, but every now and then she liked something stronger than orange juice or tea.

She bent down to open the fridge. Without Caitlyn and her family, she would have been a lot worse off than she was. Tricia had fed her and mothered her as best she could, while her own mother — She stood up straight and cracked the lid off her bottle on the edge of the counter.

Drinking from the chilled bottle, she licked her lips and smiled in appreciation of the cold beverage. Leaning back against the counter, she sighed. Her father leaving was the worst thing. He had left for good, leaving her with good old Yvonne!

Darcy stood at the edge of the playing field, her hands on her hips, eyeing her competition. It was sports day. She hated sports day. Not because she was unfit, or because she didn't like physical activity. No, Darcy didn't like sports day because she was a competitor, in it to win it. And if she didn't win, she went into a sulk.

Today she was on the blue team, her favourite colour because it matched her best friend's eyes. Caitlyn was also on her team, everyone knowing the two girls were inseparable.

There were six teams all together, and Darcy's team was currently in second place, with their biggest rivals, the reds, ahead of them by five points.

"The egg and spoon race," Barry Kuffs, the self-appointed team leader, announced. "Who wants to do it?" He looked around at his team. "It can't be Niall because he just did the skipping race, and it can't be Darcy because she did the basketball challenge."

"I...I don't mind doing it," Caitlyn volunteered, drawing groans from the two other boys on the team.

Darcy turned to face the five members of her team, putting her hands back on her hips menacingly, scowling at Oliver and Niall. She was quiet and often shied away from people, unless provoked or her best friend got picked on. "I vote for Caitlyn," she declared, smiling at her friend. "I think you'll be great, Caitlyn."

"You would say that, Stretch Armstrong," Oliver grunted. "She's your best friend."

"You have a problem with Caitlyn doing the race, butt-face?" Darcy glared at the boy upon hearing the much-hated nickname. Stretch Armstrong was one of those retro re-release toys of the early nineties, which had arms and legs that could be tugged on and stretched out. Because of her height, she had been christened with the name. She stood tall, towering over the smaller boy.

Brown eyes widened as Oliver looked up into angry dark green. "No, but look at the other teams." He pointed in their opponent's direction. "They're all picking people with long legs. How's she going to keep up?"

"It's not about running fast, it's about keeping your egg on the spoon," Charlotte Fleming, the other girl on the team, spoke up.

Darcy smiled at the raven-haired girl, acknowledging her support. "Yeah. You can do that, right, Caitlyn?"

The whole team turned to stare at her, making Caitlyn swallow nervously. "I...I guess so."

"You're going to be great, Caitlyn. I know it." Darcy wrapped an arm around her friend's shoulders and led her over to the starting line.

"I don't know, Darce." Blue eyes filled with doubt looked up. "Maybe I should let one of the guys do it."

"No way!" Darcy shook her head. "They'll only try to run

really fast and end up dropping the stupid egg. Remember, it's all about not dropping the egg," she grinned. "You're going to be great, don't worry."

"Which one of you is running?" Miss Berhalter asked as they reached the starting line.

"I am," Caitlyn answered. She took the spoon the teacher held out for her.

"Darcy, go back to your team," the teacher smiled. "I assure you Caitlyn will be fine here on her own." She placed an egg on Caitlyn's spoon, then turned away to get the other racers ready.

Darcy ran back over to her team and gave Caitlyn the thumbs up when her friend looked in her direction.

The race started and Darcy cheered as loudly as she could, shouting her encouragement even when Caitlyn's egg fell off her spoon. The team jumped up and down excitedly and in expectation when Caitlyn closed the gap on the leader, their throats raw from shouting, and when Caitlyn finished third, they hid their disappointment as best they could. Most of them did.

"Jeez, Caitlyn. Could you have gone any slower?" Niall said snidely, as the smiling blonde approached the team.

"Yeah, and you dropped your egg," Oliver added. He smirked at Charlotte. "It's about keeping your egg on the spoon," he repeated in a high-pitched voice.

"Hey!" Darcy growled, shoving Oliver away from Caitlyn. "Leave her alone, Olive Oil. She did her best and got us eight points. Look at Adam, he came last and got nothing for the green team. And Janey got nothing for the yellow team."

"Darcy's right," Charlotte said, smiling at the usually shy girl.

"Yeah," Barry nodded. "As long as we pick up points, it shouldn't matter where we finish the race."

Scowling, Oliver moved away from the trio of girls.

"I'm sorry I dropped the egg," Caitlyn whispered, tears filling her eyes, happiness from moments ago gone.

"You did great, Caitlyn," Darcy reassured her. "You got points, didn't you?"

"Yeah, but...."

"No buts." Darcy grinned. "You did great and almost caught up with Dawn." She wrapped an arm around her friend's shoulders. "Don't worry, you'll catch her next time."

Caitlyn grinned and wrapped her arm around Darcy's waist, the pair following their team to the next event, the bean bag balancing race.

When a short drink break was called, Darcy followed Caitlyn to where Tricia and Joe were sitting. Joe had taken the afternoon off work and was filming everything on his new camcorder.

"Hey, girls," he greeted from behind the camera. "You're doing great out there. Wave at the camera and give a big thumbs up."

"Oh, Dad!" Caitlyn grumbled, though she did what he had asked.

Darcy looked around at the gathered parents, frowning when she didn't spot her own. "Have you seen my mum and dad, Mrs. S?"

"I haven't, honey. Sorry. Maybe they got held up." Tricia handed her a carton of orange juice.

"My dad did go to work this morning," Darcy said thoughtfully. "Maybe he wasn't allowed to come."

"So, girls," Joe said, getting them to face the camera again. "What's up next for the blue team?"

"It's the three-legged raced," Darcy replied, grinning widely.

"And me and Darcy are doing it!" Caitlyn giggled. "I said she should just carry me, and we'd get there quicker."

"A perfect race for you. You're hardly ever apart and now they're going to tie you together!" Tricia laughed.

"You better hope Darcy doesn't trip up, sweetie, otherwise you've never get untangled from her long legs!" Joe teased.

"Hey!" Darcy laughed. "I better hope Caitlyn doesn't fall over, otherwise I'll be dragging her along!"

"You would not," Caitlyn protested. "You would stop to make sure I was okay." She smiled and poked her friend in the ribs. "I know you, Darcy."

"How many points behind are we?" Joe asked.

"Seven," Darcy informed him.

"Yeah, because stupid Niall came in last in the bean bag race," Caitlyn pouted. "He had a go at me for coming in third, then couldn't even win himself."

"The one good thing was he tripped up Eve from the red team, so they got no points either." Darcy wrapped an arm around Caitlyn's shoulders.

"So, you two are going all out to win the three-legged race?" Tricia asked, smiling when both girls nodded enthusiastically. "Well good luck. We'll be here cheering you both on." She waved them off as they were called back across the field.

"Go team blue!" Joe cheered.

That had been a good day, Darcy thought, sipping at her beer. She smiled as she remembered the three-legged race she and Caitlyn had taken part in, the whole team going on to compete in the obstacle course challenge and the relay race, picking up top points in each.

She moved into the living room and sat down on the window seat, green eyes looking out at the beauty of Cascais, called by many the Portuguese Riviera. The salty sea air of the Atlantic Ocean drifted in to her through the open balcony doors, the sound of happy voices from people down on the street reaching her ears.

Her childhood had been blighted with her parents arguing fiercely, a drunken mother who cared for nothing but where her next drink was coming from, and her peers siding against her. That sports day memory was one of very few good childhood recollections she had.

The faint smile curling her lips faded as she remembered the rest of that day, still left wondering why it had gone so wrong.

It turned out to be a good day, the blue team catching up and overtaking the reds to finish in first place. They were presented with gold medals which hung on a blue ribbon and each handed a gold gilt-edged certificate.

Tricia and Joe praised Darcy and Caitlyn, congratulating them on the events they won, and for a treat, bought them both ice cream from the vendor outside the school grounds. Excited over her achievement, Darcy only wished her parents could have been there to see it.

She got a lift home with Caitlyn, eager to get home and show her parents her medal and her impressive certificate. She had never won anything before and couldn't stop staring down at the cream-coloured card with her name written neatly on it in flowing script.

As Joe pulled into his driveway and stopped the car, Darcy hurried to undo her seatbelt.

"Are you going to stay out and play, Darcy?" Caitlyn asked.

"Um, I want to go home first and show my medal to..." She frowned, not sure if her parents were home. "To my parents." Seeing the disappointed look on her friend's face, Darcy gently touched Caitlyn's arm. "I'm not going forever, goof. I'll be back out in a minute or two."

"Okay then, Stretch." Caitlyn smiled brightly.

"Don't you start!" Grinning, she climbed out of the car. "See you in a bit."

"Do you want to stay for dinner, Darcy?" Tricia called out. "You know you're more than welcome if your parents say it's okay."

"I'll ask, Mrs. S. Thank you for the invite."

"You're welcome, honey."

Singing "We are the champions" over and over because she didn't know any of the other words to the song, Darcy made her way over to her house and knocked on the front door. Not getting an immediate response, the ten-year-old guessed her parents were out, so she made her way around the house to the back, where she knew a back-door key was hidden beneath an old flowerpot.

Her dad was probably at work, but where had her mum gone? Had she gotten a new job? Gone shopping? Darcy hoped she remembered ice cream if she'd gone shopping. Or maybe she'd just gone off again.

Finding the key, Darcy let herself into the kitchen and frowned when she stepped inside. The house was quiet, but it looked like it had been burgled. She spotted her mother's handbag on the counter and knew Yvonne was around somewhere. She never left the house without her bag.

"Hello. Mum? Dad?" she called out, waiting but not getting an answer.

She cautiously made her way over the broken glass and plates and out of the kitchen, heart pounding as she crept along the hallway, heading for the living room. She stopped in her tracks when she heard a shuffling sound, eyes going wide as she spotted the shadow of a person on the floor.

Frozen in place, she shrieked when the person stepped out of the living room and turned in her direction. Yvonne jumped in surprise and dropped the glass she held.

"God damn it, Darcy! What the hell is wrong with you?"

"Sor — sorry, Mum. You...you scared me. I thought..." She wasn't sure what she thought and shook her head. "Never mind." She pressed herself against the wall and watched her mother move drunkenly. She could smell the familiar aroma of alcohol on her mother as Yvonne shuffled past her. "What happened in the kitchen, Mum?"

"What does it look like?"

Darcy stood in the doorway, watching her mother fix herself a strong drink. Her heart sank. It was one of those days. "Is Dad at work? He didn't come to my sports day. He said he would try but had to ask Mr. Welch if he..."

Yvonne snorted and turned to face her daughter. She frowned at the little girl, lifting her glass to her lips slowly. "Why aren't you in school? You skiving off, Darcy? I don't want any trouble from the school, you hear?"

Darcy frowned, pretty sure she had mentioned sports day. "School is over, Mum. We had..." She moved as Yvonne lurched her way and followed the older woman as Yvonne made her way back to the living room. "It was sports day and I...I won a medal," she told her mother, lifting the gold disk hanging around her neck. "And we got a certificate."

Yvonne took the certificate and looked at it with glazed, drunken eyes.

"I wish Dad...and you had been there to see me get it," Darcy smiled. "The red team were beating..." She frowned when her mother started to crumple the certificate. "Hey! Don't do that, Mum!" she yelled, trying to snatch it back. "I want to show it to Dad!"

"Show it to Dad! Your dad is gone, Darcy," Yvonne snapped, ripping the certificate in half. "Left because of you! He doesn't care about some stupid certificate, or your bloody sports day! He doesn't give a shit, Darcy. Doesn't give a shit about you, doesn't give a shit about me. He doesn't care!" She finished ripping the certificate into small pieces and threw them at her daughter. "He won't be back. He took all his things. Probably gone off with the bottle-blonde he works with!" She snorted. "Traded in the family he didn't want for a younger model with perky tits!"

Darcy turned and fled the house, tears flowing down her cheeks as she raced off as fast as she could. She didn't have a destination in mind, she only knew she wanted to be away from her mother. The pain of having the one thing she had ever won, the one thing she was proud of, ripped up into irreparable pieces in front of her, made her cry like she never had before.

"Hey, baby. I'm back," Lauren called out, pushing open the front door. "I bought some fresh red snapper. I thought maybe I would serve it with some sautéed onions, garlic, and tomatoes."

Darcy got up and walked to the door as Lauren stepped inside, taking the bags her girlfriend held. "Sounds good, sweetheart. Unless you want me to cook it, then..." she pulled a face, "not so good."

Lauren laughed, following Darcy through to the small kitchen. Darcy's cooking skills were well below par and an ongoing joke between them. She bent to open the fridge to retrieve a cold beer, while Darcy set the bags down and started unpacking them. "I bumped into Joaquina down at the market. She didn't know we're leaving and is very upset. It's your fault somehow."

Watching Lauren trail the chilled bottle down the side of her neck, Darcy licked her lips with sudden want. She stood up straight, eyes following a bead of moisture slowly sliding down the redhead's neck. She bit back a moan when the urge to lick it off with her tongue filled her head.

The shopping promptly forgotten, she stepped up behind Lauren and wrapped her arms around her girlfriend's trim waist, resting her chin on Lauren's shoulder. "You are so beautiful."

"She wants us to, uhh! She wants us to go out for...drinks. Ooh, Darcy!" Lauren moaned as Darcy swept her hair aside and placed hot kisses down the side of her neck. "Tonight. She wants us to go out tonight."

"Uh-huh," Darcy murmured, taking Lauren's ear lobe between her teeth. "We're busy tonight." At a leisurely pace, she slid her hands from where they rested on Lauren's stomach to the tops of her thighs, fingers beginning to lift the thin material of the summer dress. With the dress held securely in one hand, Darcy caressed the smooth, silky skin at the top of Lauren's leg with her free hand, soon moving in to trace a soft inner thigh.

"Mmm, baby!" she groaned huskily when Darcy's fingers traced the crease of her groin. Feeling suddenly shaky, Lauren set her beer down and braced her hands against the counter in front of her, pushing her butt back against Darcy's crotch.

"What?" Darcy murmured softly, grinding herself against Lauren. "What do you want, sweetheart?"

Lauren panted for breath, her body responding to the touch, to the teasing, even as she tried to get her brain working. "You!" she gasped. "I want you, baby!"

"You've got me, baby. But..." Darcy smiled while she worked Lauren's underwear down. She threw the black lace knickers off to the side once Lauren stepped out of them, then caressed her way up shapely legs, momentarily distracted by the feel of silky skin against her palms.

"I...I want..."

"What do you..." Darcy trailed her fingers through swollen, wet folds, making Lauren shudder and cry out, "What do you want me to do?"

"God, I want..."

Darcy nibbled her way along Lauren's shoulder, talented fingers teasing an exposed bundle of nerves, driving Lauren to greater heights. She felt Lauren's clitoris pulse against her fingertips and knew it wouldn't take much to make her girlfriend come. "You want?" she encouraged, the words murmured hotly into the redhead's ear, trailing a hand up Lauren's torso to a breast. "You're not wearing a bra," she noted huskily, pinching the rigid nipple she was playing with. "Giving the market boys an eyeful in order to get a good deal?" she teased.

Lauren groaned wantonly, her head tipping back at Darcy's shoulder at the sensation of stroking fingers gently playing between her legs, while the other fingers pinched and tugged on an aching hard nipple. "Oh, God! Oh, Darce! Fuck me, pleeeaassse!"

Darcy pulled the redhead more firmly against her body, holding her as close as possible, while driving her to the brink of orgasm. The small apartment filled with the sounds of sexual symphony, their panted breathing, their guttural moans, as Darcy stoked the fire burning fiercely within Lauren.

She captured Lauren's hard, throbbing clit between her fingers, squeezing, then softly caressed over the pulsing muscle. Having teased Lauren to lofty heights, it only took a few masterful strokes to make her come.

Lauren cried out, hips jerking in climax. Darcy slipped two fingers inside her girlfriend and curled them to stroke the soft, contracting walls, until they clenched tightly around her, her name spilling from Lauren's lips as she came again. She held Lauren up as her girlfriend's knees buckled, placing soft, loving kisses wherever she could reach and ignoring her own pounding need, savouring the feel of having Lauren in her arms.

"God, baby!" Lauren exclaimed, once she got her breath back. "What got you worked up while I was out?"

"Nothing wrong with a little afternoon delight, is there?" Darcy smiled charmingly as Lauren turned in her arms and looked up at her with eyes full of love. She ducked her head to kiss neglected lips.

"Nope, nothing wrong with it at all." She started undoing the buttons on Darcy's shirt. "In fact," she kissed the hollow of Darcy's throat and along her collarbone, spreading the shirt open, "how about we continued this," she cupped Darcy's breasts firmly, drawing a lusty moan from her girlfriend, "somewhere more comfortable?"

"You mean the kitchen doesn't qualify?" Darcy offered her girlfriend a lazy, content smile.

"Been there, done that. Why don't we try..." Lauren ducked her head and nibbled at a bra-covered nipple, "the bedroom?"

Darcy sucked in a sharp breath when Lauren lightly bit her protruding nipple. "Been there, done that," she teased.

A perfectly sculpted eyebrow lifted, an amused smile curling her lips, Lauren stepped back. "Oh, well then. I suppose I could get on with cleaning the apartment. The floors could do with...."

Grasping Lauren's hips, Darcy pulled her back. "Changed my mind. The bedroom," she groaned as Lauren sucked on her neck, hands cupping her buttocks firmly, "sounds good, baby."

Smiling seductively, the redhead took a step back. With their eyes locked, she started undoing the buttons on the front of her dress while walking backward out of the kitchen. She licked her lips provocatively as the dress slipped from her body in the living room, landing in a puddle at her feet. "What are you waiting for, stud?"

Grinning devilishly, Darcy stripped off her already undone shirt and her bra, stalking after her girlfriend. Her trousers were unbuckled and loose by the time she reached the side of their large bed and pooled at her feet as she hungrily took in the curvaceous form sprawled out before her.

"You are so beautiful, Lauren," she murmured, eyes trailing along the redhead's body. Naked, Darcy climbed onto the bed and settled herself next to Lauren. "Hi," she greeted softly, a small smile tugging at the corners of her lips.

"Hi." Light green eyes studied the contours of Darcy's face. Now that she had time to think and ponder, she wondered what had put the other woman in such an amorous mood. She knew her girlfriend of three-and-a-half years was anxious about them returning home, and she knew Darcy was doubting her decision. She had her own concerns about them going home but hadn't yet let on.

Manoeuvring Darcy onto her back, Lauren decided she wouldn't let her fears of what lay ahead intervene right now. For now, they were away from home and Darcy was hers. She was determined to take her time making love to her, wanting to make this special, memorable, not wanting her girlfriend to forget what she meant to her.

Like it was their first time together, Lauren explored every inch of her lover. She caressed soft, tanned skin, traced small scars, and kissed wherever took her fancy. Darcy's musky aroma quickly filled the bedroom, along with her guttural moans and pleading whimpers.

Lauren suckled on a warm lobe while she explored the dips and rises of Darcy's body. Nipping and marking a slender neck, she traced soft, wet folds with a single fingertip, making Darcy gasp and arch up into her touch. Moving slowly up and then circling down to gather more spilt desire on her fingertip, she smiled, knowing exactly what she was doing to her girlfriend.

"Please!" Darcy finally cried out, eyes closed, body trembling, hovering on the precipice of ecstasy. "Lauren, please!"

Lauren ignored the desperate plea, removing her hand from between Darcy's spread legs. She coated a rigid nipple with Darcy's desire, her smile broadening as the action drew a groan of frustration. "Patience, baby," she murmured, meeting green eyes darkened with arousal. Lowering her head, she softly blew against the nipple, watching as Darcy groaned and shivered. Lowering her head farther, she teased the nipple with her tongue, waiting until Darcy pleaded with her again before drawing the rigid nub into her mouth.

Darcy's back arched and she curled her fingers into red locks as her girlfriend's hot tongue circled and flicked her aching nipple. It felt divine. Each flick, each swipe, each swirl, sending jolts of pleasure down her body to between her legs. She couldn't help but groan in need as she grew ever wetter.

Lauren didn't linger for long. She kissed her way down Darcy's sweat-dotted body and settled herself between Darcy's spread legs. Pausing, she inhaled deeply, taking in the aroma she had helped to create, before delicately parting the soft folds hiding the treasure she sought. She blew softly on the now exposed bundle of nerves, making Darcy cry out and squirm.

"Jesus, Lauren! Please, baby! Have mercy!" Darcy begged, fingers curling around the sheet she lay on and gripping tightly.

Mouth watering in anticipation and having teased enough, Lauren lowered her head and slowly proceeded to lap up every spilt drop of desire from the source, and the flow that followed as she caressed Darcy's throbbing clitoris, not stopping until her name was screamed in climax.

WHILE LAUREN DOZED, Darcy lay staring up at the cracked ceiling of their bedroom. She couldn't move. Not that she wanted to, but Lauren effectively had her pinned. She stroked red strands of silky hair slowly, as her thoughts, much to her shame, returned to Caitlyn.

Whenever things fell silent and she started thinking, she

found her thoughts almost always returned to the family she had left back in England, almost always returned to Caitlyn and their childhood, their teenage years, and early adulthood.

She sighed and closed her eyes, tired of the sight of the chipping white paint above her. I miss her, she thought morosely. And thinking about their lives that were so entwined with each other made her feel like Caitlyn wasn't so far away, like Caitlyn wasn't out of reach. Sleep crept up on her and her thoughts turned once again to her childhood and the day her father left.

Darcy ran until her sides ached, ran until she couldn't draw a breath properly, ran until her legs burned and she wasn't sure where she was. Stopping, she doubled over, panting hard, tears still trailing down her cheeks. Why had Yvonne done that? Why did she have to rip it up? Where'd her daddy go? Was he really not coming back? Would she ever see him again? Would her mum stop being nasty now? Would she stop drinking?

Standing up straight and looking around, she recognised the area. Grove Park was up ahead, so she made her way there, wanting to sit for a while. Entering the park, her legs felt like jelly, but she made herself walk on, looking for somewhere to sit. The afternoon sun had children and adults out. Dogs were running enthusiastically back and forth chasing sticks or balls. Darcy ignored them all.

Spotting an empty bench as she neared the pond, she hurried over and plopped down wearily. Rubbing her face, she wiped away her tears and sweat before staring blankly ahead at Lower Pond. She watched the ducks swimming, not really seeing them, as her rampant thoughts kept her occupied. Would things change now? Would her mum be better? She scowled angrily. She didn't seem better. She seemed drunk.

Fresh tears falling, Darcy let them, not caring. Her day had gone from great to disastrous in the blink of an eye. The joy of sports day, the joy of winning, the joy of a medal and certificate, it all meant nothing now. The memory of the day ruined forever once she got home and was confronted with the truth of her life.

Sniffling and rubbing her nose, Darcy looked down at the gold medal still hanging around her neck, eyes filling with tears again. It hurt to look at it and she knew she could never again look at the medal and not remember what had happened. Her bottom lip trembling, a lone tear slid slowly down her cheek as she took the medal off and stood up to stuff it in her pocket.

Maybe she'd give it to Luke, she thought sadly. Dark green

eyes widened as she remembered Caitlyn. She had told her she would be right back! She hoped Caitlyn hadn't gone to her house looking for her! She got up and started jogging back the way she had come. Worried about her best friend being yelled at by Yvonne, Darcy picked up her pace, her own worries forgotten as she thought of Caitlyn.

It didn't take her long to get back to her own street, and as she approached the Swailes' house, she spotted Caitlyn sitting on her front steps. Darcy offered her friend a small sheepish smile. "Sorry."

"Where did you go?" Caitlyn stared back, a frown creasing her brow even as she tried to hide how hurt she was.

"Just ran." Darcy shrugged.

"Do you want a drink?"

Darcy nodded and walked over to offer the girl a hand up, then followed her friend inside the house, the pair walking through to the kitchen.

"I told you I'd be right back. I'm sorry, Caitlyn."

"It's okay."

"It's not. I can see you're upset."

"Why didn't you come here? I told you..." Caitlyn glanced at Darcy, watching her friend stare at the kitchen floor in misery.

"I know," Darcy interrupted, looking up and meeting concerned blue eyes. "I know I can always come here, but this time I didn't think, I just ran."

Tricia walked into the kitchen. "Oh, hello, Darcy," she greeted with a warm smile. "Everything all right, honey?"

"Yes, thank you."

"Here you go, sweetheart," Tricia said to her daughter, handing over her now framed certificate. "Ready to be placed in a prime spot on top of your bookcase, or wherever you want to put it."

"Thanks, Mum."

"I have a spare frame if you would like me to frame yours, Darcy," Tricia offered.

The colour drained from Darcy's face. "Oh, um...no. No, thank you, Mrs. S."

"It's no trouble, honey. I don't mind."

"I uh, I don't want it framed."

"Are you sure?"

Darcy nodded, ducking her head to discreetly swipe away a tear. "Thank you anyway."

Seeing that her best friend was upset for some reason, Caitlyn walked over and took her hand. "Come on, Darce. Let's go up to my room." She led the way upstairs to her pink bedroom, closing the door behind them, while Darcy sat on the bed. "What happened? Something did, otherwise you wouldn't have run away, and you wouldn't have told my mum no to a frame. I know you, Darce, you were really proud of your certificate."

Darcy looked up from the pale pink carpet and into compassionate blue eyes. "My mum ripped it up because...because my dad left."

Eyes widening, Caitlyn hurried over to the bed and sat next to Darcy, taking her friend's hand. "Oh, Darcy! I'm sorry." As Darcy's shoulders started shaking, she wrapped her arms around her friend and held her while she cried silent tears.

Lauren stroked Darcy's hair while her girlfriend traced patterns into her naked stomach. They lay quietly, neither needing to say anything, while they basked in the afterglow of their afternoon of lovemaking.

The redhead knew this was as perfect as it got. She also knew that soon they would be returning to the real world they had left behind and would be faced with new challenges, like Darcy's love for her lifelong best friend. Stroking soft locks of sweaty hair, she wondered what Darcy was thinking about. She wasn't sure she wanted to ask in case she didn't like the answer.

Feeling Lauren tense beneath her, Darcy lifted her head and looked into troubled green eyes questioningly. "You okay, babe?"

"Fine. I was just thinking." Lauren smiled weakly.

"Want to talk about it?" Darcy shifted until she was lying next to Lauren.

Lauren rolled onto her side, so she was facing Darcy and sighed heavily. "I was thinking about how great the last five years have been."

"Nothing's going to change, babe. Just because we're going back home, it doesn't mean I'm going to stop loving you. Unless..." she frowned, "unless you don't want us to stay together?"

"I do! Of course I do," Lauren quickly replied, reaching out to caress Darcy's cheek. "God, Darce, don't you know by now how crazy about you I am?" She leaned forward to claim Darcy's lips in a slow, loving kiss that was meant to portray all her feelings. She smiled and hummed in delight when she finally ended the kiss and pulled back. "Better?"

Darcy grinned. "Much."

Lauren's smile slowly faded away and she sighed again. "I...I wasn't sure if you would want to keep seeing me," she confessed quietly.

"Why would you think that, sweetheart?" Concerned, Darcy reached out and gently lifted Lauren's chin so she could gaze into the light green eyes that she loved. Not getting a response from Lauren, who looked away, refusing to meet her gaze, she suddenly realised the truth. "Caitlyn."

"You love her, Darcy. You always have."

"Jesus, Lauren!" Darcy growled in frustration, rolling onto her back. She covered her eyes with an arm. "I've moved on. I've stayed away all these years. I've worked her out of my system. And, I'm with you. I've been with you for the past three years! I don't know what it means to you, but it means a hell of a lot to me!"

"It means everything to me, Darcy!" Lauren answered, snuggling closer. "I wanted you for so long and waited while you struggled with your feelings for her, waited while you got over her. But I can't help thinking you only feel how you feel because we're away from home, away from...her. When you see her again, it could all be different."

"She's probably married by now," Darcy murmured, heart aching as she said the words. "Probably got a couple of kids and is living the perfect life she always wanted." She tugged Lauren closer and kissed her forehead, "I love you. You make me happy, you love me. The last five years travelling around Europe together have been great. The three years we've been a couple have been a little slice of heaven. Nothing is going to change, babe."

"Okay." Lauren kissed Darcy because she could and smiled. "So, what got you worked up while I was out shopping?"

"You got me worked up," she answered, not wanting to talk about what she'd been thinking about all day. Darcy caressed naked skin, hoping to distract Lauren. She leaned into her girlfriend, easing Lauren onto her back, her intention to make love to the beautiful woman again. Smiling lovingly as she looked into amused light green eyes, she lowered her head and kissed waiting lips. "Thank you for the last five years, Lauren. Thank you for coming with me, travelling all over with me, thank you for loving me."

Opening her mouth to respond, Lauren blushed crimson when her stomach rumbled loudly, making Darcy burst out laughing.

"Jeez, baby, better feed that thing, it don't sound happy."

"It's your fault, lover." Lauren slapped Darcy's arm. "We missed lunch because we were otherwise occupied."

"Come on then, let's cook the red snapper you bought." Darcy jumped up out of bed and grabbed a T-shirt. "And feed your beast." She left the bedroom laughing.

"Keep teasing me, Darce, and I won't feed you at all!" Lauren called out. Getting up, she walked to the drawers to find her faded jeans and a T-shirt. A photograph on top of the dresser caught her eye, as it always did. A photograph of two smiling girls with their arms around each other. A photograph with the note "Caitlyn and Darcy, New Year's Eve" written on the back.

"You coming, babe?"

"On my way." Slipping the T-shirt over her head, Lauren pulled free her hair and turned toward the doorway.

Chapter Three

WALKING INTO THE hospital where she worked, Caitlyn smiled at Vivian Sammon and Brenda Hayes, two of her colleagues on the children's ward. "Good morning, ladies. How's it looking this morning?" she greeted as enthusiastically as she could.

"Not too bad," Vivian replied with a smile. "But then it is early yet. Do you want a cup of coffee?"

"The good stuff?" Caitlyn asked, eyes pleading.

"Nothing less for you, hon." The older woman chuckled.

"Are you all right, Caitlyn?" Brenda asked. "You look a little weary."

"I didn't sleep very well," Caitlyn confessed, rubbing her forehead. Looking in the mirror that morning, she had looked like death warmed up with dark smudges beneath her weary eyes, baby blue missing their usual sparkle. "I had one of those nights where I just couldn't seem to switch off."

"Couldn't your lovely fiancé help you switch off?" Vivian chuckled, wiggling her eyebrows.

Caitlyn blushed. "Stop that!" she scolded, though smiling. "He tried, but I got news from an old friend and I guess it's thrown me. I wasn't expecting it at all."

"Bad news?" Brenda asked.

"Not at all. She's coming home after five years away travelling."

"You don't want her home?"

"I can't wait for her to get home," Caitlyn replied instantly. "Only...she hasn't been back once during all those years and I'm a little hurt by that." She sipped at the hot brew Vivian had handed her and hummed her satisfaction. "Okay, now I can face the day."

"Good to know," Vivian smiled sadly, "because little Jacob was asking for you earlier."

"Was he all right?"

"Bad dreams, I think. You know he likes to have you nearby afterward."

"I'll dump my stuff in the locker room, then I'll go in and see him before I do anything else." Bidding goodbye to her two friends, Caitlyn made her way along the corridor toward the locker room, waving at familiar patients and fellow colleagues as she walked. She was a favourite of many of the patients because of her gentle, friendly nature. And she always had a smile for everyone.

The heavy antiseptic smell that was common to hospitals was muted this morning by the coffee she cradled, but the hustle and bustle was the same. She could hear someone somewhere singing "Twinkle Twinkle Little Star" slightly off-key.

Poor Jacob, she thought, entering the locker room. The poor little lamb was in the same predicament Darcy had to grow up with. Only he didn't have neighbours he could run to, or family who could take him in. Caitlyn opened her locker and deposited her winter coat and handbag. Jacob was going to end up in care and perhaps a foster home, she thought sadly. She could only hope it would be a good house, with kind people.

A door slamming somewhere drew Caitlyn's attention, dispersing her thoughts of Jacob. She remembered another door slamming shut, only this one shutting in anger and a none-too-happy Darcy storming out into the night.

It was August 2007 and approaching midnight. Caitlyn sat out on her front steps watching the world go by. Despite the late hour, it was still too hot indoors to sleep, so she had come outside to stare at the stars for a while. Because it was the summer holidays, her parents had given her their blessing, and Caitlyn was in no rush to go back indoors, feeling very grown up sitting outside at such a late hour.

Hearing a familiar voice shouting, then a door slamming, she watched Darcy race out of her house. Another fight with her mother! At this hour too. She supposed Mrs. Kenton was drunk as usual.

She got up and hurried after her best friend, having to run to catch up with Darcy, who was already halfway down the street.

"Darcy!" Caitlyn called out, knowing Darcy was about to break into a run. "Hey, wait up!" Darcy didn't stop, but she did slow down, and Caitlyn caught up and valiantly tried to keep pace with her friend's longer strides. "Hi, Darce."

"Hi, Caitlyn."

"Are you all right?"

"Peachy."

Knowing something was wrong, Caitlyn pulled her taller friend to a stop and turned her around, gasping when she saw the blood on Darcy's face. "Oh, Darcy! What did she do?" She cupped

Darcy's cheek gently, eyes full of compassion as she tried to determine how bad the wound was.

"It's nothing. I'm fine."

"Come back to my house," Caitlyn pleaded. "Let me patch you up." She took Darcy's hand and gave it a little tug. "Please?"

Slowly, Darcy nodded and with a sigh of resignation, allowed Caitlyn to lead her back down the street.

Tricia and Joe had gone to bed by the time they got back to the house, so the two teenagers quietly made their way upstairs to the bathroom. Darcy sat on the end of the bathtub and let Caitlyn take care of her.

"What set her off tonight?" Caitlyn asked gently, looking in the medicine cabinet for what she needed.

"She's missing some money and figured I must have taken it."

"Are you okay?" Caitlyn glanced at her friend, who looked back at her sadly, dark green eyes swimming with a lifetime of hurt. "Other than the cut you have."

"I'm good."

So stubborn! Darcy always had to be tough, strong, and detached. Caitlyn turned her attention back to the cabinet. Moving over to her friend, she looked down at the cut. Opening a bottle of antiseptic, she dribbled some onto a cotton ball. "This is going to sting a bit," she cautioned. She winced when Darcy hissed. "Sorry."

"You did warn me," Darcy smiled.

Cleaning the wound and seeing it wouldn't need stitches, Caitlyn washed away the blood then taped down a small bandage to the corner of Darcy's eye. "There you go."

"Thanks, Catie. I uh…" Darcy stood, gaze on the far wall, anywhere but on her friend. "I should go." She left the bathroom before Caitlyn could say a word and reached the top of the staircase before she could stop her.

Surprised at how quickly Darcy had fled, Caitlyn was caught on the back foot. Hurrying out of the bathroom, she grabbed the nearest hand and stopped Darcy from getting any farther. "Stay," she whispered desperately. "Stay with me tonight, please? Give your mum a chance to cool off."

"She's probably crashed out by now."

"And if she hasn't and is still looking for a fight?"

Taking a deep breath, Darcy slowly nodded.

Caitlyn smiled in relief and still holding her friend's hand, led the taller girl into her bedroom. Turning to shut the door behind them, she spotted her mother's head poking around her own door. The pair smiled at each other, then retreated and shut their respective doors.

"Do you want some clothes to sleep in, Darce?"

"Will anything fit me?" Darcy laughed softly.

"I'm not that small!"

"Neither am I!" Darcy slipped out of her jeans, standing up abruptly as Caitlyn laughed out loud. "What?"

"Taz boxers!"

"What's wrong with Taz?"

"Nothing. I just...I never pictured you as a cartoon-on-boxers fan," Caitlyn chuckled. "Now I know what to get you for Christmas."

"You pictured me as a boxer's girl?"

Caitlyn sobered quickly. "Wh—what?"

"You said you never pictured me as a cartoon-on-boxers fan," Darcy reiterated. "And I said, you pictured me as a boxer's girl. As in you were imagining me in my underwear."

"Well, I...you...I've known you my whole life," Caitlyn stammered, cheeks beginning to burn crimson. "I've noticed and..." Panicked eyes flitted around the bedroom, Caitlyn was unable to look at her grinning friend. "You hate anything girlie. It makes sense you'd wear boxers."

Darcy slipped into a T-shirt that had originally belonged to Caitlyn's older brother Brian, then stood awkwardly in the middle of the room. "Um, where exactly am I sleeping?"

"With me, silly. You've always slept with me."

"Caitlyn, I don't think...."

"Would you rather sleep on the floor? Come on, Darcy, don't be daft."

"I don't want to get blood on your pillow."

Caitlyn tut-tutted. "I put a bandage on your cut. I don't think it's bad enough to seep through. Come on, stop being silly."

Darcy nervously slid into bed and backed herself closer to the edge as Caitlyn slid in next to her and turned the lamp off. They lay facing each other, their eyes slowly adjusting to the darkness settling around them.

"I went to the park this afternoon and Janey Inglis was going on and on about some new boy band," Caitlyn whispered. "Duty Free. Have you heard of them?"

"No."

"She wouldn't shut up about them. I told her they probably won't last six months, because boy bands hardly ever do."

"Right."

"And then, we were standing on the playing field, you know near the cluster of trees? And Barry Kuffs and his new best friend, Wayne Jarvie, came up to us and the girls got all giggly. I don't know why they do that, it makes them look stupid, like airheads, right?" Caitlyn barely paused for breath. "Anyway, Janey and Gemma Hegan, I'm not sure if you know her, were flirting and giggling, and then Wayne asked me out." She laughed. "It was so funny because they suddenly stopped talking and giggling and stared at me open-mouthed, like they couldn't believe what had happened."

"What did you say?"

"Barry asked Gemma out and everyone decided we should go to the cinema this weekend." Caitlyn frowned. "I don't think you can class it as a date if everyone is coming along, right? Anyway..." She sensed the change in Darcy, a sudden tension in the body next to her. "Um, Janey turned into a real bitch for the rest of the day, I guess because no one asked her out." she finished, frowning as she tried to work out what was wrong. "Darcy," she murmured, inching closer to the warmth of her friend.

Darcy rolled over onto her other side, away from Caitlyn. "I'm tired, Catie. Good night."

Disappointed because she wanted to talk, Caitlyn sighed. "Night, Darce." She rolled over, her back to her friend and snuggled down. What had just happened?

It seems obvious now, Caitlyn thought with a small smile. Her talking about bloody Wayne Jarvie and Darcy getting jealous. Why hadn't she seen it then? Shutting her locker, she left the room, making sure the door was locked behind her, before making her way back along the corridor toward the ward where Jacob Harduval was.

"Caitlyn!" Jacob called out in delight, his little face lighting up as she appeared on the children's ward.

"Good morning, Jacob," she greeted with a smile. "How are you today?"

"Fine."

"Oh, really? Then you weren't asking for me earlier? Oh, well, I may as well go and—"

"I asked for you! I asked for you!" the six-year-old giggled.

Smiling affectionately, Caitlyn turned back and took a seat next to the bed. "Did you have bad dreams?"

"The bad man was going to get me," he whispered.

"The bad man is gone, Jacob." She leaned in closer. "He can never hurt you again, okay?" She smiled as she got a vigorous nod from the little boy. "Okay. Now, how are you feeling? Is your leg all right?" She patted the hard cast covering the entire length of the boy's right leg.

"Itchy."

"Ah, unfortunately there's nothing I can do about that. But, if you're a good boy today, maybe later I'll take you for a spin around the hospital. How about it?"

"Now?" he asked excitedly.

"Not now. I have work to do first. But later before I leave, okay?"

"Okay. Don't forget, Caitlyn."

"I won't." She offered him her little finger. "Pinkie promise."

"Pinkie promise." Giggling, Jacob hooked his finger around hers.

Waving goodbye, she made her way back along the ward, stopping at the nurses' station. Humming a song she didn't know the words to, she smiled when she spotted Doctor Roycroft walking toward her. "Good morning, Doctor Roycroft."

"Hello, Nurse Swailes." The older man smiled brightly at her. "A little bird tells me you've been working your magic on the patients again."

She blushed at the praise. "I don't know who told you that, but I've done nothing special."

"You've been you," Quinton replied. "That is the best cure I can think of."

"Thank you, doctor," she said, unable to stop her blush from deepening. "Anyway, I best let you get on. I'm sure you have surgery to get to."

"Uh-huh." Quinton glanced down at his watch. "In half an hour or so. See you later, Nurse Swailes."

Seeing Brenda frantically waving up ahead, trying to get her attention, Caitlyn hurried over, her amusement on her face. "Can I help?"

"I need a hand with Nick. He slipped earlier and has broken his wrist."

"Sounds pretty straight forward, Brenda. Unless he's making naughty comments again and you want me to threaten him with an anal probe."

Brenda let out a sharp bark of laughter and slapped her colleague's arm. "It's nothing like that! It's his damn girlfriend. She turned up and I can't get her to leave. She's in the way and causing problems."

"Problems?"

"Questioning everything, mouthing off, blaming me for him falling over in the first place!" She sighed. "Can you lead her over to the waiting area? I'd be ever so grateful." She batted her eyelashes.

Rolling her eyes and chuckling at her friend's antics, Caitlyn followed Brenda to her patient's bed. Stopping next to the bed, she smiled at the two teenagers. "Good morning, Nick." Blue eyes drifted from the boy to the girl seated beside the bed. *Oh, good Lord!* she thought, taking in the slapped on make up, the attitude radiating off her, and the many piercings on view. And her mum thought she gave her problems!

"We need you to go in the waiting area, please," she said politely to the girl. "This shouldn't take too long."

"I'm not leaving him," the girl huffed. "I don't know what you maniacs might do to him next."

"I assure you, no harm will come to Nick."

"He's broke his bleeding wrist!" the girl screeched.

"He's in good hands," Brenda said calmly. "I only need to put a cast on. You could go off to school and come back later."

"I'm not leaving."

"Are you family?" Caitlyn asked. "Because if you're not, you're not allowed in here." She smiled sweetly when the girl huffed and got to her feet.

"I love you, babe," she called back. "I'll be right outside."

After that, it didn't take Brenda long to set Nick's arm in fibreglass mesh and all too soon his girlfriend barrelled her way back in to take a seat next to his bed. The two nurses took their leave, heading for the nurses' station.

"Ah, young love!" Brenda said sarcastically.

"Oh, come on. Don't you remember being young and in love?"

"Yes, but I'm sure I didn't have such an attitude."

"I don't know about you, but I certainly had attitude! The world was wrong and always against me, everything was unfair, and no one understood me at all!" Caitlyn laughed.

"You know, that does sound kind of familiar," Brenda nodded, breaking into laughter. Taking out a pen, she started to write up her notes.

"Do you remember your first love?" Caitlyn asked thoughtfully, having been thinking of her own earlier.

"I do, yes. I remember him fondly," Brenda smiled wistfully.

"Still see him?"

"Every now and then, along with his wife and children." She chuckled. "Poor woman. Seven children!"

"Wow, you had a lucky escape."

"Definitely. How about you? Do you remember your first love?"

"I do."

"Still friends? See him around?"

"No," Caitlyn shook her head. "God, no. I think I heard he's in prison these days! Shows what a bad judge of character I was. Darcy knew. She knew he was no good, but would I listen?"

It was now September 2007.

The local park was the place to go after school, at least it was for Caitlyn and her friends. Having been in the park for the last hour, Caitlyn was growing annoyed with her circle of friends, their immaturity grating on her nerves, along with the nasty comments about other people from school.

She smiled at Wayne as he caressed her thigh. They had been seeing each other for a month now and she still found herself amazed that he had asked her out. He was a dish and could be with anyone. All her friends were jealous, even if they pretended they weren't.

He stood up and offered her his hand. Frowning at him, she watched him nod his head in the other direction and got the hint. Taking his hand, she got to her feet, allowing him to lead her away from their group.

She felt her heart pick up in pace, knowing they would soon be making out, as was common whenever they got together lately. She knew he liked her and was aware he was eager for more than just a make-out session, but she wasn't sure she was ready for that.

He led her around a cluster of high bushes surrounding an old horse chestnut tree, so they were out of sight of their friends, and sat down at the base of the tree, pulling her down beside him.

"You don't mind slipping away, do you?" he asked. "Sometimes those guys are too loud. Sometimes I'm just thinking shut up, you know what I mean?"

"I feel the same way sometimes. Anyway, I like it when it's only us."

"I like being alone with you, too," he replied, eyes on her lips. Closing the gap between them, he kissed her. "I also like kissing you." He wrapped an arm around her, his tongue teasing her lips into parting, his hands roaming over her back.

She scooted closer to the raven-haired boy and wrapped her arms around him when his tongue slipped into her mouth and caressed her own. She stroked the nape of his neck, moaning in a way she knew he liked. Not that she was any kind of expert, but in her opinion, he used too much tongue. Feeling his hand slip beneath her school blouse and stroke her bare skin, she whimpered and pulled him to her, her nipples hard and pressing deliciously against his chest.

Kissing her neck, Wayne worked his hand around to her front and cupped her breast. She moaned aloud and arched her back, pushing herself more firmly into his hand, wanting the stimulation on her aching nipple. When he started nipping at her neck, she knew she had to put a stop to this soon, otherwise it would get out of control.

"Wayne," she murmured, trying to ease back.

"You feel so good, Caitlyn. Smooth and soft." He squeezed the breast he held, making her gasp and clutch tightly at him.

"Wait, Wayne!" she persisted. "We should stop! I want to stop."

"What? Why?" He pulled back and looked at her in disbelief. "No one can see us, don't worry."

"It's not that, Wayne." She scooted backward when he reached for her again. "I should get home and...it's not like I want to do this in the park where anyone could see us or find us."

He exhaled deeply, rubbing a hand through his dishevelled hair in frustration. "Running home to your dyke friend?" he asked grumpily.

Caitlyn frowned and slowly shook her head. "She's not a dy—she's not that way. Who said that?"

"Everyone says it," he snorted. "What, you haven't heard? Everyone thinks she's a fag with the alkie mother."

"Don't say that!" she snapped. "And she's not gay. I would know if she was, I'm her best friend." She stood, more than ready to leave now.

"Yeah, well, maybe you shouldn't be. Who knows what she might try with you?" He got to his feet, towering over her. "Have you not noticed how she doesn't date? Keenan asked her out 'cause she ain't bad looking, but she turned him down three times. Then his brother asked her out, she still said no. They figure it's because they're twins and look alike, but then Adam Roffe asked her out and she still wasn't interested."

"That doesn't make her gay, Wayne. It means she has good taste."

"Keenan said he saw her peeking at girls. You know, like looking at their legs and stuff."

"I don't believe that. Nor anything else he says. I'm going home. See you tomorrow."

"Why is she always over at your house?" he called out, watching her walk away. "Hanging around, getting friendly with your parents, waiting to make a move on you."

Caitlyn continued walking without bothering to reply. She didn't even stop to say goodbye to her friends. Walking home, she couldn't help but think over what Wayne had said. Despite him being a jerk, and the things he said being horrible, he did make some sense. Darcy had never shown an interest in guys. She didn't wear make-up or nail polish. She disliked anything girlie, preferring sports over shopping. Was she gay?

"Hey, Caitlyn," Darcy greeted, falling into step with her friend.

"Oh. Hey, Darcy. You only now coming home from school?"

She wiggled the bag she held. "No, I've been to the shop. You okay, Catie? You look kinda...I don't know, sad."

"I'm fine, Darce." She offered her friend a small smile.

"You sure?"

"Yeah. I was with Wayne and he said some things." She looked at Darcy when she thought she heard her friend growl.

"He's an idiot," Darcy growled. "A pot smoking, moronic, class clown. I bet you anything he either ends up in prison or lounging around on benefits. I don't know what you see in him. You could do much better."

Feeling a sudden surge of anger, Caitlyn picked up her pace. "Who I date is none of your business! And I would appreciate it if you wouldn't insult my boyfriend. You don't even know him!" She stormed off.

"Caitlyn! Hey, Caitlyn, come on."

She heard Darcy calling after her but didn't slow down or stop, knowing Darcy could easily catch-up if she wanted to. She found herself grateful her friend decided to leave her alone.

Wayne Jarvie. What had she seen in him? "I best get on," Caitlyn said to Brenda. "I told Jacob I'd take him for a spin before I leave tonight. Give me a shout if you need a hand or anything."

"Sure thing," the distracted nurse replied. "Don't forget to drop in on Lindsey Underwood. I don't think her mum has left the room since we moved her in there. If anyone can get Freya to go for a coffee, it's you."

"I'll see what I can do." Caitlyn smiled sadly.

Lindsey Underwood had been brought in three days previous after being hit by a van while crossing the road. After many hours in surgery, the teenager now lay in a coma and her doctors could only tell her family that they had to wait and see. It was Caitlyn's job to offer the family some comfort and support, while attempting to ease their anger, anxiety, and feeling of powerlessness, while they waited and prayed for their daughter to recover from her injuries.

Entering the private room, Caitlyn's heart ached at the sight that greeted her. Freya Underwood was asleep in a chair next to her daughter's bed, one of Lindsey's sweaters wrapped around her, her fingers barely touching her daughter's hand.

Caitlyn was a compassionate woman, sometimes too compassionate for the job she did. She hated to see children suffering or in pain, and she occasionally had trouble separating work from her outside life.

Looking at Freya, Caitlyn wondered when the older woman had last left Lindsey's bedside. A quick trip to the cafeteria might do her some good. She walked over to the slumbering woman and gently lay a hand on her shoulder. "Good morning, Freya," she greeted. She moved to check her patient over.

"Oh." Green eyes blinked rapidly. "Good morning."

"Have you eaten?" Caitlyn asked. "Or even left her side?"

"No," the woman shook her strawberry blonde head. "Not yet. I will," she promised emptily. "Later. When I'm sure...when I'm sure she doesn't need me. I mean she might wake up while I'm gone, and I don't want her to think she's alone."

"I know you don't want to, but will you join me in getting something to eat from the cafeteria?" Caitlyn asked delicately. "I can't promise it will be good or in any way edible, but we both need something in our stomachs."

"I don't know, Caitlyn." Green eyes darted back to her daughter. "What if...?"

"I'll have one of my colleagues come in and read to Lindsey for half an hour. If there's any change, they'll page me, and we'll come running."

The two women made their way through the hospital's winding corridors to the newly installed cafeteria. It was much bigger than the old one, now able to provide hot and cold meals, snacks, fast food, and vegetarian options. Rather than sterile white, the walls had been painted a light peach colour. The pair queued up and got themselves a meal and a hot drink, then sat at a table in the corner of the room.

"How are you holding up, Freya?" Caitlyn asked, after the woman had eaten half her meal.

"I don't know," Freya answered honestly. "I just can't believe this has happened. Not to Lindsey, not to my baby girl." She reached for her cup of tea, trying to take in some of the warmth it offered. "It's odd seeing her lying there so still," she said. "If you knew her," she smiled and shook her head, "she's never still! Always dancing, or playing some sport, off with friends—" Her voice broke and she lowered her head.

"I'm sorry," Caitlyn told her sincerely, reaching across the table to cover the other woman's hand. "I know what you're going through, and I wish I could make it all better."

Freya looked up, meeting understanding blue eyes. "I suppose you've seen this sort of accident a lot with the job you do."

"I've seen a few," Caitlyn admitted. "But I have personal experience as well. It wasn't a traffic accident, or even a fall..." she trailed off, not really wanting to go into it. "I um, I know how hard it is dealing with the aftermath, the questions you find yourself asking, the what ifs, the feeling of hopelessness while you sit there waiting for them to wake up, waiting for them to give you a sign that they're okay." She shook her head. "If you ever need to talk, don't hesitate to ask for me."

"Thank you, Caitlyn. I appreciate that." Freya sipped at her tea, watching the nurse poking at the remains of her meal. "Can I ask what happened?" she asked impulsively. "I'm sorry. That's rude of me!" she added hastily, shaking her head at herself. "Forget I asked."

"No, it's fine." Caitlyn offered the woman a small smile, knowing that she just wanted a distraction. "It was my best friend. We were fifteen," she said, thinking back. "And...we had a falling out."

For the first time in their lives, the two girls had seriously fallen out. They ended up not talking to each other after Caitlyn had said something deeply scathing. Darcy avoided her at school and at home, hurrying away if she spotted Caitlyn approaching and not answering her front door when Caitlyn knocked. It almost ended so badly, Caitlyn thought with trepidation, lost in her memories from long ago. She very nearly lost Darcy forever!

October had set in and Caitlyn mooched into the kitchen and

sat at the table, elbows resting on the surface, her chin settled into one palm.

"Hello, honey," Tricia greeted her grumpy daughter. "Did you have a good day?"

"I guess."

"Do you have lots of homework?"

"Not really."

"Will you set the table for dinner, love?"

Caitlyn shuffled despondently over to the drawer where the place mats were kept. Walking through to the dining room, she set everyone a place, then returned to the kitchen for the cutlery.

Walking to the table with a jug of juice, Tricia frowned as she watched Caitlyn setting out the cutlery. "Honey, you've set too many places."

"No, I haven't." Caitlyn blinked, looking around the table to check. "I...I set a place for Darcy."

"Oh. Of course, silly me." Tricia set down the jug, eyes on the teenager. "I hope she's all right," she said conversationally. "She hasn't been around all week."

"She's fine," Caitlyn replied, reminded that it was her fault Darcy was staying away. "She's been at school."

"Well, it's Friday now, sweetheart. Movie night. I'm sure she'll come over."

After dinner, Tricia smiled at her sons as Brian finished doing the washing-up and Luke finished drying and putting everything away. "Okay, everyone. Let's get comfortable in the living room. Brian, why don't you put some popcorn in the microwave. Luke, you get everyone drinks."

The family moved to the living room and took their usual seats, Tricia and Joe snuggled up on the sofa, Brian lay on the floor, Luke took the armchair and Caitlyn sat alone on the two-seater sofa, very aware that Darcy was missing.

Joe popped open his can of beer and poured the chilled beverage into a pint glass. "All right, Lukey, it's your night, son. What movies have you picked out for us to watch?"

"We can't start yet!" Caitlyn protested. "Darcy isn't here."

"She didn't come to dinner, honey," Tricia pointed out.

"I know," Caitlyn pouted, arms crossing defensively. "Maybe...maybe she got held up."

"Yeah, right!" Brian scoffed. "After what you said, I'd be surprised if she was still your friend! I know I wouldn't be."

"Brian!" Tricia scolded.

"That's enough, Brian," Joe warned the eighteen-year-old.

"Shut up, Brian." Caitlyn scowled as tears clouded her vision. Her brother's words were painful, but frighteningly, quite possibly true. She didn't like him reminding her it was her who had driven Darcy away though.

"I tell you what," Tricia spoke up. "We'll give it a few more minutes. It won't hurt to wait, will it?" She looked pointedly at Brian, who shook his head.

Fifteen minutes ticked past, then half an hour, still with no sign of Darcy.

"Honey, we're going to have to put on the first film," Tricia eventually said, as it neared the hour mark. "Otherwise we won't get through them. It wouldn't be fair to Luke, would it? It is his night tonight and he's picked out films he wants to watch."

"Fine," Caitlyn mumbled. "Put on the first film, Luke."

"We can wait," Luke offered. "I don't mind waiting a bit longer."

"No, it's okay. You can go ahead." Caitlyn sank down on the sofa she occupied. While Brian got up to turn out the lights and Luke put in the first movie, she fought valiantly not to cry in front of her family.

Up in her bedroom getting ready for bed, Caitlyn wiped away tears that refused to stop falling. Usually, Friday was her favourite day of the week. It was movie night and after having dinner at the table, they stayed up late watching a trio of films. Then Darcy usually stayed over, and the two girls would talk long into the early hours until they fell asleep.

Tonight, Caitlyn had hated the whole evening. She was used to Darcy being beside her, their feet sharing the footstool, occasionally rubbing against each other affectionately, giggling at funny movies, cuddling when it was scary. But tonight, Caitlyn had sat alone and been very aware of the fact.

"Come in," she called out in response to the soft tap on her closed door.

Luke poked his head in and smiled at her. "Hey. I just wanted to tell you to ignore Brian. Darcy will come around, you'll see."

"Thanks, Luke." She smiled at her brother.

"Night."

"Good night." As the door closed, she climbed into bed and reached out to switch off her lamp. She lay back and waited for sleep to come. What if Darcy never forgave her? What if the last thing she said was the last ever thing? She glanced in the direction of her unlatched window. Was today payday? A frown creased her brow as she tried to remember. Or was it last weekend and that was why Darcy was over here when she got home? She nibbled on her bottom lip. Surely if today was payday Darcy would have come over?

She wasn't sure when she fell asleep, but it was a hand on her shoulder that woke her. Her mother's hand gently rousing her.

"Caitlyn, come on, honey. Wake up."

"Mum?" she questioned groggily, cracking open one blue eye and seeing it was still dark. "Mum, it's still dark out," she whined, snuggling back into her covers, the warmth inviting.

"I know, honey, but we have to go to the hospital."

Caitlyn sat up instantly, eyes wide open now with fear. "The hospital? Is Jeremy all right?" Her oldest brother had moved out of the family home when he started university. If they were lucky, they saw him once every two weeks when he returned with his dirty laundry.

"Jeremy's fine, sweetheart. It's Darcy. Now, be as quick as you can, all right?" Tricia hurried out of her daughter's bedroom.

Caitlyn scrambled out of bed, kicking at her covers frantically to get herself free. Darcy was at the hospital. Was that why she hadn't come over tonight? Why was she at the hospital? Burst appendix? Broken leg? Or was it Yvonne? How did her mum know Darcy was at the hospital? She put on an old pair of jeans and a sweater, then grabbed her trainers and hurried from her room.

Downstairs, Brian and Luke were bleary-eyed as they fumbled to put on their shoes, awake but not totally with it. Caitlyn sat down on the second from bottom stair to put on her shoes.

"How do you know, Mum?" she asked as she tied her laces.

Tricia met her husband's eyes, a silent conversation going on between them. Joe gave a little shrug, leaving it up to Tricia. "Your father and I were watching television, when I noticed blue lights playing across the ceiling. I got up to look through the curtains and spotted an ambulance and a couple of police cars outside." Her children ready, she shepherded them outside to the car.

"But how do you know Darcy's involved?" Luke asked.

"They were at her house, honey."

"Yeah, but..." He climbed into the back of the car with his siblings.

"I popped over to see if everything was all right and it

wasn't," Tricia told them, her tone telling them she didn't want any more questions.

The drive to the hospital was made in silence. Caitlyn desperately wanted to ask more questions but didn't dare. Instead she sat worrying, her imagination coming up with worst-case scenarios.

The parking lot was almost empty at such a late hour and Joe picked a spot as close to the doors as he could. The Swailes family hurried inside, Joe directing his children to the seats, while Tricia strode up to the reception desk to try and find out about Darcy's condition and what was going on.

Caitlyn sat next to her father on a hard metal chair. Luke and Brian sat on Joe's right side talking quietly. She ignored the walking wounded, the man with his bleeding head temporarily bandaged, the group of party girls one of whom had her shoes off and swollen ankle raised. She watched her mother, sure if something terrible had happened she would see it on her mother's face first. She watched Tricia turn to a nurse who appeared, watched them exchange words, frustratingly unable to gauge anything.

Tricia finally turned away from the nurse, her face taut with worry. Making her way to her family, she took the seat next to her daughter, wrapping an arm around her.

"What did they say?" Joe asked his wife. "Would they tell you anything?"

"Darcy's in surgery. That's all she would tell me because I'm not family, even though I explained the situation."

"Will she tell us when Darcy's out of surgery?" Caitlyn inquired, voice laced with fear. She felt sick to her stomach, one of her worst fears come true.

"She said the surgeon would come when he could."

"Mum, where's Yvonne?" Luke asked. "Shouldn't she be here? I mean Darcy is her kid, right?"

The Swailes siblings watched their mother share a look with Joe and knew then that their parents knew something and were keeping them in the dark about it.

"Mum?" Caitlyn pressed. "What did she do? She did something, right?"

"Why don't I take the boys to the vending machines?" Joe suggested. "Do you want a hot chocolate, Caitlyn?" he asked kindly. Getting a nod from his daughter, he looked to his wife. "Trish?"

"A coffee would be wonderful, love. Thank you," Tricia smiled wearily.

"Come on, boys. We're going to get drinks."

Left alone with her mother, Caitlyn knew she was going to be let in on the secret. "Mum, where is Yvonne?"

Tricia sighed and hugged her daughter closer to her side. "Honey, Yvonne's been arrested along with some man named Ricky." She brushed a hand through dishevelled blonde hair. "I can only assume he is Yvonne's man of the moment."

"What...what did they do, Mum?" Caitlyn asked, feeling a swell of nausea rush through her as the word surgery flashed in her head.

"I don't know what went on, sweetheart. Like I said, I went over and Darcy was..." She licked dry lips, blue-grey eyes on her daughter. "Darcy was being brought out on a stretcher."

Caitlyn inhaled sharply. "Was she...did she see you? Did you tell her we'd be here?"

Tricia shook her head. "She wasn't conscious." She squeezed her trembling daughter. "But try not to worry, Caitlyn. Darcy's in good hands here."

They sat quietly then, the sounds of the hospital keeping it from being truly silent.

Caitlyn chewed on her bottom lip as her imagination ran riot. What if Darcy was really, really hurt and didn't make it? Why hadn't she come over? Had she tried to, and Yvonne caught her? You didn't have surgery unless you needed it and mum said Darcy was unconscious.

Joe, Luke, and Brian returned from the vending machines and handed Tricia and Caitlyn their drinks.

"No news?" Joe asked.

"Nothing yet."

Caitlyn cradled her hot cup, staring blankly at her surroundings, while her parents spoke softly around her. Worried eyes watched the women at the front desk, tracked a nurse as she wandered by, listened to the ringing of a phone. She wondered how long Darcy would be in surgery and how long it would take the staff to inform them.

Their drinks were long gone by the time a man in scrubs headed in their direction. He looked around the waiting area, seemingly looking for someone, then focused on them. "Are you here for Darcy Kenton?"

Tricia jumped to her feet, looking nervous and apprehensive. "Yes, we are. Is she all right? We've been waiting so long."

"Why don't we go somewhere a little more private." He pointed to a nearby door.

In what turned out to be an office, the doctor perched on the front of the desk, while the family settled into available chairs.

"My name is Doctor Roycroft and I operated on Darcy," he started. "Now, I'm only talking to you because one of the nurses and the police have informed me a little about the situation. Usually, it's only the family spoken to, but Darcy has no one else I hear."

"How is she, doctor?" Joe asked, irritated by the man's rambling.

"Darcy has some head trauma and we had to operate to relieve the pressure on her brain."

"What caused the head trauma?" Caitlyn asked, bewildered by what she was hearing. "Did she bang her head on something? Was she...hit?"

"I don't know what went on, but Darcy has three broken ribs, two fractured ribs and a badly broken wrist. We had to insert a metal rod. Her skull has been fractured by blunt force trauma and will be closely monitored."

"The head injury...it's not bad, is it?" Tricia asked. "I mean I know it's bad, but...there won't be lasting damage, will there?"

Doctor Roycroft folded his arms across his chest, his face grave. "We don't know right now. We'll have to see when she wakes up. She was unconscious when she arrived and we now have her in a barb coma, or induced coma."

"What does that mean?" Caitlyn asked, hysteria swelling in her chest.

"It's a temporary coma brought on by a controlled dose of a barbiturate drug," he explained. "It's used to protect the brain during major neurosurgery and reduces the metabolic rate of brain tissue, as well as the cerebral blood flow. What that means is the blood vessels in the brain narrow, decreasing the amount occupied by the brain and the cranial pressure." He looked around at their blank faces.

"In English?" Joe requested.

"We're keeping Darcy asleep to give her body time to adjust to what's happened and to help with the healing process."

"So, this coma is stopping her brain from swelling?" Joe asked.

The doctor nodded. "The hope is that with the swelling relieved, the pressure decreases and some or all brain damage, if there is any, may be averted."

"Can we see her?" Caitlyn asked desperately. "Can I see her?"

"For a moment, then I suggest you go home and get some rest. We'll be keeping an eye on Darcy tonight, or this morning rather, to see how she responds." He stood as the family did and followed them out of the office. Taking the lead, he led them through the hospital and upstairs to the intensive care unit.

Caitlyn swallowed hard as her gaze fell on Darcy, her breath catching as she bit back a sob. Her friend was hooked up to machines and lying ever so still. From where she stood, she could see the thick bandage around Darcy's head, the white of it standing out against her tanned skin. She didn't hear what the doctor was saying to her parents, didn't hear them calling out to her as she moved into the room, she only wanted to be with Darcy, wanted Darcy to know she was there and that she did care.

She stopped next to the bed and choked back a sob as she saw up close her friend's bruised and cut face. "Oh, Darcy!" She delicately picked up Darcy's hand and cradled it, her thumb slowly stroking back and forth, watery blue eyes watching Darcy's face. "Why didn't you come over, Darcy?" she whispered brokenly. "You always come over." She felt her heart clench in pain as she realised it was probably because of her thoughtless words that Darcy had stayed away.

"If only I hadn't said what I did." Caitlyn swiped at suddenly falling tears. "You're so damn stubborn, Darcy Kenton! You could've been killed! You should have come over, no matter what!" she whispered fiercely. "I know there are times you feel unloved, unwanted, but you are loved, Darcy. You are."

"Honey," Tricia called out. Coming up behind Caitlyn she put her hands on her daughter's shoulders. "Come on, love. Let's go home."

"We can't leave Darcy alone, Mum!" Watery blue eyes looked up at her mother. "What if she wakes up? She'll think no one cares!"

"Honey, she's in an induced coma. She won't wake up until the doctors think it's time."

"What if something happens and they have to wake her up? We should be here just in case. Please, Mum. Please can I stay? There's no school tomorrow, it's the weekend."

"Oh, sweetheart! Nothing's going to happen to Darcy. She's in good hands now, they're keeping a close eye on her." Tricia glanced at her watch. "Why don't we head home and get some rest? We'll have a nap, have some breakfast, then be back in time for visiting hours."

Caitlyn stubbornly shook her head. "Something could happen

while we're gone. The doctor said they're keeping an eye on her to see how she responds after surgery. She could respond badly."

Seeing her daughter wasn't going to budge, Tricia sighed heavily, then smiled lovingly at the younger blonde. "Peas in a pod!" she teased. "Let me go and see what the doctor says then."

"I felt so guilty," Caitlyn recalled. "Blaming myself for the argument, which made my friend stay away from my house, for being such a bitch, for not trying harder to make up with her. Then there was the fear. The fear that she wouldn't get better, or she would but she would have brain damage, or she would have amnesia and wouldn't remember me or our lifelong friendship."

"I'm sorry you went through that," Freya said sympathetically. "At a young age as well."

"Me?" Caitlyn blinked. "I was fine, it was Darcy who nearly died."

"Your friend was hurt, but you were beating yourself up over your argument," Freya replied. "It must have been hard for you to deal with. How old were you, fifteen?"

"I did give myself a hard time. And every day I sat there and waited, not knowing if she was going to wake up or give up." She exhaled, hating to think about it. "It was hard."

"But she got better?" Freya asked, hoping for a happy ending.

"She did," Caitlyn smiled brightly. "The doctors woke her, and things weren't easy, but we got there in the end."

"That's good."

"Doctor Roycroft was one of her doctors, so I assure you, Lindsey is in good hands."

"All the staff here have been wonderful."

"And what I was trying to convey is, don't be too hard on yourself, Freya. What happened has happened, but Lindsey is young and fit and has a very loving family waiting for her, along with many friends by the sound of it."

"She does, far more than she probably knows," Freya smiled. "I meant to ask, my husband told me he's had numerous phone calls from her friends asking if they can come in and visit her. Would that be all right?"

"That's fine." Caitlyn smiled. "Familiar voices around her might tempt her into waking. It is said some people in comas can hear what's going on around them, so by all means have a few come in when they can."

"Thank you, Caitlyn," Freya said sincerely. "You have been a godsend. I'm very grateful, my whole family are."

"It's nothing, Freya. It's why I'm here." The nurse blushed.

"Thank you anyway. You no doubt don't hear it enough." Freya looked down at the remains of her now cold meal. "Um, have I been away long enough now?" she teased.

"Yes, I suppose." Caitlyn laughed. "You go on, I'll clean up here."

"Thank you again. For everything."

Caitlyn watched the woman stand and hurry away, sending up a prayer for Lindsey, before she got to her feet and cleared up their plates and cups. She had gone into nursing after seeing the care Darcy got when she was in hospital.

It was hard to witness sometimes, the devastation, the suffering and pain, but then there was the other side of the job, the gratefulness, the children smiling and laughing, relieved families looking your way and thanking you for your input into their child's recovery.

It may be tough, but it was definitely worthwhile at the end of the day. She allowed herself a small smile. They were so lucky with Darcy. The injuries she had sustained could have changed her life forever. She couldn't even imagine what would have happened if there had been brain damage. Their lives would have been completely different. She nibbled on her bottom lip. They wouldn't have... She shook her head. No, don't go there, Caitlyn! It won't do anyone any good to drag up those memories!

Glancing down at her watch, she hurried for the exit, knowing she had other duties to take care of before she could call it a day.

Chapter Four

LAUREN STOOD IN the kitchen humming softly while she prepared breakfast. She had been woken by soft kisses and a wandering hand. A nice way to wake up if she were honest. The only thing puzzling her was why Darcy suddenly couldn't get enough of her. Not that she was complaining. They had always had a great sex life, but now it was as if her girlfriend were in super active mode and the reasons why concerned her.

Stirring the scrambled eggs she was making, she could hear Darcy singing in the shower slightly off-key and smiled. Her girlfriend was unable to carry a note if her life depended on it. Bending to check on the toast she had under the grill, she thought back to Darcy's mood before she had left to go to the market and her mood once she had returned and smiled as she fondly remembered exactly how they had spent their afternoon and early evening.

Walking into the kitchen dressed in a bathrobe, a towel around her neck to catch droplets of water from her wet hair, Darcy stepped up behind Lauren and wrapped her arms around her girlfriend, bending to nuzzle her neck. "Mm, baby. You smell good." She kissed Lauren's neck. "And that food looks to die for."

"It's plain old scrambled eggs on toast, babe."

"Yeah, but you're making it."

"All right, charmer, go sit down. Or better yet, set the table, please." She watched Darcy collect the cutlery and prepare them both a glass of milk. She couldn't help but think that this simple life they had carved out for themselves away from home was about to be lost. Darcy had assured her nothing was going to change, but she was adult enough to know that it might.

Plating the food, she walked to the table and set one of the plates in front of Darcy, hating how insecure she felt. She had been tormenting herself with maybes and what ifs ever since Darcy had mentioned wanting to go home. The truth was she didn't know what was going to happen and simply had to wait and see.

"Thanks, babe. Do we have any ketchup?"

Lauren nodded and walked to the fridge to retrieve the red sauce. "So, what are the plans for today? Do you need to go off somewhere to get more photos?"

"No, I think I've been pretty much everywhere of interest. I'm happy with the shots I've got." She took the bottle offered to her.

Whilst at college, she had discovered a love of photography and had taken it up as a hobby while travelling. A woman named Margo, a friend of a friend, owned an art gallery and after seeing some of Darcy's work, offered her some wall space to see if her photos would sell. They had and Darcy's work was now very popular among Margo's clients.

"You always take great shots, Darce. You know I love your work."

"You're biased, sweetheart, but thank you anyway," Darcy grinned. "I thought maybe we should go and meet up with Joaquina, seeing as how we blew her off last night."

"Yeah, that's a good idea. I'll shower after we finish up here, then we can go looking for her." She smiled. "She's probably incredibly pissed off at you."

"Me! What did I do?" Darcy asked as innocently as she could.

"Whenever we're late turning up, or if we don't show up at all, it's always down to you, my love. I'm the innocent party here." Lauren laughed.

"Didn't hear any complaints last night," Darcy replied, wiggling her eyebrows.

The couple found Joaquina at her father's café, a welcoming place situated in a beautiful spot on the coast, with views of both the ocean and the Sintra mountains. True to Lauren's warning, the raven-haired woman was annoyed at Darcy, but not for very long. She liked the couple and had become a good friend to both during their stay in Portugal. The trio took a seat at an outside table, enjoying the warmth of the sun, while they people watched and relaxed.

Joaquina worked for her father, though she was very laid back about it, often spending more time chatting to the customers than serving them. Her father didn't mind. He said the relaxed atmosphere kept people coming back.

"I should have known," Joaquina said, an eyebrow raised in Darcy's direction. "You are so...*apaixonado!* It takes you over!"

Lauren looked at Darcy for a translation, her girlfriend having picked up more Portuguese than she had.

"Passionate," Darcy grinned. She looked at a smiling Joaquina. "*Desculpa*," she apologised. "Lauren *é lindo*."

"That she is, my friend," Joaquina nodded, still smiling.

"What did she say?" Lauren asked their friend. "Something insulting, or...?"

"No, nothing like that." Joaquina laughed. "She said you are beautiful."

"Oh." Lauren blushed and glanced at her girlfriend. "Thank you."

"*Eu te amo.*"

"I love you, too," Lauren smiled adoringly and leaned over to kiss Darcy's waiting lips.

"Ugh! Doesn't it make you sick how in love they are?" Kendall Grenier flopped down into a chair at their table. The bottle-blonde hailed from New York and was loud and brash, but at the same time, willing to do anything to help someone out if she could. She smiled brightly at Darcy and Lauren. "How are you, love birds?"

"Good," Lauren replied for them both. "Yourself?"

"Great! The couple I'm working for now are agreeing with all my suggestions," Kendall smiled. "I love it when they do that." As a wedding planner she travelled the world searching for beautiful places to host weddings. "So, Darce, tell me you have some new photos due out." She had become a big fan of Darcy's work and had already purchased five framed photos.

Darcy nodded. "I went to the Belém tower last week and have some great shots. I also went to Cape St. Vincent and took some panoramic shots of the views. And almost ready to go on sale are the photos I took at the Knights Templar castle in Tomar."

"Excellent! I can't wait to see them," Kendall smiled. "Heard you two were heading back to England, is it true?"

"Yep. Have to go back some time."

"Why? Is this place not heaven?"

"We can always come back," Darcy told her. "But I have family I should really go and see, and Lauren has to check up on her business affairs."

"True, very true." Kendall sat back in her chair and lit a cigarette. She frowned as she studied Darcy, exhaling smoke before speaking. "I thought you left home because...what was it, some girl?"

The colour drained from Lauren's face, the redhead hating to be reminded of Caitlyn and the hold she had on Darcy.

"I left because I wanted a change," Darcy replied. She reached out to take Lauren's hand.

Kendall laughed out loud. "That means it was some girl!

Don't worry, Darcy, it happens to us all eventually. One gets under your skin and gives you hell!"

"Kendall!" Joaquina shook her head at the American. "You have no...." She searched for the right word.

"Tact," Lauren suggested, smiling to ease the blow. "I'm sure that's because she's a New Yorker."

"Too bloody right!" Kendall boasted. "Tell it how it is and let the world know when you're not happy."

"Do you want coffee?" Joaquina asked Kendall, knowing she had a love for the stuff. "Do any of you want coffee?"

"You know me, honey," Kendall replied, smiling at the waitress. "Besides, if we don't order something, I'm fairly sure your father will be out here like a shot demanding to know why!"

"I'll have an orange juice, please, Joaquina," Darcy said politely.

"You see?" Joaquina directed at Kendall, whilst pointing at Darcy. "That is the way you get good service." She left her three friends sitting in the sunshine and making small talk.

"Will you be returning to America for Christmas, Kendall?" Lauren asked.

"Oh, yeah. The whole family gets together. They're kind of pissed at me for not returning for Thanksgiving, but I had to work." She stubbed out her cigarette, a naughty grin spreading across her lips. "Did I tell you of my trip to Sagres the other day?"

When Joaquina returned with their drinks, she found the three women laughing and in good spirits. "What did I miss?" She set down the tray, which held not only their drinks, but pastries also.

"Kendall was telling us how an older gentleman was trying to get fresh with her when she went down to Sagres," Lauren replied, smiling.

"Enough about horny old men trying to seduce me!" Kendall laughed. "Tell us your coming out story," she said to no one in particular. "Everyone has one."

"Why would you care to know?" Darcy blushed and found something interesting to look at across the street.

"Ah, honey, you're blushing!" Lauren chuckled and rubbed her girlfriend's arm affectionately. "Shall I go first?"

The women laughed when Darcy nodded enthusiastically.

"I was twenty-one..." Lauren started.

"Late bloomer, huh?" Kendall interrupted.

"To each their own," Lauren shrugged. "Or it could have just been my family's views on gays, which caused my hesitation to explore my true feelings."

"Homophobic?" Kendall asked.

"Very," Lauren nodded. "Though, I think that was due to their age. You know how it is with the older generation. Anyway, I got a job working in my uncle's bar and one night in walked a vision," she smiled in remembrance. "An angel."

"Love at first sight, hmm?" Joaquina smiled.

"I don't think I breathed for about two minutes!" Lauren chuckled. "And, of course, she came over to the bar and stood in front of me. Blonde, statuesque, the greenest eyes you will ever see!"

"What happened?" Darcy asked in amusement, never having asked about her girlfriend's past.

"I nearly swallowed my tongue!" Lauren laughed. "She tried starting up a conversation with me and I kept stammering and tripping over my words. It was so embarrassing!" She hid her face in her hands, cheeks tinged red. "She told me later that she found it very cute."

"You ended up together?" Joaquina asked in surprise.

"She stayed all night and as it neared closing time, business died down and she came over to the bar. She asked me if I wanted to play pool," she recalled, a faraway look in her eyes. "And asked if I was interested in making a bet. If she won, she got a kiss and a night out with me sometime, and if I won, it was up to me to choose."

"You won?" Joaquina guessed.

"She kicked my butt!" They all laughed. "So, we kissed and," Lauren sighed dreamily, "it opened my eyes. After a couple of months of sneaking around, I boldly decided to tell my parents and..." She shrugged. "They kicked me out."

The three women looked at Darcy, waiting for her to contribute her coming out story. "Oh, all right!" she sighed in mock annoyance. "Can I get another drink before I start?"

"You are stalling!" Joaquina rolled her eyes. She smiled good-naturedly. "A good idea though. The sun is warm today. Beautiful. Does everyone want a fresh drink?" Getting nods all around, she weaved her way between the outdoor tables, smiling and conversing with other customers as she headed for the café entrance.

Watching her friend walk away, Darcy heard Lauren and Kendall start up a conversation about New York in winter, Darcy's photos, and the suggestion of Darcy opening her own gallery. Darcy allowed the conversation to drift past her, her thoughts instead turning to Caitlyn and the autumn she had realised her preferences.

Ever since her father had left, Darcy's mother had embraced her wild side even more and with more regularity. It was September 2007 and Yvonne Kenton thought nothing of waking up to a glass of vodka, or cider, or if she wanted to be discreet, an Irish coffee.

As the years ticked by, she started coming home later and later and sometimes not alone. Darcy would often sit in awkward silence while her mother entertained some man she had picked up at one of her haunts. She would stay seated until she grew tired of them and their behaviour, then slip away to the sanctuary of her bedroom, or over to Caitlyn's house.

This Thursday was like every other Thursday when it was payday. Yvonne had returned from her favourite bar with a "friend." Darcy watched on uncomfortably as the two adults flirted outrageously over dinner, lewd comments being said none too quietly, Yvonne giggling like a schoolgirl and continually running her hand along the man's bare, heavily tattooed arm. The man, Ricky Prunty, returned the caresses whenever he got the opportunity, and not only to Yvonne's arm.

After dinner, Yvonne disappeared into the kitchen to get fresh drinks for herself and Ricky, Darcy following with the dirty dinner plates.

"Hey, Mum," she started, wanting to talk to her mother about her juvenile behaviour.

"I wish you wouldn't call me that when I have company!" The older woman turned around holding two full glasses of whiskey. "I don't want my friends knowing I'm a..." She trailed off, shaking her head. "I never wanted you in the first place. I don't understand why you can't move out and find your own life."

"Like I chose you!" the teen muttered.

Yvonne lurched toward her, causing half of the amber liquid to spill onto the newly mopped floor as she stumbled. "God damn it! Look what you made me do!"

"Sure, it's my fault you decided to get drunk so early in the evening!" Darcy rolled her eyes. Why was it always the same?

"I don't know why I kept you! I should have got rid of you when I had the chance!"

Though said slurred, the drunken yet heartfelt words were too much for Darcy. Her jaw clenched tightly, her fists balling up as she fought the urge to strike her mother.

"Nobody is ever going to love you, Darcy! You're...you're unwanted!"

Instead of attacking Yvonne, Darcy stood to her full, imposing height, turned, and stormed out of the kitchen. She slammed the front door behind her, nearly smacking into Caitlyn standing just outside. "Jesus! Sorry, Catie, I didn't see you."

At the age of fifteen, Darcy stood at five foot nine and was still growing. Caitlyn had just topped five foot four, much to her annoyance. All her brothers were six foot or close to it, while she was the smallest of the bunch.

"Was that a joke about my height?" Caitlyn teased, watching her friend shake her head.

Darcy stood waiting for her friend to say something, wanting nothing more than to run, desperate to be away from Yvonne, if only for a while. "What's up?"

"I was um...I was going to uh...Darcy, are you all right?" Caitlyn stuttered, head tilting to the right as she regarded her friend. "You've got your 'I want to run' look on."

Should she tell Caitlyn? Confide in her the way she used to. Darcy sighed, a frown creasing her brow. No, everything was different between them now. Everything changed when they started high school. "I'm fine, Caitlyn. But I have to go." She started walking.

"Would you like some company?"

"Sure. Come on," Darcy nodded, sensing her best friend needed some time away from her own house.

Caitlyn looped an arm around Darcy's once she caught up, remaining close to the taller girl. "Where are we heading?"

"The park. I was going to sit by the lake for a bit."

They walked in a comfortable silence, the two lifelong friends not needing to fill the gap with mindless chatter. Their old neighbourhood hadn't changed much over the years. Shops had closed and been replaced with something new, families had come and gone, graffiti had been updated, but overall, the neighbourhood was still the same.

Grove Park had been given a much-needed face-lift by the local council, and Darcy took a seat on one of the new wooden benches that faced the Lower Pond, which flowed through the park as part of the River Wrythe. She felt her anger, fear, and anxiety start to fade away. The hurtful words spoken by her mother not forgotten, but not as prominent as they had been.

Caitlyn sat next to Darcy, blue eyes following a pair of geese swimming by. "Were you fighting with your mum?" She looked at her friend when she got no response. "I heard shouting when I reached your door."

"You know Yvonne," Darcy shrugged, not really wanting to talk about it. Not here where she often found peace.

"Darcy." Her voice sounded loud in the stillness of the early evening around them. She took her friend's hand.

"Yeah?" She held onto Caitlyn's hand, their fingers entwined. She didn't know why her friend reached for her, but the contact felt right.

"Darce, you know you're my best friend."

"I thought so. You gonna tell me different?"

"No! No, of course not."

Darcy waited, but Caitlyn said nothing more. "Catie," she sighed softly, finally breaking the silence that had fallen between them. "Whatever it is, just say it."

Caitlyn took a deep breath and focused her attention on the swimming geese and ducks, unable to look at her best friend. "Darcy, are you...are you gay?"

"What?" Darcy exhaled in surprise. She had been expecting Caitlyn to tell her she was pregnant. This hadn't crossed her mind. She cleared her throat, trying to think. "Why are you asking me that?"

"I heard some stuff at school. There are rumours, comments, insults. People say stuff about you."

"Oh, I see!" She dropped Caitlyn's hand and jumped up from the bench. "Your so-called friends at school have said something and what they say goes!"

"It's not like that, Darcy." She watched her friend pace. "I heard things and I got thinking. You've never had a boyfriend, never shown an interest in any of the boys, and you're not...you're not like other girls."

Darcy swallowed hard at the lump suddenly filling her throat. Was she gay? Did she have to be labelled because she wasn't like everyone else? Had she said anything to make people think she was gay? Done anything to make them think that? She shook her head. She couldn't have done, she was a loner. She shied away from them all. Darcy glanced at the patiently waiting blonde and wondered if Caitlyn hated her.

"You don't wear dresses or skirts, you've never worn nail polish in your life, or makeup, and you don't care one way or another about your hair as long as it's not in your eyes!" She took a deep breath and found the courage to glance in Darcy's direction. "You are, aren't you?"

Hurt and afraid once again, Darcy glared at the small blonde. "I don't have to answer you one way or the other. Fuck, Caitlyn! I just got grief from dear old Yvonne and now I'm getting it from you as well! I'm going home. Don't follow me!" She raced away, leaving Caitlyn to sit on the park bench alone in the waning light.

Later, Darcy lay on her bed in shorts and a sleeveless T-shirt. It was hot and stuffy in her bedroom, even though the window was open and summer was technically over. After returning from the park, she had locked herself in her room, choosing not to confront Yvonne again that night. Now, as the sound of creaking from her mother's bed drifted along the hall, panted breathing and heated moans and groans following, the teenager sighed heavily, wishing she hadn't argued with Caitlyn so she could escape over to her friend's house for some respite.

With nothing else to do, she found herself thinking back over her short life. It had never been easy living with Yvonne and Colin and when her father walked out on them things had gotten even worse.

Yvonne was an alcoholic. Though, if you asked her, she would tell you that she only liked a drink or two to relax, liked having a good time because there was nothing wrong with that, and truth be told, she was a bit of a party girl at heart. To Darcy, she was an unbearable alcoholic who only cared about where her next drink was coming from. Yvonne spent most of any pay packet she got on drink, filling the house with her favourite tipples before disappearing down to the pub or to local bars.

Darcy took it upon herself to steal what little she could from Yvonne's purse to keep the fridge-freezer and cupboards filled with food. Things were okay when there was little money available, but come payday, Yvonne would go into work half-cut and lose yet another job, making life a struggle again.

Yvonne constantly directed blame Darcy's way, making it clear she never wanted a child and didn't know how to care for one. Darcy had only ever known love from Caitlyn and her family. It was the Swailes family who gave her hugs and showed her she was loved. It was Tricia who cleaned up her cuts and scrapes, Tricia who made sure she got a warm dinner and fresh veg.

Rolling onto her side, Darcy felt her chest ache from years of hurt and neglect at the hands of her own mother. And the added torment of being rejected by her peers. Tears stung her eyes. Peers who seemed to be spreading rumours about her, even though she hadn't done anything. She barely talked to them!

What's made them turn their attention to her?

She knew she was different. She had always known. And now it seemed others knew as well. The children at school had always thrown taunts her way. Adults and children alike gave her "looks" that reminded her she didn't fit in. She had learnt to ignore it over the years, had learnt to pretend she had missed the not-so-quiet comments, pretended not to notice the glares and looks of distaste turned in her direction.

She wondered why people hated her for something she couldn't change. She was only being herself. It wasn't as if she were hurting anyone. She was just trying to make her way in the cruel world just as they were.

Rolling onto her back, she wiped away the tears that stung her eyes, then stared unseeing up at the ceiling. She realised the sounds from her mother's room had ceased for the time being. A trembling breath escaped her lips as she frowned and thought again about what Caitlyn had asked, trying to analyse what she felt.

Caitlyn was her best friend. She'd always been her best friend. Only these days she wasn't exactly thinking of her as only a friend. She hated that they weren't together as much now as they used to be. Whenever they were apart it felt like an eternity. And when she was with her... Darcy smiled. When she was with Caitlyn, the world was right. Her world was right. She loved it when Caitlyn held her hand and missed her touch the moment she let go.

Darcy sighed and rolled back onto her side, restless and unable to remain still. She watched the net curtain fluttering from the breeze. She had gotten jealous when Caitlyn told her about stupid Wayne Jarvie asking her out. Darcy snorted. And now they were dating and he was around Caitlyn's house after school and most weekends, or she was off with him....

Knowing she wasn't going to sleep for a good long while yet, she got up and paced back and forth across the room, her carpet soft underfoot, her arms swinging as she tried to burn off excess energy. In the silence of the night, she argued with herself about her life, who she was, and how she felt about those in her little circle.

"Hey, baby," Lauren waved a hand in front of Darcy's face. "You with us?" She smiled lovingly as her girlfriend blinked and came back to the present. "Drifted off somewhere nice I take it?"

"Sorry, babe," Darcy grinned sheepishly. "Just thinking back to my childhood."

"Your coming out story?" Kendall asked. "Going to share?"

"Why the interest?" Darcy asked, a dark eyebrow raised in question.

"Something to talk about."

"Why not tell us yours?"

Joaquina returned with a tray of drinks and set the cups and glasses in front of the women. "Tell us what?" She took a seat.

"Kendall was about to tell us her coming out story," Lauren informed her.

"Ooh," Joaquina clapped her hands in delight, eyes on the New Yorker. "Tell us!"

"All right, fine," Kendall rolled her eyes. "I was fourteen and a real wild child. I used to disappear with my friends until all hours of the morning, drinking and smoking, mostly pot, no doubt driving my poor parents insane!" She reached out for her coffee. "That's how I met Paisley. She was the older sister of one of my friends."

"She was your first girl crush?" Lauren questioned.

"My first everything," she replied with a wistful smile. She sipped her steaming coffee, the roasted aroma wafting up her nose. "My first crush, first kiss, first love." She set the cup down and licked her lips. "My parents were delighted," she chuckled, "because I suddenly calmed down, no more wild parties and too much drink and pot. They adored Paisley. We told each other we would be together forever, but when she went off to college and met new people, our relationship fizzled out." Done with her story, she levelled her gaze on Darcy. "So, Darce, I've told you mine, are you going to tell us yours?"

"Nothing to tell. I haven't technically come out yet," Darcy smirked.

"What?" Joaquina frowned. "How is this possible? You are, how old?"

"Don't tell me you're a classic closet case!" Kendall exclaimed.

"I fell in...lust with my lifelong best friend. She's straight and broke my heart a hundred times as we grew up. There were rumours about me, but I never confirmed nor denied. I never cared for anyone other than Caitlyn. Until I started travelling with Lauren." She looked at her girlfriend. "Then I fell for her charms."

"Just my charms?" Lauren smirked.

"Among other things," Darcy laughed.

"Did you ever tell her how you feel?" Joaquina asked curiously.

Sighing heavily, Darcy felt a dull thud in her chest from long ago hurt. Her head tilted as she frowned, trying to recall if she ever had said the words out loud. "Maybe I did, or maybe I never actually said it, just thought it. A lot."

"Okay," Lauren said suddenly, sitting forward in her seat. "We've done coming out stories —"

"Except me," Joaquina spoke up, a small grin gracing her lips.

"You have a coming out story?" the redhead asked in surprise. "But I thought..."

"Are you holding out on us, Joaquina?" Kendall laughed.

The waitress shook her head, laughing at the looks on their faces. "No, I like men. But it's rude not to ask."

Lauren laughed, thoroughly amused. "My apologies," she conceded. "Joaquina, do you have a coming out story you'd like to share with us?"

The women laughed as Joaquina tilted her head in thought. "No, I don't have one to share. But thank you for asking."

Shaking her head at her friend's antics, Lauren looked around the table. "Okay. How about confessions of our most embarrassing moment?" She stared at Kendall, her eyebrow lifted in challenge as she waited for the American's tale.

"Oh, all right!" Kendall threw her hands up. "My most embarrassing moment was when I was in London. I got roaring drunk with a few friends and they dared me to strip and go paddle in the Trafalgar Square fountains." The women laughed while Kendall had the decency to blush and look around to see who else had heard her confession.

"My most embarrassing moment was when I spotted this absolute Adonis," Joaquina confessed, a faint blush already colouring her cheeks. "I was trying to act so cool. Like I didn't care if he noticed me or not. Then I walked into a streetlight and fell flat on my butt!" She laughed along with her friends. "He came running over and tried to help me up while laughing at me and telling me I should get my eyes tested. I jumped to my feet and ran away."

"Mine?" Darcy frowned, trying to think. "I went skidding across a supermarket after treading on a dropped grape. Hoping no one had noticed my flailing, I tried to style it out by pretending to grab something down low on a shelf and split my trousers!" She ducked her head while the other women laughed, tears springing to their eyes as they imagined the scene.

"You win, honey!" Lauren caressed her girlfriend's thigh.

"How about worst memory?" Kendall asked, wiping her eyes. "Mine has got to be breaking both legs on the first day of a family skiing trip! God, that was the worst vacation ever!"

"No!" Joaquina gasped. "How long were you in a cast?"

"Six weeks!" Kendall groaned. "Six weeks of hell!"

"Mine is when my uncle died," Lauren confessed. "He took me in when my parents kicked me out and let me work for him at the bar. He was my family, my friend, then one day he was gone."

While Joaquina regaled them with her worst memory, Darcy thought back to her own. The time in her life when she was at an all-time low. And, of course, it involved Caitlyn. Lifelong best friends, inseparable, no one could come between them...until they started high school. Then everything changed.

Friday night was movie night at the Swailes' house and Darcy always attended. She had been going every Friday since the idea was thought up by Joe. The whole family, including Darcy, would sit down to dinner at the dining room table, then afterward, they would move into the living room to watch back-to-back movies.

Every week it was the same, Tricia snuggled up with Joe on the sofa, Brian sprawled out on the floor if he was in, Luke sat sideways on an armchair, his head hanging off the side, and Darcy and Caitlyn sat together on the two-seater sofa, their feet up on the footstool.

Darcy had always liked it when it was Jeremy's turn to pick what they watched. He liked horror films, which scared Caitlyn to no end, meaning she would snuggle up against Darcy's side. She wasn't sure why, but she liked having her best friend close to her. But since Jeremy had moved out to go to university, horror films were a rare choice these days.

That wasn't the only change. Now, Darcy wasn't sure of herself, or her place in Caitlyn's life.

Ever since they had started high school, things had been different. Caitlyn made a new circle of friends and had at first tried to include Darcy, until it became painfully obvious her best friend didn't fit in with them and that her new friends didn't like her. Whilst Caitlyn was outgoing, friendly, and the girl everyone wanted to know, Darcy was shy and detached, didn't like big crowds, and preferred to be by herself rather than with a group of people.

The two friends rarely spoke in school and now that Caitlyn had a boyfriend, they rarely saw each other out of school.

Kicking a stone out of her way, Darcy heard a car pull up beside her but didn't turn to look. If they were going to kidnap her, they could at least take her somewhere nice, she thought morosely.

"Darcy, would you like a lift home, honey?"

At the sound of the familiar voice, she turned and smiled at Tricia. "Hi, Mrs. S." She walked over to the car, affectionately called the mum-mobile by Joe, as Tricia pulled to a stop at the kerb.

"We haven't seen you at the house lately, Darce. Is everything all right?"

The teenager shifted from one foot to the other, fidgeting as she debated whether to tell the older woman the truth. Tricia had always been like a mother to her, but she wasn't her mum, she was Caitlyn's. "Everything's fine. I've been busy with...stuff."

"Oh. Well, it's Friday now. Movie night. You can't miss movie night, honey," Tricia said cheerfully.

Darcy found herself grinning. "A lift home would be good. Thanks, Mrs. S." Walking around the car, she slid into the passenger seat.

Tricia drove toward home, trying to engage a naturally shy Darcy in conversation. She finally gave up on trying to draw her out of her silence and instead told Darcy about her afternoon and what she planned to cook for dinner that October evening.

Pulling into the driveway, Tricia stopped the car and climbed out as Darcy did, the pair of them heading to the rear of the vehicle to get the shopping from the boot. Tricia led the way to her house, getting the front door open and leading the way through to the kitchen, complaining about prices rising.

"Let's get this shopping put away, then we'll start on dinner," she announced, smiling warmly at Darcy." How would you like to chop up the potatoes? I know you proclaim to being unable to do anything in the kitchen, but I've had you chopping veg for years."

"All right. I can do that," Darcy smiled.

The front door opened as Darcy returned to the kitchen after setting the dining room table, Caitlyn's voice drifting along the entrance hall.

"Hello, sweetheart," Tricia called out. "You're late getting home."

"Hi, Mum." Caitlyn stopped in the kitchen doorway, blue

eyes flicking from her mother to Darcy then back again. "Wayne and I were with friends at the park."

Tricia glanced in her daughter's direction and lay eyes on the tall, scruffy-looking Wayne. She smiled politely. "Hello, Wayne. It's nice to see you again."

"Hey."

"You'll have to send Wayne home, Caitlyn. Tonight is family night."

"Darcy's here, she's not family," Caitlyn argued, not looking Darcy's way.

"Caitlyn!" Tricia warned.

"You only invite her 'cause you feel sorry for her," Caitlyn continued, Wayne barely hiding his sniggering. "Her dad's gone and her mum's a waster—"

"Caitlyn, that's enough!" Tricia snapped. "Show Wayne to the door, then get your butt back in here." She and Darcy watched Caitlyn take Wayne's hand and storm away. Tricia turned her attention to the silent Darcy. "Ignore her, honey. She's showing off."

Darcy's jaw twitched as she clenched her teeth. She cleared her throat, wrestling with her emotions. "I forgot, I can't have dinner tonight. I have to um...I have to go to the library 'cause I have an essay to do."

"Oh, I see." Blue-grey eyes remained on the teenager.

"I know it's Friday, but I...I want to get the books I need so I can work on it all weekend." She felt uncomfortable under Tricia's scrutiny and shifted her weight nervously from one foot to the other.

"That sounds very sensible, Darcy," Tricia smiled, eyes softening. "Though I'm disappointed you're going to miss the dinner you helped prepare. Perhaps you'll be back for the movies tonight?"

"I'm not sure." Darcy shrugged, not wanting to say no but knowing she wouldn't be.

"You're always welcome here, Darcy. Don't forget that."

"Thanks, Mrs. S. Bye."

"Bye, Darcy."

Leaving the Swailes' house via the back door, not wanting to see Wayne and Caitlyn, Darcy walked with shoulders slumped, her heart aching. Her one friend had turned against her. She didn't belong anywhere. No one wanted her around.

They didn't talk all that week, Darcy thought, coming back to her senses and smiling as the women around her laughed at something she had missed. Every time she had spotted Caitlyn coming in her direction at school, she turned and hightailed it away. Darcy reached for her orange juice, the glass chilled and slick from condensation. She winked at her girlfriend, who beneath the table, caressed her thigh. Lauren always seemed to know when she'd drifted off to memories of her past. Caitlyn and she weren't talking, so she had nowhere to escape to the one time she really needed to. Yvonne and her man of the month kicking off and her getting caught in the middle!

"Are you all right, sweetheart?" Lauren asked quietly, leaning in so she wouldn't be overheard.

Darcy nodded, turning her head to kiss Lauren's cheek. "Thinking about a bad time in my life. One that I don't want to share with everyone."

"Hospital?"

"Before that. An incident with Caitlyn. We had a falling out."

"Oh." Lauren rubbed Darcy's thigh.

"What are you two whispering about?" Joaquina asked, spotting the couple talking in low tones. "Planning your escape from our company so you can run back to your love nest?"

"You know us so well, Joaquina." Darcy lifted Lauren's hidden hand from her thigh to rest on top of the table.

"No, my friend. I know you so well!" Joaquina teased.

"It's Friday," Kendall chipped in. "That means date night. You should be out partying, not rolling around like dogs in heat!"

"I'm sure the dating gods will forgive us," Lauren replied, lips curling into a naughty grin. "I call out for him or her enough times!" The women laughed in surprise while Darcy turned a deep red. Getting to her feet, she looked down at her girlfriend. "Shall we go, honey? Or did you want to stay here chatting to these two troublemakers a bit longer?"

"How about we meet up tonight and go out on the town?" Darcy looked at each of their friends.

Kendall and Joaquina looked at each other, then back at the couple. "Sounds like a plan," Kendall nodded. "What with you two leaving soon, we should go out dancing or something. When are you leaving?"

"Next week," Darcy replied. "We haven't booked the tickets yet, but I'm aiming for next week."

"I'm in for tonight," Kendall smiled.

"Me too," Joaquina nodded. "How about we meet up at the Cinco Lounge?"

"Eight tonight?" Lauren suggested.

"Yeah, that gives you two enough time to get your fill of each other," Kendall smirked.

"I could never get enough of Lauren," Darcy retorted, making her girlfriend blush. "See you later, guys."

"Be good." Lauren waved goodbye. "Kendall," she added, laughing as Darcy led her away from the café.

As they strolled slowly toward their rented apartment, oblivious to the wide-eyed tourists around them, she broke the silence. "What was this bad memory you were thinking about?"

"A week before I ended up in hospital, it was a Friday and I was at the Swailes' house. Caitlyn came home with her then boyfriend, Wayne Jarvie," she said the name with distaste, "and she said something hurtful, something that I really took to heart. I ended up avoiding her the next week at school and at home and, unfortunately, the next Friday was after a payday and I had nowhere to go."

"And it all kicked off," Lauren finished, having heard her girlfriend's sorry tale before.

Darcy nodded. "I honestly don't remember much about it. Maybe I don't want to and have blocked it out, but..." She sighed deeply. "I woke up in the hospital and was told I had been put in an induced coma to aid my recovery."

Returning slowly to consciousness, Darcy became aware of two things: one, she wasn't in her bedroom, and two, there were people in the room whose voices she didn't recognise. She tried to open her eyes but found her eyelids incredibly heavy for some reason. She frowned and mumbled in protest, causing the voices to cease.

"Darcy?"

That voice sounded familiar, but Darcy couldn't place it through her fogginess.

"Darcy, can you hear me?"

The voice held a hint of excitement and Darcy felt a gentle squeeze to her hand.

"Come on, Darce. Open those green eyes of yours for me, hmm?"

"Caitlyn?" she mumbled, fighting against the heaviness that was preventing her from waking up properly. Her voice sounded incredibly rough and she wondered if she'd been drugged.

"Yes!" Caitlyn half-sobbed excitedly. "Yes, Darcy, it's me." She squeezed the hand she held again. "Open your eyes, baby."

Baby? Darcy expelled a deep breath, coming over sleepy suddenly. "Tired, Catie," she murmured.

"Okay. You sleep now, okay?"

"'Kay."

"I love you, Darce," Caitlyn whispered close to her friend's ear.

The next time she became aware of her surroundings, Darcy heard other members of the Swailes family talking, along with a voice she didn't recognise. Curious, she tried opening her eyes again, this time managing to do so a little before the lights overhead forced her to close them swiftly once again. She squeezed the hand holding her own, wondering who the owner of the appendage was.

"Darcy?"

Caitlyn. Was she here earlier? Was earlier today or yesterday? "Caitlyn?" she murmured, not realising she was smiling.

"Darcy? Can you hear me?" the voice she didn't recognise asked.

"It's okay, Darce, he's the doctor," Caitlyn reassured her.

"Can you open your eyes, Darcy?" the doctor enquired.

"Too bright."

"Okay. Let me turn the lights down, then I would like you to try again, all right?"

"All right." She heard footsteps moving away from where she was lying, a click, then the footsteps returning.

"Okay, Darcy, the lights are off."

Slowly, her eyes fluttered open, blurred sights greeting her. "It's all blurry," she announced, blinking to try and clear her vision. She turned her head to the small figure sitting by her bed and smiled when Caitlyn slowly came into focus. "Hey."

Caitlyn promptly burst into tears and launched herself forward, hugging her fiercely. "Oh, Darcy!"

Startled by her friend's reaction, Darcy wrapped her arms around the trembling girl and held her, a comforting hand trailing slowly up and down Caitlyn's back. "Hey, it's okay, Catie." Worried and confused, she looked to the other people standing nearby, seeing Tricia and Joe, Luke with a tear in his eye, and Brian and Jeremy. "What's going on?"

"Darcy, I'm Doctor Roycroft," the voice she hadn't recognised told her. "You were brought in two weeks ago unconscious. We had to operate because you sustained some bad head trauma, and afterward, we put you into an induced coma to aid with your recovery."

"Oh." Darcy lowered her head to where Caitlyn's head was resting on her chest, picking up the aroma of her friend's shampoo and lightly sprayed on perfume. "It's okay, Catie," she whispered. "I'm okay." She looked back up at the doctor. "How did I get head trauma?"

"We're not sure," he answered. "But from the injury, I would say you were hit with a heavy blunt object."

Tricia moved closer to the side of the bed and sat down next to Caitlyn, reaching out to soothe her daughter's crying. "Something happened at your house, Darcy," she explained. "There were police cars and an ambulance parked outside. When I went over to see what was going on, you were being brought out."

"Where's...where's my mum?"

"She was arrested, honey. Along with a Ricky Prunty."

Darcy frowned as the name triggered a flash of memory, making her tighten her hold on Caitlyn.

Feeling Darcy tense, she looked up, her eyes red and puffy. "What is it, Darce? Do you remember something?"

Darcy tried to grasp the fragments of the memory. "They...they came home drunk," she recalled. "They started arguing about..." She shook her head, unable to recollect. "I don't know. Something. They were shouting and fighting each other. Ricky got nasty. I saw him grab my mum and he slapped her hard. I...I tried to help."

Getting a good idea of what had happened, fresh tears filled Caitlyn's eyes and swiftly fell. "Oh, Darcy!" She clutched her friend as tightly as she dared. "Why didn't you come to me? Why didn't you come over like you always do?"

"I..." Darcy shrugged, not wanting to go into it in front of everyone. "I don't know."

"Bet I do," Brian said none too quietly.

"It...it was because of me, wasn't it?" Caitlyn asked softly. "Because of what I said?"

"No. No, Caitlyn. I didn't want to come over to your house." She had heard what Brian had said and could see the guilt on Caitlyn's face and wanted to reassure her best friend. She didn't want this eating her up inside. "I can't keep coming over to your house, I have to grow out of the habit." Not wanting to discuss the matter further, she looked at the silent doctor. "How long will I be here for?"

"Your wrist was badly broken, and we had to insert a rod to help the bone knit, that's going to take at least six weeks to heal. As you can see, it's been put into a cast. You have fractured and broken ribs, not much can be done about them, but we can give you some pain reliever to ease your discomfort. The head injury you sustained is a little more difficult and the injury we're most concerned about. It could take a few weeks, or a few months. We would like to keep you under observation."

"I'm tired." Darcy settled back, suddenly feeling drained of energy.

"You rest, Darcy. I know it's a lot to take in," Doctor Roycroft said, smiling kindly. "I'll drop in later to check on you."

"And I'll be right here when you wake up," Caitlyn promised, her smile small.

Reaching their building, Darcy lifted Lauren into her arms and carried her inside.

"Darcy!" Lauren squealed, grinning happily. "Put me down!"

Laughing, Darcy started making her way up the stairs. "No. I rather like having you like this." Quickly reaching their apartment, she waited while the redhead got the front door open, then strode in and kicked the door shut again with her heel. She grinned lasciviously. "You're mine now!" She captured soft lips in a heated kiss that stated her intent.

"Honey, as much as I would like to fall back into bed with you, we should really start packing."

"Why?" she pouted, not liking the sound of that at all. "We can do it tomorrow, surely?"

"We have a lot of stuff, baby. After all the travelling around Europe we've done, we've picked up numerous knickknacks, clothes, and other such things. I'd rather get a start on it now." She smiled at her girlfriend and kissed Darcy's pouting lips. "Come on, baby, it's not like we haven't had sex all week, is it?"

"No, but..." Darcy pursed her lips, "deciding against sex in favour of packing a suitcase is damaging my ego. But I guess you're right. We should get started." She followed Lauren through to their bedroom and flopped down onto the bed, watching the redhead pull out a suitcase from the bottom of the wardrobe.

"If I left things up to you, we'd be packing at the very last minute. Do you remember when we left Switzerland?"

Nodding absent-mindedly, Darcy ran her fingertips over the covers she was lying on. "Lauren, are you okay with us going home?"

"Of course."

"Are you sure?" Darcy persisted. "I get the feeling you're...I don't know, having doubts."

Lauren set the suitcase on the bed and focused on opening it. She glanced at her waiting partner and sighed. "I do have doubts, but they're silly doubts, so it doesn't matter."

"It does matter, sweetheart. I know you think I'm going to get back home and fall at Caitlyn's feet, but it's not going to happen. I've moved on from that chapter in my life."

"You didn't really move on though, babe. We ran away," Lauren said delicately.

"Doesn't mean I haven't dealt with my unrequited feelings. I'm over her, Lauren. As for the rest of them, they're my family and I miss them, and Christmas is fast approaching, and I want to be at home for this one."

Sitting down on the bed, Lauren rubbed Darcy's outstretched leg. "I know, love, and I understand. It's just…she has such a hold on you, and I can't help but fear that." She smiled sadly as she got back to her feet. "Now, stop distracting me, I have to pack."

Darcy watched Lauren turn her attention to the old, mahogany wardrobe, eyes on the numerous items of clothing within. "I don't think we're going to be able to take everything."

"I was just thinking that. Do you think Joaquina would mind taking care of what we leave behind until we can arrange to have everything shipped to us? If we decided to stay in England."

"We can ask, sweetheart." Dark green eyes glanced toward the framed photo sitting on her bedside table. "Do you think they're going to be mad at me?" Her voice was soft and tinged with worry and fear. She never wanted to disappoint Tricia and Joe.

Lauren looked over at Darcy, seeing where her attention was. "I don't know, sweetheart. You never gave them a reason for leaving, simply told them you wanted to travel for a bit. But despite not having been back, you have at least kept in touch over the years."

"So, they're going to be mad?"

Lauren smiled lovingly at Darcy's childlike tone. "I doubt it, Darcy. They love you. You're part of the family."

"My friends think it's great you're getting so much time off school," Caitlyn mentioned, lying next to Darcy on her hospital bed. "I told them you were really hurt, but they said they'd swap places with you any day."

"They're idiots," Darcy muttered.

"Yeah, I know," Caitlyn agreed softly. "But you're okay, you're getting better."

"Yeah, I'm getting better."

"Hello, girls," Tricia greeted. "Caitlyn, I told you before about getting onto that bed," she scolded lightly.

"I don't mind, Mrs. S," Darcy told her, knowing Caitlyn remained close to her out of fear and the need for physical contact. She really didn't mind at all. "There's plenty of room." She smiled as Caitlyn squeezed her around the waist in silent thanks. "Catie was filling me in on what's going on at school."

"I see," Tricia smiled. That faded as blue-grey eyes focused on her daughter. "Honey, why don't you go over to the vending machines and get yourself a hot chocolate."

"I don't want a hot chocolate," Caitlyn replied stubbornly.

"Honey, please. I need to speak to Darcy alone for a minute."

"Go on, Catie," Darcy urged softly. "While you're there, could you get me some gummy bears if they have them?"

"You and your gummy bears!" Caitlyn grinned.

"What?" Darcy gave her a lopsided smile. "I like them. Except the —"

"The green ones, I know," Caitlyn finished. "Because they're evil looking." She laughed and got up. "All right, I'll go. Mum, do you want anything?"

"A tea would be nice, love. Thank you." Tricia handed over some money, and once her daughter had left, she sat down in the chair next to the bed.

"Is it about my mum?" Darcy asked quietly, knowing the talk was going to involve something serious.

"No. It's about you, Darcy," Tricia told her. "The authorities have decided it's not safe for you to live with your mother."

"I've been living with her for years," Darcy protested.

"She has a drinking problem, Darce. She goes on bar crawls and brings strange men home with her. She doesn't take care of you the way she should."

"What...what does that mean then?"

"They want you to go into care."

"No!" Darcy protested loudly, throwing back her covers, ready to walk out of the hospital and disappear before anyone could come and take her away. "I'm not going to be taken away!"

"Darcy!" Tricia jumped up and put her hands on the teenager's shoulders to stop her from getting out of the bed. "Darcy, wait! Let me finish, honey."

Darcy lay back against the pillows and folded her arms,

scowling at Tricia. "I'm not going," she said defiantly.

"Good, God! This is your reaction, can you imagine Caitlyn's?" She chuckled again and brushed a hand over her tied back blonde locks before sitting back down. "Joe and I have been talking to social services. They haven't been able to find any sign of your father unfortunately, but we found out..." She paused to clear her throat. "Joe and I could become your legal guardians."

"What does that mean?" Darcy asked, frowning. "You would look after me?"

"Yes," Tricia nodded. "If it's something you're interested in, Joe and I would then undergo an assessment by social services, which would include how we interact with you and how we would deal with you, how we would support you, and how we would make sure your upbringing continues in a suitable manner. Social services would then submit reports and their findings to the family proceedings court."

"Then I could stay at my house?"

"No." Tricia picked up Darcy's hand. "You would move in with us. With Jeremy off at university now, we have a spare room."

"I can't take his room. What about when he comes home?"

"He can stay in Brian and Luke's room. He won't mind." She squeezed the hand she held and smiled. "This won't be a swift thing, Darcy. These things take time."

"I...I want to come and stay with you, Mrs. S," Darcy decided. "I don't want to go away."

Tricia smiled. "I'm glad to hear that, honey. We all want you to stay. And you're already family in our eyes, so this won't be such a big change."

"Thank you for this, thank you for everything."

"Oh, honey!" Tricia stood up and gently embraced the teary-eyed teenager. "There's no need for thanks. I'm only sorry it came to this sort of situation."

"What's going on?" Caitlyn demanded, returning to the bedside and eyeing the situation suspiciously.

Tricia released Darcy and stood back from the bed, smiling over at her daughter. "I'll let Darcy fill you in, honey. I have to go and make a phone call."

"I really do miss them," Darcy admitted softly, glancing over at Lauren. "I haven't thought much about it, but I've missed so much," she said sadly. "Birthdays, Christmases, who knows what else. God, it seems so daft now that I stayed away so long."

"Well, you are stubborn, love," Lauren replied affectionately.

"Stubborn, yeah. I think that might be an understatement, sweetheart." She sighed deeply. "I hope they forgive me."

"They will, don't worry." Lauren flopped down on the bed next to her girlfriend. She kissed soft lips and caressed Darcy's cheek. "How about tomorrow we look into booking our flight home? See what's available and get ourselves sorted out so we can leave?"

Grinning, Darcy captured soft lips that had briefly touched her own a moment ago. "I love you, you know?"

"I do know," Lauren replied softly, rolling onto her back and pulling Darcy on top of her. "But thank you for reminding me."

"Let me remind you in another way," Darcy murmured, trailing kisses down Lauren's neck, a hand caressing the redhead's side.

Lauren couldn't respond as she groaned aloud and closed her eyes, fingers tangling in dark locks, the packing forgotten, her fears about being faced with Caitlyn Swailes again fading. All that mattered right now was Darcy's expert touch.

Chapter Five

CAITLYN STARED AT herself in the mirror, wondering if she had changed much over the last five years. Personally, she didn't think she had as she looked at herself from every angle. Would Darcy notice any changes in her? Had Darcy changed much herself? Would she recognise the woman who turned up or confuse her for someone random knocking on the door?

"Sweetheart?" Ian Moran called out before appearing in the bathroom doorway. "Which tie do you think I should wear?" He held up a selection for her to view. "A joke tie, or perhaps a more sensible one?"

"Honey, you aren't going to a meeting." Caitlyn fought the urge to roll her eyes. He was trying too hard. He always tried too hard. Putting on a smile, she turned to face him. "This is a casual family get-together. You don't need a tie at all." She walked up to the dashing brunette and kissed his clean-shaven cheek, taking the ties from his grasp.

"But I want to appear smart," Ian protested. "I want to give a good impression."

She wanted to tell him it didn't matter what he wore, or how he acted, her family would never accept him completely. Her brothers were especially bad, regularly making jokes at Ian's expense, or leaving him out when they planned a night out or a get-together to watch sports on the television. "I guess a cartoon tie," she suggested. "At least that will impress the nieces and nephews." She walked over to the large pine wardrobe.

"You're going to make a great mum someday, sweetheart," he smiled, bringing out his dimples. He wrapped his arms around her waist. "Someday soon, hmm?"

"Let's not have that conversation now. We should get going," she replied, evading his question. "I'm sure my mum will need a hand with something in the kitchen."

"Will your brothers be there?" He took the tie she held up and stepped in front of the standing mirror to put it on.

"I assume so. Mum said she was inviting the family."

"I was told a great joke the other day," Ian smiled. "I'm sure your brothers will appreciate it. It's a bit...risqué, but that seems to be their sense of humour."

She did roll her eyes this time. He tried too hard to make

them like him! "I'll meet you downstairs." She walked out of the bedroom before he could say anything more, fairly sure he would bring up something else she didn't want to discuss.

Making her way downstairs, she had to get her house keys and car keys, as well as make sure everything was locked up. She should have told him Darcy was coming home. She didn't know why she hadn't. Actually, that was a lie. She did know precisely why she hadn't told him. She sighed as she made her way into the dining room. Picking up a discarded mug from the solid oak dining table, she walked through to the kitchen with it.

If she had told him, he would have brought up the subject of them getting married, setting a date, telling her family they were finally going to do it. She set the mug in the sink and turned to make sure the back door was locked. He was her fiancé but she didn't want to think about marrying him, let alone entertain the thought of them starting a family!

With the door and all the windows locked, Caitlyn left the kitchen and headed for the living room to collect her keys. It wasn't that she didn't want to ever marry him. She loved him dearly. It was just…Darcy was coming home. After so long away, she was finally coming home and she had to deal with that first and not be worrying about planning a wedding.

She had met Ian when they were both in college. Wandering along a corridor during her first week, completely lost and in a panic, Ian had boldly approached her and smiled brightly, his adorable dimples on show. Feeling instantly at ease in the handsome man's company, she accepted his offered help and agreed to let him walk her to her class.

They had bumped into each other again and again around the college, always stopping to say hello and making small talk. He had eventually asked her to join him for lunch one afternoon and they spent the hour getting to know each other properly, Ian telling her he was studying to become an accountant or financial consultant, and Caitlyn confessing she wanted to be a nurse and the reason why.

Life was so simple back then, she thought, standing at the living room window and staring out at her street. Well, sort of.

"Are you ready, sweetheart?" Ian asked from behind her.

She turned to face him and smiled when she saw he had changed into clothes more suitable for a casual get-together. "Just waiting for you, love."

TRICIA HAD ONLY invited immediate family for the Sunday lunch she was making, planning a bigger affair for when Darcy returned home. Jeremy, her eldest son, and his wife, Stacey, arrived first, along with their four children. They had been happily married for six years, despite the long hours Jeremy worked.

He had obtained a business degree at university and gone on to open his own bar. Over the last few years, he had managed to buy the property next door to his establishment and had expanded his business to include a restaurant as well. Though the endless work kept him busy, he loved it and loved the fact he had something he could pass down to his children if they were interested.

"Hello, Mum," he greeted with a weary smile, his screaming children having given him a headache on the drive over to his parents' house. "Kids, go on through to the back. Go play outside in the cowboy cabin or the Wendy House."

"And behave!" Stacey called after them as the two boys and two girls ran away squealing excitedly.

"Don't worry, Joe's out there. He'll keep an eye on them." Tricia shut the front door behind the couple and followed them back to the kitchen once they had discarded their winter coats.

"I brought a cheesecake from the restaurant," Jeremy informed his mother. "Some sort of new creation the chef wants my opinion on."

"Thank you, sweetheart. Can you put it in the fridge?"

"Can I help with anything, Tricia?" Stacey asked.

"No, everything's done for now. Thank you for offering though, Stacey. That was nice of you," Tricia said, louder than necessary as she watched her eldest open the fridge to deposit the cheesecake and grab a beer.

"What?" Jeremy questioned, turning to find both women staring at him. He looked from one woman to the other and finally the conversation he had partly heard sank in. "Oh, sorry, Mum. Would you like a hand?"

Tricia laughed and shook her head. "How do you put up with him, Stacey?"

"I don't know," Stacey replied, smiling at her husband. "He drives me mad most of the time!"

"Jeremy, did it occur to you that you should offer your wife a drink?" Tricia asked. "And your long-suffering mother?"

"Oops, sorry again," the handsome blonde apologised sheepishly. "Would you two lovely, long suffering, ladies like a drink?"

Tricia smiled and looked at her daughter-in-law. "I have a bottle of wine chilling in the fridge, if you're interested?"

"Sounds wonderful, Tricia. Thank you."

"So, have you got around to telling Caitlyn that Darcy's coming home?" Jeremy asked, sitting down at the table with his wife.

Tricia opened a drawer and rooted around for the bottle opener, a novelty gift Darcy had sent. "Your sister was around the other day," she mentioned, her back to the couple. "She saw the letter Darcy sent then."

"And what did Catie have to say?"

"Not a lot." Tricia triumphantly pulled out the bottle opener. "She was angry at Darcy. It seems our Darce hasn't written to her once since going away."

"Did they fall out?" Stacey asked.

"Luke asked me that the other day and I honestly don't know the answer." Tricia poured two glasses of white wine, then put the bottle back in the fridge.

"Yeah, but we can all guess. They were thick as thieves when they were little, rarely ever apart," Jeremy said. "It's odd that Darcy went off and stayed away for five years. Not making one trip back, not even for a Christmas, and not keeping in touch with Catie."

Tricia nodded in agreement as she walked over to the table. "I agree," she said, handing Stacey a glass. "But none of us know what went on and Caitlyn is unlikely to tell us."

"Nor Darcy!" Jeremy chuckled. "I don't think I've ever known someone so reserved and quiet!"

The doorbell interrupted their conversation and Jeremy left to go and answer the door.

"Hi, Jeremy." Caitlyn smiled when her eldest brother opened the front door. "Have you gained weight?"

Jeremy scowled at his baby sister and stepped outside to grab her and lift her over his broad shoulder. "It's all muscle, baby sis!"

"Ahhh, Jeremy! Put me down!" Caitlyn squealed. "I'll tell Mum!"

Laughing, Jeremy turned and started running through the house with Caitlyn over his shoulder. "Lookit! Lookit, everyone! Look what I caught!" He ran into the kitchen, going past a startled Tricia, his wife, and Brian's wife, Isabella, then changed course and raced into the open-plan living-dining room, handing his sister to Brian and Luke, who were seated on the sofa.

"Jeremy!" Caitlyn growled, though she was smiling. "I'm

going to set your wife on you!"

Stacey walked into the room laughing. "Just say the word, Caitlyn."

"No fair!" Jeremy pouted. "You're my wife, you should side with me."

The raven-haired woman walked up to her husband and kissed him softly on the lips, ignoring the gagging from his siblings. "Behave," she warned, pinching his cheek before stepping back.

Ian walked in and waved nervously at the group. "Hello, all. Is everyone well?"

The good humour died instantly, the energy sucked out of the room at his appearance. The Swailes brothers looked from Ian to each other, then back again.

"Hey, Ian," Brian greeted, the only one willing to. "How are you? Still trying to marry our sister?"

Ian blinked, digesting the question. "I'm fine, thank you. Could do with getting away from work, you know how it is I'm sure." He smiled at Caitlyn. "As to marrying your sister, I would wait an eternity."

"Probably have to," Luke muttered, making his brothers snigger.

Hating the noticeable change in the room, Caitlyn stood up, annoyed at her brothers for treating Ian like an outsider even after all the years they had been together. "Where's Dad?"

"In the garden with the kids," Jeremy replied. He wrapped an arm around his sister's shoulders. "Mum mentioned you cleaned up your old Wendy House."

"The other day, yes," Caitlyn smiled and nodded. "Are your girls out there enjoying it?"

"All the girls are in the Wendy House, the boys are in the cowboy cabin," Brian told her. "They're taunting each other. The girls claiming the Wendy House is best, while the boys are insisting the cabin is better."

"It is," Luke spoke up. "I vouch for it."

"Me too," Jeremy grinned.

"The Wendy House is better." Caitlyn slapped him in the stomach with the back of her hand. "Darcy and I took such good care of it, unlike you lot and the cabin. Wasn't there a hole in the roof at one point?"

"That was Luke's fault," Brian chuckled. "Hammered straight through it!"

"Darcy and I were always out there and spent many a night

camping out."

"It's great Darcy is coming home!" Brian reached for his bottle of beer. "We'll have to plan a big night out."

"Definitely!" Jeremy nodded in agreement. "Remember the last time we were all out together?"

"Yeah, it was when..." Luke trailed off, blue eyes flicking over to a scowling Caitlyn. "Uh...it was a while ago." Brian and Jeremy sniggered again.

"Darcy's coming home?" Ian asked in confusion.

"Yeah, didn't Caitlyn mention it?" Jeremy asked, acting innocent and earning another slap from his sister.

"No, she didn't," Ian smiled tightly, wondering why his fiancée had neglected to mention her best friend was returning after so many years away. He opened his mouth to question her, only to be interrupted.

"I didn't know Darcy was coming back," Isabella said, walking into the living room and hearing the tail end of the conversation. "When is she due back?" She sat down next to her husband.

"Sometime next week, according to Mum," Brian replied. "Not that you even know her, sweetheart!" he chuckled, earning a slap on the thigh from the redhead, much to the amusement of his siblings. "What? It's true!"

Brian and Isabella had been introduced to each other by friends five years previous and had fallen in love. After a brief, whirlwind romance, they had married.

"I've heard so much about her, I feel like I know her," Isabella argued. "I can't wait to meet her."

"Does this mean we can actually set a date for our wedding then?" Ian asked suddenly, eyes on Caitlyn and missing her brothers rolling their eyes.

The room went very still and very quiet. The Swailes boys silently waited with bated breath for Caitlyn's response, knowing what they wanted to hear.

"She is the reason you wanted to wait," Ian continued. "Perhaps now that she's returning, we can finally tie the knot?"

"Soon." Caitlyn smiled weakly at him. "Let's get Darcy home and settled first before planning anything, sweetheart."

"I'm sure she won't mind if our wedding is—"

"I need a drink," she interrupted, not wanting to deal with the subject of their wedding in front of her family. "Would you like one, Ian?" Without waiting for an answer, she left the room.

Tricia looked up and smiled as her daughter walked into the kitchen. "Are you all right, honey? Jeremy didn't actually hurt you, did he?"

Caitlyn smiled and shook her head. "You know the boys, they come over all rough but are actually as gentle as teddy bears."

"Uh-huh," Tricia nodded. "They're good boys," she said proudly.

"It smells gorgeous in here," Caitlyn mentioned, picking up the mouth-watering aroma of a beef joint in the oven. "Do you need a hand, Mum?"

"No, everything that needed to be done has been, thanks, honey. Though, when I need a sample tasted, I'm sure you want to be the one to do it?"

Growing up, all the Swailes siblings and Darcy loved Sunday roast afternoon. Each week one of them would be picked to sample the fare close to serving time to make sure it was cooked and ready to be eaten. It was a favourite memory of Caitlyn's.

"After the way I was just jostled through the house, I think I've earned it," Caitlyn joked.

Laughing, Tricia placed the last of the dirty bowls and dishes she had used into the sink to soak, then reached out for the tea towel to dry her hands. "Did Ian come with you?"

"Yeah," Caitlyn nodded, humour fading. She opened the fridge and looked inside for something to drink. "I didn't tell him Darcy was coming home," she admitted. "And Brian just blurted it out." Spotting the bottle of wine on the counter, she closed the fridge and walked over to grab it.

"Why didn't you tell him?" Tricia asked in interest.

"I don't know why I didn't mention it." She got herself a glass out of the cupboard. "I just..." She shrugged. "I always got the impression they didn't really like each other, you know what I mean?"

"It happens, sweetheart. Friends and boyfriends clashing. I think they worry they'll lose out on time with the one in the middle, or perhaps lose that person all together." Tricia watched her daughter, noting the way she avoided looking at her.

"Maybe," Caitlyn mumbled, not knowing what to think. "Do you want a top-up?" She jiggled the bottle at her mother.

"No, thank you."

"I think I'll go out front for a bit, get some peace and quiet before we all sit down for dinner. Shout if you need any help."

"Sure, honey." Tricia watched her daughter leave the kitchen and shook her head. How could Caitlyn not know why Darcy and Ian never got along? She couldn't really be that blind to Darcy's feelings, could she? And how could she deny having feelings for Darcy? Tricia sighed. Stubborn. They were both always so stubborn.

Caitlyn stepped outside her parents' house and took a seat on the front step, like she had many times throughout her life. She breathed in the winter air and looked out at the neighbourhood where she had grown up.

She smiled as she watched Sofia Emelin and the Bethune twins riding bikes and taunting each other. She wondered what had happened to old Mrs. Wildeve as she watched a little boy and girl playing with the snow that had fallen the night before. She didn't recognise the pair and realised a new family had moved in. Blue eyes watched Aimee Tenma skip down her garden path, the teen laughing loudly while she talked on her mobile phone. Caitlyn smiled, remembering the girl when she was younger and scared of her own shadow.

Sipping her wine, she let her thoughts drift back to her childhood. When Darcy was well enough to leave the hospital, she had been brought home to the Swailes' house. In Caitlyn's mind, it had been the best thing ever. Certainly better than the alternative.

Darcy had told her the other option, the possibility of her being sent away to some foster home, and she was glad it hadn't come to that. The thought of losing her best friend had filled her with dread.

With Jeremy off at university, Darcy was given his old bedroom as her own, with his blessing. Though, with nightmares plaguing her, she didn't often sleep in there in the beginning. Not that Caitlyn minded Darcy's company at night.

"Caitlyn?"

Smiling in the darkness, Caitlyn lifted her covers in invitation and laughed softly as Darcy hurried across the dark bedroom to climb into her bed. "Another bad dream, Darce?" She wrapped an arm around her trembling friend.

"Yeah. Do you think they'll stop?"

"Eventually," Caitlyn promised. "You don't have them when you share my bed with me, do you?"

"No," Darcy replied in amusement. "But I can't sleep with you for the rest of my life!" They fell silent as her words registered with each of them. "Um..." She cleared her throat. "How uh...how are things going with you and Wayne?"

"He's not happy," Caitlyn sighed. "He's grumpy about me not letting him..." she trailed off, embarrassed by what she had been about to confess. "Never mind."

"Not letting him what?"

"It doesn't matter. Forget it, Darce."

"Don't let him pressure you into anything," Darcy murmured. She wiggled closer to Caitlyn and wrapped an arm around her waist. "If you're not ready, don't do it." She let out a nervous, tremulous breath as she felt warm lips on her neck.

Caitlyn started off only wanting to give Darcy a comforting, thank you kiss. She had kissed her before, on the cheek on birthdays and over the holidays. But as she trailed soft kisses down Darcy's neck, she admitted to herself she was curious about the difference and wanted to experiment a little.

"Caitlyn, I don't think we should do this."

"Shh," Caitlyn soothed, wanting more and knowing Darcy did too. "Have you ever kissed someone?" She watched her friend shake her head. "Haven't you ever wondered, Darcy? Wondered what all the fuss is about?"

"I...I guess."

"My first kiss was with Wayne. It was awful!" Caitlyn confessed. "He thrust his tongue into my mouth, and it was all slobbery."

"Oh."

"I um..." She hesitated, shy about confessing her feelings. "When you were in the hospital, I found myself wondering what it would be like to kiss you," she admitted nervously. "That's weird right? I would sit beside your bed, watching your lips."

"Total weirdo," Darcy teased.

Caitlyn snorted and slapped the nearest body part she could reach. "Are you telling me you've never thought about kissing someone?" She waited for an answer that never came. Sitting up, the blanket they were sharing fell away and pooled at her waist. "You have. I bet you have." *Was it a girl?* she wondered. *And that's why she doesn't want to say.* "Darcy, are you...I mean it's okay if you are, but I want to know if...if you're gay."

"Uh..."

"The outcome of this discussion won't change anything," Caitlyn assured her. "I'm not going to have my parents kick you out and put into care."

"I think I...I don't know."

"Why?" Caitlyn asked softly. "Why don't you know? When you people watch, who do you watch more, boys or girls?"

"That doesn't mean anything," Darcy protested. "That's just something I do to pass the time."

"When you think about kissing, who do you imagine kissing? What about when we're older and married, who do you imagine being married to? Robert Pattinson or Scarlett Johansson?" she grinned.

"Um, I don't um..." She shrugged, not wanting to answer. "Does it make you uncomfortable?" she asked after a long period of silence between them. "I'm sharing your bed and you don't know how I feel or who I feel it for. Do you...do you want me to leave?"

Did it make her uncomfortable? Caitlyn pondered, seriously thinking it over. She smiled suddenly, the answer obvious. "No," she replied firmly. "We've shared a bed loads before, Darcy. Why would it be different now?" She laughed.

Darcy chuckled awkwardly.

"I mean, it's not like you want me that way, is it?" Caitlyn stroked Darcy's belly over the T-shirt she was wearing.

Darcy inhaled sharply as Caitlyn bent down and kissed her cheek. "Turn...turn over," she stuttered.

"What?"

"Turn over."

Frowning at the request, Caitlyn rolled over and held her breath as Darcy moved closer to her, managing to bite back a heated moan when her friend spooned up behind her and wrapped an arm around her waist, her hand accidentally brushing against her breast. Strangely, it felt right to be held intimately by her best friend.

"Night, Catie," Darcy murmured.

Darcy's breath warming the back of her neck made her shiver. "Goodnight, Darcy."

How Darcy felt seemed obvious now, Caitlyn thought, finishing her wine. Why hadn't she seen it then? She smiled sardonically. The inexperience of youth, she supposed. She groaned as she got to her feet. Though it wouldn't have changed anything back then anyway. She was dating Wayne and Darcy didn't know what she wanted.

Heading back inside, she realised she had left her fiancé in the company of her brothers for far too long and hoped Ian was handling them okay.

"Jeremy set up this big old..." Brian struggled to find the word. "What was it?"

"It was a bit of plywood, I think," Jeremy filled in.

"Whatever it was, he leaned it up against the front of Mr.

Tenma's car out on the street and dared Darcy to ride up it on her bike and try and fly over the car behind."

Jeremy and Luke started laughing, while Caitlyn smiled fondly as she hovered in the doorway, listening to the story.

"Darcy didn't hesitate! Peddling as fast as she could, up she went, flying through the air, leaving us all sitting there idolising her," Brian finished.

"She made it over then?" Stacey asked, eyes wide in amazement.

"Almost," Luke told her with a chuckle.

"Her back wheel clipped the back of the second car, and she was sent sprawling," Jeremy recalled. "She ended up with cuts and bruises, and we were all grounded, but she had bragging rights. She didn't let us forget for the rest of that summer what chickens we were!"

"She sounds like she was a handful," Ian said with a shake of his head.

"Darcy was as good as gold," Caitlyn spoke up. "Shy and quiet and polite." She walked farther into the room. "Until one of this lot dared her to do something, or someone started picking on me." She shared a smile with her brothers. "Then she turned into a wildcat!"

"She could have died," Ian argued, not impressed. "That kind of stunt could have broken her neck."

"God damn it, Ian! We were doing what kids do!" Caitlyn snapped. "Do you have to be so bloody righteous?"

The room fell silent, the atmosphere thickening as the brothers and their wives looked from Caitlyn to Ian and back again, all of them waiting to see what would happen between the couple.

"I'm not being righteous. How many times do you come home from work and tell me about stupid stunts kids have done which landed them in hospital? Where were her parents?"

"So," Isabella said suddenly, with far too much enthusiasm. She had heard Caitlyn's sharp intake of breath and had a feeling things would only get worse if she let the argument continue. "First kisses?" she threw out, completely changing the subject. "Brian would never tell me about his."

"Flora Narkus!" the Swailes siblings called out together.

"Oh, thanks a lot, guys!" Brian blushed.

"Who was Flora Narkus?" Isabella grinned triumphantly at her husband and reached over to rub his thigh.

"The most unfortunate teenage girl you could ever meet," Jeremy laughed. "She had frizzy red hair, prescription glasses that were too big for her, braces on her teeth, asthma, and really bad acne."

"She was a nice girl," Brian protested.

"She was doing your homework," Luke laughed.

"Brian!" Isabella slapped his leg, less than impressed.

"Not all my homework!"

"Only maths," Luke said, smiling at his siblings.

"And history," Jeremy added.

"And geography," Caitlyn put in, getting an outraged look from Brian.

"Thanks a lot, Caitlyn!" Brian pouted. "I wasn't going to mention Wayne Jarvie, but you've forced my hand."

"Wayne Jarvie," Tricia repeated, entering the room. "I vaguely remember the name."

"I don't think I ever met him," Jeremy said, head tilted left as he tried to think back to teenage Caitlyn's life.

"Lucky you," Luke replied, face distorted with dislike. "The boy was a prick. I'll never understand what you saw in him, Catie."

"I was thinking the same thing the other day," Caitlyn admitted. "Brenda and I got on the subject of first loves and it got me remembering dear old Wayne."

"Wasn't he the one who tried to drive a wedge between you and Darcy?" Brian asked.

"And very nearly succeeded," Caitlyn nodded.

"What made you see sense in the end?" Stacey asked.

"Darcy ended up coming to live here with us," Caitlyn replied, not wanting to get into the reason why. "I think it made Wayne insanely jealous. I was worried about Darcy and spending more time with her and less with him and he...he turned nasty."

It was February 2008.

"Hey, Caitlyn," Darcy called out. She raced up the stairs, heading for Caitlyn's bedroom. "Your mum said to tell you we're having another movie night 'cause tomorrow is Valentine's Day and she said it gives her a chance to watch chick flicks without complaint." She walked into her friend's room and faltered as she found Caitlyn applying makeup. "Uh...Luke and I think we um...we can overrule her if we can find support from other sources," she grinned. "Meaning you and your dad."

"Sorry, Darce," Caitlyn glanced at her friend and smiled apologetically. "I told Wayne and the guys I would go to some party that's being thrown by a friend of a friend."

"Oh." Darcy turned her gaze to the lilac carpet. "Never mind."

Watching her friend turn, ready to retreat, Caitlyn swivelled sideways on the stool she sat on. "Hey, Darcy." She waited for the tall teen to face her again. "How about you come with me?"

"I don't know, Caitlyn." Darcy toe-poked the carpet with her socked foot. "Your friends don't like me, and to be honest, I don't really like them."

"I know, but how about if I promise not to leave your side all night?" Caitlyn offered. "Come on, Darce, you should totally come out and socialise after...after what happened. You're a teenager, be a little wild and reckless. It'll be fun. It's a party."

"I don't like crowds and you're going with Wayne," Darcy protested. "He won't be happy with me hanging around."

"Well tough," Caitlyn rolled her eyes. "He'll just have to like it or lump it." She jumped up and walked to her taller friend, placing her hands on Darcy's hips. "I want you to come. You're my best friend and I want to spend time with you."

"Catie, I live in your house. You see me all the time," Darcy laughed.

"Well, yeah, but not surrounded by party people," she smirked. "Totally different."

Grinning, Darcy slowly nodded. "All right." She put her hands up in surrender. "All right, I give. I better go tell Luke he's on his own."

"I'll come with you." Caitlyn took Darcy's hand. "I can't wait to see the look on his face!"

The group of mostly teenagers gathered at Oaks Park, laid out for the Earl of Derby in the 1770s in a fashionable style with trees forming a perimeter screen and placed in artful clumps to suggest a natural landscape. Music was being provided by Adam Roffe's stereo and a little light provided by fires that had been lit in a few steel barrels as well as from headlights on cars and mopeds. With the tree screen, there wasn't a house in sight, so they knew they wouldn't be spotted easily and ordered to move on by the police. Exactly why the location had been picked.

Darcy was handed a bottle of alcopop as Caitlyn led her through the crowd to where Wayne was standing with their friends. Darcy held onto the drink though she had no desire to drink it, not after what she had been through with her mother.

"Hey, guys!" Caitlyn greeted her friends cheerfully, smiling big and bright.

They all turned at the sound of her voice, smiling until they spotted who had tagged along with her.

"What is this, babe?" Wayne grumbled. "Charity night?"

"Shut up, Wayne," Caitlyn warned. "I asked Darcy to come along. She didn't want to, but I wanted her here. And if you don't like that, then you can all take a hike." She smiled at her best friend and felt her heart flutter when Darcy smiled back gratefully. "Now, how come my best friend has a drink and I don't?" she questioned, laughing when her friends thrust several bottles in her direction.

The group stood huddled around one of the flaming barrels, some swaying to the music, others talking.

Wayne grabbed Caitlyn's arm and started to drag her off. "Can I have a word with you?"

Caitlyn shrugged herself free and shook her head. "Whatever you have to say can be said here. I'm not leaving Darcy."

"Okay, fine, whatever," the taller boy rolled his eyes. He glared at Darcy, then looked down into Caitlyn's eyes. "Babe, I thought tonight would be just you, me, and the guys. I've missed you, missed spending time with you. You're always off with her now. You're my girlfriend and I never see you!"

"You're such an arse, Wayne," Caitlyn hissed angrily.

"Right, I'm an arse for wanting to spend time with my girl-friend," he grumbled. "I don't suppose I'll be seeing you tomor-row, will I? Valentine's Day being on a Sunday, you'll want to be spending the day with your family 'cause mummy makes a roast. Why do I even bother with you?" He stalked off.

"Hey there, Darcy," Charlotte Fleming greeted. "And Cait-lyn!" she laughed. "You two never were far from each other's sides. Good to see some things never change."

Charlotte had attended the same infant and junior school as the two friends. But when it came to high school, she had gone elsewhere, while they had stuck together.

"Hi, Charlotte. How are you?" Darcy asked with a smile.

"I'm feeling pretty good right now," the raven-haired teen-ager replied, smiling lopsidedly. She held up a joint. "Do you want a hit?"

"Oh. Uh, no, thanks."

"Cool, that's cool," Charlotte grinned, before taking a deep drag from the joint. She looked at Caitlyn. "Did you?" She wig-gled the joint at Caitlyn who shook her head. Charlotte turned her attention back to Darcy. "I heard some bad shit went down for you, Darcy." She squinted at the other girl. "I like, heard you were in a coma or something. That true?"

"Yeah. I was put in an induced coma because of a head injury."

"Damn!" Charlotte blinked. "I'm sorry to hear that. If I had known, I would have come to visit you." She frowned. "Not that you would've known I was there, but anyway, thought that counts, right?"

"That's nice of you to say, Charlotte," Darcy smiled.

"Yeah, well, I know you from way back and I've always thought you were pretty cool."

"Thanks," Darcy replied softly, blushing in embarrassment.

Wayne walked up to the trio, sneering in Darcy's direction. "Can we at least dance?" he asked Caitlyn. "Or does she have to come too?"

Sighing in annoyance, Caitlyn looked to Darcy. "Hey, will you be okay for a minute while I go dance?"

"Sure, go have fun. Do you want me to hold your drink?"

"Thanks, Darce." She leaned in close to her friend. "I'll be back as quick as I can be." She winked before turning away and following Wayne into some space for them to dance in. She tried not to sigh in annoyance when he wrapped his arms possessively around her and held her close to his body, his lips trailing sloppy wet kisses down her cheeks to her neck.

"Missed you, babe."

"Ease up, would you. You're acting like one of those horny little dogs that go around humping legs."

"You're my girl, Caitlyn. I want to remind everyone."

Caitlyn rolled her eyes, feeling his hands start to wander up and down her back, slowly falling to her backside. She found herself looking past Wayne and over in Darcy's direction, watching her best friend talking to Charlotte and another girl she didn't recognise.

She watched Darcy smile as the two girls laughed at something that was said, finding a smile curling her own lips in response. When dark green eyes drifted her way, she winked to let her best friend know she was still around and keeping an eye on her, and watched Darcy relax and go back to talking. Why was it she wanted to be over there with Darcy rather than here in her boyfriend's arms?

As Saturday turned into the early hours of Sunday, a lot of the teenagers were drunk or high, or a mixture of both. Darcy had a slight buzz going, having succumbed and drunk a little and been surrounded by lit joints all evening. Caitlyn had been less reserved and was past feeling any pain. Sitting on the bonnet of a car, she leaned heavily against Darcy's side and had come over all affectionate in her drunken state, much to Darcy's amusement.

"Hey, baby. Where ya been?" Caitlyn smiled as Wayne approached.

Wayne stepped between his girlfriend's legs and leaned in close to nuzzle her neck. "Off thinking about you," he murmured into her ear, before nipping her ear lobe. "How about we slip away for a while and kiss goodnight?" Without waiting for an answer, he took her hand and led her away from the group, heading out of range of the fire light and deeper into the darkness.

"Wayne!" Caitlyn giggled as he led her into the cluster of trees and leaned her back against a solid trunk.

He kissed her, tongue thrusting into her open mouth, his hand settling on her breast and squeezing in time to the thrusts of his tongue. "I love you so much, Caitlyn," he murmured, kissing a path along her jaw. "I've missed you these last few weeks."

"I've...I've missed you, too." Caitlyn moaned at the feel of his touch on her breast, his palm rubbing her suddenly hard nipple pleasurably. She tipped her head back, offering her throat to his hungry mouth. She felt him tugging on her leg and willingly lifted the limb, hooking it around his waist. She groaned aloud when he thrust his hips forward, feeling him hard and ready against her.

"Been aching to be with you, babe. Wish you had come alone tonight."

"Wait!" she gasped, surprised at how far things had gotten so suddenly. "Wayne, wait!" She pushed at his shoulders, trying to stop him, not happy about his hand slipping between her legs and rubbing painfully hard. "Wayne, stop!"

"Come on, babe," he groaned, ducking his head to kiss her neck again. "I'll make you feel good." He grasped her hips and tugged her back against him, thrusting his hips into her a couple of times. "That feels good, right?"

Caitlyn gasped at the unexpected sensation of him rocking against her. Surprised as her body responded, she allowed him possession of her lips. "No!" she cried out, jerking her lips away from his. "I can't!"

"You can."

"I don't want to!"

"Why not?" Wayne pulled back slightly and looked at her in disbelief. "No one's around, they won't know what we're doing."

"I'm here with Darcy, I have to get back to her," she insisted, again shoving at his shoulders. "She was hurt so badly."

"But she's better now," he growled. "They let her out of hospital, didn't they?"

"God, you don't get it!" Caitlyn pushed at his chest, trying to wiggle herself free. "She could have died! I could have lost her forever, all because of you, Wayne! I was horrible to her because you were standing there watching on and for that reason she stayed away and nearly got herself killed!" She squirmed, head moving as he attempted to kiss her, trying to get what he wanted despite her protests.

"Damn it, Caitlyn, will you shut up about bloody Darcy!"

"She didn't even want to come tonight and I've let you take me away, despite telling her I wouldn't leave her side. She hates mingling, hates crowds and I've left her."

"She's a big girl. Literally. She can take care of herself." He tore at her shirt, thrusting his hips against her desperately, not to be denied. "Uh, Jesus, Caitlyn!" he groaned as she continued to struggle. "Will you hold still, I promise it won't hurt."

"Get off me, Wayne! Get off!" she squealed. "No! I don't want this!"

Suddenly Wayne was gone, and Caitlyn looked down wide-eyed to see Darcy straddling him, raining down furious punches to his face.

"Fuckhead! Did you not hear her? She said no!" Darcy growled, oblivious to Wayne's nose crunching beneath her fist. "Did you choose to ignore her, huh? Determined to get what you want no matter what!" She punched and punched and punched, not caring when his lips split, his eyes blackened, and he groaned pitifully beneath her, barely conscious.

Coming to her senses, Caitlyn hurriedly moved forward toward the pair. "Darcy," she called out desperately, truly scared she was going to kill him. "Darce!" She reached out to gently touch her friend's shoulder, flinching back when blazing eyes glared her way. Swallowing nervously, she moved forward again, confident Darcy wouldn't hurt her.

"Honey, get off him," she said tenderly, offering Darcy her hand. "Leave him be now, okay?" She watched, wondering if Darcy was herself. "No, Darce," she beseeched as Darcy's head turned back to Wayne. "Come on, baby. Let's go, okay? We're going to go home. I...I want to go home, Darcy. Please?"

Eyes on Caitlyn, Darcy took the offered hand and got up, crushing Caitlyn to her in a fierce embrace. "Are you all right, Catie?" she whispered, lips against her friend's head. She pulled back to look down into Caitlyn's watery blue eyes. "Did he hurt you?"

Caitlyn shook her head. "I'm fine." She clutched at the taller teen's shirt, snuggling into her familiar warm embrace as she began to tremble from the realisation of what had almost occurred. "You rescued me, Darcy. He was...he was going to..." The tears that had been building fell then. "Thank you! Thank you so much, Darcy!"

"Come on, let's go home. Yeah?" Darcy pressed a kiss into Caitlyn's hair.

Caitlyn nodded and without looking back at Wayne, kept hold of Darcy as her best friend led her away.

"Darcy was furious!" Caitlyn finished retelling. "Absolutely furious."

"Wow, how awful!" Isabella breathed, shaking her head.

"Yeah," Jeremy agreed. "Thank God Darcy was there."

"You never told me this!" Tricia said disapprovingly. "Thank God Darcy went with you that night."

Embarrassed, Caitlyn looked down at the carpet, knowing her mother was hurt and upset that she had been kept in the dark. "It was the very early hours by the time we got home, everyone was in bed. Then the next morning, I just wanted to forget the whole incident had happened."

"It's a good thing he's locked up now, or I'd hunt him down and slap him around myself!" Brian growled, outraged some little punk had attempted to rape his baby sister.

"You and me both, brother," Luke nodded.

"I didn't notice anything," Tricia said, more to herself than the others. "The things you lot got up to! It's a wonder I'm not locked away in a madhouse!"

"Flora Narkus is a total babe now, by the way," Luke said out of the blue. "I bumped into her a while back. I was in the pub garden and this gorgeous woman approached and started up a conversation. I didn't recognise her until she laughed and told me exactly who she was."

"Oh, yeah?" Brian asked, slightly curious as to how his first crush had changed.

"Hh-hmm," Isabella interrupted. "Your loving, pregnant wife is sitting right here, Brian."

"I know," Brian grinned sheepishly. "And I love you more than life itself. I'm just curious. If you had known Flora back then, you'd be too."

"Do you have any old photos?"

"I might have," Tricia mentioned. "Or Joe might have captured her on film. He forever had his camcorder in hand."

"Oh, the camcorder," Luke chuckled. "He loved that old thing."

"Hey, is dinner going to be ready any time soon, Mum?" Jeremy asked. "I'm starving and fancy eating before we start watching old family movies."

Stacey rolled her eyes at her husband. "There are some days when I could throttle him!" she teased.

"Now you know how I felt whilst growing up," Caitlyn laughed.

"Let's all go through to the kitchen and have a peek," Tricia spoke up, rubbing her daughter's shoulder as she walked past Caitlyn. "Even if it's not quite done, I'm thinking we could all use fresh drinks, and I'm sure Joe could use a hand in keeping the children occupied."

Caitlyn paid no attention to the chattering and joking of her family as they headed for the kitchen. Her thoughts still lingered in the past, on Darcy, her knight in shining armour. They were so close once, cared so deeply for each other. How on Earth did she let them fall apart, the wall between them growing so thick and so high, Darcy felt she had no choice but to leave the country?

Entering the kitchen, she smiled at her family, as always, heart warmed by the obvious love between them all. With Darcy coming home, she could fix this. She could fix some of the problems that drove a wedge between them. If Darcy was willing.

Chapter Six

UNABLE TO SLEEP, Darcy sat in the dark at the bedroom window and marvelled at the world in the still of the night. She had been out at this hour before, capturing images usually only seen in the glare of daylight. Over the five years she had spent travelling, she had seen many different things, some breathtaking, some unique, some downright scary. But one thing remained consistent, her favourite time of the day was the very early hours from midnight onwards.

Her gaze flicked over to the bed where her girlfriend lay sleeping peacefully and she smiled, knowing how lucky she was to have someone as sweet and understanding as Lauren in her life.

After recovering from a late Friday night out with Kendall and Joaquina, the couple had gone out Saturday afternoon to see about booking tickets home. Darcy had continually had a change of heart as they strolled toward their destination, making good arguments for why they should stay in Portugal, arguing for them to move on to somewhere new. Lauren patiently reminded her she had already written home to let the family know she was going to make an appearance, and Darcy knew it wouldn't be fair to back out now.

They spent some time debating on exactly when they should leave. Finally, the couple returned to their rented home with their tickets and focused on packing. They dined out on their balcony, enjoying the mild weather and vibrant life going on down below, then spent the rest of their afternoon recalling their favourite moments from their time in Europe. The evening had been spent in the company of their friends, sharing drinks and memories, promising this wasn't the last time they would see each other.

Yesterday had been a lazy Sunday, the couple not venturing out at all. Their packing was done, the apartment had been cleaned, and the countdown was on to leaving it all behind.

Hearing Lauren moan unhappily in her sleep, Darcy glanced over to their bed again, watching her girlfriend roll over and settle back down. She recalled meeting Lauren for the first time and smiled fondly. It had been her eighteenth birthday, and Luke, Brian, and Jeremy had taken her and Caitlyn to a bar, which happened to be where Lauren worked for her uncle.

"This is the place, Darce," Luke announced, grinning broadly. "The place where you have your first grown up drink."

It was May 2010, and Darcy's birthday.

"Your parents let me have a glass of wine at Christmas."

"Yeah, but..."

"And I've tried other drinks here and there, beer, alco-pops...." she listed.

Luke blushed while his brothers laughed and shook their heads at him. "Way to kill my moment, Darcy," he pouted.

"Sorry, Luke." She laughed and wrapped her arm around the handsome blonde's shoulders, taller than him now by a few inches. "Lead the way and you can buy me my first drink of the night."

Inside, the bar was dimly lit and mostly decorated with dark mahogany wood panelling. The long bar was to the left as you entered, with several stools chained to the metal footrest in front of it. On the right side were tables and chairs for seating. For entertainment, up on the wall was a large eighty-inch flat screen television and toward the back of the property, on a slight elevated level, were three pool tables, a line of fruit machines, and a jukebox, lit up and blaring out The Carpenters.

"Hello," a beautiful redhead greeted the group with a radiant smile. "What can I get you?"

"Two bottles of Magners, a pint of John Smiths," Luke ordered, before looking to his sister. "Caitlyn?"

"Coke with ice, please."

"And you, Darce?" he asked, smiling at the birthday girl.

The barmaid looked with uncertainty at Darcy, who despite her height looked baby-faced. "It's illegal to sell minors alcohol," she said in warning.

"It's illegal to sell a minor orange juice?" Darcy asked, a hint of a smile gracing her lips.

"Depends on what else you want in the glass," the redhead retorted with a smirk.

"A little umbrella. Make it tropical looking," Darcy laughed. "Just orange juice, please." She pulled her new ID out of her pocket and handed it over to the woman. "To prove I can have a real drink if I want one later."

The barmaid took the small card and glanced over the important details, a smile dancing along her lips. "Happy birthday, Darcy Kenton."

"Thank you, Miss...?" A dark eyebrow lifted in question.

"Cansdell. Lauren Cansdell."

"Do you think we could perhaps get our drinks, Lauren Cansdell?" Caitlyn asked in annoyance, making both women glance in her direction in surprise.

"Of course. Sorry," Lauren apologised with a small smile.

"That was a little rude, Caitlyn," Darcy pointed out, once the barmaid walked away.

"Why? We asked for drinks and she was just standing here questioning you. She's a barmaid, Darcy, she wasn't doing her job."

Was Caitlyn jealous? Darcy grinned and bumped her shoulder against her best friend. "You're right, but you should be careful upsetting someone who is serving you, Caitlyn. She could spit in your drink."

"Yeah, right," Caitlyn laughed before doubt set in and a small frown creased her brow. She looked at Darcy in disbelief. "Do you think?" Blue eyes looked into amused green briefly before finding Lauren along the bar and watching her carefully.

"Come on, grumpy," Darcy laughed and turned Caitlyn away from the bar. "Let me beat you at pool."

Darcy took her shot and groaned when she missed the pocket. They had been occupying one of the pool tables since arriving, taking turns to play each other. Darcy was currently playing Caitlyn again, only her best friend had lost interest in the game and was instead entertaining a couple of guys who had arrived shortly after they had.

Standing up straight, Darcy sighed, watching her best friend flirting with the strangers. "Hey, Caitlyn, it's your turn." Getting no response from her distracted friend, she growled quietly and walked to the table where Luke and Brian were sitting watching the drinks.

"She being a pain, Darce?" Brian asked.

"She's found something more interesting to do." Darcy picked up her glass and drained what was left.

"We could have left her at home," Luke grinned. "You're the one who invited her."

"Mm. I'm going to get another drink. Do you guys want one?" Getting nods from the two brothers, she looked around for Jeremy. "Where's Jeremy disappeared to?"

Brian rolled his eyes. "Gone off to make a phone call to lover girl."

"Oh, right. Here," she handed him her cue stick. "If Catie eventually tears herself away long enough to take her shot, take my turn. I'm reds."

"Here, Darce," Luke stood up and rummaged through his pocket. "To pay for the drinks," he said, handing over a banknote.

"You don't ha—"

"You're not paying on your birthday, Darcy," Luke interrupted. "So, stop complaining."

Smiling, she grabbed the empty glasses and made her way over to the bar, taking a seat on a free stool while she waited to be served. Giving her order to the barman, Darcy turned in her seat as she heard Caitlyn's laughter, her heart aching as she watched her friend with the two men, both vying for her attention.

Darcy found herself smiling as her gaze lingered on the beautiful blonde. She'll be a great catch for any guy, she thought, her smile fading. And there was her problem. Caitlyn liked guys, not girls. Not her.

Paying for the fresh round, she returned to her table and set down Luke and Brian's drinks, seeing the brothers over at the pool table playing a game. She returned to the bar to retrieve Jeremy's pint, then, rather than disturb the game, she caught Luke's eye and let him know they had fresh drinks, before she made her way back to the bar and took a seat.

"Hey there, birthday girl," Lauren greeted, walking up to the despondent Darcy. "I thought you were drinking orange juice?" she mentioned, eyeing the bottle of beer Darcy was nursing.

"Not really the best way to toast a birthday," Darcy muttered without meeting the barmaid's eyes. "Figured I'd have a real drink."

Lauren leaned on the bar in front of Darcy and sighed sadly for the teenager. "How long have you been in love with her?"

Dark green eyes looked up in surprise. "What made you think...who said...I'm not," she stammered, shaking her head.

"It's written all over your face. Though, I take it she hasn't got a clue?"

Darcy shook her head. "I don't think so." She sighed heavily and looked up to meet sympathetic light green eyes. "My whole life." Seeing confusion etched on Lauren's face, she smiled sadly. "I think I've loved her my whole life. That's how long we've known each other."

"And she's not interested? Or..."

"Straight," Darcy exhaled. "She's straight."

Lauren sucked air through her teeth. "Ouch! I'm sorry."

"So am I." Darcy frowned, eyes on her bottle. "Is it obvious? How I feel?"

"Maybe only to me. Maybe your friends are too close to see it for what it is."

Darcy watched the attractive redhead turn away, someone calling for another drink. Left alone, she turned her attention back to Caitlyn, watching the blonde with her brothers, her interest in the men fleeting it seemed. Turning back around to face the bar, she sighed deeply.

Why did she always set herself up for heartache? she wondered, beginning to pick at the label on her bottle. Caitlyn was never going to be hers. Caitlyn was never going to give her a chance. She was straight, she had always been straight, and yet...Darcy lived in hope. She picked up her bottle and sipped at the beer, trying not to cringe at the taste.

Tonight, she wanted the oblivion that alcohol would provide. Her chest ached, or rather, her heart ached, as she felt the weight of her unrequited love.

"Hey, baby," Lauren greeted, bending to kiss the top of Darcy's head. "You're looking very troubled. Everything okay?"

"Troubled?" Darcy murmured. She pulled Lauren down to sit between her legs. "I was thinking about the first time I met you."

"Your eighteenth birthday," Lauren said fondly. "I was so sure you were underage!"

"Yes, I remember," Darcy chuckled.

"It was also the one time I sort of met Caitlyn. She didn't like me, if I remember correctly."

"Could've been because you were talking to me rather than serving us."

"How could I resist?" Lauren turned her head to kiss waiting lips. "You were quite...devilish!"

"Devilish!" Darcy squawked in outrage. "I was not being devilish!"

"You were. I was merely trying to do my job, positive you were underage, only for you to ask for orange juice! And then, to add insult to injury, you produced your ID and proved you were legal anyway!"

"You shouldn't have been so presumptuous," Darcy laughed.

Smiling, Lauren moved to get up. "Do you want some warm milk? Or perhaps a hot chocolate?"

"Hot chocolate sounds good." Darcy let her girlfriend up, then stood herself, following Lauren through to the kitchen. "I'm nervous about going home. That's why I'm not sleeping very well lately."

"I know, baby. You should try not thinking so much about it. It's not like they're going to slam the door on you, you're family to them, you know that."

It wasn't the family she was worried about. Darcy leaned back against the counter and nibbled on her bottom lip. She watched her girlfriend grab two mugs and the tin of powdered chocolate. "I can't help it," she said aloud. "But the tickets are booked and one way or another, for better or for worse, I'll soon know where I stand."

"And I'll be by your side no matter what," Lauren promised.

"Even if I want to jump on a plane and flee to Avarua?"

Lauren turned and blinked at Darcy, a blank look on her face. "Um, sure! Why not?"

"That's the national capital of the Cook Islands," Darcy grinned.

"God, you're smart!" Lauren praised. "Sure, babe. Wherever you go, I'll go." Drinks made, she handed Darcy one of the mugs and picked up her own, before following her taller partner through to the living room.

The couple sat on the sofa next to each other. "Out of curiosity, what happened after you left the bar that night?" Lauren asked shyly. "I heard Caitlyn tell her brothers she was going to take you home."

Darcy studied Lauren's poker face, trying to work out why she would be asking now and never before. "She took me home and put me to bed, where I didn't stay because I was as sick as a dog in the early hours. Then in the early afternoon when I finally managed to drag myself out of bed, she teased me mercilessly."

"Oh," Lauren grinned. She sipped at her steaming chocolate, the heady aroma conjuring memories from her childhood. "Beer didn't agree with you then?"

"I always thought it might have been the damn orange juice."

"Hey!" Lauren protested while Darcy laughed. She cringed suddenly. "You might be right. Orange juice and beer, ick."

They fell quiet, content in each other's company, at the stage in their relationship where they didn't have to talk meaninglessly just to fill the silence.

"Are you going back to your flat when we get home?" Darcy asked, her thoughts having turned to home once again.

"Mm-hmm. Have to sleep somewhere."

"You could stay with me," she offered, looking down at her mug and its contents. She looked up to meet Lauren's gaze. "I have a very cosy single bed that I am willing to share."

Lauren laughed out loud at the thought of them squeezing into a single bed. "Tempting," she nodded. "But I think you should have some time with the family on your own. I've had your company for the last few years. And hey, it's not like they know about us anyway."

"I'm going to tell them," Darcy replied quickly. "You're not a secret, Lauren. I'm not ashamed of you. It's just…it's not the sort of thing I wanted to write in a letter or on a postcard, you know?"

"Yeah, I know. And I understand." She smiled, reaching out to caress Darcy's hand. "If you need to get away from the madness, you can always come over to mine, honey. It's going to be very weird sleeping alone after so many years next to you."

"Maybe we should get a couple of walkie-talkies."

"Okay," Lauren said slowly, not following.

"To save on a big phone bill," Darcy explained, making the redhead chuckle. She lifted an imaginary walkie-talkie and started speaking into it. "Lauren? Lauren, you there, over? I miss you, over."

That made Lauren laugh out loud again. "God, you are too adorable sometimes, Darcy Kenton!"

Darcy blushed crimson. "Thanks."

"Anyway, sweetheart." Lauren got up. "I'm going back to bed. Are you coming?"

"In a minute. I'll finish this first."

Stopping in front of her girlfriend, Lauren bent to kiss Darcy's head. "Okay, babe. Don't be too long. You know I don't sleep well without you snuggled up next to me."

"Ooh, the lies!" Darcy chuckled. "This building could come down around you and you would sleep right through it!" Tilting her head back, she smiled at her girlfriend and accepted the kiss the redhead bestowed upon her. "I'll be there soon, sweetheart. Promise." She watched Lauren walk out of the room, appreciating the sway of her hips as she went.

Left alone once again, she finished her chocolate before it got cold and as she set the now empty mug on the coffee table, found herself thinking back to the night of her eighteenth birthday.

Caitlyn couldn't help but smile as she and Darcy made their way home from the bar. Away from the main streets, things were quiet and they were the only two out it seemed. Caitlyn was holding onto her best friend to keep Darcy on her feet, the brunette having decided to try every beer available and drinking a few bottles too many.

"You look like an angel in the moonlight, Catie," Darcy declared, stopping in the middle of the pavement, making Caitlyn stop as well. "An angel of the night!" she said loudly, not caring if it was after midnight. "An angel of the night, who doesn't know it. So, I have to tell her. I have to tell you," her voice softened, eyes settling on her friend. Pulling the smaller girl in front of her, she looked into Caitlyn's eyes. "You, Caitlyn Eleanor Swailes, are an angel."

Caitlyn smiled lovingly. "You know, you're quite sweet when you've had a drink."

Darcy laughed and took her friend's arm, starting them walking again. She almost stumbled as she glanced at Caitlyn, a deep frown creasing her brow. "You mean I'm not when I'm sober?"

"You hardly talk when you're sober," Caitlyn replied with a chuckle.

Reaching their home, the pair stopped at the front door, Darcy fumbling in her pockets for her door keys and Caitlyn rummaging through her handbag.

"Where did the brothers go?" Darcy suddenly asked, frowning at her dropped keys.

"They've gone on to a club."

"A club! We should go! Why didn't they invite us? Let's go to the club, Caitlyn. We can...we can dance and drink!"

Bending to pick up her friend's dropped keys, Caitlyn stood quickly and grabbed hold of her drunk friend, slapping a hand across her mouth to silence her. "Darcy, honey, I'm seventeen. I won't get in. And you, my dearest friend, are incredibly drunk."

"I know," Darcy sighed, suddenly tired. "It's my birthday."

"Yes, I know, Darce," Caitlyn smiled.

Darcy watched Caitlyn watching her, a look she didn't recognise on her friend's face. She blinked, but the look didn't go away. "Caitlyn?" she questioned softly as the other girl stepped forward, her blue eyes on Darcy's lips.

Without saying a word, Caitlyn closed the gap between them and kissed her best friend on the lips, her hands on either side of Darcy's face to keep her in place. Not that Darcy had any intention of moving. Stepping back far too soon for Darcy's liking, Caitlyn smiled brightly. "I just um...wanted to say happy birthday, Darce."

"Okay."

"Come on." Stepping back completely, Caitlyn turned her attention to the front door and getting it open. "Let's get you to bed. You'll share with me, won't you, Darcy?"

"No. Not tonight." Darcy shook her head and reached for the wall, almost stumbling over again. "I think...tonight I'll sleep in the bathroom...next to the toilet." She frowned as her stomach started to rebel. "Don't feel good."

"I know, honey. That's why I want you to sleep with me. I can keep an eye on you and look after you. Okay?" She glanced over at her friend. "Please, Darcy? Let me look after you, hmm?"

How could she say no when Caitlyn looked at her like that? She found herself nodding and smiled when Caitlyn smiled, pleased she had made her friend happy.

"Okay. Let's get you inside." Caitlyn wrapped an arm around Darcy's waist. "Hey, did I tell you Ian finally asked me out?"

Ian. Darcy growled as she got to her feet, taking her mug to the kitchen. The moron, as she liked to call him. Otherwise known as Ian Moran. She sighed and ran a hand through her tousled hair. Why did Caitlyn have such rubbish taste in men? First Wayne the pain, then that other guy briefly. What was his name? Garry? Jackson? Or maybe it was Phillip? Anyway, he didn't last long. Then it was the moron. She rolled her eyes.

Knowing it was going to be a while until she could sleep, Darcy padded quietly back into the living room, switching off the kitchen light as she left. She stood at the window, gazing out at the quiescent and silent town. If the weather was warmer, she would have stepped out onto the balcony, loving the view it provided. But temperatures had dropped low and weren't helped by the sea breeze that drifted lazily through town. It had been perfect in the summer.

Her deep, sad sigh fogged the glass in front of her and she traced a smiling face into it, smiling herself. She wondered if Caitlyn had forgiven her for leaving. Would she forgive her for having stayed away for so many years? She gave her little smiling face a hat and drew a palm tree next to him.

Caitlyn was probably even more beautiful now. And married. She's probably married to... Darcy shook her head. Nope, don't think about it. She remembered meeting Ian Moran for the first time. She remembered she had instantly disliked him, not because he was dating Caitlyn, but because he was a smarmy arsehole. She remembered that her barely disguised dislike for him caused an argument between herself and Caitlyn.

The group of teenagers walked into the bar in July 2010, laughing and talking loudly to each other, all except Darcy, who remained her usual shy and quiet self. Today was Caitlyn's eighteenth birthday and she had invited not only her boyfriend, Ian, but Gemma Hegan, Janey Inglis, Charlotte Fleming, and Adam Roffe to celebrate with her. Darcy couldn't help but wish her best friend had done what she had done and just celebrated with her and the brothers.

Walking up to the bar, Darcy took a seat on a stool and smiled when she spotted Pat on duty behind the bar. Her attention was swiftly caught by Ian when the pompous git started ordering drinks for everyone. Loud and centre of attention.

"Two bottles of WKD for—"

"The red one, please," Janey interrupted, looking around the bar distastefully.

"A pint of Strongbow, a pint of Carlsberg, a brandy and coke, and Caitlyn will have a red wine. Oh, and Darcy? What are you having?"

Darcy looked disdainfully at the man, then at Caitlyn. "What do you want, Caitlyn?" she asked, an edge to her tone.

"She's having—" Ian started.

"No," Darcy interrupted, hard green eyes settling on him. "That's what you ordered for her. But what does she feel like having?" She looked back to her best friend. "Caitlyn?"

"It's fine, Darcy. I've had wine before, at least I know what I'm getting."

Seeing she was giving in to what Ian wanted, Darcy held back from saying anything else. If she wanted some dickhead dominating her life that was her business. "Suit yourself. I'll have an orange juice, no ice."

"Orange juice?" Adam laughed. "You do know this is a bar, don't you, Darcy?"

Darcy looked at the small balding man, to Janey and Gemma laughing behind him. "I know where I am, thanks." She looked at Pat and saw the sympathetic look he shot her. "An OJ, no ice, please, Pat."

"Sorry, ladies and gents, but I'm going to have to see some identification," Pat told the group. "Except you, Darcy. I remember you," he smiled and gave her a cheeky wink.

While the group of teens sorted out their IDs to show the barman, Caitlyn took Darcy's arm and tugged. "Come with me a minute, Darcy."

Darcy sensed her friend was angry but couldn't figure out why. She was looking out for Caitlyn, or at least trying to. She allowed the smaller woman to drag her away from the group and when they stopped, she waited, watching Caitlyn's face in puzzlement.

"What the hell is wrong with you?" Caitlyn growled. "Making a scene like that in front of my friends!"

Darcy blinked, taken aback by her friend's outburst. "Caitlyn, he ordered for you. He didn't ask what you fancied, what you like, he just ordered for you. That doesn't bother you?"

"God, what is it with you? You never like the guys I date for stupid little reasons! Is this because you're gay? Or because you think you might be gay? You still haven't told me your preferences. Either way, I'm not gay, Darcy. I'm not interested in dating you, or having you act possessive all the damn time!"

"I'm not possessive. I was being protective. You shouldn't let that idiot be so domineering. It starts with him ordering for you, where will it stop?"

"I wish you could just be happy for me."

"This has nothing to do with me or my preferences, Caitlyn. You are your own woman, strong and independent. You're more than capable of choosing what you want to drink without being told. I'm just looking out for you. You do remember how things turned out with Wayne, don't you?"

"Ian is nothing like Wayne," Caitlyn scoffed. "He's kind and attentive and cares about me. He's not looking for a quick shag. And he's got a job goal, he wants to be an accountant, or financial adviser."

"Oh, how good of him. I must run out and start up a petition to get him made into a saint! A fucking accountant! How noble, how courageous!"

"Stop that!" Caitlyn slapped Darcy's arm, though unable to hold back her smile.

"Accountants are boring, everyone says so," Darcy pouted.

"Be happy for me, Darcy. Please?"

"I'll try." She shrugged as Caitlyn looked at her sternly. "What? That's the best you're getting."

"What am I going to do with you?" Caitlyn muttered, turning away and making her way back to the bar.

While Caitlyn and her friends went off to play pool, Darcy sat at the bar, moping over what would never be, who she could never have.

"Hey, Darcy," Lauren greeted cheerfully as she walked behind the bar. "What's got you looking down in the dumps?"

"Hi, Lauren. Just coming to realise that some things aren't meant to be. How are you?"

"Good, thanks," the redhead smiled as she stored her jacket beneath the bar. "Back on the orange juice I see."

"Yeah, you know I like to start out slow," Darcy chuckled.

"Ah, yes, I remember," Lauren laughed. She glanced around the crowded bar, spotting the small blonde her new friend was in love with. She watched Caitlyn for a few moments before turning her attention back to Darcy. "Is that her boyfriend?" she asked softly.

Darcy glanced over her shoulder and saw Ian all over Caitlyn. "Yeah. He's a dickhead." As Lauren laughed, Darcy met her eyes and grinned. "And I'm not just saying that because of how I feel. He really is. Even his name suits him. His surname is Moran."

"Let me guess, you like to call him moron?"

Darcy's grin widened. "I'm not the only one."

Lauren turned to grab a bottle of whiskey and two glasses. Turning back to face the teenager, she wiggled the bottle. "Fancy joining me for a real drink?"

"Sure, okay."

Lauren poured them each a small measure and slid one of the glasses to Darcy. "I wouldn't guzzle that."

"Understood. Thank you." Darcy wrapped a hand around the tumbler. "Will you get in trouble?"

"I doubt it," the redhead chuckled. "I know the owner." Leaning on the bar, she cupped her chin in one hand. "This place was my uncle's," she explained. "When he died, he left it to me."

"Oh. I'm sorry."

"Don't be. He enjoyed life a little too much and it caught up with him." She downed her tot of whiskey. "You know, maybe you should make her appreciate you more," she suggested, eyes drifting over to Caitlyn again. "Make her realise how great you are and just what she has."

"You mean like...make her jealous?" Darcy asked uncertainly.

"No, not necessarily. Perhaps distance yourself from her life a bit, don't be around as much as she's used to."

Darcy's gaze drifted to Caitlyn interacting with Ian, thinking over the bar owner's words, a thoughtful look on her face. "Perhaps."

That's what planted the seed, Darcy thought, covering her mouth as she yawned. That's what got her thinking about leaving. She turned and walked away from the window, ready to try and sleep again.

She quietly made her way to the bedroom and gently slid into bed, careful not to disturb her girlfriend. Lying on her back, she stared up at the cracked ceiling, smiling when Lauren rolled over and snuggled against her. She wrapped an arm around the slumbering redhead, holding her close and savouring the warmth Lauren's body provided.

Of course, something happened to make her put off the thought of leaving. She thought back to a certain New Year's Eve. If she had got her act together and just left, maybe...maybe she wouldn't have stayed away as long as she had. Darcy kissed her girlfriend's head as Lauren mumbled in her sleep. But if she had left sooner, the greatest night of her life would never have happened.

Darcy walked into the packed pub and looked through the masses of men, women, and children, for Caitlyn. She had been debating whether to meet up with her best friend all evening, knowing New Year's Eve 2012 would be a big celebration with lots of alcohol flowing and kissing when Big Ben struck midnight. Not a good combination when she was trying to keep her feelings in check.

Spotting Caitlyn standing with Ian and his friends deep in conversation, Darcy couldn't help but pause and admire the small blonde. She's so beautiful, she thought, eyes drinking in Caitlyn, dressed to the nines in a sexy little black dress. And she's straight. She had to keep reminding herself of that.

As though she felt she was being watched, Caitlyn glanced around even as she continued talking, light blue eyes finding Darcy in the crowd. A beautiful angelic smile lit up her face when their eyes locked. "Darcy!" she squealed in delight, pushing through the crowd to get to her best friend. "Where have you been?"

"I was at Lauren's," Darcy explained, seeing what she could have sworn was jealousy flashing in Caitlyn's eyes. She caught her friend when Caitlyn launched herself at her and relished holding on for a few precious moments, even managing to not feel guilty. Closing her eyes, she lost herself in the feel and smell of Caitlyn, her lifelong best friend, the secret owner of her heart. A very happy smile curled her lips as she was hugged back just as tightly.

Pulling back, Caitlyn grinned and rubbed her nose to Darcy's. "I'm glad you came, Darce. I know you don't like my friends, or Ian, and you hate crowds, but I think it's important we spend these holidays together. Though, you have left it late enough, there's only ten minutes to go."

She released her hold on Darcy, heeled feet hitting the ground as she unwrapped her legs from around Darcy's waist. "Come on, come meet the guys."

Darcy missed the feel of Caitlyn wrapped around her instantly but smiled when her hand was taken, and she was dragged toward the group her friend was with. She was introduced to everyone and remained polite, though internally she was fighting the urge to run. She hated crowds and the company of strangers. Caitlyn knew this though, so remained by her side, her thumb stroking the back of the hand she still held.

Glancing down at her watch, Caitlyn excused herself and Darcy, explaining they needed drinks to see in the new year with. Surprisingly, she bypassed the bar completely and led Darcy outside into the pub's garden, making her way past the gathered smokers standing in the lighted and heated area just outside the doors, and headed for the back of the garden, which was shrouded in darkness, only the moon above showing the way.

"I figured you would like to be away from the crowd for a while," Caitlyn said kindly.

"You know me so well." She looked around the dark garden, seeing flowerbeds and tall hedges around the outer edges and tables scattered around the middle of the area for people to sit at. From what she could make out, the garden was neat and well maintained. Toward the very back of the garden was what looked like an open shack. "What's that?"

"A shed, though I don't think it always was one," Caitlyn replied, leading Darcy over to the structure. "I think it use to be a place to sit out of the sun, but now it's used to store the gardening tools, umbrellas for the tables, and other odds and ends." She leaned back against the side of the shed.

Music the DJ was playing blasted out of the outdoor speakers, along with loud conversation and laughter drifting to them from inside the pub. Two outdoor floodlights attached to the outside wall of the pub lit up the smoker's area, but the back was in virtual darkness, making Darcy wonder why they had come out there.

"Come here often?" Darcy asked suddenly, confused as to what was going on.

Caitlyn laughed out loud. "Was that a chat-up line, Darce?"

Blushing, Darcy shook her head. "No."

"This is Ian's local pub. We come here every other night."

"Shouldn't we get back? I'm sure Ian will be wondering where you've got to."

"I'm where I need to be," Caitlyn murmured. When it was announced there was only a minute to go before midnight, she stood up straight and took Darcy's arms, tugging Darcy into a position in front of her.

"The freezing cold garden where the smokers gather? Neither of us smoke," Darcy replied weakly. Not at all sure what her friend was doing, she nonetheless allowed herself to be tugged this way and that until Caitlyn was apparently satisfied with her position. "What are we doing?"

Caitlyn placed her hands on Darcy's hips and stared into her eyes. Darcy swallowed hard as she swore that past the slightly drunken glaze, she could see love and desire reflected back at her. I'm seeing things, she thought. She was seeing what she wanted to see because they were out here in the dark together, for reasons Caitlyn hadn't shared.

As the countdown began, Darcy tried to talk herself into moving away, but found herself frozen in place, eyes lost in pools of blue. Oddly, she wanted to stay and see what Caitlyn had in mind.

"Ten!" People started counting down joyously.

Darcy licked her lips nervously, a crazy thought popping into her head.

"Nine!"

Caitlyn mirrored Darcy's action, a small smile curling the corners of her mouth.

"Eight!"

Caitlyn can't be planning to kiss me, Darcy thought fearfully, mouth suddenly going dry. Not out here. In the dark. Away from everyone else.

"Five!"

She is. That's what this crazy plan is all about. Oh, God! Oh, God! What if she really does kiss me? How do I react? She opened her mouth to protest, to remind Caitlyn of her boyfriend no doubt looking around for her inside the pub.

"Three!"

Caitlyn shook her head, a finger pressing against Darcy's lips to stop her.

"Two!"

Caitlyn moved closer, pressing the front of her body into her taller friend, both women groaning at the pleasurable contact.

"One! Happy New Year!"

Darcy was oblivious to the loud cheer from within the pub, the popping of party poppers, the DJ saying something cheesy. All she knew, all she was aware of, was that she was receiving the softest of kisses from the sweetest of lips. They had kissed before on other holidays and birthdays, but not like this. This was everything Darcy had ever wanted.

Sinking into the kiss, she pulled Caitlyn even closer, her hands roaming slowly up and down her back. Caitlyn moaned aloud and grasped Darcy's jean-covered butt, while Darcy's tongue sampled her lips. She parted her lips to allow Darcy's exploration to continue, and as their tongues caressed, she jumped up, hooking her legs around her friend's waist, moaning deeply when Darcy pressed her back against the wall of the shed, both of them lost in the feel of the other.

Suddenly having the very woman she had always wanted, Darcy savoured the moment. She caressed the smooth thighs wrapped around her and trailed hot kisses down Caitlyn's neck, feeling Caitlyn rocking herself against her body, seeking a more pleasurable touch.

"Oh, sweetheart!" she moaned into Caitlyn's neck, her friend's perfume intoxicating, the moment near perfect.

The softly moaned words brought Caitlyn to her senses. She opened her eyes and immediately panicked. "Put me down!" she gasped, pushing her friend's shoulders. "Put me down, Darcy!" As soon as Caitlyn was back on her own feet, she stepped backward, unable to meet Darcy's eyes. "I...I should...get back inside...to Ian," she stuttered distractedly, turning to walk away.

Heart breaking, Darcy reached out and gently took Caitlyn's arm in her grasp, stopping her from fleeing. "Stay," she pleaded softly. "Stay with me." She looked deeply into the eyes of the woman she loved, praying Caitlyn picked her for once. Tired of the games, of the flirting and the jealousy.

Confusion distorted Caitlyn's usually angelic features and she slowly shook her head from side to side. "I should get back to Ian. He'll be wondering where I am."

Darcy leaned against the wall of the shed, her heart having been ripped out of her chest and discarded carelessly. She watched through teary eyes as Caitlyn walked away, another rejection under her belt. "Oh, God!" she keened through clenched teeth, a hand covering her heart as she physically felt the pain of Caitlyn's rejection. This hurt more than ever before. This time she had foolishly believed she had been about to get everything she had ever wanted. But it was never her. It never would be her for Caitlyn.

Darcy rolled onto her side away from Lauren and let out a trembling breath. It still hurt to this day. She felt the slow trek of a single tear making its way from the corner of her eye to her temple. She probably should have stayed away that night. All night she had debated whether to show up where Caitlyn asked her to or not and eventually she gave in. She gave in to her need to see Caitlyn, her need to be with her, her need for her.

She lay still as Lauren rolled over, waiting to see if her girl-friend had woken. She wasn't sure how she'd explain the tears if she had. Barely daring to breathe, she listened to Lauren's breathing, noting it was deep and even.

Darcy slowly exhaled, still thinking of that fateful evening. If she hadn't gone... She glanced over her shoulder at Lauren, the redhead's back to her. She turned over as carefully as she could, so as not to disturb Lauren, and spooned up behind her, slipping an arm around Lauren's waist and taking comfort in holding her. But if she hadn't gone, things wouldn't have turned out how they did, and she wouldn't be here. She wouldn't have Lauren. Maybe it was always her fate to leave town? She sighed, not having an answer.

Even after all this time, she still wasn't sure if she would do things differently if she could go back in time. Closing her eyes as they finally grew heavy, Darcy felt herself start to relax, ready to give in to her need for sleep, the comfort of Lauren in her arms a balm to her. She drifted to sleep thinking about the rest of that New Year's Night, which had changed her life forever.

Chapter Seven

CAITLYN POKED AT her dinner, watching a pea roll away and the prongs of her fork graze against her chicken breast, not listening to a word Ian was saying as they shared a candlelit meal at their small dinner table. She couldn't care less about the bores he worked with, had no desire to go out for drinks with a couple who were friends to his family, didn't want to meet up with old college friends. She knew what he was doing, and it was annoying her. He was desperately trying to take her mind off Darcy, trying to distract her and remind her of her life with him.

It had all started on Sunday when he had found out Darcy was coming home. Not from Caitlyn, but from a jubilant Brian. Getting through lunch with her family, the car ride home had been made in tense silence and as soon as they got in, it had bubbled over and the couple had a blazing row, Ian demanding to know why she hadn't thought to tell him the news, asking why she had seen to him being embarrassed in front of her family.

When the arguing got them nowhere, Ian insisted they discuss their wedding. Suggesting they pick a month at the very least. She hadn't responded. She had retreated upstairs and locked herself in the bathroom to run a bath, where she had reclined until he took the hint and left her be.

"Darcy phoned up today." Caitlyn could still hear her mother's voice say again, while moving peas around her plate. She had been at work when Tricia called her to excitedly tell her the news. "She's booked the tickets and will be home Wednesday! Ooh, I can't wait to see her! Isn't it exciting, sweetheart? You will get the day off, won't you?"

Caitlyn hadn't known what to say, overwhelmed with the news, so she lied, telling her mother she had to go because a patient was calling for assistance. The news had knocked her for six once again and she spent the rest of the day distracted, much to the concern of her colleagues who had never known her to be anything but professional.

"Caitlyn, are you listening to me?"

She looked up and blinked. "Yes, Ian. I heard every word."

"Well, what do you think?"

Sighing, she set down her cutlery, no interest in finishing what was on her plate. "I have no desire to spend an evening in

Georgeanne and Emiliano's company. I don't want to go out for drinks, I don't want to go out for a meal, and I don't want to talk about our wedding!"

"I see," Ian said calmly. "What would you like to talk about, darling? How about Christmas. It's fast approaching. Where will we be spending it this year? Oh, that reminds me, Niall wants to meet up. It's been over a year since we saw him last and he's back in town for a while. I thought it would be nice to see him over Christmas."

Knowing Ian wasn't going to drop it no matter what she said, Caitlyn sighed and nodded. It was easier to give in to what he wanted. "Fine. Whatever you want, Ian." While her fiancé started rambling on and on about their old college friend and his new wife, Caitlyn found herself thinking back to the last Christmas she had spent with Darcy.

So much happened that Christmas, she thought sadly. She was off with Ian as often as possible, much to the family's annoyance. And then Darcy got news. News she wasn't sure was good or bad, news she didn't know how to handle. She ended up a mess, though she pretended to everyone she was fine.

It was December 2012. Humming "White Christmas," Caitlyn couldn't help but smile happily as she made her way up the snow-covered garden path, the beautiful white powder crunching under foot. She had spent the day Christmas shopping and despite the crowds of crazy people elbowing her out of their way, despite the shops all playing the same irritating songs over and over, despite the long queues and less than helpful shop assistants, she loved every minute of it.

She loved Christmas. It had always been her favourite holiday and this year she had Ian to celebrate it with as well. Even though her family seemed standoffish with him, she was determined he should join them for dinner and be made welcome, like she had been when meeting his parents.

The house had been fully decorated. Every window facing the street had festive lights in them, though they weren't switched on now during the day. A halo of holly was hanging on the front door, and a waving Santa figure stood proudly on the lawn alongside a team of reindeer. Inside was even better, with the large decorated tree in the living room and tinsel and garlands hanging everywhere. It looked as if Christmas had thrown-up and Caitlyn loved it.

"Hello," she called out, getting the front door open, despite all the bag handles tangled around her fingers.

Tricia appeared in the kitchen doorway looking worried. "Hello, honey. Did you get everything you were after?"

"Yes, just about." Caitlyn stepped inside and shut the door behind her. "It smells divine in here, Mum. What are you baking?"

"Cinnamon cookies."

"Ooh, lovely. Crazy shoppers! Every year I say I'm going to do my shopping earlier, but I always end up leaving it until the last week!" She headed for the closed living room door, wanting to put down her bags and get her winter gear off.

"You can't go in there, Caitlyn," Tricia called out, stopping her in her tracks.

"Why? What's going on, Mum?" Frowning, Caitlyn walked toward her mother.

Leading her daughter over to the kitchen table, the two women took a seat. "Darcy's in there with the family lawyer. He turned up on the doorstep and asked to speak with her about something urgent and apologised that it was so close to Christmas."

"I didn't know Darcy had a family lawyer."

"Neither did Darcy. Do you want a cup of tea, love?"

"Yes, please." Caitlyn watched her mother head to the kettle. "If he's not Darcy's lawyer, then is he Yvonne's? Or Colin's?"

Tricia got two mugs ready with sugar and a teabag in each. "I wonder if they would like a cup?" she pondered, staring down at the mugs. "I would assume it was one of them, yes.

"That's odd, isn't it?" Caitlyn queried. "When Darce was in the hospital, Colin couldn't be found, and Yvonne disappeared off the radar once she was released by the police." Caitlyn had a sudden terrible thought. "You don't think something's happened, do you?"

Tricia glanced at her daughter. "I don't know, love. We'll have to see what Darcy says. If she says anything."

While they drank their tea, Caitlyn shared with her mother what she had gotten everyone for Christmas. Tricia smiled and refused to reveal what she had bought, knowing Caitlyn wouldn't keep it a secret no matter how hard she tried. Tricia knew her sons had ways of making their baby sister talk.

The two women fell silent when they heard Darcy and the lawyer come out of the living room and start talking in the hallway, the pair moving toward the front door by the sounds of it. Mother and daughter heard the door open, then shut, and only silence remained. When Darcy didn't appear in the kitchen, Tricia stood up and Caitlyn quickly followed.

"Darcy?" Tricia called out. "Honey, are you okay?" She walked into the living room and frowned when she found it empty.

"I'll check upstairs," Caitlyn offered. Leaving the living room, she ran upstairs to Darcy's bedroom. Pausing at the closed door, she heard nothing within. "Darcy?" she called out softly, knocking gently on the wood. "You in there, Darce?" Getting no response, she opened the door and found the room empty. She hurried back downstairs to her mother. "She's not up there."

"Where could she have gone off to?" Tricia asked rhetorically. "Surely she would have told us if she was leaving with the lawyer?"

Not if it was bad news, Caitlyn thought, knowing her best friend well. If it was bad news and she wanted time to deal with it, she would've run. "I'm going to go looking for her. I have an idea where she may be." Leaving the living room again, she grabbed her coat and scarf. "If she turns up, call my mobile and let me know." Spotting Darcy's winter jacket still hanging on the peg, she grabbed it, knowing her friend would need it if she was out in the cold weather.

"Okay, honey. Be careful."

Caitlyn headed for the local park. Having known Darcy her whole life, she knew her best friend always headed to the park when she wanted space to think. Darcy liked to sit on the benches that faced the Lower Pond, silently watching the swimming geese and ducks as she thought over whatever was bothering her.

That was exactly where Caitlyn found her.

"Hey, Darcy," she greeted softly, taking a seat next to her. "Thought you might need this." She handed over the jacket she had brought with her.

"Thanks." Darcy slipped the thick coat on and zipped it up, burying her hands in the deep pockets.

"Want to talk about it?"

Darcy shook her head. "How was shopping?"

Okay, they'd have to do this the hard way. "Great. You know I love it. Even though I had little old ladies elbowing me out of the way, bratty kids stepping on my toes and throwing temper tantrums in front of me, and the longest queues imaginable to wait in." She smiled as she spotted a small, amused smile on her friend's lips. "Should've come with me, Darce. We could've caused mayhem!"

"Yeah, I should have," Darcy sighed heavily, her breath coming out in a white cloud in front of her. The temperature was low today and dropping even lower the later in the day it got.

Caitlyn pulled out her phone and hit speed dial for home. "Hey, Mum. Just wanted to let you know I found Darcy."

"Is everything all right?"

"She's fine. We'll be home soon."

"Okay, love. See you soon."

"Bye." Caitlyn slipped the phone back into her pocket. "She was worried when we discovered you had disappeared without a word."

"Sorry about that. I just had to…"

"Run," Caitlyn finished. She smiled as Darcy glanced at her. "I've known you forever, Darce. How do you think I knew I'd find you here?"

Darcy nodded and smiled a little, before green eyes turned back to the rippling water of the pond. "Yvonne's dead," she said numbly. "Liver failure," she snorted. "No surprise there!"

"Oh, Darcy!" Caitlyn moved closer to her friend and wrapped an arm around her. "I'm sorry, honey."

"Are you?" Darcy looked at the smaller woman, a frown creasing her brow. "Because I'm not. I don't…I don't feel anything."

"I'm sorry for you." Caitlyn tightened her hold on Darcy and kissed her temple. "You went through a lot and nothing ever really got resolved. You ended up in hospital and she disappeared. She didn't once call to see how you were, didn't send a card on your birthdays or at Christmas. She was a terrible mother and I'm sorry that someone as wonderful as you had her as a parent."

Tears welling up in her eyes, Darcy wrapped Caitlyn in her arms and held on to her best friend tightly. "I feel lost now," she whispered. "My dad did a runner and I haven't seen or heard from him since, and now my…Yvonne's gone forever. I have no one, Caitlyn. It's just me now."

Caitlyn pulled back and looked into conflicted eyes. "That's bullshit and you know it!" she said gruffly. "You have me, Darcy. You'll always have me. And my family is your family. My parents took you in and love you as if you are their own. My brothers adore you as well. You have family, Darce. Maybe not blood family, but a family nonetheless."

"Thanks, Catie." She kissed Caitlyn's head, a small smile back on her lips. "I love you, you know?"

"I know. I love you, too."

That was such a difficult time, Caitlyn thought, scraping what food remained on the plates into the bin, before moving to the sink. It had been Christmas, a time for friends and family, and Darcy wasn't sure how she should feel about Yvonne dying, so she ignored her feelings and pretended everything was fine, and the family wasn't sure what to say or do, making everything awkward. Then there was Ian, who she had invited to dinner.

She turned off the hot water tap and slid the plates and cutlery into the sink to soak. Walking through to the living room, she found Ian lounging in front of the television. Taking a seat next to him on the sofa, she snuggled into his side, the familiar musky aroma of his aftershave hitting her senses. He wrapped his arm around her shoulders.

"There's a film on in twenty minutes," he told her.

"What's it about?"

Releasing his fiancée as he leaned forward, he grabbed the TV guide and flicked to the appropriate page. "Says it's about ice skating," he read. "Polar opposites unite on ice for a shot at the Olympic gold."

"I haven't seen it, so we may as well give it a chance."

"Mm."

"What, you don't want to watch it?" Caitlyn asked, not liking the tone to his response.

"I can think of better things we could do." He leaned back and kissed her on the lips.

"Talking perhaps."

"No, not talking," he smiled and placed a hand on her thigh, caressing the limb tenderly.

She shook him off by moving her leg. "I'm not in the mood, Ian. Let's just watch the film."

When the film began, Caitlyn watched. She ignored Ian's sighs and muttered comments, brushed off his wandering hands when he attempted to get his way and curled herself up into the corner of the sofa as the story on screen unfolded. She found herself enraptured until a New Year's Eve scene. Then she found herself drifting off to her own thoughts, thinking back to Darcy once again and a New Year's Eve which had changed everything between them. All because of her.

With a forced smile on her lips, Caitlyn danced with Ian. Her boyfriend was drunk and slobbering on her neck, his hands roaming her body as he tried to touch every part of her. She didn't mind, she didn't really notice.

Swaying to a slow love song she vaguely recognised, Caitlyn's thoughts were on Darcy and the kiss they had shared in the darkness of the pub garden. She had completely lost herself in the much-desired kiss, a kiss she had dreamed of experiencing many a time. For that brief moment, she had forgotten her fears and concerns and allowed herself to experience Darcy's soft but sure lips.

She knew she had once again hurt Darcy by walking away. But she'd had no choice. The rush of unexpected emotions and her desire for the other woman confused her and took her by surprise. She had been startled by her reaction to what should have been a simple kiss. A mix of every emotion except anger had run through her, as she looked into her best friend's eyes and saw nothing but love reflected back.

Caitlyn was afraid and confused by her desire to stay with Darcy when she asked her to stay, confused by her body's reaction to Darcy, confused and scared by the thoughts of wanting more, of going further. Not willing to confront her feelings or rampant thoughts, she fled. Back to Ian.

Getting back inside, Caitlyn found her boyfriend and kissed him passionately, wrapping herself around his body, trying to recreate the passion and intensity she'd experienced with Darcy. It was during the less than thrilling and sloppy kiss that she opened her eyes and spotted Darcy slipping out the front door, leaving without saying goodbye.

Now dancing in Ian's embrace, Caitlyn wanted to go after her best friend and... What? She wondered. Say sorry? Again.

"Hey, sweetheart, I was thinking," Ian murmured into her ear. "How about we go back to my place and..."

She blinked away her thoughts as she realised he was talking to her. "Um, I'm sorry, Ian. What were you saying?"

He pulled back so he could look into her eyes. "I was about to suggest we leave and head back to mine for the night." He grinned, a drunken, lop-sided grin.

"Oh. Sorry, honey, but I think I better go and check on Darcy. She was...feeling ill and I...I want to make sure she got home okay."

"It's New Year's Eve." Ian looked disappointed and did nothing to hide how he was feeling. "You went off earlier and missed the countdown with me! And now you're ditching a night with me to go off and visit your friend, who you can see any time!"

"You know how difficult this holiday has been for her."

"This was supposed to be our first New Year's together, and it's been rubbish."

"She wasn't feeling well, honey," Caitlyn mollified. "I'll only worry until I know she's all right. I don't want any distractions when we decide to finally take things to the next level. Do you?" She kissed him on the lips and smiled her most seductive smile, her mind made up and not to be changed. "I'll make it up to you."

"Okay. I can see your mind is made up." Ian sighed, knowing he wasn't going to win.

With her boyfriend placated for the time being, Caitlyn hurried off to grab her coat and handbag, then left the pub after a quick goodbye to Ian and his friends.

It was raining. Not lightly raining, it was pouring. Fat, heavy droplets that soaked through Caitlyn's coat and dress and chilled her to the bone, droplets that hit the pavement then bounced back up to attack her exposed legs. Being a night of celebration, there were no cabs around and buses were few and far between, so she decided to walk.

Reaching her street, Caitlyn quickened her pace, eager to see Darcy, though why, she couldn't fathom. Walking past Darcy's childhood home, she noticed a light on and wondered if the old place was being robbed. Caitlyn paused between her house and the Kenton's, looking from one to the other. The house had been left to Darcy and her friend had decided to do the old place up. Being the Christmas season, she hadn't had the time to do anything major yet, but she had plans.

It had to be Darcy, she thought. After what happened between them tonight, she wouldn't want to risk facing Mum and Dad. Mum would know something was wrong the moment she saw Darcy's face and would set about dragging it out of her.

Caitlyn hurried up the Kenton's path to the front door, taken back to her childhood when she used to make this same trip whenever she went to knock for her best friend after school, or during the holidays. Knocking loudly on the door, she stepped back and bounced from foot to foot while she waited, starting to feel the chill of the night. Hearing movement inside, she took it as a good sign.

Darcy opened the door and blinked in surprise when she found a drenched Caitlyn on her doorstep. "Caitlyn? Jesus, Caitlyn! Get in here, you're soaked!"

Caitlyn said nothing as Darcy, dressed in a thick bathrobe,

took her hand and tugged her inside. Stepping inside, all sense and reason deserted her. Looking up at Darcy, droplets of rain dribbling down her face from her hair and dripped off her body, she had the urge to again taste the soft lips that had driven her to distraction, the urge to feel strong arms around her, not crushing like Ian's hold, but tender as if she were the most delicate thing in the world.

She thought Darcy was the most gorgeous creature on Earth and with sudden clarity knew she wanted her best friend, despite feeling like a drowned rat. She stepped forward, closing the gap between them, blue eyes on Darcy's lips as she licked her own.

"Caitlyn?" Darcy questioned softly, recognising the look of lust on her friend's face.

Holding onto Darcy's shoulder and standing on her tiptoes despite wearing heels, Caitlyn kissed her friend and murmured in delight at how right it felt. It was everything that kissing Ian wasn't. This kiss was soft, this kiss made her tingle, this kiss set her body aflame. Caitlyn quickly deepened the kiss, her tongue teasing apart Darcy's lips and slipping inside the warmth of her mouth to start a slow exploration.

Darcy moaned aloud and pulled Caitlyn closer, sinking into the kiss rather than stopping to question it. She lifted Caitlyn with ease, feeling Caitlyn's legs wrap around her, and moved to lean her friend against the nearest wall.

Caitlyn rocked against Darcy's body desperately, trying to satiate the throbbing between her legs. She had never been this turned on before, not with any of her boyfriends. Jerking her head back and panting for much needed air, she looked into half-lidded dark green eyes and saw they were clouded with arousal.

"Darcy," she sighed, ducking her head to reclaim kiss-swollen lips again in a slower more tender kiss. It felt right. It all felt right.

Holding on to Caitlyn, Darcy made her way upstairs, her journey made arduous by her friend nibbling and nipping at her neck, fingers playing with the hair on the nape of her neck. She somehow made it upstairs and along the hall to her newly renovated bedroom.

Standing in the middle of the room, a solitary lamp on for light, Darcy set Caitlyn down on her own feet and offered her friend a small loving smile as she reached out to brush aside damp tendrils of hair. The two lifelong friends got lost in the tender moment, exchanging no words. Not needing to. They both knew where this was heading.

Darcy caressed the side of Caitlyn's face with the back of her fingers, before softly cupping her cheek, watching blue eyes flutter shut as Caitlyn leaned into the gentle touch. Eyes of green and blue locked onto each other, Darcy reached out to start undressing her friend. "We should get you out of these clothes," she said tenderly. "I don't want you getting sick," she explained, slipping Caitlyn's coat from her shoulders.

Caitlyn licked her lips, thoughts racing with what was to come, feeling gentle fingertips brushing against her damp, chilled skin. She watched Darcy place her wet coat over the back of a chair and watched her best friend turn back to face her, eyeing the dress she wore. Without saying a word, she lifted her arms and waited for Darcy to lift the black dress up and off, knowing she wasn't wearing a bra and would be left in only her underwear.

Darcy audibly swallowed, cheeks turning an adorable shade of red. Eyes locked onto blue, she stepped closer to Caitlyn and slowly reached for the bottom of the dress, expecting her friend to stop her. Not getting a command to stop, she lifted the dress up and off and was left with the most beautiful sight she had ever seen. Throwing the dress in the direction of the chair, her attention never wavered from Caitlyn.

She licked her suddenly dry lips and reached to cup the shivering blonde's breasts, a trembling breath escaping her lips as she felt the stiffness of Caitlyn's nipples against the palms of her hands. "Oh, Catie," she murmured, stroking their smoothness, filling her hands with them, gently squeezing.

Caitlyn's breathing hitched when Darcy touched her breasts, her heart pounding, her head tilting forward to watch her friend's hands on her. She gasped as Darcy pressed against her hard nipples, her breathing becoming ragged as she looked up at Darcy's face and saw the pure desire etched there, the love, the want, all for her. Darcy wanted her. And she had seen the look before but never acknowledged it, never recognised it for what it was. She watched Darcy in fascination as her friend continued to gently squeeze and caress the breasts she held.

A pink hue coloured Caitlyn's pale skin, a delicious warmth fluttering in her belly, and she knew she wanted to experience this. She wanted Darcy to make love to her, wanted Darcy to be the first, the one to show her true love.

Not wanting to just stand observing, Caitlyn reached out to undo the belt on Darcy's bathrobe, inhaling sharply when she found her friend half-naked beneath. Wrapping her arms around

Darcy, she ran both hands up and down the taller woman's smooth back, tracing skin never before explored. Sliding down, she slipped inside the waistband of Darcy's boxers and farther down to cup firm buttocks.

They kissed, happy to take things slowly, happy to explore soft skin, to tease, to heighten their arousal. Darcy moved even closer, one hand leaving Caitlyn's breast and dipping down to follow the curve of her ribs, gliding down to trace the velvety skin of her belly, then farther down to caress the baby soft skin of her inner thighs.

Caitlyn sighed when gentle fingertips traced her heated body, closed her eyes as her nipple was tweaked and rolled between two fingers. She felt the delicious warmth in her belly flow down to her groin and down farther to her tingling toes, an insistent throbbing starting between her legs at each urgent touch of Darcy's fingers.

Caitlyn took a step back from Darcy and while looking into her friend's eyes, slid her underwear down and carefully stepped out of the lace garment, before reaching for Darcy's boxers. She moaned aloud when the talented fingers found their way to the moist warmth between her thighs, hips rocking as she encouraged the touch. She drew in a ragged breath when Darcy brushed lightly over her swollen clitoris.

Wanting to move things along and knowing Darcy wouldn't, Caitlyn made her way to the bed and lay back. With one leg outstretched, the other bent at the knee, she was unwittingly striking a very seductive pose. Darcy licked her lips and knelt between slender thighs, caressing each, as she met Caitlyn's steady gaze.

"Are you sure about this, Caitlyn?" she asked tenderly, unsure herself of what was happening between them. "We don't have to continue."

"I...I want to. I want it to be you, Darcy. I want you to be my first." Caitlyn smiled and sat up to caress Darcy's cheek. "I know you love me," she said lightly. "And I know you'll be gentle." She lay back, eyes on Darcy while she waited for her friend to decide whether they carried on or not.

Darcy hesitated. She had thought about a moment like this, dreamed a hundred different ways it would play out. And now here they were on a rainy New Year's Eve, Caitlyn asking her to be her first. She settled between Caitlyn's spread legs and moved her head forward, kissing her moist sex, tasting the essence of Caitlyn. She groaned when Caitlyn's sweetness hit her tongue, Caitlyn moaning aloud at the sensation of such a delicate touch.

Caitlyn writhed as Darcy's tongue traced along the outline of her tumescent cleft. She murmured approvingly as Darcy worked her tongue expertly over her full, throbbing clitoris and labia, pushing her ever closer to the release she sought. She could hear herself panting and moaning aloud, could hear the rain hitting the windowpane, could feel her skin tingling. She felt very alive in this moment, as if all her senses were heightened, as her body responded to the teasing of the ever-moving tongue of her best friend.

Her body left the mattress she lay upon, hips rocking frantically as she raced toward climax, until quite suddenly she was poised, ready to fall, waiting for that last devastating flick of her best friend's tongue. When it came, Caitlyn grasped the sheet tightly in both hands while her body arched up, her heart seeming to skip a beat in her chest, a cry of Darcy's name passing her lips before her trembling body hit the mattress again and twitched with aftershocks of delight.

Lying next to Caitlyn, Darcy trailed her fingers over the perfect body before her, tracing every inch with a feather light touch. Following the line of Caitlyn's shoulder, she traced her way down her friend's arm, past the bend of her elbow and to her wrist. Finding her hand grasped suddenly, fingers entwining with Caitlyn's, Darcy smiled as she looked up and met Caitlyn's half-lidded eyes. Leaning over, she kissed pink lips slowly, tenderly, delighting in the fact she could. "Hi."

"Hi," Caitlyn hummed. She shifted slightly, a satisfied smile curling her lips.

Taking back her hand, Darcy followed Caitlyn's arm up to her shoulder, then slowly traced each collarbone with a fingertip, delighting in kissing and nibbling Caitlyn's neck. "Are you okay?"

Caitlyn moaned at the delightful torture of soft, feather light touches and hot kisses, left wondering where Darcy's attention would go next. "Never better." She couldn't believe she wanted Darcy again, her body ready for Darcy's touch, needing Darcy's touch, eagerly awaiting Darcy's touch. She wondered if it was the alcohol making her feel this way.

She cried out and arched her back as Darcy traced the outline of her breasts. Darcy was very careful not to touch the hard points of Caitlyn's nipples. She moaned when Darcy cupped one breast, still not touching her nipple, and gently kneaded the soft mound. She threaded her fingers into dark locks as Darcy lowered her head toward her chest, panting for breath and whimpering when she felt the warmth of breath on her heated, sensitised skin.

"Darcy!" she cried out desperately when her lover hovered, teasing her further.

Darcy's lips curled into a smile as she lowered her head farther and teased Caitlyn's nipple with the tip of her tongue, making Caitlyn cry out and arch up off the mattress. Fingers tightened in her hair as Caitlyn fought to keep her exactly where she was. She circled the hard nub, flicked over it, and finally captured it in her mouth, gently suckling.

Caitlyn gasped and moaned, body writhing, unable to remain still. Her hold on dark locks tightened as she willed her lover to never stop her ministrations. Darcy took more of her breast into the hot cavern of her mouth, grazing a now aching nipple with her teeth while she suckled, and Caitlyn wondered if she could come just from what Darcy was doing. She was certainly getting wet enough.

She squirmed, hips rocking, toes curling, searching for much needed contact where she needed it most, trickles of wet desire flowing from her. Eyes closed tight, her whole body was infused in heat as she edged ever closer to the precipice of climax.

As quickly as she had started, Darcy stopped and pulled away, smiling down at a now scowling Caitlyn. She kissed pouting lips, then returned her attention to her friend's beautiful body. She kissed her way down Caitlyn's chest, past her breasts to her stomach, placing all too brief kisses here and there, before tracing Caitlyn's ribs with her tongue. Stroking through soft curls of hair, down to where Caitlyn was slick and hot.

Caitlyn gasped aloud and parted her legs farther for Darcy's hand, hips rocking up to meet talented fingers stroke for stroke. She strove to keep her eyes open, wanting to watch what Darcy was doing, but as her friend drove her toward the highest of peaks again, Caitlyn found it impossible. Her breath caught as she felt a solitary finger pressing against her opening and opened her eyes to find Darcy looking at her, uncertainty in her eyes.

"Please," she gasped. "Do it, Darcy. Please!"

Leaning half on Caitlyn, Darcy captured kiss-swollen lips, while she slid her finger easily inside the heated canal, which had been calling to her for attention. She moved slowly, caressing the tightening walls, and waited until her friend relaxed before adding a second finger.

Caitlyn jerked her head from Darcy's kiss to groan aloud, her inner walls clamping tightly around the invading fingers. "Darcy!

Oh, Darcy!"

"Relax, sweetheart," Darcy murmured, kissing Caitlyn's neck and nibbling on her ear lobe. She felt her lover start to relax and smiled. "There you go. Just relax, Catie. I'm going to be as gentle as I can be. I promise."

"I know," Caitlyn turned her head to gaze lovingly at her friend. "I know you will be."

Darcy claimed Caitlyn's lips again as she moved to straddle her friend's thigh, ready to take care of her own need while she took care of Caitlyn. She groaned deeply when Caitlyn lifted her thigh, to press more firmly against Darcy's swollen sex.

They looked into each other's eyes as they pleasured each other, the moment intense, much more powerful than either could comprehend, and at the moment of their climax, they fell together, each shattering into a thousand pieces, only to come back together as before but completely changed as well.

That was the most amazing experience of her life, Caitlyn thought, wiping away a tear that slipped free from watery blue eyes. The one time she had ever felt truly loved and appreciated.

"You okay, babe?" Ian asked. "Not getting sucked in by this mushy stuff, are you?"

Caitlyn looked away from the images on the screen she hadn't been watching and lied. "I'm a girly-girl, you know how we get over a good romance film."

Ian smiled affectionately and reached out to caress the side of her face. "Do you want a drink, babe? I'm getting up to get one."

She nodded and watched him stand and leave the living room, letting out a wistful sigh as soon as she was left alone. She had really messed things up with Darcy, she thought sadly. Okay, so she was drunk, but she hadn't done anything she didn't want to. She brushed away another falling tear. She bit her bottom lip to bite back a sob that almost slipped past her lips. She had pan-icked. Plain and simple. She woke up and she panicked and once again she hurt Darcy.

She turned her attention back to the film when she heard Ian returning, trying to pick up what she'd missed since zoning out. Glancing in his direction as he walked in, she smiled when he handed her a glass of white wine.

"What did I miss?" he asked cheerfully.

"Nothing much. Not that you care," she smiled.

"Hey, a guy can pretend, can't he?"

She laughed and returned her attention to the film. Ian could be very sweet. He was intelligent and caring and loved her. Yes, he tried far too hard to get her brothers to like him, and told god-awful jokes, but those weren't good reasons not to be with him. She sipped at her wine, watching the main characters on the screen.

"They're going to end up together," Ian declared in a bored tone. "We know it, they know it—"

"Shut up," she chuckled, knowing he was right. Ian was a good man and she loved him, she told herself. So, why had she put off marrying him for so long? The answer was simple. She had always refused to acknowledge it. Because of Darcy, she sighed. It would have been simpler if they'd never slept together.

It was New Year's Day 2013. Caitlyn slowly woke up, acknowledging the fact she was warm and somewhere incredibly comfortable. The next thing she came to realise was that she wasn't alone in bed. Blue eyes popped open at the feel of an arm wrapped securely around her middle, a warm body spooned behind her. A naked warm body. Oh, my God! What had she done?

As gently as she could, Caitlyn lifted the arm from around her waist and slowly turned over to return the limb to its owner, eyes widening when she found Darcy behind her. A loving smile curled her lips as she watched her friend sleeping, an angelic countenance on Darcy's face, completely peaceful and without worry. Caitlyn's smile faded and was replaced by a frown of concern. She had to get out of there.

Sitting up, she ran a hand through her tangled hair, remembering she had got soaked coming home from the pub. Manoeuvring to the side of the bed, she covered up as much as she could as she reached for her underwear and discarded dress.

"Where you off to this early? Come back to bed," Darcy mumbled in an adorable sleep-roughened voice, startling Caitlyn.

"Jesus, Darcy!" Caitlyn breathed. "I...I should get going."

Darcy reached out and softly touched the silky warmth of Caitlyn's back. "Catie?"

Caitlyn didn't respond to the soft call of her name, feeling a small ball of tension settle in her stomach.

"Caitlyn, look at me."

"I really have to go, Darcy." Caitlyn stood in just her under-wear, refusing to turn around and face her friend while still nude, even though they had shared one of the most intimate acts the night before. She slipped her dress back on, aware that it was still damp.

"Go where?" the now agitated brunette questioned, sensing something was very wrong. "It's not even..." she glanced at her watch, "nine yet." She sat up. "Caitlyn, stay," she pleaded softly, her voice breaking from emotion.

Eventually turning, blue eyes briefly met hurt dark green. "I can't. I have to check in with Mum and Dad. And Ian. He'll be worried about me." She watched her best friend slump back, a look of utter devastation etched on her features. "I...I rushed off last night. Left him in the pub after lying to him. I told him you'd been feeling ill. I lied to him and ditched him on New Year's Eve, our first as a couple. I should go and make it up to him."

"After sleeping with me?" Darcy questioned softly. "After what we shared, you're going to run off and be with him?"

Caitlyn turned away to grab her coat, suddenly feeling ill. "I'll see you later, Darcy," she called back over her shoulder as cheerfully as she could manage.

Darcy swallowed hard, eyes on Caitlyn's back. "What about last night, Caitlyn? What did it...? Didn't it mean anything to you?"

Caitlyn turned to stare at Darcy, seeing the hurt she had caused. She let out a forced laugh. "Last night was...it was..." She shrugged. "We had both been drinking, Darcy. That's all. It was a drunken thing that happened because we got caught up in the moment. Girls kiss all the time."

"It was more than kissing, Caitlyn!"

"I'm with Ian," she insisted. "I love Ian."

Darcy nodded once, eyes settling on the blanket covering her body. "Right. We'll forget it ever happened and carry on like before. Okay?"

"Okay," Caitlyn smiled brightly. "See you later, Darce."

Caitlyn knocked on the door in front of her, knowing how early in the day it was. A ridiculously early time on New Year's Day, she wasn't sure if she would get an answer, wasn't sure if she really wanted an answer. Just as she was about to give up and go home, the door swung open.

"Caitlyn?" Ian greeted in surprise. He was adorably dishevelled and rubbing his eyes, while trying to focus on her. "Babe, do you know what time it is?"

She stepped inside the luxurious apartment which Ian shared with two other men and slipped out of her coat. "I know. I'm sorry for getting you out of bed, but..." She reached up and wrapped her arms around his neck. "I wanted to see you."

"Oh, yeah?" He wrapped his arms around her.

"Oh, yeah." She kissed him then. Possessively. Fiercely. Wanting to wash away memories of Darcy's lips and replace them with thoughts of Ian. "You don't mind, do you?" she asked in a husky tone. Feeling him stirring against her, she glanced down and smiled knowingly. "No, I don't think you do."

"A very good reason to be...up, at this hour," he grinned. He lifted her then and she wrapped her legs around his waist, allowing him to carry her to the black leather sofa.

She had decided today was the day. Today, right now, she wanted to go all the way with him, wanted to feel Ian's naked body on top of her, wanted to experience him inside her. Most of all, she wanted to forget Darcy and be normal. She wanted to forget Darcy's touch, Darcy's lips, the way her heart had thumped with glee and burst with love. She didn't want to be able to see the look of love Darcy had directed at her, didn't want to remember how much she'd loved every minute. She wanted to be like everyone else.

Ian lay her on the sofa and covered her smaller frame with his body, kissing her face, and her neck. He paused, eyes on her neck. "God, did I do that?" he asked of a love bite.

Caitlyn said nothing, not sure of her answer, but almost positive it hadn't been him to leave the mark.

He started kissing his way down her chest and she groaned when he pressed against her, back arching when he covered her breast with his hand. She wrapped her arms around his back, slipping beneath the T-shirt he wore to lightly run her short nails up and down his spine.

"You feel amazing, Caitlyn," he murmured into her ear, squeezing her breast. "God, I want you so badly!" Sucking on her neck, his hands desperately tried to remove her dress all without shifting himself from her body.

"Wait, Ian!" She writhed beneath him, unintentionally getting him more worked up. "Not here! Your roommates could stumble in on us!"

He stopped what he was doing and tilted his head as if listening. "I don't think they're home, babe."

"But what if they walk in while we're...?"

"You're right." He smiled and ducked his head to kiss her again. "How about we go into my bedroom?" Upon her nod, he got up and offered her a hand, then led her through to his room.

It was strangely neat, everything in its proper place.

Caitlyn laughed as she looked around. "God, you should teach Darcy how to keep everything neat and tidy! She has a habit of throwing things around and hoping it lands somewhere within easy reach!"

He looked at her, a strange look she couldn't put a name to on his face. "I like everything neat and tidy and clean. I don't understand how anyone can live in a pigsty, not knowing where things are, having to hunt around for things when they need it."

"Darcy doesn't live in a pigsty," she defended her friend. "It's organised chaos, as she so often tells my mum."

He smiled tightly. "Let's not talk about your best friend." Wrapping his arms around her, he nuzzled her neck. "There are so many other things we could be doing."

Caitlyn eased out of his hold and stepped back. Shyly removing her dress while he watched her every move, she watched his face, watched his eyes trail slowly down then back up her body. She felt self-conscious now she was with him. When she had stood naked in front of Darcy, she had known her friend loved her no matter how she looked, but with Ian it was different.

Shaking her head slightly to dislodge thoughts of Darcy, Caitlyn smiled seductively and reached for him. "You're wearing too many clothes," she told him, amazed at how controlled her voice sounded.

Smiling lasciviously, he hastily pulled off his T-shirt and moved forward to capture her lips again, a hand covering her naked breast, squeezing in time with the thrusts of his tongue into her mouth. He concentrated on her hard nipple, rolling it, pinching it hard.

Each tweak reminded her of how gentle Darcy had been. She manoeuvred them to the bed and slid beneath the covers, feeling better now she had a barrier to hide her body from plain sight.

Ian settled next to her, kissing her, a hand roaming her body. "I know you're nervous, Caitlyn. But I want you to know that I love you. I wanted you to know that before we —"

"I know. I love you, too."

He moved to lie on top of her, groaning when his body pressed into hers. He lowered his face to her neck, breathing heavily against her skin as he eased into her. "You feel amazing."

She lay staring up at the ceiling while he moved on top of her, his hot panting going directly into her ear, making her want to squirm away. She hated herself. Hated what she was doing and why she was doing it. She hated that she was here with Ian so soon after making love with Darcy, hated that she was desecrating the memory of such a sweet tender first time with something cheap and rash.

Most of all she hated the fact that she was comparing Ian to Darcy. She couldn't help but think that Darcy's kisses were softer, that Darcy's touch was more electrifying, that Darcy knew how to touch her and where to set her body aflame. Darcy, Darcy, Darcy.

Then it was over, and Ian was happy and satisfied, telling her so as he rolled over onto the other side of the bed. She felt dirty and was left wanting. She didn't mention that. Instead, she started to climb out of the bed, wanting to leave more than anything.

"Where are you going, babe?" he asked sleepily.

"I need the toilet and um...I was going to take a quick shower. If that's okay?"

"Sure, babe, go ahead," he smiled as he stretched. "Do you want some company?" he asked, wiggling his eyebrows at her.

She managed a smile and shook her head. "No, not this time." She got to her feet. "You sleep. I'll be back in a moment."

"Are you ready to go up, love?" Ian asked, frowning at his fiancée when he got no response. "Caitlyn, are you all right? You're off in a world of your own again."

Caitlyn blinked away her thoughts as she looked at him. "Fine," she replied, reaching for the remote control to turn off the television. "I'm fine. Just thinking."

"You know, you've been acting very odd lately," he mentioned, offering her his hand to help her up. He looked at her flat belly curiously. "You're not...pregnant, are you?"

"Ian!" She couldn't keep the annoyance out of her tone. "No, I'm not pregnant. I'm not on my period, and my period's not due. I've just been thoughtful lately. It's not a crime is it?"

"No, it's not a crime," he replied calmly. "But you have to admit you've been acting odd. It can't all be because Darcy's coming home, surely. I mean for God's sake, she's only a friend! Friends go off all the time, travelling, moving home, getting married. I just don't understand what the fuss is about!"

"No, you don't understand. So, mind your own business!" She brushed past him and out of the living room, her emotions all over the place. Darcy was not just a friend.

Chapter Eight

DARCY SMILED AND hugged Joaquina as the Portuguese woman embraced her tightly. She wasn't one for displays of affection, but this was one time when she was happy to go along with it. With Lauren and herself leaving, she was going to miss the daily company of Joaquina and Kendall, the two women having become very good friends. Something she didn't make easily.

"Darcy, I am going to miss you very much," Joaquina said tearfully.

"I'm going to miss you, too," Darcy replied, rubbing the woman's back. "But we'll come back. If not permanently, then at least for a holiday."

"That is not the same," Joaquina pouted. She kissed Darcy's cheek then released her. "Take good care of Lauren. She is a good woman and loves you very much."

"I will. Try and keep Kendall out of trouble. With us going home, she's likely to search for adventure elsewhere!"

Joaquina laughed and moved over to say goodbye to Lauren, while Kendall turned to Darcy.

"Darce!" Kendall threw herself at the taller woman. "I can't believe you guys are really leaving!"

Darcy hugged the New Yorker while laughing at her dramatics. "The holiday had to come to an end eventually. Anyway, you're off home soon as well, aren't you?"

"Yeah," the bottle-blonde nodded sadly. "Have to get back to the real world now that my happy couple is married. And the family want me home for Christmas because I missed Thanksgiving. I think they're expecting apology presents." She kissed Darcy's cheek. "You guys have my phone number. If you ever fancy a trip to New York, give me a call. I'll make sure I'm out of town!" She laughed raucously at Darcy's outraged countenance. "I'm joking. You're always welcome."

"The same goes for you, Kendall. Take care of yourself."

"And you. And keep taking those awesome photos. If nobody else wants them, I'll happily purchase them."

The taxi pulled up and the driver climbed out and walked to the back of the car to open the boot for their luggage. Darcy helped him load the suitcases and bags, while Lauren said a last goodbye to their friends.

"Joaquina, thank you so much for agreeing to take care of the things we can't take home this trip," Lauren said gratefully.

"It's no problem, my friend. I am happy to do it."

Finished with loading their things, Darcy returned to Lauren's side, while the driver got back in the car to wait.

"Okay, so we have to get going now." She slipped an arm around Lauren's shoulders. "I don't want him driving off with our stuff!" She gave a final hug to each of their friends then climbed into the back of the car, Lauren close behind.

They set off, leaving Joaquina and Kendall at the roadside waving and calling out until the taxi was out of sight.

"God, that was upsetting!" Lauren sighed, wiping away her tears as she turned in her seat to face the front.

Darcy pulled her girlfriend against her side. "It was. I'm going to miss them a lot."

"Me too. We'll see them again though, right? I quite fancy visiting New York," she smiled.

"It feels like only yesterday we arrived here." Darcy turned her attention to the passing scenery, drinking it in one last time, and sighed. "Nowhere to stay, not knowing anyone."

"Uh-huh. But, on to new things, sweetheart. I'm sure you can find beautiful and unique things to photograph back home."

"Perhaps," she laughed, not so sure about that. Falling quiet, she lost herself in memories of home, trying to think of anything that was worth photographing. It all seemed so dull to her, but she supposed to people not from the area it may be something of interest. There was the park with its lake, which she had always found comfort in.

"It will soon be Christmas," Lauren said, breaking the silence between them. "Are you looking forward to spending it back home?"

Darcy glanced at her girlfriend, stroking the back of the hand covering her jean-clad thigh. "Sort of. I haven't seen Jeremy and Stacey's two children since they were one year old and six months. They'll be grown up now. Brian was dating a mystery woman, who he would never bring home. And Luke is a father now. It will be nice seeing them all and catching up."

"Then there's Caitlyn," Lauren said hesitantly.

"Yeah," Darcy sighed, her attention returning to the scenery. "The last Christmas I spent at home with Caitlyn," she looked at Lauren, "it didn't exactly go well, did it?"

Darcy sat at the bar, her fourth beer in front of her, the label ripped off in little pieces beside it. She hadn't wanted to stay at her childhood home, not after what she had shared with Caitlyn, and she hadn't wanted to go next door either because Tricia would know immediately something was up and press her to talk about it.

Caitlyn's rejections always hurt, but this one had cut deep. This time it hurt more than anything else in her life. She had thought perhaps things had changed between them after what they had shared, thought she had a chance with the beautiful blonde after being given such a precious gift. But Caitlyn swiftly put a stop to any ideas she'd had by leaving as soon as she had woken up and writing the night off as nothing more than a drunken fling.

Unable to stay at home and not wanting to face the family just yet, she had decided to drown her sorrows at Lauren's bar for the few hours it was open.

"Happy New Year, Darcy!" Lauren greeted cheerfully. Stopping next to Darcy she frowned at the misery her friend was radiating.

Darcy looked up at the bar owner and smiled weakly. "Hey, Lauren. Happy 2013."

"Hey, Pat. Can I get a lemonade?" Lauren sat on the free stool next to Darcy and leaned on the bar.

"Sure thing, boss lady."

"So," Lauren turned her attention back to her friend. "Everything okay? You're not usually one to drink." Darcy had told her about her mother and growing up living with the alcoholic. Yvonne had put Darcy off drinking to excess.

"It's the start of a new year," Darcy replied. "Can't a gal enjoy a drink or two?"

"Of course," Lauren smiled. "It's just that I've gotten to know you, Darcy, and you prefer to celebrate with an orange juice."

Darcy picked up her bottle and took a couple of long swigs, not replying. She didn't want to talk about it, not while it was still so raw. "I'm of the legal age, Lauren."

"Right," the redhead agreed. "You're right." She smiled and thanked Pat for her drink. "So, how was your New Year's? You left here early, surely you didn't go home?" she chuckled.

Darcy's jaw clenched. God, how she wished she had! "Uh, no." She looked at Lauren, a serious look on her face. "I don't know how to tell you this, but I...visited another pub!"

Lauren burst out laughing and slapped Darcy's arm. "God,

you shit! I thought something serious had happened!"

Darcy laughed for the first time that day and reached for her beer. "Couldn't help myself."

Lauren shook her head in amusement. "Did you have fun at this other pub? Was it worth cheating?" she teased.

Darcy's lips curled with a genuine smile briefly, before her thoughts swiftly returned to Caitlyn and their night. "Not really." She finished her beer and asked Pat for another. "I'll stick to this place in the future."

Long after everyone had left, Lauren placed a hand on Darcy's shoulder. "Darcy, we're closing," she told the inebriated brunette. "Because it's New Year's Day, we're only allowed to stay open until three o'clock. Not that I would allow Pat to serve you anymore," she muttered under her breath, worried eyes on Darcy. "Shall I call you a taxi, or do you want me to have someone come pick you up?"

"No, can't go home," Darcy slurred. "She'll be there. Beautiful angel who breaks my heart," she said mournfully. "Didn't happen, wasn't real, but I know," she nodded. "I know."

Lauren frowned, not sure what her friend was going on about. Sitting next to Darcy, she wrapped an arm around her waist. "Darce, has something happened between you and Caitlyn? Has she somehow upset you?"

Watery eyes turned the bar owner's way. "Can't go home," she replied mournfully. She sighed deeply, a long, tortured sigh that spoke of her heartache.

"Okay," Lauren nodded. "Okay, Darcy. How about you come upstairs to my place and have a little nap, yeah? Have a little nap and you'll feel better."

"No," Darcy shook her head. "I should go." She started to slide off the bar stool she was sitting on, Lauren grabbing hold of her, so she didn't end up on the floor.

"Where, Darcy? Where are you going to go?" Lauren asked in worry.

"Away. I'll go away."

Not sure what was going on, Lauren stood up and wrapped an arm around Darcy's waist. "Come up to my place, Darcy. Have a little nap, then you can go away later, okay?" Darcy stared at her with drunken, pain filled eyes. "Come on, Darce. Keep me company for a while."

Getting no resistance from the younger woman, Lauren led Darcy toward the back of the bar where there was a securely locked door, which would lead them up to Lauren's flat above the bar. With great difficulty, the bar owner got Darcy through the door and up the stairs to her place. In her bedroom, she sat Darcy on the edge of her bed and crouched in front of her to take off her trainers.

"I'm bad, Lauren," Darcy mumbled sadly.

"No, you're not."

"I am. No one stays. Everyone leaves. They all leave."

Lauren looked at Darcy, her hands on the other woman's knees. "I'm still here, aren't I, Darcy? I haven't left." She smiled and patted the younger woman's knees. "Lie back, sweetheart." She stood and helped Darcy into bed, settling the blanket over her once Darcy was comfortable.

"You will," Darcy mumbled. "Everyone does." She watched through drooping eyes as the redhead brushed aside dark locks and placed a soft kiss on her forehead, before falling into a deep, drunken slumber.

Waking, Darcy looked around in confusion, not recognising the room she was in. Throwing back the blanket covering her, she sighed in relief when she found herself still dressed. Where the hell was she? There were no photos that she could see, and she couldn't gauge anything from the room itself, other than it was a woman's room. She got up, hearing a television somewhere nearby.

Leaving the unfamiliar bedroom, she padded quietly along a short dimly lit hallway and found herself peeking into a living room, Lauren seated on the sofa. "Oh, Jesus!" she sighed in relief.

At the sound of Darcy's voice, the redhead gave a start and glanced over at the doorway, smiling affectionately as she lay eyes on the dishevelled brunette. "Hey you. How are you feeling?"

"Um…better." She walked over to the sofa and took a seat at the opposite end. "How did I get here? I assume this is your place?"

"It is my place. Welcome," Lauren smiled.

"Thank you for having me."

"You're above the bar, which is where I found you earlier this afternoon. You drank yourself silly and when I suggested that I phone for a taxi to take you home, you insisted you didn't want to go home."

"Oh." Darcy looked at her socked feet, knowing Lauren probably had questions and that she deserved some sort of explanation.

"How about a cup of tea?" Lauren got to her feet. "I bet your poor head is aching something rotten."

Darcy smiled and glanced up, meeting compassionate light green. She cleared her throat and nodded. "Tea would be heavenly." She followed Lauren through to a small kitchen, taking a quick look around.

"Couldn't swing a cat in here," Lauren chuckled, catching Darcy taking everything in. "But it's spacious enough for me. How many sugars?"

"Two, please." Darcy watched the older woman set out two mugs with tea bags and sugar while the kettle boiled. "Last night when I left your bar, I went to—"

"Another pub, I know," Lauren feigned hurt. "You confessed earlier." She put a hand to her brow dramatically, making Darcy smile briefly.

Leaning against the counter, Darcy folded her arms. "I met up with Caitlyn, the moron and his friends." She paused as the kettle clicked, watching Lauren pour steaming water into their mugs.

"Come on," Lauren smiled, rubbing Darcy's arm as she moved past the taller woman. "Let's leave the tea to brew." She walked back into the living room and they sat on the sofa. "Did one of them do something? Or say something that upset you?"

"No," she sighed. "Close to midnight, Caitlyn led me outside. The pub has a garden and we went down the back where it was dark. I didn't question why. Not out loud anyway. When the countdown to midnight began, Caitlyn tugged me into a position in front of her and I...I was going to ask what was going on because I had all these thoughts and questions, but at the stroke of midnight we...we kissed."

"Oh, okay," Lauren replied, confused.

"I know that's what people do at midnight on New Year's. You kiss briefly and wish each other a happy new year, but this wasn't a friendly kiss. This was...life changing. Breathtaking. Perfect and...right. It felt so right." She smiled to herself in remembrance. "We've kissed before but nothing like that. It was everything I ever wanted."

"I feel like there's going to be a but," Lauren spoke up.

Darcy shook her head to clear away the memory. "Anyway, it deepened and was very heated and passionate. Things could have quite easily gone too far. I don't know why it suddenly came to an end, but it did abruptly and she went running back to him."

"God, hon, I'm sorry," Lauren sympathised. "Let me get the tea."

"Yeah, tea fixes everything," Darcy smirked. "Or so I'm told."

Lauren disappeared briefly before swiftly returning with two mugs of steaming tea. "That's why you don't want to go home yet?" She set her mug down on the floor. "You live with her family, right?"

"It wasn't the kiss that caused the problem." Darcy set her own mug down and sighed sadly. "If it was only a kiss, I would go home and continue as usual. It was...after." Lauren patted her lap and she didn't hesitate. She lay down, her head resting on the other woman's thigh, smiling when her friend ran her fingers through her hair soothingly. "Want me to get comfortable so I answer all your questions, don't you?"

"Damn, on to me already?" Lauren smiled. "Will never find out the secret to making decent Yorkshire puds!"

Darcy laughed at the absurdity of that comment. "You're mad, you know that?"

"I try my best." Lauren shrugged, grinning. "So, what happened after the kiss? You said she ran back to him."

Amusement fading, Darcy exhaled as she gathered her thoughts. "I went to my childhood home. I've been doing up the old place with the hope of eventually renting it out, until such a time I want to live there, if ever. I went there because Tricia would've known something had happened and I didn't want to answer her questions. So, I was there and had just got out of the shower when I heard someone knocking on the front door."

"Caitlyn?" Lauren asked.

"Caitlyn," Darcy nodded. "She was soaked because of the downpour and I pulled her inside and..." She frowned and shook her head. "I don't know who started it, but we ended up in a lip-lock again. I took her upstairs to my bedroom and had every intention of just getting her out of her wet clothes and into some dry ones so she wouldn't get sick, but as we stared into each other's eyes, all thought of warm clothes disappeared. And when she stood naked in front of me...I think I initiated it."

"Darcy," Lauren broke in softly, tenderly brushing her fingers through her friend's hair. "Did she tell you to stop? Did she protest at all?"

"No, she wanted it as much as I did, and it was beautiful." She sat up and swallowed hard as a lump formed in her throat, her emotions bubbling close to the surface. Reaching for her tea, she picked up her mug and wrapped her hands around it, trying to find her composure.

Lauren picked up her own tea, sipping at the hot brew while she patiently waited for Darcy to continue.

"It was perfect." She smiled. "The whole night was perfect." She snorted to herself. "It was the morning after that was a bitch!"

"She regretted it?"

"She was up like a shot as soon as she woke up, hurriedly getting dressed so she could leave. I tried to entice her into staying, but she told me she had to get going, had to go and check in with the moron because she'd left him at the pub the night before after lying to him."

Lauren frowned at that. "She lied to him?"

"Told him I was ill, and she wanted to check up on me."

"She lied to her boyfriend so she could come after you? That kinda makes me think she wanted to be with you over him."

Darcy frowned, thinking it over. "I didn't really think about it, but you're right. She ditched him to come after me." Maybe there was hope after all. She smiled at the thought. But why had Caitlyn run back to him this morning? She finished her tea and got to her feet. "Listen, Lauren, I'm sorry for intruding on you like this."

"You're not intruding, Darce. And I'm glad I was there for you in your hour of need." She got up as well.

"I should get going. Tricia's probably climbing the walls with worry. But, thank you. For everything." She pulled the redhead into a tight embrace. "If there's ever anything I can do for you, don't hesitate to ask."

"I'll keep that in mind." Lauren smiled. "Go on then, get home. I'll see you soon hopefully?"

"I'll stop in for my usual orange juice soon. Bye, Lauren."

"Bye, Darce."

As the front door bumped shut behind her, Darcy stuffed her hands into her pockets and puffed out her cheeks. Time to face the music!

DARCY AND LAUREN waited in the departure lounge for their flight to be called. Sitting on hard uncomfortable chairs, they people watched as they usually did when in public, rather than trying to have an intimate conversation which would no doubt be overheard by all and sundry.

They watched a couple of hyperactive children running around screaming and annoying everyone nearby, their sunburnt mother running out of patience with her offspring and yelling at them to behave. A businessman stood off to the side, talking loudly on his mobile and glaring at the noisy brood. An older woman smiled and shared tales of her own grandchildren with anyone who would listen. And somehow slumbering on the hard seating was a hungover bachelor party, all wearing garish tropical shirts, one sporting black marker on his face and another cuddling a blow-up doll.

"God, I hope those damn kids aren't seated near us," Darcy murmured into her girlfriend's ear, earning a light slap to her thigh.

"Why ever not? Don't you think they're adorable?" Lauren asked sarcastically.

"I have plans to seduce you, Miss Cansdell. I don't want to look up and find them peering over a seat at us, 'What are those ladies doing, Mummy?' ringing in my ears!"

Lauren laughed out loud and slapped Darcy again, her cheeks turning crimson. "You're awful!"

"You still love me."

"That I do, sweetheart."

When their flight was finally called, the couple stood and slowly made their way to the gate, wanting to avoid queuing with the misbehaving family. Instead, they found the businessman in front of them, the arrogant man still shouting into his phone. They smiled sympathetically with the airline worker, who rolled her eyes after the man had stalked off. She smiled warmly at the couple as they stepped forward.

"He's the type to complain about everything," Darcy mentioned. "Any chance you can get him bumped from the flight?" she joked.

"Afraid not," the woman laughed. "The good news is you're not seated near him," she told them. "Have a good flight."

Strolling toward the plane, Lauren took Darcy's arm, the couple in no hurry to be seated as they knew there was still a long line of people to come yet. They said very little as they walked, everything having already been said. Now, all they could do was wait and worry about what lay ahead, both women conjuring up what may be and could be said, Darcy worrying more than Lauren.

"Do you want the window seat, babe?" Lauren asked. "I know you hate strangers starting up conversations with you."

Darcy smiled and gratefully took the window seat. "I'm not sure it's wise, I didn't exactly enjoy the first flight we took."

"That was your first time flying. You know what to expect now." Lauren found herself next to the old lady who had been telling stories of her grandchildren back in the airport and just knew she would be hearing a few during the flight. She smiled politely when the woman caught her eye and smiled.

"Guess they'll be no mile-high club for us after all," Darcy whispered into her girlfriend's ear, watching Lauren turn an amusing shade of red.

"Hello," the woman greeted the couple cheerfully. "My name's Iris."

"Lauren and Darcy," Lauren replied.

"What lovely names. Have you been on holiday in Portugal? Or were you on business? I must say, you are both very tanned!"

"We were on holiday," Lauren answered with a polite smile. "We started off in France and have been all across Europe, seeing the sights and enjoying the different cultures."

"Oh, that sounds wonderful!"

"It has been, but we're going home now."

Iris chuckled. "You have to eventually, I suppose. I live in Portugal, but I'm heading to England for the Christmas holiday, the family insisted. I don't know why they don't come to me. The weather will be nicer."

While Lauren and Iris lost themselves in conversation, Darcy stared out the small window next to her, lost in memories of why she set off travelling in the first place. She hadn't planned on not going back. When she left it had been to have some time to clear her head, to get herself together, and to get over her lifelong crush on Caitlyn. She had been hurt, angry, lost. And for some strange reason, Lauren had tagged along and stuck with her.

It was May 2013. Darcy poked at her breakfast, not paying attention to Luke's animated chatter about an amazing motorbike he had seen on sale, nor Tricia adamantly telling him he wasn't getting a motorbike, even though he was twenty-three years old and capable of making his own choices. She didn't hear the words of the song playing on the radio, nor the crinkling of the newspaper Joe was reading.

She stared blankly at her plate. She wasn't hungry, but Tricia had gone to the effort of making scrambled eggs on toast for everyone and Darcy felt bad about not wanting it. How could she eat when she didn't feel like it? she wondered. It was a common problem lately, her stomach was a twisted knot as she battled her emotions, unable to forget what she had shared with Caitlyn, even if her best friend had. And this afternoon was a family barbecue, where she'd have to pretend everything was fine and smile through her pain, her heart breaking a little more with each passing minute.

Dark green eyes flicked to the empty seat where Caitlyn usually sat. She hadn't come home the night before. It was becoming a common routine as she spent more and more time with Ian.

Everything had changed. Ever since New Year's Eve their friendship was no more. They barely spoke unless other members of the family were present, then Caitlyn would be like the Caitlyn of old, laughing and joking with Darcy like nothing was amiss. But once alone in each other's company, which was rare in itself, conversation was non-existent or stilted.

"Honey, you don't have to play with your food to avoid eating it," Tricia said fondly, getting to her feet. She had noticed something was bothering Darcy for a while now, but as yet she hadn't questioned her about it.

Darcy looked up, eyes full of apology. "Sorry, Mum. I'm just not hungry." She had called Tricia Mum one day without realising it, Tricia having always been more of a mother to her than Yvonne. The first time Darcy had slipped, Tricia hugged her tightly and told her she was very honoured to be called such. Hoping a family mindset would dampen her feelings for Caitlyn, Darcy had continued with it.

"She just wants to save space for one of my hamburgers," Joe said smiling. "And one of my steaks, and a hot dog..."

Darcy conjured up a laugh. "If you grill it, I will come," she said seriously, making them all laugh. *Field of Dreams* was selected one movie night and ever since the tagline had been altered and used in jest among the family. She got to her feet and gathered their dirty dishes. "I'll do the washing-up," she offered. "Luke, do you wanna dry?"

"No, but I have no choice now!" Luke pouted. Standing, he walked to where Darcy stood waiting for the sink to fill.

"It will be nice having everyone together this afternoon," Tricia mentioned, settling in her seat and relaxing. "The grandparents, the uncles and aunts, Jeremy and Stacey, and my two grandbabies."

"Will Brian be bringing his mystery woman?" Joe asked. "He's keeping her such a big secret, I'm beginning to think there must be something wrong with her!"

"Joe!" Tricia scolded her husband, though cracking a smile. "Have either of you two met her?" she directed at Luke and Darcy.

"I haven't," Luke replied. "And whenever he goes off to meet her, he refuses to let me go along. Maybe Dad's right, maybe there is something wrong with her. Or, she isn't even real!" he laughed.

"What about you, Darce?" Joe questioned. "Have you met her?"

Looking over at the table, Darcy smiled. "No, I haven't. But I'm going to follow him one night if he doesn't bring her around soon!"

"Is everything all right between you and Caitlyn, Darcy?" Tricia asked suddenly. "Whenever I see you two lately, things seem...tense. That's when you're in the same room together! I remember a time when you two were never apart if you could get away with it."

Placing the dirty plates and cutlery into the hot water, Darcy sighed. "Things change as you get older, I guess. She's busy with the moron." She looked up wide-eyed as she realised what she had said aloud. Luke was laughing and Joe smiling behind his newspaper, Tricia, on the other hand, wasn't so happy. "I mean um...Ian."

"That's not nice, Darcy," Tricia softly scolded, shooting warning looks at her son and husband.

Darcy looked at the older woman sheepishly. "Sorry, Mum. I guess...I don't like the guy. Anyway, I'm going to let this soak while I go have a shower." She left the kitchen quickly, her true feelings too close to the surface.

Standing between Joe and Uncle Edward, Darcy watched the meat sizzling on the barbecue, the aroma making her mouth water. The two men talked about the weather, sports, and work, while leaving her in charge of the food. She had seen Caitlyn arrive with Ian and carefully avoided the couple as they walked around socialising with the rest of the family.

She watched Caitlyn from afar, heart aching whenever the familiar laugh drifted across the garden. She tried valiantly not to glare at Ian, even when he draped a possessive arm around Caitlyn's waist, or her shoulders. She tried not to growl in displeasure as he smugly ambled around the back garden like he owned the place, and politely refused his help through gritted teeth when he asked if she wanted him to take over at the barbecue.

She hated the distance that had grown between herself and Caitlyn. She wished they could overcome the abyss that had formed between them ever since they had woken up together but knew in her heart it wasn't possible. Caitlyn wished what had happened between them hadn't occurred and Darcy wanted them to make a go of it together, that whole night having felt right.

Everything was forever changed. She missed her best friend, the one constant in her life, but she couldn't go back to denying her feelings. Seeing Caitlyn with Ian hurt more than anything though and she wasn't sure how much more she could take.

"Do you guys want another beer?" she asked the two men, wanting a reason to escape.

"Yes, please, kiddo," Joe smiled, handing over his empty bottle.

Edward shook his bottle slightly. "No, I'm fine, thanks, Darcy. Hey, don't be too long, you know my brother has a habit of burning everything!"

"Hey!" Joe protested, blue eyes darting to Darcy for support.

"I'll be as quick as I can," Darcy grinned, ducking the tongs as Joe swiped at her. Taking her leave of the men, she made her way into the kitchen via the back door.

"Hey, Darcy," Ella, Edward's daughter, greeted brightly, jumping to her feet from her seat at the table. "I've been practising a lot with my violin. Do you want to hear?"

Darcy smiled at the eleven-year-old as she handed Joe's empty bottle and her glass to Tricia. "Maybe later, Ella. The food's almost ready." She brushed a hand over the girl's hair. "Have you grown another inch? You seem taller."

"I think so. Mum says I'm going to need new clothes again."

"How's life treating you?"

"Same old, same old."

"So, Darce," Aunt Debrah started. "Found a nice young girl to call your own yet?"

Grandma Peggy slapped her daughter-in-law's arm lightly. "Leave the poor girl alone, Debrah. Love will happen when it happens."

Darcy walked over to the table and kissed the top of her head. "You always were my favourite, Grandma Peggy."

"Sweet talker," Peggy chuckled and winked.

Tricia cleared her throat to stifle a laugh. "I thought I was your favourite?" she teased.

Darcy swiftly made her way over to Tricia and wrapped an arm around her shoulders. "It's a very close tie, you're just edging ahead at the moment."

"What are you like?" Tricia laughed and shook her head at the younger woman. Smiling, she turned to open the fridge and grabbed a fresh beer. "Do you want a beer, Darce, or another soda?" She handed over the beer.

"Soda, please."

"How's the food looking out there?" Debrah asked. "You're not letting the guys burn it, are you?"

"Do I ever?" Darcy replied. "When is the last time you had a burnt burger or sausage?"

"Well, there was that one time last summer," Peggy spoke up.

"You're so not my favourite anymore!" Darcy pouted, making the other women laugh. "And anyway, that wasn't my fault. I had to go to the toilet and told Brian to keep an eye on everything."

"How soon will things be ready?" Tricia handed Darcy a full glass of soda. "Should we start bringing out the salad stuff and sauces?"

"Might be a good idea," Darcy nodded. "I better get back out there, don't want you slave drivers complaining about a bit of charring on the food!" She laughed as she ducked swipes of the hand from Tricia and Debrah, stopping at the back door to allow Caitlyn entrance. The two said nothing to each other and it didn't go unnoticed.

After the food was consumed, some of the relatives remained seated outside, enjoying the fine weather, drinks, and easy conversation while they relaxed. Others wandered inside to sit on a chair more comfortable than the outdoor furniture, or to play on one of the many computer systems one of the brothers owned.

After listening to a mini concert Ella put on, Darcy got caught up in conversation with Grandad Cliff, always enjoying the company of the older man. She loved Cliff like he was her own grandfather, the older man having always treated her as one of his own even before Tricia and Joe had taken her in. Her attention was drawn to Caitlyn when she stood, clinking her glass with the side of a fork to get everyone's attention.

"Um, is everyone out here?" She looked around uncertainly. "I'd...I'd like to share some news with all of you, so could we go inside to the living room for a moment?"

The whole family gathered in the living room, laughing and talking loudly, everyone in good spirits. Darcy waited until the last moment to go in. With everyone else inside, all the seats were taken and standing room was limited. She leaned against the doorjamb, arms folded, green eyes studying the love of her life. What the hell did she see in the moron? she wondered, her gaze flicking to Ian, who looked like a complete dork dressed in a suit and tie. He looked as if he were going to a business convention. Caitlyn could do so much better.

Tricia walked past Darcy, gently squeezing her arm in greeting, and made her way to the front of the room where she sat next to her husband.

Caitlyn cleared her throat. "With everyone I love here for the barbecue today, I...I wanted to share some happy news with you all."

Oh, good God, Darcy thought, suddenly feeling sick to her stomach, her heart thumping painfully in her chest. She's going to announce she's moving in with him. Or worse, she's engaged to him or pregnant!

Ian stepped in, sporting a bright, smug smile. He wrapped a possessive arm around Caitlyn's shoulders. "I asked Caitlyn to marry me."

"And I said yes." Caitlyn smiled up at him, looking from him to her surrounding family. "We're engaged!" She lifted her left hand so she could show off a diamond engagement ring.

Swigging from a bottle of beer she had grabbed out of the fridge once she fled the living room, Darcy gently set the bottle down on the grass and glanced over her shoulder to see who it was she heard approaching. She smiled at Luke before returning her attention back to the Wendy House, where some of the nieces were playing.

"Not like you to drink, Darce," Luke said carefully, not wanting to sound like he was judging.

"It's a celebration, Lukey-boy. Caitlyn's engaged to what's-his-face. Is that not a reason to celebrate?"

Luke sat next to her, leaning against the trunk of the tree, and sighed. The nieces were squealing at each other and laughter drifted from inside the main house, almost everyone in high spirits. "It must have surprised you?"

Darcy snorted, not replying, and picked up her bottle again.

"It surprised everyone. Did you not notice how baffled the family were?" he smirked. "Everyone was looking around to see if it was some sort of joke." He watched her picking at the label on her bottle, a habit she had picked up. "I guess we all thought it would be you," he said nonchalantly. He took the beer as Darcy's head whipped around in his direction.

Dark green eyes studied Luke's face for signs of teasing, for signs of disgust. He didn't know. Couldn't know. Nobody knew. "Wha — what?"

Smiling knowingly, Luke swigged from the bottle. "It's

always been pretty obvious to me that there was something between you two. When we were kids, nothing in the world existed when you two were together. It was like," he paused, trying to find the words, "like you had each other and didn't need anyone else."

"Things change I guess." Darcy took back her beer and finished it off.

"You never gave me the time of day," he mumbled, not looking her way.

Darcy exhaled, stalling. This was becoming a day of confessions. She was aware Luke had feelings for her, but she had only ever wanted Caitlyn. "It never would've worked. You're like a brother to me, Lukey."

"We could've tried. You can't know what might have happened. We might have been great together, Darcy."

She looked at him, meeting hurt blue eyes. "I've only ever wanted Caitlyn, Luke. I can't explain why. It just...is. Anyway," she got up, having had enough emotional talk for one day, "I'm off out. I can't stay here and watch them being happy and in love."

"Fancy going out for a pint or three?" he asked. "I'll get the brothers and we'll make a night of it."

"Your baby sister just got engaged, shouldn't you stay here and celebrate with them?" Darcy asked in amusement.

Luke snorted. "You're not the only one who doesn't like the moron, Darce. I would personally prefer it if it was you officially joining the family."

Darcy grabbed him and hugged him tightly. "Thanks, Luke. I appreciate that." She grinned as she pulled out of the embrace. "I think a night out would be good for us. When was the last time we went on an all-nighter?"

"Exactly."

Holding onto Luke's arm, she walked with him back toward the house. "Lukey-boy..."

"Yeah?"

"If I was looking for a good guy, I would have given you a shot."

He laughed out loud. "If you ever decide not to be gay, will I be your first phone call?"

"I don't want to get your hopes up, but sure," she laughed.

"Good to know, Darce. Good to know."

Darcy knocked on Lauren's front door and waited, not sure if her friend was home or not. After spending all night out with the brothers, she hadn't felt like going home and had started walking, no destination in mind, until she stopped and found herself at Lauren's door.

"Darcy?" Lauren greeted, opening the door dressed in a robe and looking dishevelled. "Everything all right, hon?"

"I'm sorry. You um...I don't know why I came. I'm sorry." Darcy turned and started to walk away, getting the feeling she had interrupted something.

"Darce, you came all this way, why not come in for a cuppa?" Lauren called out.

Darcy stopped walking and turned back to face her friend. "I don't want to interrupt anything."

Lauren frowned, then laughed as she looked down at her robe. "I don't have company, Darcy. You just caught me being lazy. I couldn't be bothered to get dressed yet because I'm working the late shift."

Inside, Darcy paced back and forth across the flat, her heart painfully broken as she recalled yesterday's announcement and feeling sick to her stomach after a night of heavy drinking and little food since the barbecue. Lauren sat and watched her friend pacing, not saying anything, as she waited for Darcy to come out with what was on her mind.

"She's getting married!" Darcy blurted out suddenly, unable to hold it in any longer. "She really is sticking to the story of being straight and she's getting married!"

"Maybe she won't go through with it," Lauren offered. "Maybe she'll come to her senses and realise what a mistake she's making."

Darcy stopped moving and looked at Lauren in hope. "Do you think?"

Lauren didn't have an answer. "I don't know, Darcy. I don't know the woman. What little I do know has come from you, and you're slightly biased, honey."

"No." Darcy shook her head, not hearing Lauren. "No, she won't do that." She smiled sadly. "She's made up her mind." She started pacing again. "Jesus! She's getting married and I can't stop wanting her! I can't stop thinking about her!"

"Do you want a cup of tea?"

"First, it's a wedding, where I'll have to bite my tongue and forever hold my peace..."

"Or perhaps something a little stronger? I have scotch."

"...then it will be the happy news of the pitter-patter of tiny feet!"

"I think tea," Lauren decided. "You look like you haven't been to bed yet and tea always makes me feel better."

"And all the while I'll be dying inside," Darcy finished. She plopped down on the sofa. "I can't stop thinking about her, what we shared," she said brokenly, dark green eyes turning to the red-head. "I've tried. Ever since she made it clear New Year's was a mistake, I've tried to block it out. How do I pretend I'm happy for her, when all I can think is that it should be us together?"

"Oh, Darcy." Lauren opened her arms and embraced her tightly. "Nothing I say will make you feel better, hon. The fact is, she's straight. And, I know it hurts right now, but things will get better with time. You'll get over her and find someone who loves you dearly."

"I'm going to leave," Darcy announced. "I can't stay and..." She shook her head. "It will be torture, my heart breaking every time I see them together, knowing she picked him, she chose to be with him over me."

Lauren gaped at the taller woman in surprise. "But, Darce, where will you go?"

"Anywhere. I could go wherever takes my fancy."

"Could you really do that?" the bar owner asked in disbelief, knowing how important Caitlyn's family was to Darcy. "Just...leave?"

"Course I could. Why not?" Darcy frowned.

"What about the rest of the family? How long will you be gone? When are you going? Will you be back?"

"The family will understand, I'm sure. As for how long I'll be gone, I don't know. Europe's a big place waiting to be explored." She grinned, thinking of getting away, of making it happen. "I'm going as soon as I get my affairs in order. I'll buy the cheapest ticket I can find and...go."

"Wow!" Lauren ran a hand through her hair. "I don't know what to say."

"Say you'll come with me." Dark green eyes widened in surprise at the unplanned proposal. "I mean, if you fancy getting away for a bit."

There was silence for a moment while both women contemplated the offer.

"Is that a serious invite, or a knee-jerk request?" Lauren asked cautiously.

"It's serious. If you can get away and if you want to see a bit of Europe, I'd love for you to come with me."

"Seriously?"

"Yes, seriously," Darcy laughed, feeling light-hearted. "I consider you a friend, Lauren. A good friend. I think that's what I need right now, a good friend to make me smile and make me forget Caitlyn. Show me there's more to life than one girl. If you can find someone who will take care of your bar, I would love the company."

"Okay," Lauren nodded without hesitation. "I would love to see Europe with you, Darce. I'll look in to sorting out my affairs and let you know."

The best decision she ever made, Darcy thought, glancing at her girlfriend and smiling lovingly. She reached out to take Lauren's hand and kissed her knuckles, before turning her attention back out the window.

"You okay, honey?"

Looking at Lauren, Darcy smiled adoringly. "Was just thinking how lucky I am. I love you, Lauren. Thank you for travelling with me in the first place and thank you for sticking with me for the last five years."

"It should be me thanking you, sweetheart. But you're welcome," Lauren smiled, leaning over to kiss her girlfriend's cheek. "I just hope...." She trailed off, not wanting to ruin the good mood between them.

Darcy knew instantly what the bar owner was going to say and bit back a sigh. "That I don't fall into Caitlyn's arms as soon as I see her?" She had done her best to reassure Lauren over the last few days when it became obvious Lauren had serious concerns. She had professed her love, had promised that whatever awaited them nothing would change their relationship, and as soon as was convenient she would introduce Lauren to the family. But it seemed Lauren still wasn't convinced.

"I didn't say that."

"You didn't have to," Darcy sighed. "Sweetheart, I'm not sure how many different ways I can say I love you or tell you our relationship means everything to me. At the end of the day, you have to trust me, trust in us. Your doubts hurt."

"I'm sorry," Lauren said sincerely. "It's not my intention to belittle what we have, Darce."

"But for some reason you do. For some reason you have little faith in what we have even after these last few years together. You seem convinced that the moment I lay eyes on Caitlyn, I'm going to end things with you."

"I don't think that," Lauren protested, though she looked

slightly guilty. "And I do believe in us. I do. I know you love me, just as much as I love you. But you spent most of your life in love with her, Darcy. I can't help but think about what you'll do if we find out she's not married, if she's no longer with her boyfriend, if she's had a rethink and now wants to date you. Have you given it any thought?"

"I have wondered if she's married or not," Darcy admitted. "If she's got kids, if she's happy. But I don't think about being with her. She hurt me so many times, repeatedly. You have never done that, Lauren. Not once. You love me and want me to be happy. You've made me very happy. But if you keep doubting what we have it's going to cause problems, babe. We'll start drifting apart, because there has to be trust in a relationship."

"Surely you understand my concerns?"

"No," Darcy shook her head. "I left to travel with you, I haven't returned home once in five years, I haven't had any contact with Caitlyn at all. To me, she's a childhood friend whose family became my family. Yes, I was in love with her once upon a time, but we were kids and I thought the world revolved around her. I've grown up now and wised up. I realise that not everything is meant to be, not everything works out the way you hope or think it will."

"I'm the one who told you to distance yourself from her life, remember? Make her realise how great you are, make her appreciate you more. What if she did realise and she's waiting for you to return?"

Darcy leaned in close and claimed soft lips in a loving kiss. "I love you, Lauren. Believe that. Trust in that." While Lauren's attention was grabbed by Iris once again, she stared out the small window next to her feeling miserable. Even if Caitlyn had dumped the moron, it didn't change anything. She's straight. Was always straight. As the plane started off down the runway, a little voice in her head taunted her. If Caitlyn's so straight, why did they end up in bed together?

Chapter Nine

CAITLYN LOUNGED BACK in the bath, a Lucinda Williams CD playing on the mini hi-fi, the bathroom filled with the aroma of vanilla milk and honey. Despite the pleasant ambiance, she still couldn't fully relax. Her emotions were all over the place. She had butterflies in her stomach, and she couldn't stop coming up with different scenarios to how Darcy's return was going to play out.

I don't know why I feel nervous, she thought, lifting her hand and lightly blowing away the bubbles clinging to her palm. If anything, she should be angry. Not only did Darcy leave, she stayed away for five long years! Not coming back for a single Christmas, not one birthday, she even missed Brian's wedding and Luke's daughter being born. Nothing brought her home. Until now. Why now? Was she sick? Was there an incident?

"Sweetheart, do you know where the shoe polish is?" Ian called out.

Good grief! Why was he always asking her where his polish was? "Why do you need polish?"

"To polish my shoes, babe. Why else would I be asking for shoe polish?"

Caitlyn rolled her eyes. "Have you looked in the little cupboard near the back door?"

"Yes, there's only the brown stuff."

"Well, if there's none in there, we're out of it," she called back. Now go away and leave me in peace, she added to herself.

"Oh. I'll pop out and buy some then. Is there anything you need from the shop?"

She tried to think of anything else they might be out of. "You could pick up a bottle of wine, I suppose. I'm sure Mum will have enough drink to go around, but it's polite to take something."

"Good thinking. Back soon, sweetheart."

Left in peace once again, she settled back and closed her eyes, the words of "Reason to Cry" making her smile sadly. Darcy loved the song. Or she used to, she thought, remembering her best friend playing the song over and over when she was in a certain mood. She wondered if Darcy still cared for Lucinda Williams's music, or had she found someone new to listen to? Someone European perhaps?

Picking up her sponge, she gently rubbed her skin. She wondered if Darcy had a girlfriend. Or maybe she grew out of lusting after women and has a boyfriend? Maybe she's pregnant and that's why she's coming home. She'd soon find out. Darcy was due home sometime that afternoon. A small frown creased her brow. Would she bring whomever home with her? They hadn't seen her once in the last few years, surely, she'll realise they'd want her to themselves. Not her, per se, but the rest of the family certainly will.

Throwing aside the sponge, Caitlyn stood up carefully, water cascading off her naked frame. She still couldn't decide if she was happy Darcy was coming home or not. Carefully climbing out of the bath, she grabbed a towel from the heated rail and wrapped the warmed, plush towel around her body, before sitting down on the closed toilet seat lid.

Grabbing another towel, she dried her smooth freshly shaven legs and found herself looking at her engagement ring sitting proudly on her ring finger. She gasped as her chest ached suddenly, thoughts of her engagement announcement drifting back to her.

Caitlyn sat at Ian's small kitchen table, moving her breakfast around her plate. He had cooked for them both, burning the toast and drying out the baked beans, and whilst she appreciated his effort, she missed sharing breakfast with her family in the mornings, missed her mother's cooking. But going home would mean seeing Darcy and that was something she was desperate to avoid.

Ever since she had slept with Ian, Caitlyn found herself spending more and more time with him. She had told herself repeatedly it was what she wanted. Their relationship had evolved for the better he had said. He had started talking about them setting up home together and had hinted at marriage. She nodded every now and then, though very sure she wasn't ready for any of that just yet. She was still confused over what had happened between herself and Darcy and what it had made her feel.

Not wanting to confront her feelings, nor wanting to be subjected to Darcy's mournful looks her way, or her mother's questions, she was staying at Ian's more often to avoid going home and dealing with any of it.

Everything had changed the moment she and Darcy slept together, and their friendship was no more as far as she could see. They barely spoke unless other members of the family were present, and only then would Caitlyn make a token effort, attempting to pretend nothing had changed and everything was as it always had been. She laughed and joked with Darcy, managed a little conversation, until they were alone again, then everything became stilted and tense once more.

The fact she could barely look at Darcy without remembering her friend's gentle caress and soft breath-taking kisses was no one's business but her own. For the last few months, she had been trying to put it out of her mind. Avoiding Darcy helped some, but she knew it wasn't the solution. She would eventually have to confront her best friend and they would have to clear the air.

Ian had surprised her by proposing over a romantic meal on Valentine's Day and she had done the only thing she could do, the only thing that made sense. She said yes. Knowing they didn't have to get married right away, she hoped she would get over her fling with Darcy before they decided to settle down.

"Caitlyn, do you know where the polish is?" Ian called out.

"This is your place, Ian, shouldn't you know where things are?"

"I was just wondering if you had noticed it around."

"Why do you need polish anyway?" She pushed back her plate.

"To polish my shoes, darling. Why else would I be asking for polish?"

She sighed, looking at him as he stopped in the kitchen door-way. "We're going to a family barbecue. You don't need to dress up smartly, you don't need to wear polished shoes, you don't need to wear a tie. A pair of knackered old trainers, some ripped jeans and a T-shirt will do."

Ian stared at his fiancée as if she had grown another head. "I don't think I even own a pair of ripped jeans," he said finally. "And besides, I wouldn't be comfortable wearing that sort of thing."

Caitlyn eyed the cream-coloured trousers he was wearing and smiled as she thought of the disasters that could happen. "I wouldn't wear those trousers, babe. I can see barbecue sauce dripping onto them, or even little handprints creating a nice mess on them." She frowned. "Or you might sit on something left lying around carelessly, or someone could drop food or drink on you." Her brothers or Darcy, for example.

He frowned down at his trousers. "Oh. Maybe you're right. Good thinking, sweetheart." He walked over and bent to kiss the top of her head. "Are you getting ready any time soon? Or do you plan to go dressed in my robe?" he asked, eyeing his fluffy robe that was far too big for her.

"At least I'll be wearing something no one else is," she joked. Standing, she kissed his clean-shaven cheek. "Thank you for breakfast. It was lovely," she lied, having scraped most of it into the bin. "I'll go get ready while you hunt down the polish."

Arriving at the place she would always call home, Caitlyn was relieved when the front door was opened by Luke, her brother a more welcome sight than Darcy right now, even if he was rude to Ian. Taking Ian's hand in a show of silent support, she led her fiancé through the house to the kitchen, smiling and greeting her mother, her Grandma Peggy and her Aunt Debrah, the three women standing at the counters preparing salad and side dishes.

"Hello, love," Tricia greeted her daughter with a hug. "It's nice to see you as well, Ian," she acknowledged him, almost politely.

"Thank you for inviting me, Tricia."

"It's the only way we get to see Caitlyn these days," Tricia retorted, not quite joking.

"We uh…bought a couple of bottles of wine and a tub of ice cream, which Catie said the younger members of the family would love."

"How thoughtful, thank you." Tricia took the two bags Caitlyn held out. "Nearly everyone is in the garden, why don't you two grab a drink, then mingle. I'm not sure how long the meat's going to be, but Darcy's on the case."

Taking Ian's hand and waving goodbye to her relatives, Caitlyn stepped out into the back garden, blue eyes instantly finding Darcy through the crowd of people. Looking away when dark green eyes drifted in her direction, Caitlyn led Ian to the table where a variety of drinks were standing.

"There's one of my favourite granddaughters!" Grandad Cliff called out, approaching the couple.

"Oh, you liar! I know you prefer Darcy over me, Grandad!" Caitlyn laughed, turning to face the grey-haired man.

"Not true," Cliff replied, almost straight-faced. "How are you, sweetheart?" He wrapped the small blonde into his arms.

"I'm fine, thank you. How are you? Mum said you got food poisoning."

"Nonsense, I just ate something that didn't agree with me. I'm perfectly fine."

She hugged her grandfather, then pulled back as she remembered Ian. "Grandad, this is Ian Moran. Ian, my grandfather, Cliff."

"Hello, young man," Cliff greeted, intelligent grey eyes studying the immaculately dressed Ian. "Dressed far too smartly for a barbecue, aren't you?" He turned away before Ian could reply. "Have you told Darcy to remember I like my steak more rare than medium?" he asked his granddaughter.

"I haven't spoken to her yet."

"You two are usually attached at the hip. Come on, sweet pea. Come and say hello to your Uncle Andrew." Wrapping an arm around Caitlyn's shoulders, Cliff led her away, paying no mind to Ian.

"Come on, honey," Caitlyn called back over her shoulder, though not pausing in step. Approaching her uncle and his wife, Tara, she smiled warmly. "Hello, you two. Long time no see."

"Caitlyn!" Tara greeted, moving forward to immediately hug the younger blonde. "How are you, sweetheart? I heard you're focused on becoming a nurse?"

Caitlyn nodded as she released her aunt, smiling as she turned to hug her uncle. "I'm fine, thank you. And yes, I'm studying to become a nurse. It's hard work but will be worth it in the long run."

"Very rewarding work," Tara nodded.

"I think you'll make a great nurse," Andrew said. "I can remember when you were small, you had an obsession with wrapping your teddy bears up in bandages and poor Darcy if she'd sit still long enough for you to do it!"

Caitlyn laughed, feeling her cheeks heating up in embarrassment. "That's not why I'm going into nursing, but thank you for reminding everyone of that, Uncle Andrew!"

"My job here is done," he chuckled, buffing his nails against his shirt.

Tara slapped her husband's arm. "What type of nursing are you thinking of going into, honey? Or haven't you decided yet?"

"I want to work with children," Caitlyn replied instantly. "After what happened with Darcy, I know children need the most support at such a scary time." Her eyes sought out her best friend, spotting the tall brunette standing at the barbecue with her father and Uncle Edward. "The nurses were amazing with Darce and it appeals to me. I want to be there for someone who needs a smiling face, or a quick joke to ease their nerves."

Ian wrapped his arm around Caitlyn possessively. "You're an amazing woman, darling. They'll be lucky to have you."

"Oh, Ian." She looked up at him in apology. "I'm sorry. This is my uncle, Andrew, and aunt, Tara. Guys, this is Ian Moran."

"Hello, it's very nice to meet you both," Ian greeted, offering his free hand to the couple.

"Nice to meet you, Ian," Andrew greeted. "Are you training to be a nurse with Caitlyn?"

"Oh," Ian laughed nervously. "No, I'm the supportive boyfriend." He smiled at Caitlyn.

"New boyfriend? I don't think Catie's mentioned you."

"Uncle Andrew!" Caitlyn gasped in horror.

Ian cleared his throat and shifted uncomfortably. "We've been dating since college."

"Ian, why don't you go and get a drink," Caitlyn told him, whilst glaring at her relatives, knowing exactly what they were doing.

"Sure, sweetheart. Back in a moment."

Watching Ian walk away, Caitlyn suddenly turned to glare at her guilty-looking uncle once her fiancé was far enough away not to hear her. "What is wrong with all of you?" she growled. "Why is no one nice to Ian? What is so wrong with him?"

"Nothing, honey," Tara appeased. "We're just being protective of you, that's all."

"Right! I don't believe that for a second!" Spinning on her heel, she marched toward the main house. She faltered when she saw Darcy about to exit the house, their eyes locking briefly. They said nothing to each other as Darcy stepped aside to let her pass. Caitlyn quickly stepped inside. "God!" she sighed in frustration, taking a seat at the table with Aunt Debrah and Grandma Peggy.

"What's going on with you and Darcy?" Debrah asked in concern.

"Nothing's going on with me and Darcy!" Caitlyn exclaimed in a high-pitched voice, exasperated. "Why would you think something was going on between us? We're friends, we're fine, everything is fine."

Debrah blinked, surprised by her niece's outburst. "I've never known you two not to at least say hey to each other, or to hug. You breezed past her like she was invisible."

"Oh." She frowned, trying to think of an explanation. "It's nothing. I'm just annoyed at Uncle Andrew. We'll talk later I'm sure." She watched her aunt glance over at Tricia, who smiled and picked up a salad bowl.

"Let's get this lot outside, shall we?" Tricia said, not commenting on the obvious situation. "I'm sure everyone's hungry by now."

After the food had been consumed, no one left hungry, some of the relatives remained seated outside enjoying drinks and easy conversation while they relaxed and let their food digest, while others wandered inside to find more comfortable seating, to watch television or play on computer systems.

Caitlyn found herself at the other end of the long picnic table to Darcy during lunch, her gaze drawn to her best friend time and time again, despite her best efforts to completely ignore her. She smiled warmly when Darcy complimented Ella on her violin playing and chuckled lightly as Darcy spoke heatedly about football with Uncle Andrew. She missed having Darcy next to her, missed the comfort of her presence, little things that she hadn't really noticed at the time, like a light touch to her lower back or her hand, Darcy siding with her in a friendly argument, food being swapped from one of their plates to the other, all obviously absent now.

Eventually she found herself being led away from her relatives by Ian to a quiet spot. She had noticed all afternoon that he didn't fit in, despite his best efforts at conversation and jokes. "Ian?" she giggled, the wine with her meal going to her head.

Ian pulled her to a stop in front of himself and looked into her eyes. "I think we should tell."

She blinked at him, not understanding. "Tell who what?"

"Tell your family we're engaged. You told me yourself that pretty much everyone in your family is here. Now is the perfect time to tell them about us."

"You don't think it's too soon?" She frowned, nibbling on her bottom lip as she glanced over to her family members.

"No." He smiled and took her hands in his own. "We've been together for just over three years. And it's not like we're getting married tomorrow, we're only engaged." He pulled her into his arms. "I want them to know that I want to make an honest woman out of you, that we love each other and make each other happy."

Caitlyn found herself smiling. "You're right," she nodded. "You're totally right. This is happy news. They're all here, it's a good time to announce it. Come on, let's go finish our drinks, then I'll make an announcement."

Walking back to the table, blue eyes once again fell on Darcy, who was now deep in conversation with Grandad Cliff, her friend's face lit up as she smiled at something the older man said.

She sat down and reached out for her wine glass. Was she doing the right thing? She couldn't be with Darcy. She wasn't gay. What happened at New Year's was... She sipped her wine as thoughts of their tryst filtered through her mind. It had been a drunken mistake. It had. It never would have happened if they hadn't both been drinking. And no matter how amazing... A small moan escaped her lips as she recalled the intimacy between herself and Darcy. She shook her head to get rid of the thoughts. No matter how amazing, she loved Ian and she wanted to be with him. She wanted to build a life with him. He was a good man, he loved her.

Having talked herself around, she got to her feet and clinked a fork against the side of her glass before she could change her mind. "Uh...I'd like to share some news with you, but not everyone is out here." She hesitated, small doubts filtering back. She had to get on with it before she changed her mind. "So, can we all go inside to the living room?" She smiled and thanked them as her relatives got up and made their way indoors.

The whole family gathered in the living room, laughing and talking loudly, everyone in good spirits. Caitlyn stood nervously in front of them, very aware of Ian grinning beside her. Blue eyes flicked around the room, not finding the one person she was looking for. That was probably a good thing, she decided, smiling at Ian when he placed a hand on her lower back.

Watching her mother finally take a seat, Caitlyn knew it was time to get on with her announcement. Or back out. She cleared her throat to get the room's attention. "With everyone I love here for the barbecue today, I...I wanted to share some happy news with you."

Ian stepped in, sporting a bright smile. He wrapped a possessive arm around her shoulders, just to emphasise the fact she was his. "I know at the start of today some of you weren't sure who I was. I am the boyfriend. We've been together just over three years and Caitlyn is the love of my life. So, on Valentine's Day I asked her to marry me."

"And I said yes." Caitlyn smiled up at him, her belly doing flip-flops as she looked from him to her family, who admittedly looked a little shell-shocked. She lifted her hand to show off her engagement ring. "We're engaged!"

The room was deathly silent, eyes darting this way and that, everyone looking at each other in surprise. Caitlyn frowned as she watched her mother glance toward the back of the room, as though looking for someone. Looking back there herself, she didn't see anyone, but knew without doubt that Darcy had been standing there. Oh, Darce, I'm sorry, she thought, knowing how her best friend felt about her. Where was she now? she wondered, feeling very guilty suddenly.

Hearing Ian clear his throat, Caitlyn came back to her surroundings. "Well, don't all congratulate me at once, will you?" she laughed nervously, wondering what had gotten into everyone.

Tricia was the first to get up and approach the couple. "Congratulations, you two! It's...wonderful news!" She hugged her daughter tightly. "It's such a surprise!"

"We love each other, Mum. And we've been together a few years now, it's the next step." She did her best to hide her annoyance as Joe approached, then her two grandmothers and Aunt Debrah. She smiled and thanked them as they congratulated her, but internally, she couldn't help but dwell on their original silence and surprise at the news. Had she done the right thing?

"Let's all get fresh drinks and toast the couple," Joe called out, wrapping an arm around his wife's shoulders.

While her family members filtered out of the room, Caitlyn turned to embrace Ian. "It could have been worse," she chuckled.

"What the hell was that reaction about?" Ian asked softly, frowning. "Jesus, anyone would have thought I had announced the world was going to end!"

"I've got no idea," Caitlyn sighed, also puzzled over the family's reaction and the look her parents had shared before leaving the room. "Maybe...maybe it was just a shock. I am still only twenty-one."

"Couples used to marry straight out of high school," he grumbled. "And why is it half your family don't even know I'm your boyfriend, Caitlyn?" he demanded, easing her back away from his body so he could look into her eyes. "I've met some of them before now when you've invited me over for one of these get-togethers."

I've never gone out of my way to tell them we're together, she thought, knowing that in itself was odd. "I guess they forgot. They do have busy lives, Ian. They can't be expected to remember every guy I bring home and introduce them to."

"Every guy? I thought I was your first serious boyfriend?"

"You are, but I have dated a couple of other guys. Sweetie, let's put this odd reaction behind us." She smiled at him, wrapping her arms around his waist. "They know we're together now, that's what matters, right? How about we do some celebrating?"

Appeased, he ducked his head to kiss her. "Come on then. I'm sure some of the older relatives have sound advice to share with you, and I'm sure your brothers will want to threaten me!"

"Why would they threaten you?"

"Well, if I ever hurt you, they'll probably want to break my legs. That sort of teasing thing," he grinned crookedly at her. "I don't have brothers, but I've heard they can be quite protective of younger siblings, especially sisters."

"Are you sure you want to go looking for them then?" she laughed.

"May as well get it over with." He led them out of the now empty living room and along to the kitchen, all smiles as they met a cluster of Caitlyn's relatives standing around in conversation. They thanked the group when they were congratulated again before moving out into the back garden in search of refreshments and her older brothers.

Standing at the drinks table, Caitlyn looked around the garden while Ian rummaged through the cooler for an ice-cold beer he liked, and spotted her mother and father talking to Stacey, Jeremy's wife, and to Uncle Edward. She didn't see Jeremy, nor any of her brothers. And even Darcy was missing. If Stacey was there, then Jeremy must be around somewhere.

"Here you go, sweetheart," Ian said, handing her a glass of white wine.

"Thank you. Will you be all right for a moment? I'm going to go and ask Mum where my brothers are hiding. I can't see them anywhere."

"I'll be fine. Don't be too long, hmm? No one exactly knows me well. I think I make them nervous."

Smiling, she kissed his cheek and headed into the house, having seen Tricia enter a moment before. Walking through to the dining room, she found her mother setting out a range of desserts and snacks for people to help themselves to. "Hey, Mum, where's Jeremy? In fact, where are Luke and Brian as well?"

"Oh, they've gone off to the pub," Tricia smiled. "Do you want to give me a hand setting things up in here?"

"And Darcy?" Caitlyn enquired, already suspecting she knew the answer.

"With the brothers. Apparently, they decided it had been a while since they had all had a big night out."

"Seriously?" Caitlyn exclaimed in annoyance. "I announce I'm engaged, and they go off with the girl next door! Why didn't they invite Ian to go with them? He's going to be a part of this family." She followed her mother as Tricia walked into the kitchen. "And what the hell was wrong with everyone earlier? I tell them I'm engaged, and they sit there looking like it's the worse news in the world!"

"Well, honey," Tricia started in a low, calm voice. "I guess we all thought..." she trailed off, opening the fridge to grab an indulgent chocolate cheesecake she'd been defrosting. She shut the door with her hip and turned to head back to the dining room.

"Thought what?" Caitlyn huffed, following her. "Mother?"

Tricia sighed and turned to look at her daughter. "We thought you would end up with Darcy," she confessed. "You two girls have always been like peas in a pod. Where one went, the other wasn't far behind. And how deeply you care about each other was always so obvious."

"I don't believe this!" Caitlyn threw her hands into the air in disgust. "There are families in the world who pray their children aren't gay. My family was apparently praying I was!"

"Oh, Caitlyn, it's not like that at all," Tricia attempted to soothe her daughter. "Not exactly."

"Well, tough luck!" she snapped. "Whatever you all want, whatever you all hoped for, it's not going to happen! I'm with Ian, I'm engaged to Ian. Darcy is nothing more than a friend. The little girl you took in when she needed a place to go. That's it!" She spun on her heel and left her mother gaping after her, not stopping to wonder why her words had caused her chest to ache something fierce.

Jesus, what a day that had been! Caitlyn thought as she finished dressing. She looked at her reflection in the mirror, turning this way and that as she studied her figure in the outfit she had eventually chosen to wear. After much deliberation, she had opted for smart black, figure-hugging trousers, and a cream-coloured sweater. Her black ankle boots would finish off the outfit nicely.

Studying her reflection, she frowned as it occurred to her something was missing. Jewelry, she thought in sudden realisation. A necklace and some earrings. Moving away from the mirror, she walked to the vanity where her jewellery box sat. Opening the lid, blue eyes landed on a familiar pendant that she hadn't worn for the longest time.

She picked up the chain and looked at the delicate gold heart pendant, eyes filling with tears. The last gift Darcy ever gave her, she thought bitterly. Blinking back tears, she unclasped the catch and put the necklace on, returning to the mirror to check her reflection once again. God, why did it still hurt like it only happened yesterday? She lifted a hand to touch the pendant laying against her chest. She could still hear the words clearly, still feel the pain in her heart.

"Caitlyn? Are you still in the bath?" Ian called out from downstairs.

"I'm in the bedroom."

"I'm ready to leave when you are."

Now that Darcy was due back, Caitlyn thought, eyes roaming up and down her figure, will it hurt all over again? "I'm coming, Ian." She thought again of her past.

Caitlyn sat at the kitchen table, avoiding looking at Darcy and Luke opposite her. She was still furious with the pair over what had happened two months previous on the day she had announced her engagement, not understanding why they had left to go out on the piss with no thought to her or Ian.

Of course they hadn't invited Ian, she thought bitterly. They had made it perfectly clear they didn't like him since the first time she brought him home. Now it made sense. Darcy was in love with her and the family seemed to want her, Caitlyn, to settle down with her. They didn't want Ian in the family because it would remind them that she chose him instead of Darcy.

"I hope you're hungry, sweetheart." Tricia walked to the table with a dish filled with scrambled eggs. "I've made eggs, toast, sausages, bacon, fried tomatoes, baked beans, mushrooms, hash browns."

"Anything you didn't make, Mum?" Luke asked cheekily.

"Everything you need for a good fry up," Tricia finished. "But for that cheekiness, you're not getting any," she teased him.

Caitlyn looked at her mother. "I'm not very hungry, Mum."

"Oh. Well, eat what you can. I don't want you wasting away. Would you like a cup of tea? Or a glass of juice perhaps?"

"Tea, please."

After a strained breakfast, Caitlyn followed Darcy when she made her way upstairs. She said nothing as her friend walked into her bedroom, merely following Darcy inside and closing the door behind them. She wasn't entirely sure that being alone with Darcy was a good idea, but she had something to get off her chest.

Darcy lay back on her bed, her arms behind her head, and sighed heavily as she looked to Caitlyn hovering by the door. "I'm not apologising, Caitlyn, if that's what you're waiting for."

"Whatever could you have to apologise for, Darcy?" Caitlyn asked sarcastically.

"I told Luke I was going out for the night and he invited himself along. It was then suggested we invite the brothers and make a night of it because we hadn't been out together for a while."

"And none of you thought to invite Ian?" She folded her arms across her chest when she caught Darcy's gaze on that part of her body.

"Why would we invite the moron?" Darcy snorted.

"Darcy!" Caitlyn snapped in irritation, arms unfolding as she stepped toward the bed. "That's my fiancé you're talking about."

"There's no accounting for taste," Darcy huffed. "Look, whatever. I'm not going to lie to you, Caitlyn, I don't like the guy. I never have. That is why I didn't invite him along. The brothers don't like him, that's why they didn't invite him along."

"Did you not think of me?" Caitlyn asked quietly. "Did you not consider my feelings?"

"I'm always thinking about you, Catie," Darcy sighed, looking up at the ceiling. Swallowing hard, she inhaled a shaky, tremulous breath. "I'm sure you can understand why I didn't want to stick around."

"You have to get over your feelings for me, Darcy. I love Ian, I'm going to be with him, I'm going to marry him and build a life with him." Caitlyn moved to the side of the bed, seeing the pained look on her best friend's face. "Darcy, you're my best friend. You've always been my best friend. I...I want you to be my maid of honour at my wedding. Don't," she held up a hand, "don't answer now. But please think about it. And remember that if our roles were reversed, I would just want to see you happy." Without another word, she left the bedroom, not wanting to see the crushed look on Darcy's face any longer.

Jeremy brought his young family over for Sunday dinner that afternoon and Brian cancelled his plans with the mysterious Isabella so he could be home, after Darcy asked him to stick around. While dinner was roasting, the family sat together in the living room, talking and playing on Luke's computer system, challenging and insulting each other while they played.

After Darcy disappeared upstairs to the bathroom, Caitlyn headed up and waited outside for her friend, wanting to know if she had given any thought to her request of being her maid of honour.

Opening the bathroom door, Darcy blinked in surprise at finding Caitlyn waiting outside. "You stalking me now?" Her lips curled into a smile.

"No, I...I wondered if you had thought about what I asked

you this morning. I was hoping to tell the family while we're all here together, you know, if your answer is yes. Ian and I are thinking of having a winter wedding, so..." She trailed off and shrugged.

"This year?" Darcy asked in surprise. "You don't think that's rushing things?"

Caitlyn scowled. "When it's right, it's right."

Darcy took Caitlyn's hand and felt her friend tense at her touch. Sighing, she dropped the appendage. "Come into my bedroom for a second." She walked into her room and went to stand by the window, not wanting to make Caitlyn any more uncomfortable than she already was. Facing her friend, she watched Caitlyn hover by the door and felt an ache in her chest as she realised just how far apart they had grown, how damaged their once close friendship was. She looked into light blue eyes. "I love you, Caitlyn. I'll always love you. But I...I have to let you go." She swallowed hard and blinked away the tears that filled her eyes. "I can't keep living in hope that you'll give me a chance, give us a chance."

"Darcy..." Caitlyn frowned, remembering the last time her friend had sounded so sad, so defeated. It was one of the nights she had sneaked over during one of her parents' fights and had softly asked her why her parents didn't love her.

"What happened between us, you will never convince me that you felt nothing more than drunken lust. What we shared was special, really special. But you want to deny it ever happened, want to ignore the emotion we shared that night, write it off as drunken sex."

"Where are you going with this?"

"I can't be your maid of honour," Darcy sighed. "I'm not going to be here."

"What do you mean you're not going to be here? Where will you be?"

"I've decided to go travelling for a while. I've bought a ticket to France and plan to go all around Europe. With the family all here today, I'm going to break the news that I'm leaving."

"When?" Caitlyn choked out, looking into watery green eyes, green eyes she had always known, green eyes that had always shown her love.

"Tomorrow."

"What do you mean tomorrow? How long have you been planning this?"

"Ladies?" Jeremy called out from the bottom of the staircase.

"If you're done gossiping, dinner is ready. You know, if you're interested."

"Wait!" Darcy called out to Caitlyn as she turned to flee the room, openly crying now, her emotions a mess. She pulled a small box from her desk drawer and held it out for her friend to take. "I'm going to miss your birthday, so I got you a present early," she explained, her thumb tenderly rubbing over the top of the box. "You own mine already, I thought it was fitting."

Frowning, Caitlyn reached out and took the box. Looking into Darcy's eyes before opening it, she found a delicate gold chain and in the centre of the box, displayed proudly, a beautiful, intricately designed gold heart pendant. "Oh, Darcy..." She choked, tears returning and flowing freely.

Darcy stepped closer to her friend and tenderly wiped away the tears. "I bought it so that no matter how far I go, you will always have a part of me close to you," she said lovingly.

"I—"

Darcy shook her head. "Don't say anything. Just accept it with a smile and let's get down to dinner before they bloody eat everything!"

Caitlyn closed her eyes and summoned all her strength to smile. She watched her best friend return the smile with a small sad one of her own, both realising this was a pivotal moment in their once close friendship. She followed her taller friend out of the bedroom, knowing once again everything had changed in their lives. Nothing was the same, nor would be again.

"Hello, you two," Tricia greeted warmly upon opening the front door to her daughter and Ian. She was excited about Darcy's return and it showed.

"Hi, Mum. She's not here yet, is she?" Caitlyn asked nervously, not sure whether she wanted Darcy to be there already or not. She felt as if she needed some time to prepare herself, some time to get comfortable before being faced with her one-time lover.

"No, not yet," Tricia smiled. "Come on in and get settled. I'll sort you both out with a drink." She stood aside so the couple could enter. "You know what our Darcy's like, she'll probably keep us waiting all day!"

"No, Darcy never was one for scenes," Caitlyn murmured, taking off her coat. "She's probably on her way right now."

Tricia rubbed her daughter's back. "You know her best, love." She knew a huge rift had occurred between the pair. Something happening that had driven Darcy away. At first, she had assumed it was Caitlyn's engagement announcement, but then she remembered they had barely been speaking before that day.

Not knowing if something had happened, or if something hurtful had been said, she consoled herself with the hope that they would eventually find their way back to each other. They had known each other their entire lives, had always been close. If you found one, the other wasn't far behind.

"It smells like fresh baking and sweet pea in here," Caitlyn mentioned.

"I was up early and decided to bake Darcy's favourite biscuits. And the sweet pea is an air freshener. What do you think?"

Caitlyn inhaled and smiled. "I like it, it's not too overpowering."

"Would you like a drink?" Tricia asked, smiling at the couple to hide her inner turmoil. "Then you can catch me up on life at the hospital, Caitlyn." She led the way to the kitchen. "I'm surprised you took the day off work to be here, Ian. I didn't think you and Darcy really knew each other."

As Ian started on about being there to support Caitlyn, both mother and daughter wondered how much longer they would have to wait before Darcy arrived home.

Chapter Ten

DARCY KISSED LAUREN on the lips as they stood at Lauren's front door, oblivious to the taxi waiting at the kerb for her. "So, I'll call you later?"

"Honey, you're going to be fine," Lauren said lovingly. "They don't hate you. I'm sure they're not even mad at you. It will all work out, you'll see." Seeing the doubtful look that still lingered on Darcy's face, she caressed her girlfriend's cheek tenderly. "And if it doesn't work out, you know you're welcome here. I'll be waiting with open arms."

Darcy grinned and kissed the soft lips close to her own again. "See you in half an hour then," she joked, letting go of the redhead. "I better get going, otherwise the cabbie's going to drive off with my stuff."

"Call me tonight."

"I will. Bye, babe."

"Bye." Lauren sighed as she watched her partner climb into the taxi and waved when the car started off down the road. "Please let things go well for her," she said aloud, watching the taxi until it disappeared from her sight.

Darcy watched her old hometown flash past as the taxi headed for her street. It looked the same but older, with chipped paint, faded graffiti, and shops that had closed and not been bought by new owners dotting the streets. She sighed and wondered for the first time if the people she loved had changed much. Reviewing herself, she didn't think she had changed much at all. Maybe a wee bit wiser and more mature, she thought with a smile.

When the taxi pulled to a stop outside the Swailes' house, Darcy thanked the driver and paid him before climbing out, making sure to add a little extra as a tip. Grabbing her suitcases and bag from the boot, she took a deep nervous breath while she stood looking at the house. Her heart was thundering, butterflies in her belly fluttering wildly. She smiled when she realised the house at least hadn't changed any.

The front garden was neat, the lawn covered with a fine dust of snow that had fallen that morning, winter flowers blooming with colour stood fluttering in the slight breeze of the early afternoon. The path was clear, signs of it having been swept of any snow and debris evident. Home sweet home, she thought, glad she had returned now and sorry she had stayed away so long. Now to see how they reacted to her being back.

Puffing out her cheeks, she knocked on the dark blue door and grinned lopsidedly when Tricia opened it and gaped out at her. "Hello, Mum. You going to let me in, or just stand there gawping all day?"

"Oh, my God, Darcy!" Tricia squealed in delight and stepped forward to embrace the tall, tanned, dark-haired beauty standing on her doorstep. "It's so good to see you!"

Darcy dropped her suitcases and hugged the smaller woman tightly, breathing in the perfume she remembered fondly. Tricia still looked the same, give or take a wrinkle or two and a few more grey hairs to the collection. "It's good to see you, too. I missed you all so much!"

"Not enough to come home and visit," Tricia teased lightly, pulling back to look into amused green eyes. "Gosh, look at you! All grown up and...and even more beautiful than I remember!"

Darcy felt her cheeks heat up and knew she was blushing from the compliment. "Gee, thanks for embarrassing me out on the street!"

"It's what we mothers do best," Tricia laughed and swatted at Darcy's shoulder. "Come on, honey, let's get you inside. Everybody is waiting eagerly to see you."

Stepping inside, Darcy was taken back to her younger years, some great memories coming to her and some not so great memories shifting through her head in quick succession. She dropped her suitcases and smiled brightly as Joe appeared from the living room, closely followed by Luke carrying a little girl she assumed was his daughter, and lastly Caitlyn and Ian.

"We should at least let Darce get inside the house proper!" Tricia fretted.

"It's good to have you home, Darcy," Joe greeted, wrapping her in his arms. "Did you have a good trip?"

Even as Darcy smiled and greeted Joe, then Luke and his daughter, Olivia, her eyes remained fixed on her best friend. Caitlyn was as beautiful as ever. Her hair was a little shorter, but other than that she looked the same. "The flight was okay, the passengers were spawn from hell, but what can you do!" she chuckled. Not knowing what to expect as Caitlyn approached her, she opened her mouth to say hello, only to find warm, supple lips covering her own. As quickly as it happened, Caitlyn pulled back.

"That's because I missed you," the nurse murmured softly.

Before she could respond, Darcy felt the stinging blow of a slap to her cheek, hearing a gasp behind her from Tricia.

"And that's for not coming back for five bloody years!"

Everyone watched in shocked silence as Caitlyn stormed past Darcy and Tricia to the front door, leaving the house without another word.

Darcy blinked, reaching up to touch her still tingling lips. Not sure what to say, the sound of the front door slamming shut echoed in her head. "I better go after her."

"I'll go," Ian spoke up, a deep, confused frown creasing his brow. The family looked at him, almost having forgotten he was there to begin with. He looked at Darcy strangely, then made his way past her.

They silently watched Ian leave, then looked around at each other as the door bumped shut. Luke set Olivia down and grinned as he grabbed Darcy, pulling her into his arms for a tight embrace. "Nice entrance, Darce!" he chuckled. "What's your next trick?"

"I better go after Caitlyn," she said distractedly. "The moron's probably got no clue as to where she would go." She looked around at Joe, Luke, and Tricia and grinned. "It's really good seeing you all again."

"It's good to have you home, honey," Tricia replied, confused over what her daughter had done, but lit with a spark of hope that the two would sort themselves out and end up together.

"It smells gorgeous. Do I detect freshly baked ginger biscuits?" Darcy directed at Tricia.

"They're your favourites."

Crouching down, Darcy offered her hand to Olivia. "Hello, little one. My name's Darcy."

"I know."

"You do?" Darcy asked in amusement.

"She's seen your picture, Darce," Luke explained. "We tell all the kids about you, especially our childhood adventures."

"Oh, God!"

"Go on now, Darcy," Joe said affectionately. "Go and find Catie, then get back here so we can celebrate properly."

Standing up straight, Darcy smiled. "You haven't planned a family get-together, have you?"

"Not me!" Joe protested, blue eyes flicking to his wife, making Darcy laugh.

"I'll be as quick as I can," she said, pretty sure she knew where Caitlyn would have gone. She wasn't sure she could convince her friend to return with her, not certain she was the one Caitlyn would want to see, but she had to try. And maybe a little space away from everyone else would be good for them, a chance to clear the air. She hugged everyone, because she could, then headed back out.

DARCY HEADED FOR the cascade near the footbridge toward the Stone Court corner of the park. Whilst her favourite spot had always been on a bench in front of the Lower Pond, Caitlyn preferred a spot at the one and a half meter tall ornamental fall. When they had been thirteen, Caitlyn took a brief interest in poetry and had stumbled across a poem about a cascading waterfall. The spot appealed to her ever after.

"Hey, you," Darcy greeted softly. "You always did love this spot."

"Go away, Darcy," Caitlyn mumbled despondently. She couldn't believe what she had done. She couldn't explain what had come over her. But seeing Darcy suddenly there in front of her looking tanned and gorgeous, she just had to kiss her. Then, of course, she was angry at herself and so she saw fit to slap her old friend.

Darcy sat down, close but not too close, respecting the need for space between them. "I can't. Told the family I'd do my best to bring you back so we can all eat cake and drink tea." Looking across the shimmering lake, she sighed happily as birdsong reached her. "God, I forgot how beautiful this park is." She glanced at her silent friend and saw tears trailing slowly down her cheek. "Hey." She moved closer then, though still not reaching out to touch Caitlyn, not sure how her touch would be taken. "What is it, Catie? What's wrong?"

Caitlyn sniffed and swiped away her tears before turning her head to look directly at Darcy. "How could you stay away so long, Darcy? Not only that, but you never once got in touch with me. Do you hate me that much?"

"Oh, Caitlyn, no! I don't hate you at all. You know that." She wrapped an arm around her friend then, not caring if her comfort was wanted or not. The hurt and undertone of anger in Caitlyn's voice near enough broke her heart. "I loved you," she confessed softly. "That's why I stayed away."

"You never wrote to me," Caitlyn snapped angrily. "You never even sent me a postcard! Something to let me know you were okay."

"I wanted to. I can't tell you how many times I stood in front of a postcard stand and spotted one I thought would amuse you, fingers twitching to pick it up and buy it so I could make contact. Ultimately, I just didn't think it would be wise. I thought a clean cut would be better for both of us."

"Seriously? That's your excuse?"

"I also didn't want you knowing where I was, and I didn't want to complicate your life with Ian. I thought I was doing the right thing, Caitlyn. I thought it was best if I just disappeared from your life."

"For the best! Darcy, you've been my friend my whole life, you've always been there, always been around. You turned my world completely upside down by leaving!"

"Sweetheart, we were barely talking in the end," Darcy argued, the endearment slipping easily from her lips. "You could barely look at me, barely tolerate being in the same room with me. I don't regret what happened between us, Catie, not one second of it. To me, it was the greatest gift. But you...." She trailed off, swallowing hard as the old pain of rejection came to the surface.

"Me?" Caitlyn pressed.

"You're straight," Darcy murmured. "What happened was a drunken mistake according to you, a mistake you wanted to forget. I understand that now. I've grown up and realised that sometimes things just aren't meant to be no matter how much you wanted it."

Caitlyn wanted to dispute that belief, wanted to confess just how special their night together had been for her, wanted to confess that she often thought about that night. She had been so scared at the time, so certain she was straight and that her feelings for Darcy were the result of the drink. She bit her tongue. She couldn't disrupt her whole life the second Darcy returned. She wasn't sure what she wanted with Darcy and there was still Ian to think of.

Darcy got to her feet and inhaled the crisp cold air deeply. "I better get back. I told the family I would come and try to convince you to come back, but maybe you need some time alone to adjust to me suddenly being home." She smiled sadly and turned to walk away. "Oh." She paused and half turned back. "Ian left the house looking for you. Does he have any idea where to start?"

"You let him leave?"

Darcy grinned and shrugged. "I said I was coming to find you, he decided he should be the one to find you and left. How about you come back with me to piss him off a little more?"

Caitlyn couldn't help but laugh. "You're awful, you know that? You're all awful to him."

"What can I say, time away hasn't altered my opinion of him. He's a controlling moron who doesn't deserve you." She offered her hand to the still seated blonde. "Come on, let's go home and eat. I'm starving and Mum has baked my favourites." She wiggled her fingers.

Shaking her head at her much-missed friend, Caitlyn took Darcy's hand and got to her feet. She felt lighter than she had in a long time and could only assume that it was down to Darcy being home, being safe. Wrapping her arms around the taller woman's neck, her lips curled up in amusement. "I missed you. A lot," she declared, hugging Darcy tightly.

"I missed you, too. It's good to be home."

"I'm still angry at you by the way."

"I figured." She wrapped her arm around Caitlyn's shoulders. "Come on, let's go home."

They strolled side by side, happy to put aside their problems for the time being. Being the middle of a workday, people were scarce in the park. But even the chilly winter weather hadn't deterred some. Older men and women were out walking their dogs, a couple of mothers were out with wrapped-up toddlers in pushchairs, and smartly dressed office-bods strode along with phones pasted to their ears.

Having nothing of interest to distract her, Darcy soon grew to hate the silence between herself and Caitlyn. She'd never admit it, but she had missed her friend's gentle tone, her friend's laughter, and now that she was in Caitlyn's company she wanted nothing more than to hear her talking about anything at all, she didn't care what. "Did you become a nurse in the end?"

Caitlyn smiled, touched that Darcy sounded genuinely interested. "I did. I even got a position at the local hospital, thanks to Doctor Roycroft."

"That's great," Darcy smiled, pleased for her. "Do you enjoy it? Or do you wish you had chosen to pursue a different career?"

"I enjoy it for the most part. The people I work with are great, we keep each other sane, especially on the difficult days. And I meet so many different people, all with different personalities, not all good, and from different walks of life," she chuckled. "But because I work with children, it can be utterly heart-breaking." She rubbed Darcy's arm, thinking back to her friend's troubled childhood. "I have a patient under my care at the moment, a teenager who has been left in a coma after being hit by a van," she sighed sadly. "It has absolutely devastated her family, particularly her mother. She hardly leaves Lindsey's bedside."

"Will she recover?"

"The signs are good, but things could take a turn at any time. Then if she does wake up, there could be lasting damage we don't know about yet, and there will be a long recovery in store for her." She glanced at Darcy as they left the park. "I ended up talking about you to the mother, your coma, your injuries. I remember it all so clearly."

"I was lucky."

Caitlyn willed away the memories, not wanting to drag them up again. "So, what about you, Darce? What's kept you busy over the years?"

"Photography. I started taking pictures of things that caught my eye and it went from there. I got some interesting shots of people caught unaware, buildings at dawn and dusk, scenic views at dawn and dusk, that sort of thing."

"You always did notice beauty in odd places," Caitlyn mentioned wistfully. "Do you remember when we were kids, Mr. Vandeleur had that dark coloured twisted old tree? It scared me, but you said it had just had a tough life and was making the best of what it had been given."

"I remember," Darcy chuckled and gave a little nod. "Is that tree still around?"

"No idea. He doesn't live there anymore, a new family moved in."

"Oh. What about Mrs. Wildeve?"

"Her family moved her into an old people's home, I think."

Darcy's thoughts drifted to memories of the kind old lady who used to hand out ice lollies during the summer to the neighbourhood kids. "Doctor Roycroft," she mused. "Is he still working at the hospital?" she asked, changing the subject.

"Why wouldn't he be?"

"Caitlyn!"

The pair turned and spotted Ian hurrying toward them. Caitlyn took a step away from Darcy's side, very aware she had kissed her old friend with no thought for her fiancé. "Hi, Ian. Sorry I ran off without a word." She smiled weakly, wondering why she felt disappointed he had turned up.

"I've been looking all over for you, Caitlyn," he said sternly, coming to a stop in front of her, not acknowledging Darcy at all. "I was worried, sweetheart."

"I'm sorry. I had to get out for a bit."

"Your behaviour was—"

"I know. I'm sorry."

"Yes, well." Grey eyes flicked to Darcy, dislike etched on his face. He couldn't say for sure, but he was almost certain something had happened between Caitlyn and Darcy and he didn't like it. Looking back at his fiancée, he smiled lovingly and wrapped his arm around her shoulders. "I've found you now. Let's get back and let your parents know you're okay. I'm sure they're worried."

THE FAMILY SAT around the dining room table, Joe and Tricia next to each other on one side, Ian as close to Caitlyn as he could get on the other side. Luke sat at the head of the table, while Darcy sat at the other end with Olivia on her lap, the four-year-old having taken a shine to her new found friend.

"So, Darcy, tell us what you've been up to," Joe speared a bit of cake off his plate. "How have you paid your way around Europe?"

"I take photographs," she replied, glancing in Caitlyn's direction and smiling, not missing the scowl on Ian's face.

"Photographs," Joe repeated.

"Of places, of people, of the unusual, the sunset, sunrise, anything that caught my eye. I have some I can show you later. Most recently in Portugal, I travelled to Sintra, a beautiful little town surrounded by wooded hillsides. The former summer residence of the Portuguese Royal Family was there, and I got some great shots of the Sintra-Cascais natural park. In Venice, I took several shots of the old architecture. I travelled to Pamplona in time for the San Fermín festival, which has the running of the bulls. That was interesting, to say the least," she chuckled.

"So, you were selling your photos then?" Tricia asked in interest.

Darcy nodded. "In Germany, I met this woman at a party I attended. She owns her own gallery and after she saw some of my photos, she offered me some wall space. We framed the photos she thought might sell so they looked professional and they flew out of the gallery. She begged me for more and that's how I've earned my keep ever since."

"Where did you move on to after I bumped into you in France?" Luke asked.

"That was strange, wasn't it?" Darcy laughed. "Meeting each

other so randomly."

"I thought I was seeing things!" Luke laughed.

Darcy glanced around the table at the amused faces. "I was on my way back from this great little patisserie and who do I spot seated at an outdoor table in front of a café?"

"Me!" Luke put in.

"I thought for sure you had come to spy on me, until I realised you couldn't have possibly known I was in France." She looked at Tricia and Joe. "Did he mention bumping into me?"

"He did." Tricia smiled as she gazed in her son's direction. "Though I don't think he could quite believe it!"

"I didn't believe it!" Darcy laughed. "After France, we went to Belgium, Germany, down to Switzerland, Italy, over to Greece. Eventually we ended up in Spain, then finally Portugal."

"We?" Caitlyn enquired, her fork hovering in the air as she stared Darcy in the eye, a hint of jealousy in her tone.

With her dark green eyes locked onto Caitlyn's unwavering blue, Darcy nodded. "Yeah. Lauren and myself."

"Lauren?" Caitlyn frowned, recognising the name but not sure why. "Lauren who?"

"Caitlyn don't give poor Darcy the Spanish inquisition," Tricia cautioned, not sure Darcy wanted to discuss such things in front of everyone.

"Cansdell," Darcy filled in, deciding it was better out in the open. "Lauren Cansdell."

Caitlyn dropped her fork, the clattering of it hitting her plate echoing around the now silent room. "The bar owner? What, did you bump into her as well?"

"No. She came with me when I left."

"You travelled for five years with the local bar owner?" Icy blue eyes darted around the table, looking for any signs that her family were as surprised as she was.

"Caitlyn..." Luke started, guilt written all over his face.

They knew! Oh, my God, why hadn't anyone told her? Why hadn't they told her Darcy was writing home? Why hadn't they told her she wasn't alone? Why had she been kept completely in the dark? She turned her gaze back to Darcy. "You didn't think to ask any of us?" she asked tightly. "You asked the bloody bar owner!"

Setting down her cutlery, Darcy cleared her throat as she sat back in her seat. "I told her I was thinking of travelling around for a while, we got talking, and I asked her to come along if she was interested."

"You asked some...some bar owner, who you'd only known a few years, to go travelling around Europe with you?" Caitlyn asked in disbelief.

"She is a friend of mine," Darcy said calmly, though her heart was hammering. "She was a friend of mine. Now we're dating." She smiled as her gaze flicked to Tricia and Joe. "We've been together for the last three years."

"Oh, honey, that's wonderful!" Tricia smiled, eyes switching from Darcy to her daughter and back again. She knew that throughout the years Darcy had been hurt deeply by Caitlyn's thoughtlessness, and whilst she had lived a long time hoping the two girls would sort themselves out and end up together, at the end of the day she just wanted them happy. If anyone deserved some happiness it was Darcy.

"Unbelievable!" Caitlyn stood up, her chair jerking backward and almost tipping over, getting everyone's attention. "I suppose that's why I never heard one goddamn word from you! Ian, I want to go home."

"Caitlyn." Darcy stood, handing Olivia to Joe. "Caitlyn, wait a minute." She followed her and Ian as they left the dining room, the couple swiftly heading for the front door.

"I don't want to hear it, Darcy. Leave me alone! I feel so raw right now. You've suddenly come home and...and..." She shook her head, eyes shining with tears. "Please leave me alone."

Darcy watched the front door close and rubbed a hand over her face as she exhaled heavily. "Damn, what the hell was that about?" she mumbled, leaning against the wall. First, Caitlyn kissed her, then she slapped her, now she's stormed off after yelling at her. She smiled in amusement. Could have been worse she supposed. All that could have happened without the kiss!

Moving away from the wall, she turned and headed back into the dining room, meeting four sets of eyes looking her way. "Wow, great homecoming, huh?" she joked, smiling tightly. Sitting down, she looked at a wide-eyed Olivia, still on Joe's lap. "You okay, little one? Didn't get scared, did you?"

"Why was Aunty Caylin shouting?"

"I have no idea, Olivia," Darcy mumbled, rubbing her jaw.

"Jealous," Luke muttered.

"Luke," Tricia warned.

"Oh, come on, Mum, everything she's done today could be interpreted as jealousy. I cannot be the only one who thinks so!"

"So, me dating Lauren, it's...not a problem, is it?" Darcy looked around the table nervously.

"Of course not, Darcy," Joe reassured her, reaching to pat her arm. "You're part of this family no matter what. We didn't kick Caitlyn out for dating Ian, did we?" he chuckled.

"Joe!" Tricia scolded, while Darcy and Luke laughed. She stood to collect the plates and dishes. "Out of interest, why didn't you ever write to Catie, Darce?"

"It's...complicated."

Having an idea where the conversation was going and knowing Darcy well enough to know she wouldn't want to talk about it, Luke intervened. "Hey, Dad, would you and Mum mind looking after Olivia for a couple of hours? I was hoping I could take Darcy out for a drink or two so we can catch up away from little ears."

"I don't mind at all," Joe smiled, tickling his granddaughter's sides. "Ask your mother to be sure."

"Great." Luke got to his feet and took his plate through to the kitchen.

"I suppose he'll take you to Jeremy's place," Joe said to Darcy.

"It will be good to catch up with Jeremy if he's around. How's business going for him?"

"Good. Better than good, honestly. He bought the place next door on the cheap when they went under and remodelled a bit. He now has a restaurant for when customers get hungry, hired a proper chef as well who serves up top-notch food."

"Yeah? Good for him. I'm glad he got his dream."

Tricia walked in with Luke close behind. "I think it's a wonderful idea," she said, smiling at Darcy. "We don't mind looking after the little one for a bit, do we, Joe?"

"Not at all, love."

"Thanks, Mum," Luke said, kissing Tricia's cheek. "We won't be out long."

"I've heard that before! Make sure you behave, Darcy," Tricia teased, smirking at her.

"Me! I don't think I ever gave you trouble."

"Oh, you don't remember the time I found you and the boys in the kitchen at three in the morning, drunk and trying to make fried egg sandwiches?" Tricia laughed.

"I forgot about that," Darcy grinned. "Happy memories."

"I don't suppose you'll be seeing Lauren, will you?"

"Not tonight I don't think. Why?"

"You'll have to invite her over this weekend," Tricia said joyfully. "The boys will be here to help put up the decorations, she can meet everyone whilst lending a hand, then stay for dinner. We'll want to get to know the woman who has managed to steal your heart."

"Poor Lauren," Darcy groaned. "Is it a wise idea to thrust her into the lion's den?"

"She'll have to meet everyone sooner or later, why not get the lot of them out of the way all in one go?"

Smiling affectionately at the older woman, Darcy got to her feet. "I'll ask her if she's free the next time I speak to her." Walking to Tricia, she dropped a kiss on the top of her head.

"Good girl. Go on then, you two. We'll see you later." Blue-grey eyes landed on Olivia. "Movie night for us."

CAITLYN WALKED INTO the house she shared with Ian, silent and thoughtful as she reflected on the day. On the drive home she could feel the tension coming off Ian, but he remained tight-lipped, no doubt waiting until they were home before saying his bit. She dropped her handbag on the entrance hall table and undid the buttons of her coat, silently counting down for him to start.

"Do you care to explain what the hell is going on with you?" he growled. He shut the front door and stood watching her, waiting for answers.

Caitlyn hung up her coat and walked toward the kitchen. "What do you mean?" Her voice void of any emotion, placid, neutral.

"What do I mean?" he repeated in disbelief. He followed her into the kitchen. "How about starting with you kissing your best friend when she walked in the front door. And don't tell me it was a kiss between friends, Caitlyn. It was more than that!" He stopped beside her, frowning as he watched her prepare a cup of tea, stunned by how eerily calm she seemed. "Caitlyn?"

She looked at him, blinking once, twice. "Yes, Ian. I kissed her. I kissed Darcy like I would a lover. I missed her. She's been gone from my life for five bloody years after being the one constant. Suddenly, there she was again. I saw her and I had to kiss her."

His mouth worked up and down, trying to make sense of what she was saying to him. "You had to kiss her? Like she was your...*lover*?" He shook his head, not sure how to respond. "And you slapped her and stormed off because?"

"Because I'm angry with her," Caitlyn replied, like it was the most obvious thing in the world. When the kettle clicked, she picked it up and poured boiling water into her mug. "Would you like a cup of tea, Ian?"

He looked from her to the mug of tea she was making, a deep, concerned frown on his brow. Looking back to the face of his fiancée, he shook his head. "You're like a stranger. I don't know this Caitlyn at all!"

"Tea?" she repeated.

"Why are you so eerily calm about all this, Caitlyn?" he snapped. "I'm your bloody fiancé and you've just humiliated me in front of your family by acting like...like a jealous lover! You...you kissed your best friend in an inappropriate way, stormed off after slapping her, then flew into a mood when she announced she hadn't been travelling alone! What the hell is wrong with you?"

Caitlyn sighed heavily and turned to face him. She looked at him, really looked at him, taking in his handsome features, which at that moment were pinched in annoyance and frustration, his eyes a stormy grey. "I don't know what you want me to say, Ian."

He looked at her in disbelief and shock. "Tell me you're having a breakdown, tell me you lost your senses for a moment, tell me you've got your fucking period. Tell me anything other than you're in love with her, because that's what it bloody looked like!" He ran a hand through his wavy brunette hair, pushing back the dark locks. "Jesus, Caitlyn, we were so happy and now..." He shook his head. "What the hell is your family going to think? We've been engaged for the last —"

"Goddamn it, Ian!" Caitlyn snapped, at her breaking point. "My family will never accept you completely, will never welcome you with open arms, no matter what you wear, no matter what you earn, no matter what you do! You'll never be accepted as one of the family because they all love Darcy!" Leaving her half-made tea, she stormed away, hurrying upstairs and locking herself in the bathroom.

DARCY SAT AT a clean, two-person, chrome table in Jeremy's bar and looked around while Luke left her to get the drinks in.

It was a modern place, with metal tables and comfortable chairs or stools for seating. The bar was central, set in the middle of the large room with a three hundred and sixty degree view of everything. There were three members of staff behind the bar serving and a couple of girls walking around collecting glasses and keeping the tables clean. Ninety's music blasted out of a lit-up jukebox standing by the far wall.

She had seen the bar when Jeremy first bought the property and had seen the finished article before she left. He had since changed a few things while she was gone, but it was still the friendly place she remembered, with a comfortable atmosphere, everyone welcome.

She smiled and thanked Luke when he set a tall glass of orange juice in front of her. "Haven't spotted Jeremy, is he not in tonight?"

"I was told he's around," Luke smiled. "I'm sure it won't be long until he's over here giving you grief."

Picking up her glass, Darcy chuckled. "How are you enjoying life as a daddy?"

"It's an amazing feeling, Darce. The moment she was put in my arms I knew I loved her more than life itself and would do anything for her. She keeps me on my toes, always looking for trouble and asking embarrassing questions!" He reached for his pint and sighed. "It's a shame I had her with Natalie. We're really struggling."

Darcy nodded as she set her glass down, remembering Luke telling her about his girlfriend, Natalie, when they had met up in France. "Don't stay together if you're both miserable, Luke. Children pick up on bad vibes. Trust me, I know."

"I want what's best for Olivia. I want her happy. I want her to have a happy, carefree childhood, being brought up in a stable environment. But you're right, if Natalie and I keep arguing the way we are, it's not good for her. It's not good for any of us. A home should be a home."

"Talking of home, catch me up on the family. How are Jeremy and Stacey doing? They're still together I take it. And Brian? You told me he married the mysterious Isabella after all."

Chuckling, he nodded. "Jeremy and Stace are still together, even though he's always working long, hard hours here. They have four children now. Devon and Anya, who you know of, and the recent additions, Harry, who is three, and little Marissa, who is nearly two."

"Wow! Where does he find the time?"

"Then there's Brian and Isabella. They got married and have two children, with number three on the way. They've got two girls, Zerenity and Ruby, so I think he's hoping for a boy."

"Blimey, busy boy!" Darcy laughed, reaching out for her

drink. "Zerenity?"

"Yeah!" Luke laughed. "You should have seen Mum's face when they announced that!"

It was a new one on her, but then she had read somewhere that parents were opting for original names these days, rather than old traditional ones. "And Caitlyn?"

Luke sipped at his pint, watching her try and pretend she didn't care one way or the other. He licked his top lip as he set his glass down. "She hasn't married him, you know?" he eventually said, wiping his hands along his thighs. "She's kept him waiting all these years for you to come home."

"Why would she do that?" Darcy asked with a frown.

"They told me my baby brother had come in with a beautiful woman, tanned and exotic-looking. I didn't believe them!" Jeremy announced his presence loudly. "Jesus! Stand up, Darce, and let me get a good look at you."

Smiling and blushing in embarrassment as people stared their way, she got up and hit the slightly taller man on the shoulder. "Hey, Jeremy. Good to see you." She snuggled into his embrace, inhaling the familiar cologne he had always worn. Pulling back from him, she tugged at the beginnings of a goatee. "What's this?" she chuckled. "Did it slip from the top of your head?"

Jeremy scowled while Luke burst out laughing. "Back two minutes and already you're picking on me! You're barred," he pouted. "You look good, Darce. Tanned, beautiful, still as young as ever."

"Thank you. You're not looking too bad yourself, despite being a busy businessman with a wife and four kids."

"Shouldn't have stayed away so long. None of us are happy with you about that."

"Yeah, I know. I had my reasons though." Releasing her hold on him, she sat back down. "This place is looking great, Jeremy. I'm very impressed."

He looked around with pride. "It's been a lot of hard work, far too many long hours, missed family time, but I'm happy with what I've achieved. Finally." Grabbing a free stool, he sat down. "Bought the place next door when they went under and expanded."

"Yeah, Dad told me. Got yourself a top-of-the-line chef and serve up good food."

"I'll book us all in for a meal, you can tell me what you really think."

"I'm sure it will be top-notch."

"So, why were you gone for years rather than a few weeks? Where've you been? What you been doing? Are you back for good?"

"Jeez, Jeremy, take a breath will ya!" She smiled while he blushed. "I was gone so long because I travelled all around Europe. I saw as many places as I could, staying until I grew bored and wanted a change. I tried everything that took my interest, so skiing, cooking classes that didn't really work out well, a couple of pottery classes. Am I back for good?" she pondered. "I'm not sure. I had a yearning to come home, so here I am, but will I stay put..." she shrugged. "I don't know, I guess time will tell."

"Just before you arrived, I was telling Darcy how Catie hasn't married Ian yet," Luke told his older brother.

"Thank God," Jeremy smiled. "We don't want that berk in the family!"

"You know what I think?" Luke asked. "I think she doesn't actually want to marry him."

"Then why would she stick with him for all these years?" Darcy questioned. "She was probably just holding out for my return so I would be her maid of honour. Did you know she asked me before I left?"

"She didn't!" Luke exclaimed in surprise.

Darcy nodded. "I told her I couldn't because I was leaving. Not that I would have done it even if I hadn't been leaving. I was madly in love with her, why on Earth would she think I could stand there and watch on while she married the moron?"

"So, you've finally come out," Jeremy smiled big. "'Bout bloody time, Darce!"

"She's not only come out, she announced this afternoon that she's got a girlfriend!" Luke proclaimed.

"No kidding! Well, good for you, Darcy." He knocked her arm affectionately.

"Cheers, Jeremy." She finished her drink. "Do you want another, Luke?"

He finished what he had left and handed her his glass. "Please."

"Do you want a pint, Jeremy? Or a soft drink?"

"Yeah, go on then, I'll have a pint. May as well enjoy your company while I have you here."

Walking to the bar, she was served promptly, much to her surprise. She guessed it might have been because she was sitting with the owner and boss. Making her way back to the small table, she handed around the drinks. "What did I miss?"

"Luke was telling me you're dating Lauren, owner of the bar we used to go to," Jeremy replied. "How did that happen? Did you bump into her abroad, like you did Luke?"

"No. When I decided to go, I asked her to come along with me. We've been travelling together since the beginning."

"No kidding!"

"I was miserable a good long while, my head was a mess. All I ever wanted was Caitlyn and she spurned me time and time again. Lauren was a good friend to me, a good travelling companion. It was two years into us being away and we were in Italy. We were strolling around one afternoon, taking in the sights and the beauty and it just felt right to take her hand. In the evening, we went out for a romantic meal and we went from there." She smiled lovingly.

"You're happy then?" Luke asked, genuinely caring.

"Very happy."

"That's good, Darce," Jeremy said, smiling at her. "If anyone deserves a bit of happiness, it's you, kiddo."

"Gee, thanks, Dad."

"Don't get smart with me," he teased, wiggling his finger near her face. "Or you'll be over my knee for a spanking."

"Tempting, but what would your wife say?" she grinned.

Jeremy shook his head as he laughed out loud. "You're as terrible as always. Some things never change." He picked up his pint. "What have you been doing for work? Odd jobs?"

"I take photos."

"Then sell them?"

She nodded. "Right. Buildings, people, whatever catches my eye."

"Got any spare?" he asked in interest, setting his glass down.

"A few. Why, you interested in seeing them?"

"Could do with something on the walls," he said, glancing around. "Why not my favourite sister's work up there?"

"You don't have to sweeten me up to get a peek at them!" she laughed.

"Damn, wish I had known that before," he teased. "I'm serious though, Darce. I have the wall space."

"Sure, when we next get together, I'll give you a look at what I have."

Jeremy's attention turned to his younger brother. "Where's Olivia? With Mum and Dad, or home with Natalie?"

"With Mum and Dad. Natalie threw a strop when I said I was going home this afternoon to welcome back Darcy. She stayed home sulking." He sighed like a man with the weight of the world on his shoulders. "Darce reckons we shouldn't stay together if we're both so miserable."

"She's right," Jeremy nodded in agreement. "You two are arguing all the time, she's always moody and throwing a tantrum, you're miserable and stressed. It's not good, Luke. Sometimes people are better off apart than they are together."

Darcy tapped Jeremy's forearm. "Lukey told me you have new additions. Got any pics?"

Grinning proudly, he got to his feet and pulled out his wallet. "Of course I have." He flipped it open as he handed it over to her. "Harry's three," he told her. "And Marissa is nearly two."

"They're beautiful, Jeremy," she said, looking at the happy photos of his family. "She is the spitting image of Stacey."

"Thanks. We had Devon, then accidentally had Anya, as you know. Then I got busy with this place and Stacey was stressed out with two little ones to look after, things were strained between us for a while. It got so bad I thought the worst, so I took time out and whisked her away for a short holiday, just us, so we could reconnect, and along came Harry. Not at the best time, in all honesty! We learnt our lesson after his arrival and took precautions more seriously, but then found out we were expecting again."

"Family complete now then?" She handed back his wallet.

"Who knows, accidents happened," he grinned. "What about you, Darce. Going to settle down with Lauren? You've been together, how long?"

"Together three years," she smiled. "But settling down officially?" She puffed out her cheeks, never having given it any thought before. "That's a big step. But maybe, eventually."

Luke finished his pint. "We better get going, Darce," he said, setting his glass down. "I told Mum we wouldn't be out long. And I better get Olivia home. The last thing I need tonight is Natalie kicking off."

Darcy nodded and finished what was left of her drink. "Jeremy, it's been good seeing you."

Jeremy stood and embraced the younger woman again. "Just don't go running off again. We like having you around, Darcy."

"Thanks. Tell Stacey I said hello and send my love."

"I will," he smiled. "I don't suppose it will be too long until Mum plans a family get-together, but you're more than welcome to come over to my house any time. I know Stace would love to see you. She was delighted to hear you were coming home."

"Talking of get-togethers, I'll be seeing you Sunday, won't I? For the annual decorations fiasco?"

Jeremy slapped his head. "God, is that already upon us?" He winced. "Yeah, we'll be there."

"You might get to meet Lauren," Luke spoke up, grinning at his brother. "Mum asked Darce to invite her over to officially meet us all."

"Thanks a lot, Luke," Darcy pouted. "I was hoping to get out of it."

"No way. If anything, you have to invite her just so we can see Caitlyn's reaction!"

Darcy hugged Jeremy again and smiled. "I'll see you and the brood Sunday then. Now, get back to work, you bum!" she teased.

"Someone has to work! See you later," he waved. "Stay out of trouble."

"Bye." She followed Luke toward the exit, growing more and more happy with her decision to return home. So far, so good.

Chapter Eleven

DARCY MOVED UP the bed and collapsed onto her back next to a breathless Lauren.

"God, baby! That was...wow!" Lauren panted, turning her head to look at her flushed and panting girlfriend.

"I do what I can." Darcy smiled in satisfaction.

Rolling onto her side, the bar owner curled up against her girlfriend's side, an arm slipping around her waist, a toned thigh draping over Darcy's legs. "Are you nervous about later?" she asked softly, tracing patterns into sweaty skin.

"I don't know, I guess a little." Truth be told, she was more than a little nervous. She hadn't spoken to Caitlyn since the day she had arrived home and Caitlyn had stormed off. She was worried about what might happen if Caitlyn turned up today. With any luck, Caitlyn would be working.

"I'm nervous too," Lauren admitted. "What if they don't like me, Darcy? What if they don't think I'm good enough for you? What if I upset one of them? Or say the wrong thing."

"Hey." Darcy shifted so she could lift Lauren's chin, then kissed her softly on the lips. "Just be yourself, babe. As to them not liking you, come on, you're amazing, how can they not like you as much as I do?" She smiled when her reassurance drew a small smile from her girlfriend.

"Here I was under the impression you loved me?"

Darcy grinned at Lauren's teasing. "I do, you know what I meant."

Settling with her head resting on Darcy's shoulder, Lauren inhaled, detecting hints of jasmine lingering on her bed covers, along with the undisputable scent of sex. "I'm still going to worry though. We can't know what's going to happen."

"Seriously, sweetheart, try not to. They dislike Ian a whole lot more!"

Lauren went back to tracing patterns against Darcy's belly. "Don't they hate him because..." she trailed off, not sure she wanted to bring it up.

Waiting but getting nothing further, Darcy shifted again, pulling Lauren more firmly against her. "They dislike him because he's an idiot. He tries far too hard to get them to like him. He's smug, he's not right for Caitlyn, he's..." She growled, her temper bubbling. "He's a moron, plain and simple."

Not wanting to put her doubts and thoughts into words, afraid of what truths may come forth, Lauren sighed heavily, fear and doubt consuming her.

"Sweetheart, we've just made love and...I don't know, shouldn't we be basking in the happy afterglow?" Darcy asked. "You feel tense, baby. You're sighing." She frowned in concern. "Is there something on your mind? Other than the fact you're meeting everyone later?"

Lauren sat up, her back against the headboard, and pulled the blanket up to cover her naked chest, feeling the chill in the room now she was cooling down. "Are you sure that's the real reason they dislike Ian?" she questioned. "Are you sure it's not because they want their little girl, their baby sister, to be on your arm? To live happily ever after, a real family in every sense."

"What?"

"I'm worried they hate Ian because he's not you, Darce. I'm worried they're going to hate me because I'm not Caitlyn."

"Sweetheart, they didn't even know I was gay until I told them about you and me the other day. And Caitlyn! She's only ever dated men, only ever been interested in men. Why would the family think of there being a me and her all this time? Where's this coming from, Lauren?"

Lauren slid out of bed, padding to the where her robe was hanging. "When I first met you, it took only minutes for me to figure out you were in love with Caitlyn. They were around you every day. Trust me, they would have noticed the way your eyes followed her, the way you smiled when she spoke, the need for contact between you!"

"Well, if they did, they never said anything," Darcy grumbled, annoyed that her peaceful morning lie-in had been disrupted by this discussion. She thought back to the afternoon of Caitlyn's engagement, more specifically, her little talk with Luke in the garden after the announcement. He knew, she recalled. They all knew! He said the family had thought it would be me. Taken completely by surprise at that revelation, she climbed out of bed, not wanting to deal with it. "I'm going to take a shower."

Light green eyes watched Darcy go, the bedroom door swinging shut behind her. Lauren felt awful for ruining their morning together, but she was worried, and Darcy had asked if everything was all right. Sure, she could have lied, but what good would that do? Standing alone, she brushed a hand through her tangled locks, and sighed deeply once again. "Today is going to be hell!"

she muttered morosely. With her robe tied shut, she left her bedroom and padded through to the kitchen and set about making herself a coffee.

Was she worrying too much? she pondered, spooning a couple of sugars into her mug. She thought over their history, how Darcy had taken time to sort out her head before getting into a relationship with her, how they had been happily together for three years with very few arguments between them. She felt her belly clench with tension again as she wondered if that had been because they were away. She couldn't help but think that now the two old friends were back in each other's lives, a little older, a little wiser to the world, things would turn in the direction Darcy had always wanted.

Walking to the fridge sitting in the corner, she retrieved the milk, thinking about the fact Caitlyn was still engaged and not married. Picking up her mug, she walked to the living room and curled up in a corner of the sofa. "I'm overreacting. I know I am," she acknowledged. "So, Caitlyn hasn't married the guy yet. I completely trust Darcy. She's never given me a reason to doubt her. We're happy and our relationship is solid."

"Hey," Darcy called out softly, a small frown creasing her brow. "You talking to yourself, babe? That's a sign of madness, they say."

"You should be more worried if I was having a full-blown conversation with myself," Lauren grinned. Her gaze dragged down her girlfriend's body and she unconsciously licked her lips.

"Showers free."

"I'm sorry about before, honey. I'm just overreacting. Now I've had my morning coffee, I feel much more rational."

"It's fine," Darcy smiled lovingly.

"It's not. I was letting my fear of today get to me. I'm super nervous about meeting everyone because I know how important they are to you. But I trust you. I trust our love for each other. I was being silly."

Taking a seat next to Lauren, Darcy caressed her girlfriend's thigh. "It's fine, babe. Really. But honestly, try not to be too nervous, hmm? They're going to love you."

"Okay," the redhead smiled. "Remind me again who is likely to be there?"

"Two wives, one fiancé, and..." She quickly totted up all the nieces and nephews she now had. "Seven nieces and nephews. The three brothers and Caitlyn. Oh, and of course, Tricia and Joe. Though, I'm not entirely sure Ian and Caitlyn will be there. She may be working, and he won't turn up on his own."

"Wow!" Lauren blinked, letting it sink in. "You're going to be there, right? You didn't mention you, so I assume..." She smiled while her girlfriend rolled her eyes.

"I'm going to be there right beside you. I'm not going to let them tear you to pieces or anything, okay?"

"Okay," Lauren smiled and nodded. She handed her mug over. "Here, you finish that, I'm going to jump in the shower, then get started on making myself beautiful."

"Too late, you're already beautiful."

Smiling, Lauren bent to kiss waiting lips. "Now I remember why I love you. If you need me, I'll be in the bathroom."

CAITLYN STIRRED THE cereal in her bowl, not hungry, but unwilling to get rid of it. If she didn't have something in front of her to distract herself, she knew she would have to make small talk with Ian, which she most definitely didn't want to do. He wanted answers that she didn't have, and she was tired of them going around and around.

Ian silently watched his fiancée. He noted she was distracted and wondered what she was thinking about, or rather, who. His jaw clenched tightly, muscles bunching and rippling beneath the skin, as he thought of the woman who had been gone so long, only to return to disrupt his happy life.

He loved Caitlyn, had since the moment he set eyes on her in college. He wanted to make a life with her, but she seemed reluctant to commit completely to him. She was happy for them to continue plodding along. After proposing, he thought he had gotten the ball rolling. He was happy, Caitlyn was happy, they had announced their engagement to her entire family. He thought they would start planning their wedding, had envisioned little details, their two families coming together to celebrate at an official engagement party. That was before Darcy left.

Caitlyn had been putting him off year after year with the excuse that she wanted her best friend to be her maid of honour, that she could not, would not, get married without Darcy there. She flat out refused to discuss it. He had reluctantly accepted that, hoping one day things would change. With Darcy finally returning, he had thought that at last he would get the wife he always wanted, only for Caitlyn to confuse matters by kissing Darcy in front of her family like they were long lost lovers.

He expelled his breath loudly to get her attention. "Do we

have to go today?" he asked, more than a little put out.

Caitlyn looked up from her bowl and blinked as she looked across the table. "It's a family tradition. You usually love going."

"Yes, well, things change, Caitlyn."

"Why?" she asked suspiciously. "Why have things changed now?"

He stared levelly at her. "I don't understand why we should go around to your parents' house to put up their decorations when we have our own home to decorate. Why don't we stay home and decorate this place together?" He smiled, hoping to entice her into agreeing.

She sighed and pushed back her bowl, noting that he had barely touched his toast. "My brothers and their families all go around to my parents' house. They too have homes of their own, but it's a family tradition and gives us a day to be together. We go every year, Ian, and you've never complained before. Why is it this year you don't want to go?" She waited for his response, an eyebrow raised in question, already knowing the real reason. "Because Darcy's back," she stated. "And you're worried something might happen between us again."

"I have reason to worry, don't I?" he snapped, his own eyebrow lifting in challenge. "Will you be kissing her today?"

She deserved this, she thought. She had kissed Darcy because it was the right thing to do in the moment, but God, how she'd paid for her decision since! "No, Ian. I won't be kissing her again. It was merely the heat of the moment. Relief that she was home and in one piece."

He scowled. "I don't want to go, Caitlyn. As your fiancé, I would like you to respect my feelings on the matter."

"As my fiancé, I want you to respect mine!" she snapped back. "This is a family tradition. I'm not going to phone up and cancel because you don't want to face Darcy."

"And your family," he added softly. "Who, according to you, will never accept me or welcome me into the family because I'm not bloody Darcy!"

His voice grew louder the more he thought of the tall brunette, his dislike for the woman coming to the surface. It had always been there, since meeting her he had taken a disliking to her, not liking the influence she had in Caitlyn's life, the way she was always around. It became clear she felt the same way about him.

"What is so bloody wonderful about her?" he questioned. "Why is it they accept her and welcome her with open arms? I've met her, a number of times, and I don't get the appeal!"

Caitlyn stood, her chair scraping back across the kitchen tiles. "Come or don't come, Ian. I don't care. I'm going and that is final."

DARCY SQUEEZED LAUREN'S hand in silent support and encouragement, both women smiling as Tricia opened the front door to them. "Hello, Mum. You're looking as lovely as always."

"Hello, Darce. Late as usual and trying to charm your way out of trouble," Tricia greeted, smiling warmly as she reached out to embrace Darcy. "Everyone else is here."

"That's because they want to sit and stare at us as we walk in," Darcy replied, returning the hug. Pulling back, she reached for Lauren's hand and smiled. "This is Lauren Cansdell," she introduced. "Lauren, this is Tricia Swailes."

Tricia smiled politely and embraced Lauren. "It's very nice to meet the woman who has been taking such good care of our Darce." The redhead was older than she expected, but very beautiful, with kind eyes.

"It's a pleasure to finally meet you, Mrs. Swailes," Lauren said nervously. "Darcy has spoken about you and the family so much, I feel like I know you all already. All good things, of course."

"Oh, none of that!" Tricia scolded. "Call me Tricia. I must admit, we haven't heard much about you, Lauren. Hopefully we'll learn a bit today. Come on in, you two. I'll get the kettle on to make tea, while the rest of the gang treat you to an inquisition."

"Don't say that, you'll scare her off!" Darcy groaned. "I don't suppose you want a hand making the tea?"

"No, I can manage."

Smiling, Darcy looked at her girlfriend. "You ready?"

Lauren inhaled deeply and slowly exhaled. "As ready as I'll ever be."

Darcy led her the short distance to the living room. "Hello hello," she greeted everyone cheerfully, stepping into the room where the family was sitting in wait.

All eyes turned their way, conversation halting. Lauren shifted closer to Darcy's side, incredibly nervous, and, as she caught Caitlyn's eyes, insecure.

"Oh, my God, Darcy!" Stacey squealed in excitement, jumping up from the sofa. She hurried over to the taller woman and hugged her tightly. "It's so good to see you!"

"Hey, Stace. Good to see you, too," Darcy grinned. "Heard you've been a busy girl over the last few years."

"I don't know what you mean." Stacey smiled as she stepped back. Grey eyes flicked to Lauren standing slightly behind Darcy, almost using the brunette as a shield. "Hello," she greeted warmly.

"Typical Darcy," Jeremy piped up with a grin. "No introduction, just expects everyone to know each other!"

"Oh, um..." Darcy wrapped an arm around her girlfriend's shoulders. "Everyone, this is Lauren. Lauren, this is Stacey. The loudmouth is her husband, Jeremy. Sitting next to him are Luke and a lady I don't know. Next to her is Brian, and over there is Caitlyn and her moron. Sorry, I mean her fiancé, Ian."

The three brothers sniggered, while Caitlyn glared at Darcy. "Goddamn it, Darcy!" she growled. "Do you have to start?"

To defuse an argument, Brian got to his feet and walked to Darcy, embracing her. "It's good to see you, Darce. It's been too damn long!"

"Yeah, I know. Sorry." She smiled and hugged him back.

He walked back to the lady Darcy didn't know. "This is my wife, Isabella," he introduced. "My daughters are around somewhere, probably in the back garden."

"The mysterious Isabella," Darcy smiled, offering the woman her hand. "You know, we did begin to doubt you even existed!"

"So I've heard. It's nice to finally meet you. Brian and the family have told me so much about you I feel like I know you already."

Dark green eyes flicked to Brian briefly before returning to Isabella. "I assure you, it's mostly all lies." She smiled charmingly.

"So, you didn't go flying over a car on a bike because Jeremy dared you?" she asked in amusement.

"Ah, that rumour is true, I'm afraid. But, to reassure you, if I was to do the same stunt again today, I'm fairly sure I'd make it this time!" Darcy laughed along with the brothers.

"So, Darce, where did you go for five years?" Brian enquired.

"Tea for all," Tricia announced as she walked in carrying a tray full of mugs.

Caitlyn stared critically at Lauren. She remembered she hadn't liked the redhead when they first crossed paths years ago, and now, as she watched Lauren cling to Darcy, she liked her even less. Blue eyes followed the thumb caressing the back of

Darcy's hand and she felt a surge of jealousy building within her chest at the intimate touch.

Tricia set the tray on the coffee table. "Where's Joe got to?"

"Garden?" Jeremy suggested, more question than answer.

Caitlyn tried valiantly to bite her tongue and not say anything scathing, but suddenly she couldn't hold back. "You don't have to hold onto her so tightly, Lauren. Darcy's not going anywhere, I'm sure."

Conversation came to an instant halt, all eyes darting to Caitlyn before flicking to Lauren, confusion and nervousness and a hint of interest in most.

"She's nervous, Caitlyn," Darcy said calmly. "Everyone staring at her isn't helping." She led Lauren over to a free armchair and took a seat before settling her girlfriend on her lap.

Tricia handed around the cups, leaving everyone to reach for milk and sugar and cream if they wanted it. "I better go and find Joe."

"How did you manage to stay away from your bar for so long, Lauren?" Caitlyn asked as nicely as she could manage.

Lauren started playing with the hair at the nape of Darcy's neck. "I have people I trust. They took care of things for me so I could go." She smiled lovingly at her girlfriend. "It was very worth it." She knew she was playing with fire by winding Caitlyn up, but she wanted her to know in no uncertain terms that Darcy had moved on, wanted her to know Darcy was hers now.

Darcy smiled awkwardly, feeling very uncomfortable. She felt like a piece of meat stuck between two lionesses who were about to kick off. This is not going well, she thought, gaze flicking from one woman to the other, noticing Ian glaring at her and Caitlyn smiling sickeningly sweet at Lauren, while her girlfriend offered the same back. Dear God, please don't let them have a cat fight! "We uh...we visited a lot of great places and had a lot of fun. But we weren't completely slacking off. I took a lot of pictures and brought some with me today for you to have a look at."

"She ended up selling them," Jeremy informed Brian, who hadn't yet heard.

"How did that come about, Darce?" Stacey asked in interest, more than happy to ignore the weird tension in the room.

"In Germany, we threw a party and this woman named Margo turned up and happened to see some of my photos hanging on the walls. She's a gallery owner and offered me some space. Lucky for me, the pieces put up for sale were sold."

"Let's see them then, Darce," Jeremy said. "I would love

some for the bar."

Tricia walked back in, this time bringing biscuits, Joe following behind her, carrying a couple of cardboard boxes.

"What are we talking about?" Joe asked. "Something about the bar, son?"

Tricia smiled as her grandchildren charged in. "Careful everyone, there's hot tea and coffee."

"I'm hoping Darcy has some shots left that I like," Jeremy explained to his father. "The walls could do with something on them."

"What a good idea."

"Oh, Joe, this is Lauren, Darcy's...friend," Tricia said tactfully, eyes falling on the youngest members of the family.

"Hmm? Oh," Joe looked at the couple and smiled warmly. "Hello, it's nice to meet you."

"And you," Lauren replied politely, managing a small smile.

"It's okay, Mum, we explained to the kids about Darce having a girlfriend," Jeremy informed her.

Taking an envelope out of her handbag, Lauren held it out for Jeremy. "She's very talented," she told the family proudly. "Darce has a real eye for beauty."

Darcy blushed. "Thanks, babe." She concentrated on her cup of tea while her photos were shared around. She had never cared what people thought of her shots before, but now while the family studied each and pointed things out to each other, she wanted desperately for them to like her work.

"You have some great photos, Darce," Luke commented, looking at a photo of the Matterhorn mountain in the Pennine Alps. She had captured the shot on a perfect day. The sky was a brilliant blue and she had photographed the mountain reflected in the Riffelsee Lake.

"Thanks, Luke," she smiled, relieved and pleased. "I think that's one of my favourites," she said of the photo. "We were staying in a town called Zermatt, which the mountain overlooks. It was beautiful there, even more so because it wasn't the tourist season!"

"What would I have to do if I wanted a couple of these up on my walls?" Jeremy asked, looking at the Mediterranean Sea at dusk. She had captured a spray of waves hitting the shore, the sky purple and peach in the background, the dipping sun just peeking on the horizon, soon to slip from sight.

"I can get them blown up for you and framed, then they're good to go."

"What about a price?"

"I'm not going to charge you, Jeremy. Think of it as a gift."

"I can't do that, Darce," he argued. "It's how you make your living."

"True, but if you have a couple of my shots up on your walls, they'll get seen, then maybe those same people will go out and buy others."

"But that only works if one of the galleries gives you space, right?" He looked over at her, a light bulb going off in his head. "You can sell them from my place!" he said excitedly. "I'll give you the wall space. I get free art on the walls and you get to pre-view your work. When one sells, you can replace it with a new one."

She liked the idea a lot but didn't want him rushing into any-thing. "You have a bar and restaurant to run, you don't need the extra hassle of selling my photos."

"I like the idea," Stacey spoke up. "It's like Jerry said, we'd get free art on the walls, good stuff, and you can make some money out of it. It's win-win for all of us, Darcy."

"Well..." Darcy looked at Lauren, who smiled back and rubbed her shoulder. "Let me think about it over Christmas, okay?"

"Sure," Jeremy nodded in agreement. "Don't rush into this because it's me, Darce. Take your time deciding." He held up the photo he still held. "How much for this one? I really do like it."

"Then it's yours," Darcy insisted. "Most definitely a gift for my potential new seller."

Finishing their tea, they turned their attention to Joe and the two boxes he had brought in with him. They were the first of many, most having been stored in the loft, along with the artifi-cial tree.

"You better untangle the lights, Joe," Tricia said suddenly. "You know how frustrated and angry the children get...Jeremy and Darcy!" she teased the pair.

Darcy looked at Jeremy, the dark blonde-haired man looking right back. "I got dibs on putting up the tree," she announced as his mouth opened.

"Oh, fine!" He scowled at her. "I'll help the kids hang tinsel or whatever up." His scowl deepened when Darcy stuck her tongue out at him in triumph.

Joe peeled the tape off one of the sealed boxes. "The tree is up in the loft, Darcy. Along with the other boxes of decorations. I can't get up there so easily these days, would you?"

"Of course," she nodded. "Are the baubles up there? You

remember what happened that year you sent Brian up there? He nearly killed himself tripping over them!"

The family laughed while Brian blushed crimson. "Thanks a lot, Darcy! I have stories about you, you know?"

"Yeah, but they're not as funny."

"The cheap ones are up there, Darcy," Joe answered, pulling out a delicate tree decoration from the box standing open in front of him. "I put these safely in the downstairs cupboard because I didn't want them getting broken," he said, smiling at the plump snowman he held. "I'm guessing the many sets of window lights we own are in that box."

"You know, we really shouldn't store them away in one single box," Luke said, frowning. "It's no wonder they come out tangled every year."

"Will you be sticking around after Christmas, Darcy?" Ian asked suddenly, eyes on her as the room fell silent. "Or will you be off somewhere else?"

Darcy exhaled loudly, hating the man for ruining the cheerful mood and for bringing up a subject she had no desire to think about yet. "I don't know, Ian. I'm thinking about sticking around, this is my home after all." She looked at Tricia and Joe. "I plan to get next door fixed up and looking good enough to rent out. That should bring in some money."

"Good idea," Joe nodded. "Some good money to be made in property, I hear."

"I sort of started before I jetted off travelling. Managed to do a few bits that needed urgent attention. Now, after five years I guess a lot more will need seeing to."

Joe shook his head. "It's not too bad over there. I go over at least once a week to check on things, making sure it's still locked up tight and secure. It'll need airing out, maybe a wipe down with a duster and a new coat of paint."

"What, you mean you didn't do that?" Darcy teased, smiling broadly. "I appreciate you keeping an eye on the old place. It never occurred to me before I left to have someone check over there occasionally. But then I didn't expect to be gone long."

"It was no problem," Joe assured her. "And now you're back, we can do it up properly. Anything serious needs doing, I'll give you a hand, if you like. I know the boys won't mind helping out," he said, glancing at his sons. "And the uncles also."

"It'll be nice when the weather warms up a little," Luke said. "We could barbecue and make a real family day of it. I'm in."

"Me too," Brian nodded.

"Definitely," Jeremy added. "As long as I'm not working."

"Would you go with Darcy, Lauren?" Caitlyn asked, caressing Ian's thigh. "If she left again. Or would you stay behind to run your bar?"

Darcy clenched her teeth tightly together. She would like to say it was because of the question, but the truth was it irked her to witness Caitlyn's fingers trailing slowly up and down Ian's leg. "Of course she would come with me, we're a couple," she replied a little more harshly than she intended. "We've been together three years now," she continued, softening her tone as she looked at Lauren.

Lauren smiled lovingly and caressed Darcy's cheek. "We've had our ups and downs, but we're very happy," she declared. "Where she goes, I go." She chuckled, remembering a conversation they'd had in Portugal. "The other day, Darce mentioned the Cook Islands. That could be our next destination."

"But nothing's...nothing's decided," Darcy stammered, looking around the room and seeing looks of disappointment reflected back. "I could get an offer from one of the local galleries and end up staying put."

"I'll start threatening them to offer you some wall space then!" Luke spoke up, smiling at Darcy.

"Thanks, Luke. I think," she chuckled. She patted Lauren's leg to indicate she wanted to get up. "Do you want to give me a hand getting the tree and other decorations?"

"Sure," Lauren nodded, setting her cup on the coffee table. "I'll help you put it up, if that's okay?"

"So will I," Caitlyn announced. She smiled lovingly at her friend. "You remember how annoyed you get when things don't go well."

Luke laughed. "Like that year she didn't attach the stand properly and the whole tree collapsed halfway through us decorating it!" he recalled, making the Swailes family laugh.

"There was nothing wrong with it!" Darcy protested, a hint of a smile gracing her lips. "I'm sure someone, Luke, tampered with it!"

He put his hands up in a show of innocence. "No comment."

Shaking her head, Darcy took Lauren's hand. "We'll be upstairs if you need us," she said, leading her girlfriend out of the room, knowing they were going to be the hot topic while they were gone.

THE HOUSE WAS filled with the sounds of giggling children and Christmas songs playing on the stereo. Brian, his family, and Luke and Olivia were out front making a winter wonderland of the front garden. Once complete, the garden would draw people from miles around, everyone coming to view the snow, the LED reindeer statues, a Santa Claus that spoke when its motion detector was triggered, a holly wreath on the front door, and the many multicoloured lights lighting up the windows.

Jeremy and his family set about decorating the interior with tinsel, a garland cord wrapping around the banister, mistletoe hanging in the doorways, and stockings hanging on either side of the fireplace. Joe sat on the living room floor untangling the window lights, and Tricia retreated to the kitchen to prepare everything she needed for the Sunday roast.

"If I remember right, the branches all have a little coloured tag on them." Darcy opened the box holding the pieces of the artificial tree.

"That's right," Caitlyn nodded. "We should set them out into their groups, so it'll be easier for you to attach them when the time comes."

"Good thinking." Darcy glanced to where Ian was sitting on the sofa, watching her with contempt in his eyes, then at Caitlyn sitting on the floor, reaching into the box for the first lot of branches. "You know, I don't think this job needs four people, Caitlyn."

"I'm here to keep you calm," Caitlyn replied, smiling.

"I can keep her calm," Lauren spoke up. She reached out to caress Darcy's thigh. "We work pretty well together, don't we, Darce?"

"Um…" Darcy cleared her throat. Shit, why her? What had she done to deserve being stuck in this situation? "Why don't you two sort out the branches, while Ian and I see to the stand and putting up the trunk." Dark green eyes flicked over to Ian to see what his response would be.

"You go ahead," he waved a hand dismissively at her. "Like you said, I don't think this job needs all of us."

Sighing, her gaze flicked to Joe, who met her eyes and lifted his eyebrows. Looking back to Ian, she nodded. "Fair enough. Get to it, ladies, so I can get the base of the tree out." She sat down to wait, a hand rubbing her forehead as she felt the beginnings of a headache building.

"Do you remember the Christmas after you got out of the hospital, Darcy?" Caitlyn asked softly.

Darcy blinked at her best friend. "Uh, yeah."

"You couldn't do too much to help because your arm was in a cast," Caitlyn reminisced. "We told you to sit on the sofa and then wrapped you in tinsel," she smiled, blue eyes on her friend.

"I remember you didn't do too much to help the rest of the family. You spent most of the day sitting next to me and asking if I was all right."

"I remember that as well!" Joe laughed.

"Dad, you're supposed to be on my side!"

"Do you remember our first Christmas away from home, babe?" Lauren shifted herself over to where Darcy was sitting, settling next to Darcy's legs. "We were in Belgium, weren't we?"

"Yeah," Darcy chuckled. "We had just moved in and could only manage to get a tiny little two-foot tree that came with attached baubles!"

Laughing, Lauren caressed Darcy's leg, aware of Caitlyn's eyes on her. "It was awful, but we were together."

"I've taken the branches out, Darce," Caitlyn announced. "You can get started on putting the trunk together."

"Great." Relieved she had a task to concentrate on, she got up and walked to the box. Taking out the two parts of the trunk and the base of the tree, she started assembling it.

"What will you be doing for Christmas, Lauren?" Caitlyn asked saccharinely. "Returning home to see your family?"

The colour drained from Lauren's face and she felt her throat tighten with old hurt.

"She'll be spending it with me," Darcy answered.

Caitlyn blinked at her best friend. "But, this is your first Christmas back. I thought you'd be here."

"I will be in the afternoon, like Jeremy and his family. And I suppose Brian as well now." Again reminded of how things had changed. "I'm sure you'll be at home with Ian, won't you?"

"Of course she will be," Ian replied sharply. "We do live together, Darcy."

"Just haven't managed to tie her down officially, eh, Ian?" she replied snidely.

His face flushed red with anger and embarrassment. "It's only a matter of time. Now you're back to be her maid of honour, we can start the planning." He looked to Joe, who was watching the whole bemusing scene. "Would you like some help, Joe?"

"No, thanks, Ian. I can cope."

"I'm sure Ian could help in some way, Dad," Caitlyn said, wanting Ian to feel included. "Maybe he could hold the plug while you untangle the line?"

Darcy snorted in amusement, earning glares from Ian and Caitlyn. She coughed to clear her throat and finished tightening the screw that held the trunk in place. "All done," she declared, standing up and stretching. "Think I'll go make a cuppa, anyone want one?"

"Oh, yes please, Darce," Joe nodded. "Better ask the boys, too. I'm sure they could do with a break."

"Do you want tea, babe?" Darcy directed at Lauren.

"Yes please, sweetheart. Would you like a hand?"

"No, it's okay."

"In that case, can you tell me where the bathroom is?"

"Sure. Sorry, I should have pointed it out earlier."

After showing her girlfriend to the bathroom and sharing a quick kiss, Darcy walked around the house to find out who wanted tea or coffee, before going into the kitchen. "Do you want a cuppa, Tricia?"

"Yes please, Darce," Tricia smiled, looking up from sorting out the vegetables. "You're on tea duty, are you?"

"Wanted a breather to be honest."

"Yes, it was rather tense, wasn't it?"

"I don't understand why, but yeah, things got a little...weird."

Caitlyn walked into the kitchen and smiled at her mother. "Hi, Mum. Do you need a hand with anything?"

Tricia blinked in surprise at the offer. "Uh, no, thank you, honey. I thought you were helping with the tree?"

"I've done my bit for now."

"Right." Tricia looked from Caitlyn to Darcy and back again, picking up on the underlying tension between them. "I must use the loo."

"Lauren's up there," Darcy informed her, spooning sugar into the cups she had set up.

"Oh. In that case, I'll check on everyone's progress then," Tricia smiled.

Blue eyes remained on Darcy's back as her mother excused herself. Caitlyn wanted to talk to Darcy, wanted to clear the air, wanted their friendship to go back to how it had been when they were younger. Mostly she wanted Lauren to leave so she could have Darcy to herself.

Waiting for the tea to brew, Darcy turned to face Caitlyn, leaning back against the counter and crossing her arms. "Still mad at me?"

"I guess I always will be a little mad," Caitlyn acknowledged. "It hurt so much when you told me you were leaving, Darce. It came completely out of the blue but was obviously something you had been thinking about for some time. Then for you to stay away so long, all without a word to me." She sighed. "You were beside me for most of my life, then you were gone. Yeah, it hurt."

"I told you why I left, Catie. I couldn't stay. Don't you know how much it hurt to see you with him? To see his hands all over you. Then you announced you were marrying him! Jesus, I had to leave because seeing you walking down the aisle to him would have killed me!"

Moving forward, Caitlyn came to a stop in front of her taller friend. "We've hurt each other a lot, haven't we?"

Darcy smiled and reached out to tuck a strand of golden blonde hair behind Caitlyn's ear. "Yes, we have, but then life never is simple, is it?"

"Isn't this very intimate," Ian said from the doorway.

Caitlyn jumped back from Darcy and glanced over at him. "We were clearing the air, Ian."

"I bet you were," he growled. "Started with another kiss, did you? That seemed to be the way to do it the other day."

Lauren halted her progression toward the kitchen, frowning when she overheard what Ian said.

"That was different, Ian!" Caitlyn replied. "Darcy had just arrived home and...."

"And it felt right to kiss her, yes, Caitlyn, you told me."

Having heard enough and not wanting to be discovered, Lauren slipped back to the living room, smiling at Joe when he glanced up at her. She took a seat on the carpet in front of the Christmas tree and started fiddling with the branches. The yellow-tagged ones were supposed to be attached first, so she set about doing that, mindless work giving her time to think over what she had discovered.

Darcy hadn't mentioned Caitlyn kissing her. In fact, she hadn't said much at all about how that first day home went. Why the hell not? What else went on besides Caitlyn kissing her? Was this the start of her worst fears coming true? Was Darcy going to end up brooding over Caitlyn again? Would their relationship deteriorate?

"Look, Ian," Darcy said. "If you haven't noticed, this day has been a little tense. We were clearing the air. That's all."

He took a step into the kitchen. "I want you to stay away from my fiancée!" he growled, jabbing a finger in her direction. "I don't care if you are best friends, I don't care if you have known each other your whole lives. I don't want you anywhere near Caitlyn!"

"Ian!" Caitlyn snapped, furious with him for trying to dictate who was in her life, furious with him for implying something was going on between them, furious over his attitude of late. "How dare you!"

"Open your fucking eyes, Caitlyn!" he barked at her. "She's in love with you! That's why she bloody left in the first place!" He threw his hands in the air in disgust. "I'm not staying here. I came and attempted to fit in, but I don't, so I'm going home."

Caitlyn hurried after him as he stormed out of the kitchen, pleading with him to calm down and be reasonable. Puffing out her cheeks, Darcy turned to the cups of tea she was preparing, finishing off making them before loading them onto a tray.

"Everything all right in here?" Tricia asked, walking into the kitchen. "I heard shouting."

Darcy turned and smiled in amusement at the older woman. "How long were you lingering out of sight?"

Tricia chuckled, knowing she was caught. "Not long. I heard the tail end of the conversation."

"Do you want me to leave your tea here?"

"Yes please, Darce. Thank you."

Picking up the tray, Darcy headed for the doorway. She paused as a thought hit her and turned back to scrutinise Tricia, filled with a sudden need to know the answer. "Did you know?" she asked quietly. "Why I left."

"I had a suspicion," she admitted. "I have watched you two grow up. We all know how close you two were at one time. I remember watching you two together and randomly thinking what a lovely couple you made. You complement each other, you looked after each other, then something happened, and it all disappeared. I know you both tried to pretend nothing had changed, but I'm a mother and we pick up on these things."

"You're not...disgusted?"

"Oh, Darcy! No. All a parent ever wants is for their child to be happy. And you're one of mine, Darce, just as much as Caitlyn and the boys are. I just want you all happy." Looking into dark green eyes, she saw relief reflected back. Her head tilted slightly as she studied the younger woman. "I don't suppose you're going to tell me what went on?"

Grinning, Darcy lifted the tray she held slightly. "I better dish these out before they go cold. Shout out if you need a hand in here. You know I always was the best at peeling veg." She turned and left the kitchen, leaving Tricia laughing at her.

CAITLYN STEPPED OUT of her parents' house and shivered as the cold wind chilled her to the bone, even though she had wrapped up in her thick winter coat. The day had turned into a disaster. Ian had stormed off in a huff, which had upset her but no one else, and after dinner Lauren made her excuses and left, much to Darcy's confusion.

Glancing to the left, she saw her friend in the fading daylight standing up high on a ladder, stapling outdoor Christmas lights to her childhood home. They hadn't really had a chance to talk further, but now was the perfect opportunity. Smiling, she made her way over. "Hey, Darcy," she greeted.

Darcy glanced down in surprise and offered Caitlyn a small smile. "Hey, Caitlyn. What brings you outdoors?"

"Nothing in particular. I came over to talk to you."

"Nothing more left to say, is there?"

"There's plenty to say, Darcy."

"Like what? I left, and I would do it again even if I could go back in time."

"Are you going to come down, so I don't have to shout up at you?" Caitlyn called up in annoyance. She didn't like to imagine what could happen if her friend slipped while she was distracted.

"What for? We've got nothing left to say to each other," Darcy replied. Glancing down she saw the worried frown wrinkling her brow. Caitlyn still had her wrapped around her little finger! she thought with a sigh. Making her way carefully down the ladder, she smiled as her feet hit the ground. "Hey there."

Though desperately trying not to, Caitlyn smiled. "Hey."

"What's up?"

"Nothing, I..." Caitlyn sighed and looked down at the lawn she stood on, toe poking at the thin layer of snow. "I wanted to apologise for my reaction when you arrived home," she said, not looking at her friend. "I don't know what got into me. I never should have slapped you. It was out of order."

Stuffing her hands into the pockets of her jeans, Darcy watched Caitlyn, not sure what to say. Caitlyn's reaction to the news she had travelled around Europe with Lauren was odd in her mind, then there was how she had gone out of her way to be a bitch to Lauren all day. She stepped forward, reaching out to tenderly lift Caitlyn's chin with her fingertips. "Why did you react like that?"

Blue eyes lifted and locked onto dark green, Caitlyn getting lost in the familiar loving eyes. "I...I was hurt," she admitted. "You left, Darcy. You left and you didn't come back. I thought you were only going to be gone two or three weeks! And, I'm supposed to be your best friend, your dearest friend, and yet you asked some bar owner you had only known a couple of years to go off with you! I didn't know you were leaving until the last minute!"

Laughing, Darcy shook her head in disbelief. "You had just got *engaged*, you were barely talking to me, could barely look my way! Why would I have asked you to come travelling with me?"

Caitlyn didn't have an answer. All she knew was that she didn't like the fact her best friend had gone off with Lauren. "I'm sorry about today," she said instead. "In the kitchen with Ian. He and I...we've not been getting on lately. Things are kind of...tense."

"Oh." Darcy blinked, taking in this bit of news. She frowned and looked away from her friend. "Is it because of me?"

"No." Caitlyn sighed, lifting a hand to brush back her hair. "Not really. It's me, or rather, me kissing you," she smiled, meeting green eyes again. "It sort of brought up questions that I don't have answers to."

"Like?"

"Oh, Darcy, it doesn't matter!" Caitlyn spun away. Fear had bubbled up in her chest. This was the last thing she wanted to get into a conversation about.

"You're right," Darcy conceded swiftly. She realised nothing had changed. Caitlyn was still determined to live in denial, no matter how obvious her feelings were at times. "Your relationship is none of my business."

Turning back to face her friend, Caitlyn studied the taller woman thoughtfully. "Is it serious between you two?"

"Yes," Darcy answered promptly, giving a firm nod. "We've been together for three years now."

"That doesn't mean anything," Caitlyn argued. "Now you're back home, back to your regular lives, it could all end. I can't believe you're even dating her, Darce. I mean, she's older than you. It's practically cradle snatching!"

"She's not that much older than me. And besides, Ian's older than you, so it's not like you can talk!"

"Ian's two years older than me, it's hardly a big deal!"

"Lauren's four years older than me!" Darcy snapped back.

She felt anger surge within her, feeling like a petty twelve-year-old and very much annoyed that Caitlyn could belittle her relationship in such a way. "If you must know, Caitlyn, I love Lauren. I love her a lot. So much so I'm going to ask her to marry me." She felt an odd sense of satisfaction as she watched blue eyes widen in shock. "I'm going to fix up my house, then ask her if she'll move in with me. If not here, then I'll sell it and we'll find somewhere else. I don't care where, as long as we live happily ever after together."

Caitlyn felt as if ice water had been dropped over her. She was completely numb. It had never occurred to her that Darcy could be so serious about Lauren. Okay, fine, they had travelled together, but Darcy was home now. Back with the family. She had to catch up on everything, get settled, before making such big decisions on her future.

Darcy smirked, liking that she had shocked Caitlyn, liking that for once she had been the one to hurt her. "So, as you can see, it does mean something." She turned and started climbing back up the ladder. "Go home to Ian, Caitlyn. And shove your damn apology!"

Her own anger rising out of hurt more than anything, Caitlyn spun on her heel and marched back toward her childhood home. "I was only worried about you!" she yelled out so Darcy would hear her. The fact the rest of the neighbourhood could also hear didn't occur to her. "I don't want you rushing in and getting hurt, because it'll be me who has to pick up the damn pieces!" She opened the front door and stepped inside, slamming the door on Darcy's retort.

Chapter Twelve

STACEY LOOPED HER arm through Darcy's and smiled when the younger woman grinned at her. "Whilst I am honoured you've asked me, Darcy, I can't help but wonder why it's not Caitlyn here with you. Isn't this a best friend thing?"

"Things aren't good between us." Darcy stared straight ahead, avoiding eye contact. "And it didn't seem right to ask her."

"She's the reason you left, isn't she?"

Glancing at the other woman, Darcy saw it wasn't a question as such, more that Stacey was seeking confirmation. "Yes, she is."

"You...loved her?" Stacey watched Darcy nod. "Do you still?" she asked curiously.

Darcy remained silent for the longest time, not sure she should answer the question. "Here we are, off to a jeweller to buy an engagement ring and you're asking me if I love another woman!" she chuckled, trying to get out of answering.

"It's a fair question," Stacey argued lightly. "If you still love Caitlyn, even a little bit, maybe you should rethink proposing to Lauren. She deserves all of you, not half."

Darcy stopped walking in the middle of the pavement, forcing people around them to swerve out of the way. She glared at those who swore her way before training dark, angry eyes on Stacey. "I love Lauren. I really do. I've spent the last five years in her company, three of those as her partner. Caitlyn..." She sighed heavily. "Caitlyn is the love that never was, nor ever will be. She's straight, she was always straight. And she's engaged to the lovable Ian." She shrugged. "Now, come on, enough of this. Let's get cracking on finding the best engagement ring we can find."

They started walking again, silent for a while, each losing themselves in their own thoughts. It was a typical winter's day, cold with a sharp breeze that went right through them. The sky above was grey, the clouds fat and threatening, be it rain or snow, nobody was sure. The weather reporters had cautioned on both.

"As long as you're happy and doing what's best for you and Lauren," Stacey finally said. "Then I suppose I'll give you my blessings and best wishes."

Darcy laughed out loud. "I wasn't looking for approval, Stacey! But since you're dishing it out, thank you." She glanced at the raven-haired woman. "Caitlyn'll always have a place in my heart, there's nothing I can do about that. But I refuse to sit back with my life on hold, just in case one day she decides...you know."

"I understand, Darcy. And, I think Lauren's a lovely woman. She seems to care about you very much."

"I bloody hope so!"

"She travelled around Europe with you, hon. She wouldn't have if she didn't care."

They walked on in silence for a minute, then two, Darcy getting the sense Stacey had something else to say but hesitant to put it out there. Content to wait her out, the jingle of familiar festive songs greeted her as they walked past open doorways of the shops. She had never liked Christmas until going to live with the Swailes family, then their love of the holiday had rubbed off on her.

"Come on then," Darcy finally chuckled. "Out with it."

"What?" Stacey looked at her in surprise.

"Whatever it is you're going to great lengths not to spit out."

"Always were attentive, Darce," Stacey smiled warmly and squeezed the arm she held.

"Makes me a decent photographer. Now out with it."

"Luke mentioned Caitlyn kissed you when you got home. Don't you think that's...odd?"

"It was odd, yeah. Chalk it up to one of those weird things people sometimes do."

"She still hasn't married Ian, and she was acting rather jealous on Sunday. Maybe she feels more for you than any of us realise."

"I asked her about her behaviour and she's happy to live in denial of whatever it may be she's feeling for me. Anyway, I'm off the market. I love Lauren."

"In that case, I want the first wedding invitation, what with being supportive and all."

"I'll see what I can do," Darcy grinned at the older woman. "Have you done your shopping yet?" she asked, changing the subject.

"Most of it. Still have some little bits to get, stocking fillers and so forth." She saw Darcy's lifted eyebrow and smiled. "Oh, no! No way am I telling you what I've bought, Darcy! If you're anything like the rest of them, you'll have told everyone by lunchtime!"

Laughing, Darcy came to a stop in front of a well-lit window display. "Here we go, how about we try in here?"

"We have to start somewhere, hon. Lead the way." She nudged the taller woman with her shoulder. "What have you got me?"

"I'll never tell!"

THE DAYS ROLLED past quickly, Darcy and Caitlyn back to not speaking to each other and neither doing anything to resolve things between them. Having fallen out with Darcy again and life being strained at home with Ian, Caitlyn took as many hours at the hospital as she could, losing herself in work, rather than sorting out her problems.

Darcy stubbornly ignored all the advice and suggestions from Tricia, Joe and the brothers, who all wanted to see the two friends at least on speaking terms again, especially for Christmas. To avoid the family and their constant concerns, arguments, and advice, she spent more and more time with Lauren, often being found behind the bar serving drinks. If she returned home, it was in the early hours when she knew everyone else would be in bed. Most nights she stayed with Lauren.

The couple settled easily back into life at home, both happy for the most part. Though there were days when Darcy felt something was bothering Lauren. The redhead never brought it up though, so she assumed it was a private matter.

Christmas morning came around and Darcy woke early, giddy and excited as a child. Getting up, she left Lauren sleeping soundly and padded to the kitchen to make a cup of tea. In the living room, she turned on the tree lights and sat drinking her tea, delighting in the sparkling lights. By the time she finished her morning cuppa, her girlfriend still hadn't woken up.

With her eyes full of glee, Darcy ran back into the bedroom and jumped onto the bed, bouncing up and down and laughing out loud when Lauren shot up into a sitting position, looking around in bewilderment, her hair wild and sticking in all directions.

"What? What is it?" Lauren asked in fear and confusion, still half asleep. One look at Darcy and suddenly she realised. After spending the last few years with the brunette, she knew what Darcy was like on Christmas morning. "Oh, God, Darcy!" she grumbled, sweeping back her hair while she glanced at the clock. "Have you seen the time?" she groaned, flopping back to the mattress.

"It's Christmas, baby! You have to wake up! Have to get up! There are presents to be picked up and shaken!" She looked hopefully at her girlfriend, waiting for the words.

"All right, you big goof! Go get the presents." She laughed as Darcy jumped off the bed and raced out of the bedroom. She listened to bare feet slapping on the floor as Darcy made her way to the living room where the five-foot tree was with neatly wrapped presents sitting beneath.

"Presents, presents, presents," Darcy chanted, shuffling back to the bedroom, her arms loaded with multicoloured-wrapped presents. She dropped her load on top of Lauren. "Don't start, there's more!" She ran back to retrieve the rest, quickly returning and taking a seat at the bottom of the bed, legs crossed, eyes on Lauren.

"I love you, you know," Lauren laughed and leaned forward until she could cup Darcy's cheek. "I have loved every minute I've spent with you over the last few years," she murmured, before kissing waiting lips. "Do I not get a morning coffee before we start?"

"Later. Presents first."

"Fine. Here," She picked up the gift she had gotten Darcy. "This is from...."

"No! Don't tell," Darcy interrupted. "It'll ruin the surprise of the gift tag."

Lauren sat back smiling and watched her adorable girlfriend in amusement. "You're right, my love. Carry on."

Darcy flipped over the tag and smiled as she read the short loving note. "Thanks, babe," she grinned, putting the gift down.

Lauren laughed. "You're not going to open it? After all that?"

"You always buy me great gifts. I want to save it for last, in case I get socks off everyone else!" Picking up another present, she read the tag then held the package out to Lauren.

"Ah, bless," Lauren said, reading the tag from Joaquina. "I hope she likes what we sent her." She opened the neatly wrapped present and oohed over the framed picture. "I think this is outside her father's place, isn't it?"

Darcy studied the painting. "It does look very similar. Does it have a label on the back?"

Turning the picture over, Lauren smiled as she found a small label noting the location of the painting and the artist. "That was sweet of her. Definitely happy memories. What did she send you?"

"A check. She's requesting a couple of my pictures." She

looked up at Lauren. "I'm not accepting this. Surely, she knows she can have any photo she wants. I'll send her a couple, along with this back."

"Give her a call later and explain that," Lauren suggested. "She might be insulted if you send it back."

"Good thinking. What's next?"

"Gifts from Kendall," Lauren smiled, looking down at the closest tag. "I dread to think what she might have sent!" She opened the wrapping and found a plain box that gave nothing away. Opening the box cautiously, she stared wide-eyed, her mouth hanging open. "Oh. My. God!" she breathed.

"What? What is it?" Darcy frowned, concerned by her girl-friend's reaction. "Has she sent you something...illegal?"

"She...she's sent me a...Gucci handbag! And a Gucci fragrance set! Oh, my God, I love her! Sorry, baby, I'm soooo dumping you!"

"No fair," Darcy pouted, though she knew it was a joke. She peeked inside the box and looked at the beige and ebony handbag. She didn't know a lot about handbags, she didn't want to know a lot about handbags, but they seemed to make Lauren happy. This one in particular had Lauren grinning from ear to ear.

"You know, I bet one of her happy brides gave this to her," the bar owner speculated, delicately touching the bag with a fingertip, an expression of wonder on her face. "Remember she told us about one of her well-off brides giving her a diamond necklace worth a couple of grand?"

"Uh-huh." Darcy opened her own gift, finding a small box. Inside sat a watch. A very nice watch. Picking up a note attached to the box, she read it aloud. "Sorry I broke yours, thought it was about time I replaced it." She smiled and slipped the watch on, then looked at Lauren, who was still staring at her handbag. Rolling her eyes at her girlfriend's behaviour, she got up and walked to where her jacket was hanging, taking out her gift for Lauren. "Here, babe. Merry Christmas."

Looking up, Lauren blinked, eyes falling to the present Darcy held out for her to take. "Oh, um, sorry, honey. I'm acting like a complete spaz!"

"No problem. I know you love your handbags!"

Lauren smiled as she opened the gift, fading slightly once she got the wrapping open to reveal a ring box. She looked up at Darcy in question, not sure it was what she thought it was. "Darce?"

"Open it, baby."

Looking back to the gift, Lauren carefully opened the small box and gasped, eyes widening, as she looked upon an eighteen carat, white gold, three-stone diamond ring.

"I love you, Lauren Cansdell. You've been a good friend to me, an even better girlfriend, and after spending the last five years with you, I...I want to make us official. Will you—"

"Darcy, I..." Lauren interrupted, light green eyes darting up to her girlfriend's face. "What about Caitlyn? Your feelings for her?"

"Sweetheart, Caitlyn's in the past now. I want to be with you. I want to make a life with you."

"What about the kiss?"

"What kiss?"

"I overheard Ian that day we went to lunch," Lauren finally admitted. "When you disappeared into the kitchen. He said...he said you two kissed, or she kissed you, I can't..." She shook her head. "Whatever. The point is, you didn't tell me, Darcy. You didn't mention a thing."

Darcy took one of Lauren's hands in both of her own, hating Ian even more. "It was nothing, that's why I didn't mention it. I went home and when I got through the door, there were greetings and hugs and yeah, she kissed me, but it didn't mean anything. Jesus, Lauren! I'm trying to propose here and you're accusing me of...of...cheating!"

"I'm not. I'm...God, I don't know what I'm doing. I just...I overheard what he said and I freaked I guess."

"That's why you made an excuse to leave after dinner."

"I'm sorry." Lauren squeezed Darcy's hand. "I should have mentioned all this sooner, instead of bottling it up and letting it stew." She looked at the ring still sitting in the box and smiled shyly. "You really want to marry me?"

"Yeah," Darcy chuckled nervously and nodded. "So, what do you say? Willing to spend at least a few more years in my company?"

Lauren laughed out loud. "Gee, that was romantic!"

"I tried to do it the romantic way, but you interrupted me!"

"Good point." Lauren held the box out for Darcy to take back, then held up her left hand and smiled. "Yes, Darcy. I'll spend a few more years in your company."

Laughing as she took the ring from the box, she slipped it onto Lauren's ring finger. "After all that excitement, I don't think I want to go home to face the family. God knows what will happen!"

Lauren laughed lightly, even though she was distracted, looking at the ring she now wore. Was this for real? Was Darcy really ready to make a full commitment to her and forget about Caitlyn? "We have to go, babe, you told them we would. And we got presents for everyone."

"How about we keep them and stay here instead? In bed." As her girlfriend shook her head, she got to her feet and stretched, groaning when her shoulders popped. "Now you're up, would you like a cup of coffee?"

"Ooh, yes, please."

"I picked up some croissants yesterday as well."

Light green eyes fell on the unopened present she had got Darcy. "Aren't you forgetting something?"

Darcy turned back to look at her girlfriend, her fiancée, and followed the pointing finger to her gift. "Oops. I mean, I was saving it. I knew it was there all along."

"Uh-huh," Lauren chuckled. "I'm going to jump in the shower. When are we heading out?"

"Around ten, though there's no rush."

WITH CHRISTMAS SONGS playing on the stereo, the delicious aroma of a roasting turkey wafting through the house, Tricia looked around her decorated home proudly, counting down to the time her family was due to arrive for the traditional opening of the presents. She knew Jeremy and Brian had likely been woken at the crack of dawn by their children, keen that Santa had been. She knew Darcy had likely woken Lauren, the photographer just as much a big kid now as she had been when younger. She smiled at the thought, once again delighted that this year Darcy was back.

As the doorbell rang, she smiled as her gaze did one more sweep of the living room to make sure everything was where it should be, then went to answer the door. She found a frowning Luke on the doorstep, along with his partner, Natalie, and little Olivia. "Merry Christmas!"

"Hello, Mum," Luke greeted, looking and sounding less than happy. "Merry Christmas. We're not too early, are we?"

"Of course not, love. Come on in. Hello, Natalie, Olivia. Everything all right?"

"Fine, Tricia. Though, we might not be able to stay long. I did tell my mum we'd be round hers today," Natalie said, scowling at Luke.

"Leave it out, Natalie. We always come here for Christmas," Luke muttered. "Your damn family is a nightmare. You say so all the time."

"It's Christmas, Luke. You could at least make an effort."

Ignoring the bickering couple, Tricia picked up Olivia and carried her through to the kitchen. "Did Santa pay a visit?"

"Yeah," the little girl nodded, a big grin on her face. "I got a scooter."

"You did! Wow, just what you wanted." Setting Olivia on her own feet, Tricia handed her a festive cookie she had baked fresh that morning. The sugary treats were a family favourite but tended to make everyone hyperactive so had to be hidden. "There you go, sweetheart. Something to enjoy while we wait for everyone else to get here."

"Thank you, Ganma."

"You're welcome, my lovely. Are you looking forward to today? Seeing all your cousins and uncles and aunts?"

The little girl nodded. "We have lots of fun. And Mummy said Santa might have come here too."

"Maybe, little one." Tricia glanced out of the kitchen when the doorbell rang again. "You go into the living room, Olivia, and show your daddy what you got while I get the door." She walked the little girl to the living room doorway and ushered her inside before heading to the front door and opening it, finding Brian and his family on the doorstep. "Merry Christmas!"

"Merry Christmas, Tricia," Isabella greeted cheerfully. "Ooh, what a lovely smell. It smells like cinnamon."

"Merry Christmas, Mum," Brian grouched, not a happy bunny.

"Don't be so grumpy, Brian," Isabella scolded, her mood not to be dampened. "You're making a fuss for no reason whatsoever."

"No reason! Look at me!" Brian pouted, poking at the sweater he wore.

"Don't make such a fuss, sweetheart. I used to dress you in far worse when you were little," Tricia scolded, earning a laugh from Isabella and a deep scowl from her son. "Come on in. Luke and Natalie are already here."

"Natalie?" Brian asked in surprise. "Decided to grace us with her presence, has she? What's Luke's mood like?" he asked softly.

Tricia shook her head. "I'm sure you can cheer him up." Her eyes dropped to his sweater and she chuckled.

"Anyone else here besides Luke and family?" Isabella asked.

"Not yet, but it won't be long. I expect Jeremy got as early a wakeup call as you did." She looked down at Zerenity and Ruby. "Christmas cookies, girls?"

"Oh, I don't know about that, Tricia. I don't want them having too much sugar," Isabella warned.

"One won't hurt," Tricia insisted. "They can have it with a glass of milk. Besides, I've already given Olivia one. Can't give to one without everyone else being included." She led the way to the living room. "Look who's here!" she announced cheerfully.

"Oh, my God, Brian!" Luke exclaimed in amusement. "What are you wearing?"

AN HOUR LATER, Lauren sat on the Swailes' sofa with Isabella, Luke's girlfriend Natalie, and Tricia around her, the three women oohing and ahhing over her engagement ring.

"It's beautiful, Lauren," Natalie gushed. Her eyes flicked to Luke. "Don't you think so, Luke?"

"Very nice," he replied, not looking up from his position on the floor where he was playing with Olivia and her new Tigger toy, which was supposed to sing, bounce, roll, and talk, only Natalie had forgotten to buy batteries.

"That's the sort of ring I hope to get," Natalie continued, turning back to the three women she was conversing with and missing Luke rolling his eyes. "It's elegant, stylish, and not too big it will catch on everything. Maybe one day, I suppose."

"I don't think marriage is something that should be rushed into," Isabella said diplomatically.

"I agree," Natalie nodded. "But when you love each other, it's the next step, isn't it?"

Zerenity walked up to her father and tugged on his hand to get his attention. "When, Daddy?" She wanted to open the presents beneath the tree and didn't understand the hold up.

"Soon, sweetie," Brian replied. "We're waiting on Uncle Jeremy and Aunty Caitlyn. Once they get here, you can open your presents."

"We could give them their selection boxes," Joe suggested.

Tricia looked horrified. "And ruin their dinner? I've already spent hours in the kitchen!"

"Oh, come on, sweetheart. One treat isn't going to hurt," Joe told her.

"One treat won't, but you do remember when the boys were young, don't you? That year Luke scoffed the whole box in half an hour and spent the rest of the day complaining of belly ache."

The occupants in the living room laughed while Luke frowned. "I don't remember that at all. Are you sure it was me?"

With the children all looking at her, Tricia conceded. "All right, one treat won't hurt in the grand scheme of things."

"What time are you aiming to have dinner ready, Mum?" Brian asked while his wife knelt as near to the tree as she could get to find the long box-shaped gifts she was looking for.

"Between three-thirty and four. You know we like to watch the Queen's speech at three."

The doorbell sounded and Joe got up to go and see who it was. Devon and Anya, Jeremy and Stacey's two eldest children, charged into the living room clutching new toys and bellowing, "Merry Christmas!" They were followed by Harry, Jeremy, and Stacey, and lastly, Joe, who was carrying Marissa, decked out in a reindeer onesie.

"Hello, all," Jeremy greeted, already looking haggard. "Merry Christmas."

Brian burst out laughing when he saw what his older brother was wearing. "Hey, Frosty. How's it hanging?"

"Yeah, laugh it up, Rudolph! Yours ain't much better!" He flopped down onto the two-person sofa and grumpily crossed his arms across the "Frosty the Snowman" sweater. "Why do we let them get away with making us look like idiots?"

"Love makes you do the wacky!" Brian replied easily, leaning over to kiss his wife's cheek, before getting to his feet and heading out of the room.

Olivia walked up to Jeremy and reached out to rub his sweater. "I like it Unkey Jemmy."

Smiling, he picked the little girl up and set her on his lap. "That makes it worthwhile then, Olivia." He tickled her sides. "Did Santa visit you?" He watched her nod. "He stopped by our house as well. Every year it happens," he grumbled. "He forgot the blo—the batteries!"

"He forgot at my house as well!" Luke grinned. "Maybe we should write to him and complain!"

"Yeah, unless he left them here under Mum and Dad's tree?" Jeremy said, looking to the tree sitting in the corner. The large decorated tree had numerous presents stacked underneath, brightly coloured wrapping paper of all designs clashing garishly.

"You'll be happy to know we have batteries for all," Tricia smiled, knowing her sons would forget batteries and having purchased some of every kind.

"Do you hear that, you lot?" Stacey said to her children, none of them paying any attention as they played happily. "Grandma has batteries for your new toys."

"What have we missed?" Jeremy asked, sitting back and relaxing for the first time that day. "Where's Caitlyn?"

"Not here yet. She's late, as usual," Brian replied, as he walked in with a tray of mugs, glasses, and sippy-cups. "Thought you could do with an eggnog," he directed at his eldest brother. "Or I could make coffee."

"You're a godsend, Bri," Jeremy replied, eyes on the eggnog as he eagerly reached out for a glass. "They got us up at five!"

"Darcy had me up at six!" Lauren chuckled, looking at her now blushing girlfriend.

The Swailes family laughed. "You're not still doing that, are you, Darcy?" Tricia chuckled.

"It used to be the perk of my year!" Joe laughed. "Never failed to make me laugh!"

"My favourite memory was that year Luke and Brian snuck down and hid all the gifts," Tricia chuckled. "Poor Darcy's little face when she ran in here and found nothing!"

"Yes, thank you, all," Darcy grumbled, though grinning from ear to ear. "Now I've been thoroughly embarrassed, I think I'll go in search of those batteries."

"First drawer in the kitchen," Joe told her, winking.

Smiling, she got up from the floor and left the warm room just as Jeremy asked Lauren what Santa got her for Christmas. She found batteries of all shapes and sizes and was returning to the living room when the doorbell rang. "I'll get it," she called out, knowing who it was going to be. She opened the door and smiled at Caitlyn, ignoring the scowling Ian completely. "Hey, Caitlyn. Merry Christmas."

"Merry Christmas, Darce." Caitlyn stepped inside and hugged her friend, surprising both Darcy and Ian. "Where is everyone? In the living room?" She walked through before Darcy could respond. "Merry Christmas!" she greeted as she walked in. "Ahh, don't you two look adorable in your not matching, but equally cute sweaters!"

Darcy turned to Ian. "You coming in, or you going to stay out there all day?"

Ian's scowl returned as he stepped inside, stomping his feet on the mat to rid them of snow.

She left him to it, returning to the living room in time to stop

Jeremy and Brian from ganging up on a ticklish Caitlyn. "Right then. Who needs batteries?" she asked loudly.

"Would you like a cuppa, Catie?" Joe asked, realising his daughter didn't have a drink yet. "Eggnog, coffee, tea?"

"We've started on the eggnog," Stacey grinned.

"Some of us have," Isabella pouted, a hand on her belly.

"I'll take a cup of tea, please, Dad," Caitlyn told her father. "Ian, would you like a beverage?"

"I'll take an eggnog, please," Ian said politely. "'Tis the season, so the saying goes. You can always drive us home, Caitlyn, if it proves potent."

"Dad's eggnog is potent," she smiled. "Rum as usual, Dad?"

"Only a splash!" Joe grinned, before leaving the room.

"So, Darce," Jeremy smirked, knowing his next question was likely to rile up his sister. "Ready to make an honest woman of Lauren, are you? Very nice ring by the way."

"Thanks, Jeremy. I always did have good taste," Darcy replied, looking to Lauren and winking.

While the conversation carried on around her, Caitlyn stared at the engagement ring sitting on Lauren's finger. She couldn't believe Darcy went through with it! She actually proposed!

"Any idea on when you want the wedding?" Isabella asked. "Brian and I got married in January. Terrible weather, but then," she looked adoringly at her husband, "we didn't want to wait."

Darcy and Lauren looked at each other and smiled shyly. "We were actually thinking about doing it at the end of February," Darcy answered.

"Our anniversary is during the first week of February," Lauren informed them. "And we'd like to do it after that."

"So Darcy never forgets?" Luke asked, smiling.

"You know her so well!" Lauren laughed.

"Hey!" Darcy protested, while everyone else but Caitlyn laughed. "None of you are invited now!" She finished her tea and set her mug back on the tray.

"Oh, come on, honey," Lauren said, a devilish smile curling her lips. "We have to invite them. Think of all the free gifts."

It was Darcy's turn to laugh while the rest of the family looked outraged. "That is why I love her!"

"You don't think you're rushing in?" Caitlyn asked, eyes on Darcy. "Engaged on Christmas, married by February."

"Why wait when it's right," Darcy smiled tightly.

"What did you get for Christmas, Darce?" Stacey asked, moving the conversation on.

"A top-of-the-range camera," Darcy told her proudly. "I almost burst into tears when I opened it!" she chuckled. "But it was very much overshadowed by a gift Lauren received from a friend of ours. Tell the ladies what you got, babe."

"Kendall, our friend from New York, sent me a genuine Gucci handbag."

"Oh. My. God!" was squealed by Stacey and Natalie. "I can't believe you didn't bring it with you!" Stacey scolded.

Laughing, Darcy got to her feet, needing to use the bathroom. "Excuse me. Nature calls. Lauren? Hey, babe? You going to be okay down here with this wild bunch? Lauren, are you listening?"

"Fine, Darce. See you soon."

Darcy shook her head while the brothers laughed, taking it with good humour. She left the living room and headed upstairs, needing a breather. After years away from the family, she had forgotten how hectic Christmas could be in the Swailes' home. The house was a cacophony of noise from numerous toys, giggling and squealing children, laughing and conversing from the adults, and a continuous stream of festive songs coming from the stereo. And later, other family members would drop in as well.

She had grown used to having a quiet day with just Lauren for company and was now a little overwhelmed.

Standing at the sink, she looked at her reflection in the mirror and saw unhappiness just about hidden in her eyes. She sighed heavily, her heart aching for what she didn't have this holiday, rather than what she did have. She should be one of the happiest women on Earth right now, she thought, turning on the tap and cupping water into her hands to splash on her face. She had a beautiful fiancée, was surrounded by family, and yet... She conjured up the image of her best friend, the light blue eyes that haunted her, the smile, which caused a cute nose to crinkle slightly, a laugh that made her heart expand with love.

She thought she had left all these stupid feelings behind her. It will never happen, she told herself firmly. Lauren loves you. She wants to be with you, she wants a life with you. She has never hurt or rejected you. All she wants is to be loved in return. Be happy with what you have and don't dwell on what you don't have. She turned off the tap and reached for a towel to dry her face with. She couldn't help thinking what if, though, Caitlyn's actions making her think things she had no right thinking.

She threw the towel into the hamper and took a deep, cleansing breath, readying herself to go back out and face the family.

Unlocking and opening the bathroom door, she blinked in surprise. "Wow. Déjà vu!"

"Don't worry, I'm not going to ask you to be my maid of honour." Caitlyn smiled.

"So, what's up?"

Caitlyn's smile faded. "I um...could I talk to you for a minute?"

"You sure that's a good idea? All we seem to do is end up arguing."

"It's Christmas. I'm sure we can be civil for a few minutes."

Not wanting to leave Lauren on her own for too long, surrounded by people she was still getting to know, Darcy hesitated.

"Just a minute, Darce. Please?"

"Sure, okay. Do you want to," she nodded in her bedroom's direction, "step into my office?"

Nodding, Caitlyn smiled again, then led the way, walking inside the bedroom and stopping in the middle of the room. Blue eyes drifted around, taking note of the mementos from Darcy's travels sitting on bookshelves, the desk, and any other available surface where they would fit. Her gaze lingered on the photos, some of Lauren, some of the couple together, others showing people she didn't know. It made her heart ache knowing that was a part of Darcy's life she wasn't a part of.

Done with her assessment of the room, she turned to face Darcy, who stood patiently waiting. "I want to apologise for the last time we spoke. I shouldn't have belittled your relationship."

"No, you shouldn't have."

"It occurred to me that..." she exhaled a tremulous breath, "we've lost our way, Darce. I don't know how the wedge between us got so huge, but it did." She watched the taller woman frown. "Our friendship is the most important thing in both our lives and yet we...we lost track of that. I miss our friendship, Darcy. I miss you."

Running her tongue across her top lip while she stalled for time to think, Darcy slowly nodded. "Yeah, I miss you too, Caitlyn. But things can never go back to how they once were," she said slowly. "I love you. That's out there now, I can no longer hide the fact."

"The simple truth is you're with Lauren now. You're engaged. Just like I am to Ian. There will never be anything romantic between us, but you and I can still have friendship." She held out a small gift. "I got this for you. I've done a lot of thinking lately, and I...I want our friendship to make it."

"Thanks. I got you one. It's downstairs under the tree."

"Open it," she nodded at the present Darcy now held. "Up here, while we're alone."

Darcy chuckled nervously as she eyed the gift. "Catie, if you're going to ask me to marry you, you're far too late," she joked. Unwrapping the gift, she found herself holding a ring box. Eyebrow raised, she looked at Caitlyn curiously before opening the box and staring down at a Claddagh band ring. Glancing up, she smiled as she met blue eyes. "Thank you, Caitlyn. I...I don't know what to say."

"I hope it fits!" Caitlyn laughed nervously, watching Darcy take the ring out of the box and examine the message.

"With my two hands I give you my heart and crown it with my love," she read aloud, smiling sadly.

"You gave me your heart once upon a time, it's only fair I give you mine," Caitlyn said affectionately, watching her friend's eyes fall to the heart pendant necklace resting against her chest.

"I can't believe you still have that."

"Why wouldn't I?"

"I don't know," Darcy shrugged. Feeling heart sick, she slipped the ring onto her right index finger and smiled. "Perfect fit. Thank you."

"You're welcome."

"You'll always have my friendship, Caitlyn. I promise you that." She pulled her friend into a hug, eyes closing as her heart ached, knowing this was all she would ever get and feeling like she had closure. "Come on, we better get back downstairs. I've left Lauren alone with the brothers far too long!"

Caitlyn held onto Darcy a little longer, breathing her in, reminding herself of her touch, then let go and stepped back. "Just to warn you, when I left the living room, Mum was asking Lauren about the ins and outs of a gay wedding."

Darcy groaned. "Oh, God! What have I let myself in for?"

Returning to the living room in time to stop an argument between Natalie and Luke from taking hold, Caitlyn and Darcy found some sitting space and settled down, Darcy catching the suspicious look Lauren shot her way.

With everyone seated, fresh drinks for them on the coffee table, they all looked to Tricia for the go ahead to open their presents.

Smiling lovingly, Tricia delighted in the power she had over them. "All right, go on." She laughed out loud when Darcy and the grandchildren dived toward the tree. "Oh, Darcy, what are you like!"

"You cannot honestly tell me you're not the least bit excited?"

"I never said that."

"Good," Darcy grinned, picking up a brightly wrapped box and passing it Tricia's way. "In that case, you can have your gift then."

"Daddy, these mine?" Olivia asked, guarding the biggest presents with her small frame.

"Not all of them, bubba." Searching for one of his gifts for his daughter, Luke pulled it out from near the front. The gifts were organised into size order, the bigger ones toward the rear and out of the way, the smaller ones at the front and within easy reach. "Here we go, baby."

"It not big one," the little girl pouted.

"Start with the small ones first." He laughed as Olivia tore the paper to shreds in seconds.

"Fwozen!" Olivia squealed in delight, hugging the cuddly toy reindeer of Sven from the movie to her chest and ignoring the princess dress that was also wrapped up within.

"What did Santa get you, baby?" Natalie asked, getting the little girl's attention.

While Olivia ran over to her mother, Darcy handed gifts to all the kids first, knowing they wouldn't wait patiently. She never had.

"God, if I hear that song one more time!" Brian grumbled.

"The Frozen song?" Luke asked.

"It seems to be the only thing ever on in our house." He smiled brightly as he handed his wife a neatly wrapped gift.

"That's the first film. This is the second," Luke rolled his eyes. "You just wait until they discover that!"

Gifts were handed around to all, wrapping paper floating to the carpet, boxes being ripped open and squeals of delight filling the air. Joe appreciated the bottle of good Scotch Darcy and Lauren gave him, the aftershave from Luke and Natalie, the digital camera from his wife, the novelty socks from his grandchildren, the football ticket from Brian, and the new phone from Jeremy and Stacey, even though he hated the devices and how technical they had gotten.

Tricia smiled, thanked, and hugged everyone for her books, the crystal figurines, the bread maker, a bath set, and DVDs of her favourite chick-flicks. Isabella cried when she opened a jewellery box and found a gold heart pendant within, capable of holding pictures of her daughters. She wrapped her arms tightly around her husband's neck and wouldn't let go until Natalie squealed in a pitch only she could hit when she unwrapped the necklace she had been admiring the last time she was in the town centre.

"Okay, so it's not the engagement ring I was hoping for. But this is definitely a close second," she grinned, making Luke roll his eyes.

Jeremy adored the cufflinks he got from Darcy and Lauren, Luke loved his new tool kit, and Darcy cried, though she denied it, when she unwrapped the collage of family pictures set in a beautiful frame.

"So you don't forget us if you ever disappear again!" Brian teased.

After all the gifts had been shared around, the space beneath the tree suddenly bare, Darcy looked around the living room and smiled brightly, heart filled with love and contentment. She had missed this, the family, the love, the happiness. She regretted not coming back sooner. But she was back now, and she was going to take it all in and treasure every minute of it.

Tricia looked around her living room and smiled despite the room looking like a wrapping paper monster had exploded in it. The grandchildren were happy, Luke, Brian, and Jeremy were busy studying instruction manuals of the many new toys they would have to put up, put together, or find batteries for. Stacey was lost in reading the manual for her new mobile phone, Joe was tinkering with his new camera, and Isabella and Natalie were chatting easily with Lauren, who had fitted in nicely.

And Caitlyn and Darcy. Tricia smiled even more brightly as she watched them interact. This was the best present she could have hoped for, Darcy being home and her daughter being happy again.

Knowing she couldn't sit and observe all day, she got to her feet. "I better see to the dinner," she announced.

"I thought the turkey was already in?" Joe frowned. "Because if it's not..."

"It is. But the vegetables need peeling and cutting. Does anyone need anything? Something to snack on. Fresh drinks?"

"Would you like a hand with the veg?" Darcy asked. "I think I've shirked the duty for far too long."

"So, that's why you stayed away!" Luke teased.

"I wouldn't say no, Darcy, thank you," Tricia smiled. After taking drink requests, they made their way to the kitchen to continue the dinner preparations. Now away from prying eyes, Tricia wrapped Darcy into a tight hug. "Thank you," she murmured, her voice choked with emotion, "for coming home. I don't know why you chose now to do it, I don't care. Just know that we have all missed you very much and you being here now is the best Christmas present you could have given us."

"Sorry it took me so long to realise what's important," Darcy apologised, ashamed she had caused so much hurt.

"You're here now." She stepped back and affectionately rubbed the taller woman's arm. "Right, I shall check the turkey while you get everyone the drinks they want. Then, we'll see about the veg."

"On it, Mum." Darcy winked and turned away to complete the request.

"So, can I ask, why an end of February wedding?"

"We just don't see the point in waiting. We've been in a relationship for the past three years, have lived together all over Europe. What would be the point in putting it off?"

"Nicer weather?" Tricia chuckled.

Laughing, Darcy nodded. "Besides that."

"A spring wedding would be nice, just as all the flowers start to bloom. It shouldn't be too hot either, which would please everyone."

Finished with making drinks, Darcy placed the glasses and cups on a tray. "I'll be back in a sec. You keep plotting and planning."

Left alone, Tricia opened the oven and checked on the turkey's progress. Happy with how it was coming along, she shut the door and turned her attention to the bag of potatoes that needed peeling and washing and rubbing in duck fat.

"To make up for a cold wedding, I figure I'll take Lauren somewhere hot for our honeymoon," Darcy said on her return to the kitchen. "Maybe the Caribbean."

"What about the rest of us?" Tricia teased.

"Knowledge that we're blissfully happy?" Grinning, she looked around for something to do. "What would you like me to do?"

"The parsnips need peeling," Tricia replied, pointing to the counter on her right. "But I'm busy peeling the potatoes, so you'll have to wait."

"Can't I use a normal knife? I'm fairly sure it'll do the same job."

"Yes, but a peeler was made to peel. If we don't put it to good use, it'll feel unloved."

"You're insane," Darcy chuckled.

"Ah, but still you love me."

"I do. Don't ever change." Smiling, Darcy walked to the cutlery drawer and got out a knife. Picking up the bag of parsnips, she joined Tricia by the bin.

They worked quietly, both focused on the job at hand, laughter and small talk drifting to them from the living room, little feet stamping about as the children played. Darcy loved being home. A home that was filled with love and laughter. A home where the people she called family always made her welcome. They had forgiven her for staying away so long and had welcomed Lauren with open arms. She couldn't ask for more.

"Have you given any thought as to where you're going to live once you're married?" Tricia asked, eventually breaking the silence that had settled between them.

"Not really. I thought maybe we could live next door if I do up the old place. But I'm not sure how Lauren feels about that. She's got her flat, but..."

"But?"

"I don't think I want to live above a pub. What if someone tries to break in thinking there's money lying around?"

"It's not ideal for children either," Tricia pointed out.

Misunderstanding Tricia's meaning, Darcy agreed. "Exactly. We couldn't have everyone over. The flat is on the small side, so we would have to host down in the pub itself."

"I meant if you have children," Tricia corrected. "Next door would be perfect for raising a family. Do you think you want children, Darce?"

Blushing to the tips of her ears, Darcy focused intently on the parsnip she was peeling. "It's...not something we've ever discussed."

"That's two pretty big decisions you haven't discussed," Tricia said carefully.

"Are you suggesting we don't rush into marriage until we have everything planned out like a battle plan?"

"Not at all, love. But you do need to discuss where you're going to live, don't you think?"

Darcy conceded the point with a nod. "It will definitely be local. Lauren has the pub to run and I want to be close to you guys. Whether that means living next door or somewhere new, I'm not sure. I'll bring it up after Christmas is out of the way."

"Next door is a perfectly good house, why would you buy somewhere new?"

"I'm not sure how Lauren would feel about being so close to the family. To Caitlyn," Darcy admitted. "She...has concerns."

Tricia waited for the younger woman to elaborate, but nothing further followed. "Have you and Caitlyn made peace?"

"I guess a truce has been called for Christmas. Can't promise it's going to last though."

Glancing at Darcy, Tricia spotted the frown creasing her brow. "What happened to make you fall out this time?"

"I'd rather not say. If we keep these disagreements to ourselves, no one will be forced to pick sides."

"Did it occur when you were both here putting up the decorations? I seem to remember Ian leaving in a huff and a shouting match between you and Catie out the front."

"It's Christmas Day and there's a truce," Darcy replied, refusing to discuss it further. She grinned at Tricia. "Is it wrong I hope Ian gets drunk on Joe's eggnog and makes a total tit of himself?"

Tricia burst out laughing. "I refuse to answer that."

"On account of you're hoping he does too?"

Laughing again, Tricia shook her head in amusement and turned her attention back to peeling. "Oh, how I've missed your wicked sense of humour!"

Chapter Thirteen

CAITLYN SIGHED HEAVILY for the third time that night, unable to sleep, rampant thoughts keeping her from drifting off. She looked at Ian slumbering peacefully beside her and sighed again. She couldn't shake the feeling that everything was all wrong. Darcy was doing the wrong thing, she thought, gazing back up at the ceiling.

After Christmas, the days seemed to fly by too fast for Caitlyn's liking. January had come and gone with Darcy and Lauren arranging their wedding, rushing about trying to find a suitable location to hold the ceremony, looking into venues to host the reception, ordering and sending out invites. All too soon January was gone and had swiftly been replaced by February.

The thing that really irked Caitlyn was how happy her mother was. Tricia was delighted when Darcy included her in the planning, asked her advice on certain things, and was more than happy to help in any way.

During the first week of February, the couple had taken time out from wedding planning to celebrate their anniversary. Darcy organised a weekend break away, knowing Lauren was getting stressed over the preparations, and they left everything in the capable hands of Tricia, the aunts, and Stacey.

Once they returned, relaxed and rejuvenated, the countdown to their wedding had started.

Caitlyn smiled through it all, though she had a sinking feeling in her stomach. Darcy was happy, truly happy, but she couldn't help questioning herself, her true feelings. Now she was nearly out of time and still found herself undecided on whether to speak up or not.

She should go and talk to her, Caitlyn thought, filled with a sudden urgency. She was her friend after all. Her best friend. Friends can tell each other anything, can share concerns, worries, and problems. She should share her concerns before it's too late.

With the wedding the next day, Caitlyn had decided out of the blue to spend the night at her parents' house, telling anyone who paused long enough to listen that it would make things easier the next day when they all left. Ian decided to stay too, not wanting to leave his fiancée in Darcy's company, despite Caitlyn assuring him nothing was going to happen, especially since Tricia, Joe, and Luke would also be around.

The evening itself had been pleasant, the family sharing stories, playing a board game, and watching a movie, while drinking, snacking, and enjoying each other's company. Except for Ian
who had been in a mood all night.

Now, it was after midnight and everyone but Caitlyn was
asleep it seemed. She waited. Waited for a sign that maybe she
should let things be, let thoughts and feelings go unsaid. Maybe
Darcy was doing the right thing, she thought, eyes darting
around her dimly lit room. But then why did she have the feeling
this was all so wrong?

The bedroom remained silent and still, no obvious sign happening to deter her from doing what she thought was best. Mind
made up, she pushed the duvet back and slipped out of bed, grabbing her robe and quickly putting it on. With a last glance at Ian
to make sure he was still sleeping, she quietly left the room.

Making her way along the hall to Darcy's bedroom, her footsteps softened by the carpet, she paused at the closed door, seeing
light spilling out beneath. She didn't know whether to be happy
that Darcy was still awake or not but took it for the sign she'd
been looking for.

Without knocking, she walked into the bedroom and after
shutting the door quietly behind herself, made her way to the bed
where Darcy was sitting on the edge, staring down at the carpet.
"Darce," she whispered softly, coming to a stop in front of her
friend. She stepped between Darcy's spread legs and stroked her
friend's short dark locks. She smiled lovingly as Darcy wrapped
her arms around her body, holding her closer.

Darcy turned her head, laying it against Caitlyn's stomach.
Neither of them said a word, both savouring the intimate position
they found themselves in. Both were acutely aware of how right it
felt.

"You couldn't sleep?" Caitlyn asked softly, deciding she
should break the silence between them.

"No," Darcy sighed. "Can't seem to stop thinking."

Caitlyn's eyes slid shut, shivering when she felt Darcy's
warm breath filtering through the thin T-shirt she wore. Being
like this with her friend seemed so right, Darcy's gentle touch,
herself caressing brunette locks. The moment was perfect, like a
snapshot from their life. It took her thoughts back to the night of
passion they had shared, not the act itself, but the afterward,
when they had held each other.

She slowly ran her fingers through Darcy's hair, thinking

over every thought she had in her head, everything she was feeling and everything she wanted to say, before it was too late. "Darcy, don't marry her," she breathed softly.

Not sure she had heard right, Darcy moved her head away from Caitlyn's body and looked up into blue eyes. "What?"

"Don't marry Lauren. She's not the one for you."

"Oh, really. And who is? You?" Darcy growled, suddenly furious. Once again, here was Caitlyn trying to turn her life upside down. "No, wait a minute, you're engaged to fuck-face!"

Stopping herself from scolding Darcy about picking on Ian, Caitlyn set her hands on her friend's shoulders. "Think seriously about this. You're going to make a lifelong commitment to Lauren in front of friends and family, but do you really love her? Can you look me in the eye and tell me honestly that you love her half as much as you love me?"

Darcy couldn't. She wished she could, but the truth was Caitlyn was the love of her life. But too many times Caitlyn had made her feelings clear. She continually refused to acknowledge there may be something deeper than friendship between them. "Why are you in here, Caitlyn?"

"I'm trying to make you see sense before it's too late."

Getting to her feet, she forced Caitlyn to take a step backward. "All you needed to do was say the word and I would have been yours forever. But you didn't. You always brushed my feelings off like they were nothing and now it's too late. I will not spend the rest of my life pining for you! A woman who can't even admit how she really feels! I'm with an amazing woman, who loves me more than I deserve. Tomorrow, I'm going to marry her and spend the rest of my life trying to be the best version of me that she deserves."

"It's a mistake, Darcy."

Scoffing, Darcy shook her head. "Are you going to leave him, Catie? Are you going to run away with me and give us a chance? See if we're the real deal?"

If she said yes, would Darcy call off this stupid event? "Darcy, I..." She shook her head, flustered and confused. "What are you saying?"

"You know what I'm saying, Caitlyn. You're not stupid." Looking at her, Darcy already knew, without Caitlyn saying anything, that things were never going to be different.

Slowly, Caitlyn shook her head. She couldn't agree to anything, especially not to running away with Darcy. That had never been her intention. She had merely wanted her friend to realise that marrying Lauren was the wrong choice.

"Then how dare you come in here, after letting him fuck you no less, and tell me, the day before my wedding, not to get married. I know you don't like her, have never liked her. I know you're bitter over the fact I went travelling with her. But I love her! She makes me happy and I can make her happy. I can be a good partner to her." She exhaled, suddenly exhausted as the fight left her. "Get out, Caitlyn."

"Darcy..."

"Get out!" she growled, turning her back on Caitlyn.

DARCY WAS WOKEN the next morning by a frantic Tricia, the older woman running around like a headless chicken and cursing Darcy for over-sleeping on her wedding day. Letting Tricia rant and rave at her, she eventually climbed out of bed, kissed the woman's forehead, and smiled serenely, calmly telling Tricia everything would be fine.

Left alone in her bedroom, Darcy walked to the window and looked out on the day, staring out at a grey sky and plump clouds that were threatening rain. Hope that's not a bad omen, she thought with a frown. She wasn't really one for superstitions and signs, but she felt uneasy and couldn't pinpoint why.

Throwing on a robe over her shorts and T-shirt, she decided to eat breakfast before getting ready, just knowing that if she put on her wedding clothes, she was likely to spill something down them.

"There she is!" Luke greeted cheerfully. "The wife-to-be. How are you feeling?"

"Morning, Luke. I feel fine."

"There's still time for you to do a runner," he teased. Not long after the festive season, he had finally broken up with Natalie, much to everyone's relief, and moved back home with Tricia, Joe, and Darcy, to figure out his next move. Once Natalie had finally calmed down, the couple had spent many hours talking and decided it was for the best. It ended civilly, with Luke getting to see Olivia whenever he wanted. The family was hoping things remained amicable.

Making her way to the table, Darcy chuckled. "Now why would I do something so foolish as to run away from Lauren? You have met her, right?" She sat down and met Caitlyn's blue gaze, her own eyes cold and indifferent. She looked up and smiled at Joe as he placed a full English breakfast in front of her.

"God, how I missed your cooking when I was away!" she sighed, picking up her knife and fork and digging in with gusto. "Though, Lauren's a great cook herself. She's taken good care of me over the years."

"All these years and you still haven't learnt how to cook, Darce!" Joe teased.

"I can grill to perfection, what more do you want?" Darcy grinned.

"Ah, that's my girl," he complimented proudly. "Do you want a cup of tea or coffee?"

"Tea, please." She glanced at Caitlyn again. "No Ian this morning?"

"He's going to meet me at the church."

"You looking forward to married life, Darcy?" Luke asked, stacking his scrambled egg onto his toast.

She chewed as she thought his question over. "I guess I am. We love each other, we've lived together for these last few years, so nothing is really going to change. This will just be us living together without the beautiful sun and scenery!" she chuckled. "It should be fine, this is the next step, the official step."

"I've sampled your cooking, if she's stuck with you this long, nothing's going to scare her off!" Luke smirked.

"Ha ha," she rolled her eyes and grinned back at him.

Luke watched her for a minute, then another, knowing her well enough to sense something was off. "Everything good, Darce?" he asked, genuine concern in his voice.

She looked up from her breakfast and met his concerned gaze. "I guess I'm a little worried because of my upbringing."

"Oh, Darcy, you're nothing like your parents," Caitlyn said. "You've grown up to be a wonderful woman."

"Catie's right," Luke nodded in agreement. "And you have the added quality of not liking alcohol as much as they did."

Tricia hurried into the kitchen and looked around in dismay. "Why aren't any of you dressed?"

Joe smiled lovingly at his wife and kissed her cheek before he walked past her with Darcy's cup of tea. "Come on, love, you know how they eat like a wild pack of animals," he chuckled. "If they had got dressed up, there would now be a number of grease stains, tomato sauce stains, egg marks, and God knows what else on them!" He laughed aloud and tried to duck the paper napkins thrown his way. "Luke's already dropped his toast twice!"

Tricia smiled. "You're right. I know you're right." She moved across the kitchen and used one of the napkins to wipe Luke's egg-stained cheek. "I'm—"

"Panicking over nothing," Joe said affectionately. He pulled out a chair for his wife. "Have a seat and relax, love. This lot are almost done eating and once they are, they're going to go upstairs and start getting ready. Aren't you?" he asked the group.

"Yes, of course, Daddy," Caitlyn smiled sweetly.

"Sure are," Luke nodded.

"Well, Megan is waiting to do your hair, Caitlyn. I should probably take her a cuppa and tell her you'll be at least twenty minutes."

"I'll do it, you relax," Joe smiled, squeezing his wife's shoulder.

Eating what she could manage as butterflies invaded her belly, Darcy excused herself and retreated upstairs to start getting ready.

Changes in British Law had been made and same-sex couples could now marry in religious buildings, with the exception of Church of England buildings, as long as the religious institution didn't decline to conduct the marriage. Lauren had wanted a church service and had opted for the quaint little church she had used for her uncle's funeral service, delighted when the priest told them he was happy to marry them.

Darcy had opted for smart Oxford grey trousers, with a crisp white shirt and a grey pin-striped waistcoat. It was as close to a morning suit as she was willing to get. She had asked the brothers to be her best men, not because she couldn't choose between them, but because she loved all three equally. They would all be wearing traditional morning suits.

Looking in the full-length mirror at her reflection, she silently recited her vows, hoping that when the moment arrived, she wouldn't forget everything she wanted to say. "What am I forgetting?" she pondered out loud.

"Cuff links," Tricia said from the doorway, smiling proudly. "My God, Darcy, you look very dapper."

She blushed under Tricia's scrutiny, eyes dropping to the carpet. "Thank you. You are beautiful as ever. New hat?"

"Always the charmer," she murmured with a smile. "Yes, a new hat. New outfit, in fact. I wanted to look my very best for your wedding."

"Well, let me be the first to say that the mother-of-the-bride looks stunning in peach," Darcy smiled.

Coming to a stop in front of the taller woman, Tricia looked up into dark green eyes and smiled, tears glistening in her own eyes. "I'm very proud of you, Darce. We all are. You have grown up to be the most amazing, kind-hearted soul. A miracle after what you went through."

Smiling, Darcy embraced Tricia. "It's all thanks to you and Joe. If you hadn't taken me in like you did..." She shook her head. "I hate to think where I could be right now."

"It wasn't a tough decision, honey. You were already a part of this family, always have been." She kissed Darcy's cheek, then chuckled lightly as she wiped the lipstick mark off. "Sorry."

"I'm just glad you removed it. Not sure Lauren would've been too happy with me if I turned up sporting someone else's lipstick!"

"Would you like a hand with your cuff links?"

"Yes, please."

"Are you sure you don't want to wear a tie? It's not too late."

"I'm sure. If I wear a tie, I might pass out. I already feel far too hot. Lauren won't mind smart-casual."

"Luke's been moaning left, right, and centre about not knowing how to tie a tie, about how it's crooked, how it's too tight!" Tricia confessed. "I've had to get Joe to step in and help him with it! Though you all wore school ties, so if he would just stop complaining and concentrate, I'm sure it would come back to him." She blinked in surprise when she lifted Darcy's right hand and spotted the Claddagh ring on her finger. "You're wearing this?"

"I never take it off," Darcy admitted. "I'm not going to start today. Besides, it's my something new."

"Oh. Do you have everything else?"

"The cuff links complete the list as my something borrowed. Jeremy presented me with them yesterday."

Smiling, Tricia attached the last cuff link before stepping back to take a good look at the younger woman. "There, ready to go and get married." Her eyes watered again. "I can't believe all my babies have grown up!"

Feeling her own emotions getting to her, Darcy wrapped Tricia in her arms and hugged her tightly. "We may have grown up, but we're never far away. Where do we come to gather for a family get-together? Where do we have Sunday lunch? You and Joe are the best parents anyone could wish for. I thank you from the bottom of my heart for all the love you have ever shown me." She pulled back from the hug and smiled. "Don't cry. Your makeup will run, then you'll get angry with me and I'll have to run, then I'll get rumpled and we don't want that!"

"Truly devilish!" Tricia laughed and slapped lightly at

Darcy's arm. "You always will be!" She took the handkerchief handed to her and dabbed at her eyes. "I'm wearing waterproof makeup," she mentioned. "This isn't my first rodeo."

"The car has pulled up," Joe called out from downstairs. "Are you coming with Caitlyn and me, Trish? Or are you travelling with Darcy and Luke?"

"Go," Darcy said fondly. "Get a good seat."

Seeing the bubbling emotion in dark green eyes, Tricia realised Darcy needed some time alone to compose herself. Smiling proudly at the younger woman, she reached out and squeezed Darcy's arm. "I'm coming, Joe." She kissed Darcy's cheek again and winked. "Good luck, honey. And try not to worry or panic. If you faint, we'll have it on video and show it every Christmas!" She left the bedroom laughing loudly, while Darcy groaned in despair.

DARCY BEAMED AS Lauren came to a stop beside her. The redhead looked a vision in the cream-coloured dress she had chosen. Her red locks were pinned up neatly into a chignon, she wore a light dusting of make-up, and a thin gold chain around her delicate neck with a tear-drop diamond pendant, an anniversary gift from Darcy.

"You look stunning, sweetheart," Darcy whispered.

"You don't look so bad yourself, Darce. You've scrubbed up well."

In front of them stood the smiling priest, behind them were their friends and family. Having taken time off especially, Kendall had made it over from Greece where she was now working. Joaquina and her father had come over from Portugal, Margo from Germany, and several other friends the couple had made along their travels. Closing the bar for the day, Lauren had invited Pat and her other staff, seeing that they were like family to her.

Her actual family had refused to attend, which she had expected but still found upsetting. Darcy had refused to even try and track down her father. He hadn't been a part of her life for a long time, not even when she'd needed him most.

The priest smiled at both women. "Shall we begin?" he asked softly, watching both women nod their consent. "Ladies and gentlemen, we are here today to witness the joining of these two women, who love each other enough to want to share this moment with us," he started in a loud, clear voice.

Turning his attention to Lauren and Darcy, he smiled. "Lauren, repeat the following solemn declaration. I do solemnly declare..."

"I do solemnly declare," Lauren repeated, her voice shaky.

"...that I know not of any lawful impediment why I, Lauren Virginia Cansdell..."

"That I know not of any..." Lauren paused, a small frown creasing her brow. "Um, of any lawful impediment why I, Lauren Virginia Cansdell."

"May not be joined in matrimony to Darcy," the priest finished.

"May not be joined in matrimony to Darcy."

The priest smiled, more relieved than happy after Lauren's little wobble. He looked to Darcy and smiled encouragingly. "Darcy, repeat the following solemn declaration. I do solemnly declare, that I know not of any lawful impediment why I, Darcy Louisa Kenton..."

Darcy repeated the words, her heart pounding. She had thought for one horrible moment that Lauren was having second thoughts. "May not be joined in matrimony to Lauren," she finished with a relieved smile.

"The couple have chosen to write their own vows," the priest announced to the guests. "Darcy, would you like to go first?" He opted to give Lauren a moment or two to compose herself. She was looking a little pale.

Nodding, Darcy took a deep breath to calm her nerves, then turned to face Lauren, smiling lovingly and forgetting everyone else in the room. "Lauren, I knew I was in love with you one sunny morning in Germany. It was the day before we were due to head to Italy and I made you breakfast in bed. It was terrible," she laughed, their guests laughing with her.

"But you smiled at me with such love, I was glad I'd made the effort. I made it my goal to see that smile again. I made it my goal to make you happy. These last few years have taught me things about love I never knew, and I want to continue to learn with you by my side, both of us learning together. Lauren, you are a beautiful, smart, generous woman, with such a big heart, and I want to spend the rest of my life with you, loving you, making you smile."

She grinned and when she spoke again her tone had lowered to an intimate level. "I promise to always respect you as a person with your own interests, dreams, and desires, which are no less important than my own, and I promise to love you in good times and bad for eternity, with all I have to give and all that I am. This is my solemn vow to you."

Tricia dabbed at her eyes with a handkerchief and looked lovingly at her husband, the pair of them very proud of the woman they had helped raise.

The priest turned to Lauren and smiled reassuringly. "Lauren, it's your turn." He waited for a response from the redhead, blinking when one didn't come forth. Swallowing nervously, not liking the signs but hoping for the best, he tried again. "Lauren?"

Darcy turned fully to face her fiancée, a small curious smile curling her lips. "Sweetheart," she whispered. "This is your moment."

Slowly, Lauren turned to face Darcy, her face blank as she met worried green eyes. All their happy memories filtered through her mind, the places they'd been to together, their future plans. But even as the happy memories came to her, the biggest doubt she had ever had also played a part. "I...I can't," she murmured.

Darcy's smile faded. "Have you forgotten what you want to say?"

"I can't do this, Darcy. I...I thought I could, but..." She frowned and looked directly at Darcy as though seeing her for the first time. "Ever since we came back, I've seen firsthand how it's going to be. She'll always be in your life. Her family are your family. There'll be holiday get-togethers, weekend barbecues, and she'll always be there."

"What? Lauren, I love you," Darcy murmured urgently, starting to panic.

"But not enough," Lauren replied sadly. "She'll always be the one you love but can't have, the one who will always have a bit of your heart no matter what. I'll always be left wondering if you'll leave me if she one day decides she wants you after all. I have lived and will have to forever live, knowing I was your second choice."

"You're not my second choice. Baby, please!"

"Darcy, you're wearing her ring. On our wedding day, you're wearing the ring she gave you!"

Darcy looked down at the Claddagh ring. "It's my something new."

"I'm sorry. I can't. I...can't!" The redhead turned and fled, tears streaming down her cheeks as she raced away.

Stunned, Darcy watched her go, frozen in place. She was almost certain this was some sort of bad prank.

"I'm very sorry," the priest said sympathetically, having been privy to the whole conversation.

"What?" Feeling numb, Darcy turned to face the man, blinking at him in confusion.

"I'm —"

"What...what happens now?" The colour had drained from her face as the sinking feeling that this wasn't a prank began to hit her.

"Perhaps you should let everyone know what is going on," he told her softly.

Jeremy hurried up to Darcy's side. "Darce? What's going on? Bad case of call of nature?"

"She left."

"Left? What do you mean she left?" He looked from her to the priest.

"Maybe you should suggest that everyone goes on to the reception so that Darcy can have some time to come to terms with what's happened." He offered another sympathetic smile to Darcy. "I am very sorry." He took a step away, giving her some privacy.

Just as stunned as Darcy was, Jeremy blinked at her. "Do you want me to...?"

All the scenarios of what could go wrong on the day, this hadn't been one of them. She felt completely dumbstruck by what was going on. She blinked at Jeremy, seeing the baffled look on his face, seeing he had no idea what to do in this situation either. She turned to face the anxious friends and family who sat staring back at her, puzzled looks on many of their faces. "Um..." She licked her dry lips, wondering what the appropriate thing to say was. "We uh...paid for a location and food and drink, so...we should go and...and use it."

With nothing else to say and feeling suddenly sick to her stomach, Darcy hurried along the aisle, not as a wife like she had envisioned she would be, but as a broken-hearted woman who had just been rejected. Again.

JEREMY'S BAR AND restaurant had been chosen for the location of the reception because he had space for a sit-down meal, followed by a night of dancing and drinking. The couple had weighed up the possibility of using Lauren's bar, but Lauren had ultimately decided she didn't want the added stress it would put on her.

Darcy was immensely glad they had opted for elsewhere now. Not that Lauren was around. Darcy had tried phoning but got no answer at Lauren's flat and no response on her mobile. And if any of her friends had heard from her, they weren't saying.

Jeremy's chef and his team had put together a three-course hearty and seasonal meal. Darcy skipped it, knowing there would be questions and sympathetic looks directed her way. She didn't know where Lauren had fled to and didn't fancy sitting in front of a crowd of their confused friends and family with an empty seat next to her.

After the meal was eaten, everyone was to go through to the bar where a DJ had set up his equipment. The central tables and chairs had been moved to around the outer edges of the room, leaving plenty of space for dancing.

Before disappearing from sight, Darcy had a quick word with the DJ telling him not to play the song for the first dance. He was to keep the guests happy and dancing, playing whatever song they requested if it was available, even the cheesy ones. Through gritted teeth, she explained why there was no first dance when he taunted her about her nerves on having to dance in front of everyone. Thoroughly chastised, he apologised and promised to do as she had asked.

The bar was open to all, free drinks all night. The staff had been instructed to serve up a glass of champagne first, in celebration of the married couple. With that a moot point, Darcy had instructed them not to waste the drink and serve it anyway, then whatever people requested after that.

Standing on the roof clutching a half empty bottle of bourbon, she stared out at the distant lights of homes and office blocks in town. The loud music drifted up to her, as did the occasional muffled sound of the DJ's voice, what he was saying indiscernible. She heard laughter and people singing along to old classics, a few cheers going up when cheesy songs like "Agadoo" and "The Twist" were played.

Darcy felt numb to it all, as if this were an event she was looking in on, something that was happening to someone else. She kept expecting to wake up and find it had been a cruel nightmare. The burning of the alcohol going down told her different.

Stepping out onto the roof, Caitlyn shivered as the night air hit her. Being February, the nights were cold and this one was no different. She silently watched her best friend, knowing Darcy had no idea she was there. She was taken aback by Darcy's swaying, realising quickly that she had consumed a lot of the contents from the bottle she held.

She knew Darcy was hurting and wanted to be there for her, wanted to offer her shoulder, wanted to let Darcy know she cared and would listen if she wanted to talk. She just wasn't sure she was the right woman for the job at this moment, positive she was the last person in the world Darcy wanted to be confronted with.

"Hey, Darce," she called out softly, stepping away from the shadows and closer to her friend's position.

Recognising the voice immediately, Darcy turned to face Caitlyn and sneered. "Are you happy now?" she growled. "You got what you wanted!"

"Oh, Darcy, I never wanted this!" Caitlyn insisted. "I never wanted to see you hurt."

Darcy swigged from her bottle of Jack, her eyes never leaving Caitlyn. She looked beautiful in a cream and black knee-length dress, the matching shoes adding a couple of inches to her height. Darcy hated her and loved her at the same time. She wondered why she couldn't move on from Caitlyn, why the beautiful blonde was never far from her thoughts, why Caitlyn had such pull over her.

Lowering the bottle, she turned away from her childhood friend. It hurt too much to look at her. "That's one thing you always manage to do," she muttered in response to Caitlyn's declaration, her comment drifting away on the evening wind. "The one thing you're good at."

"Sorry, what?" Caitlyn edged closer, not catching the pain-fuelled words.

"Nothing. Never mind." Darcy moved toward the edge of the building, planning on sitting on the small wall that prevented a straight drop from the rooftop to the pavement below.

Thinking her friend was going to jump, Caitlyn hurriedly took another step forward, reached out and grasped Darcy's arm to tug her back. "Darcy! Let's...let's sit down. Over there where we'll be sheltered from the wind." Meeting no resistance, she led her away from the edge and back toward the stairwell.

Inside, she sat on the top step, Darcy eventually taking a seat next to her with a heavy sigh. "What happened today, Darcy?" The question was asked softly, but still the words echoed off the walls enclosing them.

Darcy swigged from her bottle and ignored the question. She didn't want to repeat the words, didn't want to think about the special day becoming a nightmare, didn't want to remember Lauren looking lost, then running away from her all because of the small blonde she couldn't give up.

The two lifelong friends sat in silence, Darcy lost in hurt and rejection, an unpleasant haze tinged with nausea, while Caitlyn did the only thing she could do— she wrapped an arm around Darcy's shoulder, offering silent comfort and support.

"What's wrong with me, Caitlyn? Why won't anyone love me? They...they all leave. There must be something wrong with me. I make them...everyone...go away."

"Hey!" Caitlyn said firmly, pulling Darcy tightly against her. "You listen to me, Darcy Kenton," she said in a stern tone not to be messed with. "There is nothing wrong with you. It's nothing that you do that makes them go away. They're...they're not worthy of being in your amazing, wonderful, kind-hearted company! Lauren's obviously plain mad for giving you up! And your mother and father, they didn't deserve you in the first place!"

"They must have seen something in me..."

Caitlyn shook her head. "You are so...so full of love and one day," she took a breath, "one day, you're going to find that special person who is worthy of receiving it."

Looking at her friend with tear-glistening eyes, she was touched by Caitlyn's words said with such passion, wishing with everything she had that it was Caitlyn who realised that she was the one worthy of her love. She stood on unsteady feet and offered Caitlyn her hand. "Dance with me?" she requested.

"Now?"

"Yeah, right now."

"To a Celine Dion song? You detest her ballads."

"Dance with me anyway."

Caitlyn took the offered hand and followed the taller woman out onto the rooftop. She sank into Darcy's arms as they enfolded her, her own arms wrapping around the brunette. Enveloped in warmth and love and the familiar scent of Darcy, Caitlyn sighed softly. God, it felt so right being in her arms like this, she thought, eyes sliding shut at the feeling of her world clicking into place.

Celine Dion's "If That's What It Takes" blasted from the speakers inside where family and friends were gathered, enjoying themselves despite the ceremony not going as planned. Up on the roof, Darcy and Caitlyn got lost in each other, forgetting they weren't the only two people in the world. The words struck a chord with Caitlyn as she listened and related to the song. She pulled back from Darcy's body, just enough to be able to gaze into loving green eyes, emotions she recognised swirling within her and threatening to come to the surface.

Oh, God! Caitlyn thought with sudden clarity, struck, as if by lightning. Oh, my God! I...I love her! I love Darcy!

"Caitlyn?" Darcy questioned softly, having felt her friend tense in her arms. "You okay?"

How the hell had this happened? She blinked at Darcy. Maybe it didn't happen, maybe it had been there all along and she just refused to acknowledge it. "I..." She pulled away completely, taking a step back, unable to stay so close to her friend. Her heart was hammering, and she felt as if she might be having a panic attack. "I should...I should get back to Ian," she stuttered, not meeting Darcy's worried gaze. "He's probably wondering where I am."

Darcy smiled sadly. "Right," she nodded. "Thanks for coming to search for me. I'm fine. I'm not going to jump or anything, I just," she sighed, "wanted some space from everyone."

"I understand. We all do." She rubbed a hand down Darcy's arm, needing the contact. "Come down soon, okay. Mum's worried about you and a little annoyed that you disappeared all afternoon without a word. You even missed the meal and it was delicious."

"Tell her I'm sorry and that I'll come have a dance with her later." She watched Caitlyn hurry for the stairwell, her heart breaking once again, because every time there was a moment between them, a connection, a spark, as soon as it became apparent, Caitlyn ran.

Walking farther out onto the roof, she shook her head sadly, a hand rising to her chest, fingers rubbing her aching heart. She couldn't keep going through this. She wouldn't keep going through this. There was something more than friendship between them, she wasn't imagining it, but Caitlyn was never going to give them a chance. She'll never admit she has feelings for her. She would rather live a safe, straight life with Ian bloody Moran!

Knowing what she had to do and knowing it was going to hurt not only herself, but the two people who had always been parents to her, the men who had always been like brothers to her, even Caitlyn as well, Darcy turned and made her way to the stairwell, determined to enjoy this night with them, and the extended family, before she left again. This time, for good.

CAITLYN SAT AT a table with her parents watching Ian dancing with Olivia. She couldn't deny it. She loved Darcy. She had always loved Darcy.

"You found her?"

Caitlyn whipped around in her mother's direction, eyes startled. "What?"

"Darcy," Tricia clarified. "You found her."

"How did you...?"

"You're no longer looking around in worry," Tricia smiled kindly. "How is she?"

Caitlyn felt sick as Ian winked at her. "Well on her way to being unhappily drunk."

"Oh, poor Darcy," Tricia murmured, looking sadly at Joe beside her.

"Probably be best if she drinks herself to sleep," he mentioned. "Just for tonight. Deal with it all fresh tomorrow."

"I don't suppose she told you what happened between the two of them?" Tricia asked her daughter.

"No," Caitlyn shook her head, turning in her seat to fully face her parents. "But then we don't really need to know what went on, do we? The fact is Lauren left her at the altar."

"Yes, but why?" Tricia questioned, an unsatisfied mother. "They were so happy. I don't understand it."

"Does seem strange that she suddenly got cold feet," Joe nodded.

"Hey, babe." Ian came to a stop next to Caitlyn. "Want to dance? Olivia's grown tired of me and run off with another man!" he joked, making Tricia, Joe and Caitlyn look past him to see Olivia in Grandad Cliff's arms.

Caitlyn smiled and stood up. "All right then." She took his hand and followed him out onto the dance floor, wrapping her arms around his neck as he embraced her tightly. "Jesus, Ian! A little breathing room, please."

"Sorry. I just want you close. I feel like I've barely seen you all day."

His hands are clammy, she thought, resting her head against his shoulder. And he holds onto me for dear life, like I'm going to run away and leave him standing here on his own. She sighed and came swiftly to the conclusion that they didn't fit together, not like she and Darcy did. When Darcy held her, they moulded together. Darcy's touch made her tingle.

"Ian, do you think we're compatible?"

"Of course we are, sweetheart. Whatever made you ask?" He frowned at her.

She shook her head. "Nothing, I..." She smiled for him. "I'm just being silly."

It was incredibly warm inside the bar, the sheer number of people making the space noisy and crowded. An array of cologne and perfume aromas hung in the air. Ian smelt of Old Spice and hops from the beer he'd been drinking all night. She smiled as she watched her nieces dance, her nephews taking joy out of sliding on their knees across the polished dance floor. If she hadn't known what had happened earlier in the day, she would think this was like any other reception after a wedding.

As they turned, she spotted Darcy striding toward the DJ. "There's Darcy," she mentioned. "I wonder what she's doing?"

Darcy jumped up into the DJ booth and stood next to the star- tled man. "You're doing a great job, mate. Everyone seems like they're having a great time. Can I borrow the mic for a moment?" she asked, smiling charmingly at him.

"Course you can, love. It's your do."

Taking the microphone, she tapped it before speaking. "Hi, everyone. I hope you're enjoying yourselves?"

"YEAH!"

"We love the free bar!"

She smiled. "What happened earlier is over with. I'd appreci- ate it if none of you come up to me and start asking questions. For tonight, I just want to party hard with you fine people." She laughed as that got another loud cheer. "So, Mr. DJ if you could kindly stop playing these god awful slow mushy songs and get something a little more...racy on, I think we'd all be grateful."

The man smiled broadly and nodded his head while giving her a thumbs-up.

"Excellent. Now, who's gonna drink with me?" Handing back the microphone, Darcy stepped out of the booth and headed for the bar, a string of smiling people following her, ready to party long into the night.

Caitlyn could only watch on, the sense that something wasn't quite right settling in her chest.

Chapter Fourteen

TRICIA SAT AT her kitchen table and watched Darcy pacing back and forth with nervous energy. She watched as Darcy clenched and unclenched her hands, puffed out her cheeks, paused in step to glance her way, before resuming her pacing. Her heart broke for Darcy, knowing how she felt for Caitlyn and how devastated she was over Lauren leaving her. She had tried to be happy after a lifetime of knock backs, tried to do the right thing, and had ended up with neither of the women she loved.

Tricia looked at her husband sitting next to her, his eyes on Darcy, a concerned frown etched onto his brow. They were both worried. Darcy hadn't been acting herself, which was understandable but worrying all the same.

"You see," Darcy started, pausing to lick her lips. She was nervous about telling them she was leaving again, worried they wouldn't understand her reasons, and the stress had created a tight ball of tension in the pit of her belly. "I um...I'm going to go...away." She stopped pacing and turned to face the couple, dark green eyes flicking from one to the other. "I just...I can't stay right now."

Tricia and Joe said nothing, blinking, absorbing the words, before looking at each other. Then their attention went back to Darcy.

"It's only for a little while," Darcy tried to assure them. "I need some space to clear my head."

"Is it only for a little while?" Tricia asked softly, not so sure. "You said that last time and we didn't see you again until recently." She took her husband's hand, needing the comfort.

Darcy sighed heavily. This all hurt so much and despite seeking answers to the questions she had, she still didn't have the solutions. "I don't know the answer to that," she admitted honestly. "I love you guys, I love the family, and I am forever grateful for everything you have done for me. But I'm in love with your daughter and she...she doesn't feel the same. She has never felt the same. I can deal with that. I was dealing with that, because I went away, and I found love with Lauren. But that's over now."

Standing up, Tricia walked to the taller woman and embraced her. "You're sure about this?" she asked quietly, ignoring her own feelings on the news. She wanted what was right for Darcy and if she felt like getting away for a bit was the way to cope, then so be it.

Darcy looked into motherly blue-grey eyes and slowly nodded. "Lauren won't even take my calls right now," she whispered brokenly. "I think...maybe if I give her some space for a bit, maybe she'll...I don't know, come around and at least talk about everything." She knew in her heart that wasn't going to happen. It was over. For good. Lauren wanted her to give up not only Caitlyn, but the whole Swailes family, and she couldn't do that. She wouldn't do that.

"You know we'll support your decision no matter what, Darce," Tricia told her softly, smiling at her. "If you think the best thing to do is leave right now, then that's what you should do."

"But if you stayed here, you would have our love and support," Joe spoke up, playing devil's advocate. "People whose shoulders you can cry on, arms which would hold you when you needed a hug. You should consider your options very carefully before you come to your final decision."

Pulling back from Tricia, Darcy looked at Joe, a frown creasing her brow. "You don't think I should use the..." she coughed, a lump forming in her throat, "...the honeymoon tickets to Fiji?" The day after the wedding, she had called the airline and explained what had happened. Whilst they wouldn't give her a refund, they did offer her the chance to use the tickets at a later date, if she so chose.

"But is that all you're doing?" Joe asked. "Going off on a two-week holiday to clear your head. Or are you going to stay away forever? The last time you left, it was for five years, Darcy."

Tricia rubbed the younger woman's arm affectionately. "We missed you so much in that time, Darce. And you missed so much here."

"I think I'm going to go for a walk," Darcy announced, full of doubt over her choices now. "I need to...I need to think over everything."

"We understand, honey," Tricia said, smiling sadly. She knew deep down that if Darcy left this time, she wouldn't be back. "Take your time. This is the sort of thing that requires a lot of thought."

SITTING IN THE shade of a large English Oak with a view of the Lower Pond, Darcy sighed, bending her knees and wrapping her arms around them, her chin resting on her kneecap. Was this the right thing to do? To leave the family who had always cared for her and would do so now? Essentially, she'd be doing what Lauren asked of her in the first place! Giving them up. Her eyes followed a pair of ducks swimming smoothly around the lake, the occasional quack penetrating the air.

It was. It was the right thing to do, she decided. Caitlyn was here and it ached every time she saw her with the moron. And now there was Lauren to avoid as well. It could be different this time. It didn't have to be five years away without seeing them. She could just...relocate. People did it all the time for work and...love. She could pop back for family barbecues, the odd Sunday lunch and keep in touch, but still have some space between them all.

She blinked back tears. Lauren wouldn't even take her calls. How the hell did this happen to them? They were so happy. Then they came home and... She sighed again. They came home and Lauren's insecurities kicked in, insecurities which were always there. And bloody Caitlyn confused her with her crazy behaviour!

Picking up a small pebble and flinging it at the lake, she watched the ripples she caused. A bit like her life. She made a decision and it caused a ripple and everything changed. If she hadn't met up with Caitlyn on New Year's Eve, they wouldn't have slept together, if they hadn't slept together, they wouldn't have fallen out. She wouldn't have decided to leave for Europe, wouldn't have asked Lauren to come with her, wouldn't have fallen in love with her. Jesus, how different would life be right now?

She reached for another pebble, rolling the smooth surface between her fingers. If she hadn't slept with Caitlyn, would she have married Ian that year? Would she have left to get away from them? Questions she'd never have answers for. What happened happened and there's no going back.

She got to her feet and looked around, taking everything in, knowing it could be awhile before she was back. The calm pond with swimming ducks and geese, the bench she ran to when she needed to think, the white Portland stone bridge, the cascade where Caitlyn liked to sit. It was all so familiar to her, like a comfort blanket.

She had spent the morning taking loads of photos from all around the pond, hoping the photos would sell. If she ever put them up for sale. She was doing the right thing, she decided. At least in this moment it was right. She would leave and clear her head, give everything a chance to settle down. Then maybe, maybe come back.

Turning away from the pond as it started to lightly rain, Darcy knew she wouldn't come back again. Her life would always be the same here. Caitlyn wouldn't entertain the idea of there being a them and Lauren would be around, a constant reminder that she had been stood up on her wedding day. No, her life in England was a finished chapter.

IT WAS POURING with rain, the sky a dark, ominous grey, and yet despite the bad weather, Caitlyn had travelled to her parents' house to check on Darcy. Her friend hadn't been herself lately as she tried to deal with the aftermath of the wedding that never was, and in all honesty, she hadn't exactly been around to offer support because she was trying to work out her feelings. Her real feelings, which for years she had stubbornly buried deep down inside herself.

Knocking on the familiar front door, Caitlyn smiled at Tricia when her mother opened the door to her. "Hi, Mum."

"Hello, love." Tricia opened the door wider and stepped aside to let her daughter in. "What brings you over in this weather? No work today?"

"It's my lunch break." She closed her umbrella and shook the excess rain off, before entering the house and leaning it against the hall wall. "Thought I should swing by and check up on Darcy. I haven't exactly spoken to her since...you know." Coat off and hanging up, she headed for the kitchen.

Tricia noted her daughter's dejected tone as she followed her through the warm house. "Cup of tea, love?"

"Ooh, yes, please." The nurse took a seat at the table and sighed heavily, a jumble of emotions battling within her. "Where's Dad?" she asked, focusing on something other than what she was feeling.

"He's gone to the supermarket for me. In all honesty, I think he just wanted to get out of the house." She didn't let on as to why Joe wanted to be out rather than at home.

"On his day off?" Caitlyn chuckled. "He usually likes to relax in front of the television and catch up on all the shows he missed."

"Usually, yes." Leaving the tea to brew, Tricia walked to the table and took a seat opposite her daughter. She studied the younger woman, knowing something was bothering her and wondering if Caitlyn would tell her or keep it all locked in as she usually did. "Something wrong, Catie?" For once, she decided to press the matter, if for no other reason than to take her mind off her own worries concerning Darcy. "How's Ian?"

"He's fine," Caitlyn rolled her eyes. "He keeps hinting we should get married."

"And you don't want to?"

"It's hardly an appropriate time, is it? Getting married when Darcy's just been left at the altar. He seems to think it will cheer the family up."

Tricia bit back a smile. "Perhaps he only meant you could start planning your wedding."

Caitlyn looked up from the tabletop, meeting her mother's eyes. She got the feeling Tricia knew more than she was letting on, like she had always known but had been waiting for Caitlyn to get up the nerve to face the reality. "Mum, I..." She frowned, not sure she wanted to blurt out her feelings. Sure, everyone had been okay with Darcy's confession of being in love with a woman, but this was different. She was blood, their little girl, their little sister. "I have this friend."

"I see." Tricia blinked. "Hold on, honey, let me get the tea, then you can tell me all about this...friend." She stood and retrieved the milk from the fridge, then set about making their tea. Returning to the table, she smiled as she set a mug in front of Caitlyn. "All right then, let's hear it."

Caitlyn nervously licked her lips. She was twenty-eight years old and she couldn't confess to her own mother that this is about her! She wanted to laugh at the absurdity of the situation. "Well, my...friend, she...she has a boyfriend, but she likes someone else, someone...female." She got into the role of concerned friend. "She's straight, always has been, so her feelings are confusing her."

"I imagine they would," Tricia smiled sympathetically.

"But while her feelings confuse her and scare the hell out of her, she would very much like to be with Da—I mean, this woman. Because when they're together..." her tone lowered until she was almost talking to herself, a wistful smile curling her lips, "...she knows without a shadow of a doubt that she is loved, completely and utterly. She is loved not for how she looks, but for who she is, the person inside. The rest of the world fades away and it's only them when they look into each other's eyes, and when she's held in loving arms."

Tricia hid her smile behind her mug, knowing exactly what

was going on, exactly who her daughter was talking about.

Caitlyn shook her head, coming back to her surroundings. "But the problem is she's straight, and she's worried about how those around her, mainly her family, who she's very close with, are going to react to her sudden revelation. So, she asked me what I thought, but I uh…I haven't got a clue what to tell her."

Tricia sipped her tea, watching Caitlyn over the rim, innocent blue eyes shining back. She wondered why it had taken her daughter so long to realise how she felt about Darcy, why Caitlyn would be afraid to tell them of her feelings? They had always been supportive, had never judged, as long as the children were happy, Joe and Tricia were happy.

She set her mug down and smiled. Knowing her next comment would likely confound her daughter, though why baffled her, her eyes sparkled in amusement and mischief. "Better late than never I suppose!" she declared. "Caitlyn, you two belong together. We can all see it, we've always seen it, but you refused to, opting instead to push Darcy away and deny your feelings."

Caitlyn blinked rapidly, her mouth working up and down as she tried to form words. "I…I…I wasn't talking about—"

"Yes, you were, and it's okay," Tricia said compassionately, reaching out to cover her daughter's hand with her own. "We still love you. Both of you. Your father and I have only ever wanted you all happy. Thank God you've finally woken up!" she chuckled. "Ian's a lovely man, but he really doesn't fit in at all with us. Who turns up to a family barbecue dressed like they're going to a work convention? The only problem is you've left it rather late and I…I don't know if you can catch her in time."

"Catch? Darcy?"

"Yes. While you've been avoiding her, she's been dealing with a lot. I think she's come to the conclusion there's nothing for her here. She's gone to the airport to catch a flight somewhere," Tricia explained, glancing at the clock. "She decided to get away for a while, clear her head, but didn't really say where that would be. The tickets are to Fiji, where she was going to go on honeymoon, but she mumbled something about seeing if she could change them."

"*What*?" Caitlyn gasped, her heart constricting in pain at the thought of Darcy leaving again. She thought back to the last time Darcy had left, the promises she had given that she wouldn't be gone long, that she would keep in touch. Only she didn't! Caitlyn jumped to her feet so fast her chair clattered back against the wall loudly, leaving a small mark on the paint. "I have to go!" she cried out desperately, feeling everything she wanted slipping away. "I can't let her leave, Mum! She won't come back, I just know it!"

Tricia jumped into action. On her feet, she hurried to the counter where Darcy had written down travel information. "She's leaving from Gatwick," she read.

Blue eyes flicked to the clock on the wall, knowing she should be heading back to work, only she had somewhere far more important to be. They would understand eventually and forgive her for leaving them in the lurch. "Can you call the hospital for me, Mum? Tell them...tell them I had to be somewhere else!" She ran from the kitchen, heading for the front door.

"Caitlyn!" Tricia called, almost giddy from this turn up. "Head to Victoria Station. She'll no doubt catch a train to the airport and the Gatwick express leaves from there."

Fleeing the house, Caitlyn raced down the street, knowing she could pick up a cab more easily on the main road. She couldn't drive herself, she was far too flustered and distracted. She knew she was acting crazy, but she honesty didn't care. All she knew at that moment was that she couldn't let Darcy leave, not without confessing how she felt.

CAITLYN URGED THE taxi driver to go faster, telling him it was of great importance, begging and praying to God that she made it to the train station on time. If Darcy got to the airport, that was it, she was gone.

Her desperation made no difference to the cab driver though. The journey wasn't made any easier with the bad weather, the rain hammering down in fat blobs and accompanied by the rumbling of thunder in the distance, nor the road works, which always seemed to hamper traffic in the city.

As the taxi pulled to a stop in front of the bustling train station, Caitlyn threw a ten pound note in the driver's direction and jumped out of the car, not even sure if that was enough to cover the fare. She was drenched by the time she got through the station doors, her hair a wild mess, her eyes wide and fearful.

She had no clue where to start looking for Darcy. The station was the second busiest in London and bustling with crowds of people coming and going. Travellers were standing and staring at the numerous flickering timetable boards, some ambling from shop to shop, others were seated and watching the world go by.

She was waiting on a phone call from her mother to tell her

what Luke knew. Apparently, her brother had driven Darcy to the station and Tricia was sure that her son would have found out all the little details of Darcy's travel plans before saying goodbye. There were times she was grateful her brother was so nosey.

Racing around the large station, weaving this way and that as she tried to avoid slamming into people also in a hurry, she searched the heaving crowd for a lucky sighting of her tall best friend as she fumbled with her purse, trying to get to her phone. But that would be too easy, wouldn't it? To spot Darcy in the crowd staring up at one of the boards or heading toward her departure platform. The fates couldn't make it easy for her. Not after all she'd put Darcy through!

Stopping and looking at the many timetable boards to see which trains would soon be departing, she rang home.

"Caitlyn?"

"Yes, yes it's me. Did you find out anything from Luke?"

"He says she's leaving from either platform thirteen or fourteen. They're the two dedicated to the express train."

Blue eyes widened as she read the boards and saw that the train was listed as in and already boarding. "Oh, no!" Forgetting the phone she held tightly and her mother on the other end, Caitlyn ran, racing for the ticket barriers that led to platforms thirteen and fourteen, praying that Darcy hadn't already passed through and boarded the train.

A CROWD HAD amassed at the ticket barriers that served platforms thirteen and fourteen. Darcy stood patiently in line, in no rush to get through, eyes on nothing in particular, her mind blank as she refused to think about what she was leaving behind. This was it this time, she wasn't coming back, couldn't come back and go through it all again.

Of course, this was what Lauren had asked her to do while they were at the altar, she thought melancholically. Give up the family. And she couldn't. Yet here she was, ready to leave, vowing never to come back.

The line inched forward, and Darcy sighed heavily, not sure if she was happy or not. To be honest she felt sick to the stomach. She should be happy. She was off to start a new life with a clean slate. She looked down at the ticket she held. But she was doing it alone this time.

SPOTTING DARCY IN the queue up ahead, Caitlyn felt her heart burst with joy and relief. She had made it. There was still time. "Darcy!"

Darcy frowned as she thought she heard her name being called, thinking she recognised the voice but knowing it was impossible. Caitlyn was at work and hadn't been around in recent days. She had no idea of Darcy's plans.

"Darcy!"

Darcy's frown deepened as she turned and scanned the crowd. Spotting a familiar blonde elbowing her way toward her. She felt her heart skip a beat and hated that Caitlyn could still do that to her. "Caitlyn?"

People shifted, turning to glance their way to see what the disturbance was.

"I love you, Darcy!" Caitlyn cried out in glee, not afraid to admit it anymore. "I love you and I want the world to know!" She flung herself at her friend, certain that she would be caught in strong, loving arms.

Darcy hastily dropped her bag and caught her friend, feeling Caitlyn's arms and legs wrap around her, a face buried against her neck. "Caitlyn?" she questioned again in confusion. "You're wet. Soaking wet."

"God, I thought I was going to miss you! I'm on my lunch break and decided it was time to drop in and see if you were okay, and I'm supposed to be back at work doing rounds, but then Mum said you were going and suddenly I was running and...the cab driver wouldn't speed up, I think he thought I was hysterical or something, but...here you are!" She smiled brilliantly and lowered her lips to Darcy's, kissing her with as much love as she could convey. "I love you," she murmured once she finally ended the kiss.

Darcy blinked, trying to take in everything Caitlyn was rapidly saying at her, still stunned that her friend was there.

"Don't go." She searched confused green eyes. "If you go, I will never be complete, and neither will you be. We belong together, Darcy. I know that now. I can admit it now." She kissed Darcy again, just because she could from her position, and because she hadn't for years and it turned out she had missed it, really missed it. "I love you, Darcy Louisa Kenton. I want to spend the rest of our lives together. I want you to let me make up for all the times I hurt you and rejected you, all the times I denied the love we have for each other." She caressed a soft cheek. "Stay, Darcy. Please."

Darcy stared into her best friend's eyes, wanting so much to believe the words she was saying. It was everything she had ever wanted, but she didn't trust it. Not after being hurt before. "You've broken up with Ian?" she asked in disbelief.

Blue eyes dropped. "Not yet," she muttered. "There was no time, Darce. I came to my senses while I was talking to Mum, actually it was the day of your wedding, when we danced to that stupid ballad. The words...they just made everything click into place. But I got scared again and ran. But then I found out you were leaving and ran out of the house, forgetting my umbrella, managed to hail a taxi and...here I am."

The crowd around them were listening intently, some smiling, some wide-eyed at what they were hearing.

She saw doubt in her best friend's eyes and knew Darcy wasn't convinced. Not enough to stay. "I'll tell him, Darcy," she promised fiercely. "As soon as we get back to the house. I'll call him and tell him to come over and then..." She smiled and kissed soft lips again. "With you by my side, I'll tell him it's you I want. You who I have always wanted."

Sighing, Darcy set the smaller woman back on her own two feet. "And what if he arrives and you change your mind again? Or you decide you can't face being with me after all? It's happened before, Caitlyn."

"Miss? Excuse me, miss. Are you going through?" the station employee standing at the ticket barrier asked.

"Yes," Darcy replied, deciding she couldn't take a chance on Caitlyn again, wouldn't risk her heart to Caitlyn who had always been so careless with it.

"No!" Caitlyn spoke up. Grabbing hold of Darcy's arm tightly, desperation flooded through her. "No, Darcy. I mean it this time. I realise what an idiot I've been. I've looked back over our life and have finally seen what I should have been seeing all along. We're meant to be, Darcy. The whole family thinks so!"

"Miss, the train won't be there forever. Are you boarding or not?" the woman at the gate asked in irritation, not just because of them but because the crowd around them had stopped moving as well. The scene had been interesting at first, but now they were just holding everything up.

"I want a life with you, Darcy," Caitlyn hurried on, knowing she was running out of time to convince Darcy to stay. "I want to marry you, I want to move in with you, into that evil old house you grew up in for so many years and help banish the old memories. I want us to make good memories. I want to travel Europe with you, see all the places you've already seen and discover new ones too." She searched dark green eyes. "Please stay," she whispered. "This is forever."

Swallowing hard, Darcy exhaled as she shook her head. "I can't," she whispered brokenly, stooping to pick up her bag. "I can't do this." It hurt to say it. She had known pain more than once because of Caitlyn, she didn't want to feel it again. Certainly not now while dealing with the fallout from Lauren breaking up with her. "I'm sorry. It's too late." She kissed Caitlyn's forehead then moved around the shocked woman and hurried forward to the ticket machine.

Caitlyn turned and watched in disbelief as Darcy fed her ticket into the machine, felt her heart break when her friend, her love, stepped through the barrier and made her way toward the platform and the waiting train that would take her away. Forever. Turning away, blue eyes watering, she gasped at the sudden sharp pain that hit her chest. The sympathetic noises from the crowd started to fade, her vision blurred with tears, and she couldn't seem to catch her breath.

Oh, God! Oh, God, she left! She really left! Caitlyn looked around the station with unseeing eyes, unaware of the people standing around her pretending they hadn't been listening and watching in rapt fascination, not seeing the sympathetic look the station employee shot in her direction. She felt completely numb, her heart ripped out, gone off with Darcy. *It's not over, the train hasn't left,* a little voice, which sounded a lot like Tricia, said in her head.

Turning back to the ticket barrier, she locked eyes with the woman standing guard. "Look, I know this is highly against the rules," she said to the unblinking woman. "But she's leaving. Forever. And I can't let that happen. I know I don't have a ticket, but I don't plan on going anywhere. I just need a couple of minutes to convince her not to go either."

"I'm sorry, miss. I can't let you pass without a ticket, whether you're travelling or not," the woman informed her, looking apologetic. "I have to consider the safety of all the other passengers."

"I understand safety precautions. I do. But you see, I am her first love, her childhood sweetheart. Only I'm an idiot and have spent years denying that there's anything more than friendship between us. And she left and fell in love and came back and proposed, only to get stood up on her wedding day. She was left at the altar after reciting her beautiful vows, and now she thinks she has no reason to stay in this country. But she does!" Caitlyn hurriedly explained, aware that time was getting away from her.

"Oh, let her through," someone in the crowd called out.

"I can't!" the woman protested. "I'm sorry," she directed at Caitlyn.

"I love her! I love my best friend, but I've messed her around so much over the years, she thinks she has to leave. But she doesn't! Because I can admit it now, I can admit it out loud. I just need to convince her because she doesn't believe it. Please!" she begged desperately. "The love of my life is about to get on a plane and fly away forever and you can help prevent that."

"Let her through! Let her through!" the gathered crowd started chanting, caught up in the moment.

With the crowd shouting in support of the near hysterical blonde, the station employee's features softened, heartstrings pulled by the desperation of the situation. "All right. But you have to stick with me."

Smiling brightly, tears sprang to her eyes as relief washed through her, the queue of people behind her cheering and whooping after overhearing her plight and success. "Thank you! Thank you so much!"

"Darcy! Darcy!" Caitlyn cried out as she hurried along the platform, looking in the train windows, seeking out the familiar form of her friend. The station employee hurried along with her, the walkie-talkie she held crackling with ineligible words.

Past one carriage, then two and three, in the fourth Caitlyn's heart leapt with joy until the startled woman stared wide-eyed at her with grey eyes and not familiar dark green. It was in the sixth carriage where she finally found her target. Darcy was seated on her own gazing out the window at the interior of the train station, looking utterly miserable.

"Darcy," Caitlyn whispered, skidding to a stop.

Startled dark green met watery blue. Darcy slowly blinked as if to make sure she was really seeing who she was seeing as Caitlyn boarded the train and strode toward her. "Caitlyn? What are you...? How did you...?"

"Listen, I only have a minute," Caitlyn hastily interrupted. "This woman let me through so I could convince you that I meant what I said. It's real this time, Darcy. I realised how important you are to me and I'm ready to try, I'm ready to give us a chance. Don't leave. Stay. Stay with me and let us try."

Darcy wanted to, she wanted nothing more than to believe that everything Caitlyn was saying was the truth. But too many times she had been hurt, too many times it had all been a lie. She shook her head. "I want to believe you, Catie, but I can't. You've rejected me too many times, rejected things between us. Plus, I just got dumped on my wedding day. I'm a mess, my life is a mess. I'm going away to clear my head, to think everything over."

"Think about it here! I'll leave you in peace, give you whatever space you need."

Darcy shook her head. "No. I'm going, but I will come back. I'll come back and we'll talk then. I promise."

"Darcy —"

"I'm sorry, miss, but we really have to go now," the station employee spoke up, her walkie-talkie to her ear. "The train is set to leave."

"But..." Caitlyn looked at the woman and saw there was no reasoning with her this time. Shoulders dropping, she gave a sad nod and started following the woman off the train. "I'll be here waiting," she said, stopping at the doors and glancing back at her best friend. "However long it takes." She got no response, but then she hadn't expected one.

Stepping off the train, she walked alongside the station employee as they made their way back along the platform, not hearing the woman chattering away, lost in her own thoughts of how she was losing the love of her life despite her best efforts to make her stay. It was her own fault, she thought in despair. She'd spent a lifetime hurting Darcy, telling her she didn't want her, that she was straight. Of course Darcy didn't believe her now!

A lone tear slipped down her cheek, chest aching painfully at the thought of losing Darcy for good this time. But, oh how she meant it. She had finally stopped lying to herself about who she was and who she loved. She realised she didn't have to live a lie. Her family, their family, loved them no matter what and just wanted them happy. But it was too late.

She gasped, startled, as her arm was taken and she was spun around, eyes widening when her lips were covered by familiar soft lips in a deep, loving kiss that meant so much. As strong arms wrapped around her, she wrapped her own arms around Darcy's neck and melted into her taller friend's body, the fit perfect.

Darcy finally broke the kiss and panted for breath, unaware of smiling commuters hovering nearby, and looked into blue eyes that she loved so much. "I was so ready to leave," she murmured. "I was going to get on the plane and never look back."

"What changed your mind?" Caitlyn asked quietly, not quite believing Darcy was in front of her.

Tracing Caitlyn's lips with the pad of her thumb, green eyes followed the digit along its path. "I heard this little voice in my head calling me an idiot. She was telling me everything I had ever wanted was right here, ready to give us a shot, and I was being a stubborn jerk."

"She?"

"Yeah," Darcy smiled. "Sounded a lot like Tricia's voice. When I heard the hurt in your voice, Jesus! My heart has never ached so much! And I knew," she grinned, "I knew I couldn't do it." She softly pecked pink lips. "You break my heart, Caitlyn Eleanor Swailes, and I'll never forgive you!"

Caitlyn grinned broadly and pulled Darcy toward her to place the sweetest of kisses on lips that now belonged to her. "Yeah, well, you just better turn out to be as good as I've dreamed you would be!"

Darcy laughed and kissed Caitlyn again, squeezing the smaller woman to her. "Come on," she said pulling back and taking Caitlyn's hand. "Let's go home."

Smiling lovingly, Caitlyn squeezed her hand. "You are my home."

The End

About the Author

Hartley was born and raised in South London and discovered a love of books at an early age starting with A.A. Milne and Roald Dahl. She first started trying to write her own novels around the age of ten, but as her teenage years kicked in she lost interest. Hartley later rediscovered her passion and picked up pen and paper once again and hasn't looked back.

Find her on Twitter at @Hartley_Blaze

MORE REGAL CREST PUBLICATIONS

Melissa Good	Eye of the Storm	1-932300-13-9
Melissa Good	Hurricane Watch	978-1-935053-00-2
Melissa Good	Moving Target	978-1-61929-150-8
Melissa Good	Red Sky At Morning	978-1-932300-80-2
Melissa Good	Storm Surge: Book One	978-1-935053-28-6
Melissa Good	Storm Surge: Book Two	978-1-935053-39-2
Melissa Good	Stormy Waters	978-1-61929-082-2
Melissa Good	Thicker Than Water	1-932300-24-4
Melissa Good	Terrors of the High Seas	1-932300-45-7
Melissa Good	Tropical Storm	978-1-932300-60-4
Melissa Good	Tropical Convergence	978-1-935053-18-7
Melissa Good	Winds of Change Book One	978-1-61929-194-2
Melissa Good	Winds of Change Book Two	978-1-61929-232-1
Melissa Good	Southern Stars	978-1-61929-348-9
K. E. Lane	And, Playing the Role of Herself	978-1-932300-72-7
Helen Macpherson	Revolving Doors	978-1-61929-440-0
Kate McLachlan	Christmas Crush	978-1-61929-195-9
Kate McLachlan	Hearts, Dead and Alive	978-1-61929-017-4
Kate McLachlan	Murder and the Hurdy Gurdy Girl	978-1-61929-125-6
Kate McLachlan	Rescue At Inspiration Point	978-1-61929-005-1
Kate McLachlan	Return Of An Impetuous Pilot	978-1-61929-152-2
Kate McLachlan	Rip Van Dyke	978-1-935053-29-3
Kate McLachlan	Ten Little Lesbians	978-1-61929-236-9
Kate McLachlan	Alias Mrs. Jones	978-1-61929-282-6
Hope Milam	Welcome Home, Bailey	978-1-61929-438-7
Lynne Norris	One Promise	978-1-932300-92-5
Lynne Norris	Sanctuary	978-1-61929-248-2
Lynne Norris	The Light of Day	978-1-61929-338-0
Schramm and Dunne	Love Is In the Air	978-1-61929-362-8
Rae Theodore	Leaving Normal: Adventures in Gender	
		978-1-61929-320-5
Rae Theodore	My Mother Says Drums Are for Boys: True	
	Stories for Gender Rebels	978-1-61929-378-6
Barbara Valletto	Pulse Points	978-1-61929-254-3
Barbara Valletto	Everlong	978-1-61929-266-6
Barbara Valletto	Limbo	978-1-61929-358-8
Barbara Valletto	Diver Blues	978-1-61929-384-7
Lisa Young	Out and Proud	978-1-61929-392-2

Be sure to check out our other imprints,
Blue Beacon Books, Mystic Books, Quest Books,
Silver Dragon Books, Troubadour Books,
and Young Adult Books.

VISIT US ONLINE AT
www.regalcrest.biz

At the Regal Crest Website You'll Find

~   The latest news about forthcoming titles and
     new releases

~   Our complete backlist of titles

~   Information about your favorite authors

Regal Crest print titles are available from all
progressive booksellers including numerous sources
online. Our distributors are Bella Distribution and
Ingram.